Also by Michelle Harrison

THE THIRTEEN TREASURES
Winner of the Waterstones Book Prize 2009

THE THIRTEEN CURSES

THE THIRTEEN SECRETS

UNREST

PART ONE

Death's brother, Sleep.
– Virgil

I'm not asleep . . . but that doesn't mean I'm awake.
– Author Unknown

For Darren
Fred, and Luke

With thanks to Janet
and to Emma Porter

UNREST

MICHELLE HARRISON

SIMON AND SCHUSTER

A book

Simon Pulse and its colophon are registered trademarks
of Simon and Schuster UK Ltd

First published in Great Britain in 2012 by Simon & Schuster UK Ltd
A CBS COMPANY

1 3 5 7 9 10 8 6 4 2

Simon & Schuster UK Ltd
1st Floor
222 Gray's Inn Road
London
WC1X 8HB

www.simonandschuster.co.uk
www.simonpulse.co.uk

Simon & Schuster Australia, Sydney
Simon & Schuster India, New Delhi

A CIP catalogue copy for this book is available
from the British Library.

PB ISBN: 978-0-85707-091-3
E-BOOK ISBN: 978-0-85707-092-0

Typeset by Hewer Text UK Ltd, Edinburgh
Printed and bound in Great Britain
by CPI Group (UK) Ltd, Croydon, CR0 4YY

ONE

Outside

It started the way it always did.

I sat up in bed, unsure of what had woken me. My first thought was the new family who had moved in upstairs. Rowdy, Dad called them, amongst other things. Not even a month since they'd arrived and they'd managed to upset everyone, crashing up the stairs at all hours, swearing, slurring and burping.

Not this time, though. There was only the hum of silence. Our flat, and the rest of the block, was quiet. The room was dark, apart from the light in the hallway. Dad had left it on overnight a lot recently, even though neither one of us spoke about it.

Something moved on the other side of the door, disturbing the light creeping in through the door frame. A figure, moving past in the direction of Dad's bedroom. I wondered how long Dad had been there, watching me through the gap, and whether he had been into my room while I was still asleep. I knew he lay awake some nights, thinking. Worrying. About me, about Mum. About the accident, and how different things had nearly been. The familiar guilt crept up on me. Before I knew it I was out of bed and across the room, shivering in only my boxers. The flat was freezing. I darted out into the hallway, squinting at the sudden brightness, my hand reaching for the light switch. I wanted to show him, in the smallest possible way, that tonight I was all right. I glanced at the clock at the far end of the hall.

Three in the morning.

I should have known then. The time was the first signal. That was the problem, though. I never knew until it was too late.

My fingers found the light switch just as my toes met the puddle. I froze, my hand hovering in place. The laminate flooring was dotted with patches of water, each the size of a footprint, leading to the bathroom. I was standing in one and it was icy cold.

Down the hallway, the bathroom door clicked shut. My eyes trailed over the watery footprints. My ears caught a noise – a stifled sob – coming from the bathroom, and a faint trickle of running water. Then my hand was away from the light switch and out in front of me, reaching for the bathroom door as I followed the wet trail.

I wanted to ask Dad why he was crying, even though I knew the answer, deep down. A dense wall of steam wafted over me as I pushed the door open. It wasn't warm, but instead cool and damp. I shivered again. The door continued to open without a sound and some of the steam cleared from the bathroom as it spread out into the hall.

I took a step inside, clouds of water vapour clinging to my skin. The trickling sound came from the bath. One of the taps was on. Through the haze I could just make out an arm draped along the side of the tub.

'Why are you up so late?' I asked. 'And why are you crying?'

No response came. It was only then that I noticed how thin the arm on the side of the bathtub was. How pale, and hairless . . . and *female*. I stumbled forward, glimpsing – without intending to – more than I was meant to see.

4

The woman in the bath faced forward, but she didn't see me. Her eyes were dull and empty, and her long hair trailed like seaweed. The water had a pinkish tinge to it and lapped softly at the overflow. The running tap was keeping the water warm, and the slow, steady trickle kept it at a level designed not to flood.

Most of the steam had now evaporated through the open door, making everything horribly easy to see. The slight curve of a smile on the colourless lips. The razor blade on the edge of the tub. The incisions on her wrists, red and grinning.

Too late I realised. Remembered.

This has happened before. Which could only mean one thing . . .

I turned, staggering from the bathroom and raced for my room, zigzagging one way to leap over the cat and the other to avoid tripping over my football boots. I should have been leaving the horror behind when I left the bathroom, but now I had remembered, I knew there was more.

Light from the hall streamed across my bed as I reached the door. I wanted to fall into it and huddle under the covers until I'd stopped shaking. Two things stopped me.

First, there was a shadow by the side of the bed. A tall, thin shadow that was somehow a shade darker than all the others in the room – and vaguely human. It was motionless and faceless, yet somehow, I knew what it was staring at.

A body lay in my bed. I saw the short, dark hair on the pillow. Already I knew who it was.

Me. Asleep.

A whimper tried to force its way out of my throat, but didn't quite make it. I knew I needed to get back to myself, back *into* myself, but the shadow at the bedside was even more terrifying than the woman in the bathtub.

Slowly, the shadow's head moved. Its focus changed, no longer on the me in bed, but on the me at the door. I lurched forward, scrambling for the opposite side of the bed and approached my body. The bed didn't move – I was weightless, light as air.

I needed to get back in. I *had* to get back in.

My sleeping body's mouth was open. I'd done it that way before. I leaned over, trying to prise its mouth wider while pushing my face into the tiny, impossible cavity. I felt the prickle of the shadow figure's stare on my back and knew it had taken a step towards me. Towards *us*.

I pushed again, desperate, my hands clamped round the side of my body's face. Just as I thought it was never going to work, that I'd never get back in, it happened. I felt a scratching sensation, then a rush of tightness all over, and then . . .

I was back in my body, jolted awake – for real this time. Heart thudding. Gasping, trembling, crying. Alone in the room. There was no shadow, though the feeling it brought still drenched me in sweat.

I wanted to collapse back into the covers, but there was one last thing I had to know. I eased myself off the bed and crept down the hall. This time, there was no woman in the bathroom. It was empty – and so was my bed when I returned to it.

It ended the way it always ends. With me, burrowed under the covers, too afraid to sleep again until dawn.

TWO

Traces

'It happened again last night.'

Dad stood by the living-room window, smoking what was probably the fifth cigarette of his twenty a day. His free hand held the nicotine-yellowed curtain aside, offering a view of the green in front of the flats. Green it wasn't. The tiny area of grass with its single tree and miserable *NO BALL GAMES* sign was dwarfed by grey high-rise blocks all around.

Dad tensed. He let the curtain fall and turned to me as I sat on the couch, flicking cigarette ash from the cushion.

'Want some breakfast?' he asked.

I shook my head. 'I'm not hungry.' I felt sick from lack of sleep, but already it was after eleven.

'Some coffee, then. Get yourself washed. You look like death warmed up.' He shuffled out of the room, leaving ash on the carpet like a trail of breadcrumbs.

I got up and went into the bathroom, shutting the door against the clinks and clanks from the kitchen. I couldn't help but look into the tub. A grimy tidemark sat much lower than the water level I'd seen – or thought I'd seen – in the night. In the cold morning light, I wasn't sure any more. Even so, I decided against showering if it meant stepping into the bathtub. In any case, the

7

boiler had been playing up for weeks now, running cold every few minutes – or even seconds on really bad days – but strangely, none of the plumbers Dad had called out could find anything wrong.

I walked to the sink and filled it, splashing icy water on my face and neck. I could have boiled up some water in the kettle, as Dad had been doing, but the coldness was at least helping to jerk me out of the sleepy-eyed state I was in.

After washing I towelled off, flossed and brushed my teeth, avoiding my reflection. I didn't need to look in the mirror to know Dad was right: I looked like death. The 'warmed up' bit had been optimism on his part.

I used to be okay-looking, with blue eyes – *really* blue – and dark, almost black hair, and good teeth. Not any more. My bloodshot eyes screamed out for rest. My hair needed cutting and, most days, was greasy enough to fry chips in. My teeth were still all right, but stained from the amount of coffee I was guzzling to stay awake. I hadn't done any sport for months. Oddly, I hadn't put on weight, but lost it. I hid my body under layers of clothes, but nothing short of a mask would conceal the hollowness of my cheeks or the deep smudges beneath my eyes.

I knew what I looked like. Haunted – homeless even. That part wasn't the shock. What *was* shocking was that I didn't even care.

Dad knocked on the door. 'Elliott? Your coffee's out here.'

I came out of the bathroom and nearly kicked over the mug on the floor. I picked it up and followed Dad into the kitchen. The smell of burnt toast filled the room. I sat down, sipping the bitter coffee. I reached for the sugar and dropped in another spoonful.

'Did you look in on me last night,' I asked, stirring, 'when I was in bed?'

'No. I went to bed before you. You know that.'

I did know it, but still I grasped at any possibility that the figure I'd seen at the door wasn't Tess.

'Yeah, but—'

'I heard you before,' he interrupted. 'You said "It happened again". So, which one was it?'

I tasted the coffee again. Still grim.

'The first kind. The girl, in the bath—'

'The out-of-body thing?'

I nodded. 'I saw her, Dad. Felt the wet footprints in the hall. Everything was just . . . like before. The blood in the water, the shadow in the bedroom.' I stopped there. Dad's face was already looking greyer, matching his hair.

'Why don't you call Dr Finch?' he said. 'See if he can get you in today, or maybe tomorrow. There might be a cancellation.'

'What's the point?'

'Talking about it might help.'

'I'm talking now.'

Dad reached for his cigarettes again and lit up. 'You know what I mean,' he said, calmer after the first drag. 'Talking with a *professional*.'

'I *have* talked,' I said. 'And talked and talked. All he does is tell me what it says in the books. That none of it's real and that it's all to do with waking up during REM sleep.'

Dad breathed out a lungful of smoke. 'Then maybe you should start listening.'

'Maybe *you* should!'

'I've listened, Elliott. What you're telling me isn't new. As for the woman, all of us – me, you, Adam, your mum – we all heard what happened here. Your mum and I kept it from you for as long as we could, but we knew you'd hear about it eventually. That sort of thing's bound to get round.'

'I've known since the first year of high school that a woman killed herself here,' I said. 'It bothered me at first, but gradually I stopped thinking about it. I hadn't thought about it in ages. Now suddenly, I've got this . . . this *condition* and I'm seeing her.'

'You *think* you're seeing her.'

'No, I—'

'Why is it you see her when she's in the bath, dying? Why do you think that is, eh?' he demanded. 'When people talk about Tess Fielding they don't talk about anything else but how she died. If she's a ghost – if that's what you're seeing – why's it always at the moment of death? Why not any other glimpses of her life before that, when she lived here?'

I shrugged, not meeting his eyes. 'Perhaps it's not the everyday events that leave traces. Perhaps it's the violent ones.'

'Traces?' Dad shook his head. 'If you paid more attention to the books Finch gave you instead of that mumbo-jumbo paranormal stuff . . .' He stubbed out his cigarette. 'It's not surprising you're preoccupied with death, not after what happened. That's why you've become fixated on the story of Tess. You might have *thought* living in her flat didn't affect you, and maybe it didn't. But now your mind's up to its own tricks, and Tess is an easy one for it to play.'

I got up and dumped my coffee in the sink.

'Where are you going?'

'Adam's.'

Dad raised an eyebrow. 'You're going out like that?'

I looked down at my torn jeans and rumpled T-shirt. 'So?'

He shook his head. 'Don't you think it's time you went back to college? If you're well enough to go to Adam's, then—'

'Leave it, Dad. I've told you I'm not ready.'

I grabbed my keys. The bang of the door echoed through the block as I left, starting down the three flights of stairs. The further down I got, the more it smelled like a urinal. I moved more quickly, glad to escape, and jogged to the car. I unlocked it and clambered in.

The car purred into life, the sound of the engine drowned out by Kurt Cobain screaming through the speakers. I kept the music on loud as I swung round the green and eased out of our road. The noise would help me stay awake.

Before the accident I'd enjoyed driving. As soon as I'd passed my test I'd been on the road, glad of the freedom and the possibilities. My car wasn't exactly a Ferrari, but it was decent and I hadn't done anything stupid like blacking out the windows and putting on one of those massive exhausts like all the other boy-racers. I didn't even race. That's why what happened to me was so unfair.

I stopped at the traffic lights on the high street. Somehow, one of my hands had found its way into my hair. My fingers worked over the knot of scar tissue at the back of my head, taut and smooth. I'd never grow hair there again, although the rest of my hair covered it well enough.

Ahead on the right was a parade of shops. People were queuing to get into the post office and, at the opposite end of the row outside the chip shop, I saw a huddle of girls, blowing on chips that they were eating straight from the paper. I recognised a couple of them. Juliet's friends. Tossing their hair and giggling. I searched for Juliet but couldn't see her. Then she stepped out of the chippy, pushing her dark hair back.

Like she knew she was being watched, her eyes found mine. If she didn't recognise me, which was entirely possible, she'd know the car. We'd been out a few times last year, although she'd been eyeing me up in the corridors ever since college had started.

The last time we went out had been to a party. Someone's eighteenth. Juliet was drinking but I was sober. Driving. She suggested going upstairs. I told her no way, not at a party where anyone could just walk in.

I took her back to Adam's instead.

I didn't call her afterwards. It wasn't that I didn't like her, I'd just been there before. There's something about girls. You get too close and they think they own you. Adam had warned me over and over, seen it happen to too many of his friends. One minute you can be full of ideas and ambitions. The next, your girlfriend's got a bellyful of arms and legs and you're trapped, just like that. Well, no thanks.

So I never called her. I was a coward. Gave her a cheeky wink the first couple of times she questioned me. I had the face for it back then. The kind of face that could get away with pretty much anything: forgotten phone calls, missed coursework deadlines. I knew it and I used it.

I took her number again. It was like a game. When she realised she was the one getting played her eyes went all serious and I knew she knew.

'Did I do something wrong?' she asked one day by my locker. 'Is that it? Why you haven't called?' Her chin wobbled and I had that awful feeling that you get when girls cry and you don't know how to make them stop.

'You didn't do anything. I just . . . I don't want a relationship.'

Her friends – and mine – watched from further down the corridor. I put my arms around her. She tensed and I knew she wanted to pull away, but didn't want to make a scene. She let me hold her. Slowly, I bent my head and kissed her. It was a kiss goodbye, and she knew it.

'Are you going to tell everyone now?' she asked.

'I'm not like that.'

Her eyes were full of hurt. 'Yes, you are. You're a bastard.'

I walked away from her, knowing she was right.

I hadn't lied though. I *was* a bastard, but I had morals. I never spread it around that I'd slept with her. I stared back at Juliet from the car, wondering whether to chance a smile. Over the past few months, the look in her eyes had gradually softened from being angry to dismissive. What I saw in them now was something else: pity. I didn't like it.

I felt my face twisting into something uglier, meaner.

Cars honked behind me. The lights had changed. I blinked, breaking eye contact with Juliet, only to stall the car to more hooting. Finally, crunching the gears, I got through the lights. I'd been given the all clear to drive again only three weeks ago. I tried to tell myself that I was rusty, but it felt like just another thing on the long list of stuff I was no longer any good at.

My brother lived a ten-minute drive away in a house he shared with his girlfriend and another couple. After parking, I went up the path and tapped on the kitchen window.

The front door opened seconds later and Adam stood there, wearing only his jeans. He beckoned me in. I closed the door and sat at the kitchen table as he went upstairs. I watched him go, all broad shoulders and nut-brown skin. A knot of tension in my shoulders untangled.

Adam's was the only place I could relax. It was cluttered with four people's stuff, but it always felt warm and inviting, like a home should. It smelled good, too. I eyed a pot of fresh coffee on the side.

I got up and took a cup from the shelf. 'All right if I have some coffee?' I called.

'If you must.' Adam came back into the kitchen, tugging a shirt over his head. 'You know you're not supposed to drink it.'

'A couple of cups in the morning doesn't hurt.' I helped myself to milk. 'It's only later in the day that I'm not supposed to. Anyway, that stuff Dad drinks is rank. I have to come here to get a decent fix.'

Adam's nose twitched. 'The boiler's still not fixed, then?'

'No. Why?'

'Because you're starting to smell like a tramp.'

I took a gulp of coffee. 'I washed my face.'

'Your face isn't the part that stinks. I can smell your armpits from here.'

That's what I love about Adam. He's never been one for bullshit.

He pulled a towel and some clothes from a pile of fresh laundry and threw them at me. 'Go and sort yourself out.' He glanced at his watch. 'And make it quick – I'm opening up at twelve. You're making me late.'

'Can't I just—' I began, but Adam shook his head.

'Not today. Amy's going to be home at lunchtime and she's revising. She won't want you lounging around.'

I slunk off to the bathroom and flicked the shower on, peeling off my clothes. I ducked my head to my armpit and my eyes watered. Adam was right. I felt something stir within me, some prick of shame. The warm spray hit my skin as I stepped into the

14

bath. I closed my eyes because I wasn't afraid to. There was no dead girl in the bathtub here.

Ten minutes later I emerged wearing my brother's clothes. Like my own, they hung off me as a reminder of how thin I was. In fact, everything about Adam reminded me of what I used to be. There wasn't much of an age gap between us – Adam was twenty, three years older. Before, people could tell we were brothers. We had the same features, almost identical build and colouring. Now I was just a bad version of him. Like a cheap cover song. The words are all there, in the right order and in tune, but it's never as good.

Adam gave me an appraising nod. I didn't know whether to feel pleased or irritated by it. I went to pour another coffee – the first had gone cold – but Adam was on his feet, pulling his jacket on.

'No time. Get your keys, you can give me a lift.'

Still warm from my shower, I shivered as we stepped outside. It was May, that odd, changeable time of year that's not quite spring, but not yet summer. In the car, Adam flicked through my CD collection and changed the disc, then his fingers played along over an imaginary set of frets.

As we approached the crossroads I glanced over at the chippy again. This time only workmen and school kids were outside.

'I saw Juliet earlier.'

Adam paused mid-strum. 'Juliet . . . is that the brunette you pulled last year?'

I nodded. I'd told only Adam. I knew I could trust him. We had a code, me and him. Well, mainly him. Adam always knew what to do and what to say. How to sleep with girls without getting into a relationship or pissing them off *too* badly. And the first rule of not pissing them off was not to brag about it.

'You should have seen the way she looked at me.'

'Thought she'd have got over it by now.'

'She has. She didn't look at me like she used to, like she hated me. She looked at me like I was pathetic . . .'

'That's the price you pay for dumping someone.'

'No, I mean pathetic like she felt sorry for me.'

Adam went quiet. 'You'll get it back. You just need some time, and you'll be like . . . like it never happened. You need to start looking after yourself. Come running with me again. You'll be like you always were – girls throwing themselves at you.'

'I'm too tired to run,' I said through my teeth, fighting to keep my temper. 'And I'm not interested in girls right now.'

Adam stiffened at my tone and, for a moment, the tension in the car was too thick to ignore. Then a dreamy look came over his face. 'That's what I thought until I met Amy.'

'Yeah, right . . .'

'I'm serious!' He grinned and something inside me twisted. 'You just haven't found the right girl yet. You'll know it when you do. You won't want to mess her around.'

'True.' I couldn't help myself. 'There is this one who keeps showing up naked in the bathroom every once in a while, but she's missing something . . . oh, yeah, that's it. A pulse.'

Just like that, Adam's smile was gone. He whistled through his teeth and stared out of the window. Neither of us said anything else until the car stopped.

Already I regretted my outburst. Adam made me feel better and I didn't want to leave him just yet, especially not to go back home. All that waited there for me was daytime TV and dread every time I needed to go into the bathroom. My thoughts must have shown on my face.

'Come in for a bit if you like,' said Adam.

I looked towards the darkened windows of The Acorn. 'I don't want to talk to anyone.'

Adam's hand rested on the door release. 'It'll only be the regulars and they won't bother you. It won't be busy. Come on – you can help me set the bar up.'

He got out and I found myself taking the keys out of the ignition and following him across the car park. A lone customer, a sixty-something man, waited to be let in. He tapped his watch and exchanged banter with Adam about oversleeping but didn't look at me. I kept my head down anyway. Most people knew me as 'that Drake boy from the accident'. Adam unlocked the doors and went in while the customer and I hung back, waiting as the alarm was switched off.

The place reeked of real ale and stale drip trays, the sort of smell that made you feel hungover even when you weren't. While Adam collected the till trays from the office, I filled the ice buckets and water jugs. He returned just as I was slicing some lemons, and logged the tills in. All the while the customer waited patiently at the counter, reading the paper.

'The usual?' Adam asked him, barely waiting for an answer before flipping a pint glass under the Guinness tap. He pulled half then left it to settle, then poured an orange juice for himself and a Pepsi for me. A minute later, a second man wandered in. Adam had his drink on the bar before the old guy even reached him, then went back to top up the Guinness.

'Doesn't this job do your head in?' I asked him. 'Same people, same drinks, same conversation? Day in, day out?'

Adam shrugged. 'Sometimes. But it's not for ever – just until the band takes off.' He swore as the pump gurgled. He flicked it off. 'Barrel's gone.' His eyes went to the door as more customers trickled in. 'Don't suppose you'll do the honours?'

17

I finished the lemons and put the knife down with a sinking feeling in my gut. I knew how to change a barrel. Adam had shown me a few weeks ago and it was easy enough. The problem was that I didn't want to go down into the cellar.

I went to the sink and washed the lemon juice off my hands. 'Yeah, I'll go.'

The building was split into three: the public bar, which was the busiest at this time of day; the saloon bar, which held the pool table, TV and fruit machines; and a function hall out the back. The cellar was accessed by a small door at the end of the saloon bar. I pushed it open and went through. Cold air raised the hairs on my arms. I fumbled for the light switch and snapped it on, then started down the narrow staircase.

At the bottom the cellar spread out, rows of metallic barrels, and pipes and pressure gauges on the walls. Two huge fans blasted out chilled air, whirring with a monotonous drone. The constant cold and the claustrophobia of the low ceiling was enough to spook anyone, but like most old places, that wasn't where it ended. There was a story attached.

I scanned the barrels until I found the one that had gone. In moments I'd disconnected it and shunted a new one into its place. Once attached, a quick twist and the pressure gauge popped back up. That was all there was to it. I did all this with my back to the wall, throwing quick glances into the darker corners of the cellar. As I crossed back to the staircase, a sliver of light flashed from above.

Sunlight lit the edges of the delivery hatch, two square wooden doors that opened out on to the street. This was where it had happened. In the Sixties, a landlord named Richard Stacker had fallen through the hatch. It wasn't especially high, but he'd hit some barrels before landing on the stone floor, breaking his neck. His ghost was said to haunt the entire pub, though the cellar had the most sightings. Adam had never seen anything, though he admitted that he hated coming into the cellar. The cleaning lady, a devout Catholic named Mary, refused point blank to come into the cellar and crossed herself every time Stacker's name was mentioned. Apparently she'd seen him in the doorway once.

I'd never seen anything, but the cellar always got me nervous – especially so soon after one of my 'experiences'. The creeping sensation on my arms was back, the tiny hairs rising like hackles even though I was quite far from the cold-air fans now.

I ran from the spot and clattered up the stairs, back into warmth and light.

Adam smirked. 'You survived, then? Old Stacker never showed up?'

I took a long swig of my drink. 'Not that I could see.'

Adam fetched a bucket and started pulling the new barrel through. My eyes found Stacker's picture in a grainy newspaper cutting, framed on a shelf next to the darts trophies.

'That reminds me,' Adam swilled the contents of the bucket, 'Pete wants to do one of those haunted nights. You know, like the ones they do on the telly? He's paying some guy to hold a séance overnight and charging for entry.'

I raised my eyebrows. 'Do you reckon many people will come?'

Adam nodded to a clipboard next to the phone. 'You should see the sign-up list. It'll be booked up before the week's out if it carries on like this.'

'Pretty sick, cashing in on someone breaking their neck.'

Adam shrugged. 'It's basically just a lock-in with a few spooky extras and an all-you-can-eat buffet. You should come. I can get you a free ticket.'

'Why would I want to do that? I've got enough problems at home.'

Adam leaned closer and lowered his voice. 'That's the point. Perhaps if you spent a night somewhere different you'd be able to tell whether the stuff at the flat . . . whether it's real or not. Think about it – if you *are* picking something up, then what's to stop you picking up something here as well?'

I shook my head. 'No way. People talk about me already. What if I freak out in front of everyone? It'd just make everything worse.'

Adam nodded. 'Yeah, I suppose. It was just a thought.' He crossed the bar to refill someone's glass, leaving me staring at the photograph of the dead landlord.

Because, despite what I'd said, I *was* thinking about it. I was *really* thinking about it. Even though I'd never risk a ghost hunt or séance or whatever on my doorstep, the idea had taken seed. Hauntings were big business and there were other places, away from here, where no one knew me. Where it wouldn't matter if something happened and I showed myself up. Where I could find out once and for all if what I was experiencing was real, or if I was just plain crazy.

Old Stacker grinned back at me, grainy and yellow. I lifted my glass in a toast and silently thanked him. For the first time in six months I had a plan – and some hope.

THREE

Hit and Run

I suppose I should explain what happened to make me this way.

I never thought I'd die young. Never even thought about dying at all. I thought about the same things most seventeen-year-old boys think about: nights out, driving, girls, sex, and how to get drunk without having ID. The only thing I thought of to do with The Future was getting my college grades and maybe going to university one day. So occasionally I thought about art, too, although since getting the car my social life had taken over everything else. I admit, I was slacking, but I didn't care. I was enjoying myself.

The accident made all the local newspapers and even a few nationals. *DEATH SMASH: BOY CRITICAL* and *HIT-AND-RUN MYSTERY DRIVER* were a couple of the headlines I remember. I know how it looks. Young boy, just passed his driving test. Speeding, probably showing off to a girl or his friends. Sounds familiar, doesn't it?

But I wasn't the one driving. Wasn't even in the car. Like I said before, I didn't speed or drive like a dickhead. I liked my car and wanted it – and myself – to stay in one piece.

It was a Saturday afternoon and I'd gone to meet some mates in town. I didn't plan to be long – all I needed was a new shirt for the evening. The place was heaving with Christmas shoppers. A single road divided the car park and the mall, but it was a busy one. One direction was clear, but the side closest to me hummed with traffic. I jogged to the crossing and pressed the button, waiting for the lights to change. As soon as they did, the cars stopped and I stepped off the kerb.

It went like this: I got to the middle of the road and heard a car engine, too loud and too close. It was still moving, not from behind the ones nearest that had stopped, but from the other side, the clear side with no traffic. Or at least, there had been no traffic until then. I remember turning my head at the last moment and seeing sunlight on a dark car bonnet – black or maybe blue.

Prick, I thought, running for the pavement. *Can't you see the red light?* But the car didn't stop, didn't even slow, and I stared after it speeding away. The number plate started and ended with an S but the rest was obscured with muddy splashes.

Someone screamed behind me, jerking my eyes from the road. Only then did I see that people had got out of their cars and were forming a cluster on the crossing. Voices babbled, panicked voices that drifted to me in snatches.

'. . . don't move him . . .'

'. . . just called an ambulance . . .'

'. . . give him some space . . .'

'. . . didn't stop, the bastard just kept going . . .'

'. . . number plate, but it was too fast . . .'

'. . . oh God, his head . . .'

Someone had been hit? I saw a woman crying, gripping the handles of a kid's bike, and I felt sick. Was it her child in the road? There were so many people I couldn't see anything. But then someone shifted and a little boy came into view on the other side of the woman. I saw him looking at me, his eyes huge and dark, and he shrank back, his thumb wedged in his mouth.

I loitered on the pavement, not sure what to do. It felt shitty to stand there doing nothing, but what *could* I do? I didn't know any first aid. On the other hand it would have felt callous to walk away. I noticed an odd taste in my mouth and resisted the urge to spit.

Sirens screamed, quickly getting closer until flashing lights lit up the street and an ambulance came into view. Two paramedics – a man and a woman – jumped out and urged the onlookers back. The crowd split and suddenly hushed, and I could see the legs of the person lying still in the road.

Weird, I thought, *he's wearing the same jeans as me . . .*

The taste in my mouth was back. Sort of . . . spices and meat. I ran my tongue over my teeth, but it was somehow more a *smell* than a taste. More people moved out of the way and, for the first time, I saw a middle-aged woman leaning over the body, giving it mouth to mouth. The female paramedic reached over and touched her arm. The woman sat back. There was a half-eaten sandwich by her side, scattered across the tarmac. The bread was spotted with blood.

'He stopped breathing about a minute ago,' she said, pushing grey hair out of her eyes. 'I'm a nurse . . . off-duty . . . I . . .'

Her voice was drowned out by a rushing noise that seemed to be coming from inside my head. Without realising it, I'd moved closer to the body. His eyes were closed, his mouth open and slack. Beneath his head a patch of the road was darker and shiny-wet, circled like a wreath that still grew and spread. I watched the male paramedic begin to pump the boy's chest. The woman fitted something over his face.

23

I knew that face. *My* face.

I hadn't made it across the road.

A stream of words came out of my mouth. I didn't hear or understand them. No one else heard them either, I knew that now. Because my body was over there, being pounded and pumped, and yet I was over here, away from it. Helpless. A spectator in . . . what? My own death?

'Too late.' The woman shook her head, but continued to hold the mask in place. 'There's still no pulse. He's gone.'

'Keep going.' Despite the chill in the December air, sweat beaded the man's upper lip as he continued to work. 'Just a bit longer.'

'I'm here!' I shouted at them, leaning over my body. 'I'm not gone! Don't stop – don't give up on me!'

And they didn't. Over and over again they pressed on my chest, their voices a steady beat, shouting instructions to each other. My chest rose and fell as air was forced through the mask into my lungs.

How many seconds had passed? How many minutes? There was only so much time before my body would shut down for good and then whatever part of me this was, the part of me watching it all, would be gone too. Unless . . . unless this was it – the reality of being dead. Was I dead already? My life couldn't be over, not yet. Not now, not like this . . . but there was so much blood on the road. Even if I survived, what kind of life would I be going back to? Would I be disabled? Brain-damaged?

Something was happening. A tugging sensation, almost like a magnet, pulled me closer to my body. My chest felt tight, heavy with another person's weight, and I could smell something artificial. Plastic . . .

I saw my body's eyes flick open and then . . . then I wasn't outside myself any more. The paramedics' faces loomed over mine.

'We've got him back. Hang in there, son.'

For a moment I was numb, totally numb. *Am I paralysed?* Panicking, I tried to sit up.

'No, stay still, don't try to move yet . . .'

I'd moved then. Good. I'd moved . . . I wasn't . . .

Pins and needles at first, all over. Then pain. Like nothing I'd experienced before. Each beat of my pulse jarred my smashed head. It felt like there were teeth in there. Sharp animal teeth, fighting and snarling at each other for the biggest bite of my brain. The smell of blood reached me even through the mask. The back of my head was sticky and hot with it. I hoped that was all it was. Just blood and not the contents of my skull.

The female paramedic leaned over me. Her face vanished and reappeared, vanished and reappeared, in time with the flashing lights going off behind her head, silhouetting her and then not.

Pain. It was all I could focus on. She started speaking and I tried to listen and understand but couldn't.

'We're going to move you now, love. Get you to hospital. You'll be taken care of.' She looked at her colleague. 'Ready? Lift . . .'

I blacked out.

One operation, a metal plate, and twenty-eight stitches later I woke up. Ten weeks after that, two of which were in intensive care, I was allowed home. Changed, physically and mentally. For the next two months I'd suffered crippling headaches and blurred vision. Gradually they'd subsided. The doctors said I was lucky, that my recovery was one of the most incredible they'd seen. *Lucky.* I didn't feel it.

The police still hadn't caught who'd knocked me down. Lots of

25

people gave statements at the scene of the accident. The car was black. The driver was white, female, in her early twenties or younger. The number plate began and ended with an S, but there had been mud over the rest. No one knew any more.

They also failed to trace the off-duty nurse; the eater of the abandoned sandwich that I'd been able to taste on her breath. The newspapers – and the doctors – called her a hero. By delivering oxygen to my lungs and stemming the blood flow she had almost certainly saved my life. An appeal for her to come forward never brought any results. Perhaps, like me, she didn't welcome the attention. She'd acted on impulse, done what she thought was best and gone on her way. Even though I understood, I would have liked the chance to thank her. You know how you have those little scenarios in your head, where you've worked out exactly what you'll say to a person and what they'll say back? I had it all planned out. I was even going to buy her a sandwich.

I also thought about the driver.

I thought about her a lot, at first. What I'd say to her if I ever saw her. I thought about it so much that there were a few different scenarios that unfolded in my head. Sometimes I just asked her why. Why hadn't she stopped when the lights were on red? Why hadn't she stopped after she'd hit me and I was bleeding in the road? Did she even care? Sometimes I told her I hated her and how she had ruined my life and changed me. Sometimes I imagined she had been caught and was being sentenced, and that when she tried to catch my eye from the dock to beg my forgiveness, I'd stared straight ahead, ignoring her.

I wondered if she ever thought about what she'd done. Was she sorry? Was her mind tormented? I didn't see how it could be.

Everyone who had witnessed what happened said the same thing. The driver hadn't hesitated or slowed at all.

The police questioned me, my family and friends, about any known grudge against me. They knew of none. There was Juliet, of course, but she didn't drive and the thought of her trying to run me over for dumping me was absurd. Added to the busy location, the idea that it had been deliberate was quickly ruled out.

There was another chain of thought that recurred in my head, and that was the question of what could possibly have been going through the woman's mind to warrant her not stopping.

Maybe the car was stolen. Maybe she'd been carjacked and someone was in the backseat, forcing her to drive. Maybe she'd just robbed a bank . . . or been called to the bedside of a dying relative . . . or was pregnant and in labour . . . or a government spy on her way to prevent an act of mass terrorism. Maybe, maybe, maybe. My mind reached for possibilities, excuses, it didn't matter how far-fetched. Just anything, any reason that would explain how she could disregard my life so casually.

Every day that passed left the trail colder. The police told me I should accept that I might never see justice done. I tried to tell myself that it didn't matter. That the most a conviction could bring would be a few months in prison – a couple of years, tops. Perhaps it was better this way, because she would have to live not only with her guilt but with the fear of the truth catching up with her.

But the simple truth was that she had got away with it.

Most hit-and-runs will make the news. It can vary from a small, easily-overlooked piece to a full front page, depending on the circumstances. Sometimes, there's an element that the press get hold of and won't leave alone; something that makes a story big.

The thing that made my story a big one wasn't that I was young, though I was. The stand-out thing about my accident was that I'd been clinically dead for nearly two full minutes before the paramedics brought me back.

I'd known it before I even saw the report. How else could it explain what I'd experienced in the time after the impact when I stood outside myself, watching strangers leaning over my body and seeing the culprit speed away? The doctors had theories about what I'd seen and felt. They called it a 'near-death experience'. Lots of people who'd been pronounced dead or who'd been close to death apparently had them. Some were similar to mine, with the person coming out of their body. Others detailed encounters with bright light and feelings of being at peace. I didn't relate to that at all. I remembered my panic and desperation. It hadn't been my time to go and I'd known it.

I did a lot of research in the months following the accident. Just a little at first, then more when the other stuff started happening. Psychics and spiritualists believe near-death experiences are proof of the afterlife. Scientists and doctors go with theories that it's the brain's way of coping when a human knows they're dying; a way of comforting ourselves that's genetically programmed into us.

What the doctors *couldn't* explain was how, before knowing any details of witness statements, my description of the number plate matched those of others when I was still flat on my back with my life hanging in the balance.

So that's why, the first time I came out of my body after the accident and saw myself in bed, I thought I was dead.

FOUR

Past Lives

When I stopped the car at the gates I thought there had been a mistake. They were closed, and a notice on a wooden board propped outside said as much. I switched off the ignition and reached over to my jacket (or rather, Adam's jacket because I didn't possess a suit) on the passenger seat. From the inside pocket I removed a piece of headed paper and re-read it. Right place, right time, so what was going on?

I got out, glad of the breeze and the chance to stretch after the forty-minute drive. To the right of the gate was some kind of security lodge. The blinds were drawn but there was a camera, an assistance button and a speaker. I pushed the button, not really expecting a response, but there was a crackle, then a male voice.

'Can I help?'

I cleared my throat. 'I'm here for an interview with Arthur Hodge?'

Crackle. 'Your name?'

'Elliott Drake.'

'End of the drive, main building. Someone will be out to meet you and you'll be shown where to park.'

There was a low buzz and the gates began to open. I got back in the car and nudged it forward until there was a space big enough for me to pass through. The car rumbled along the gravel drive. Either side, the grounds were impressive; leafy and green and stretching back further than I remembered, though it was a long time since I'd been here. In the rear-view mirror I caught sight of the gates swinging shut, sealing me in.

The visitors' entrance, a modern brick building, lay straight ahead and as I got closer I saw a stocky man on the steps, motioning for me to head left. Two vast gravelled car parks stretched back, the first for coaches and the second for cars. I parked as close to the exit as I could and got out, struggling into the suit jacket. I hated the feel of it. The last time I'd worn one had been for Mum's funeral almost three years ago, and that had belonged to my brother, too. The fabric stuck to my clammy neck and I wished again that I hadn't listened to Adam and bothered with a suit. I doubted I'd get the job anyway, and it was sod's law that today was turning out to be the hottest day of the year so far.

By the time I'd trudged back to the building, dust from the gravel underfoot had settled on my newly-polished shoes, turning them from shiny black to dull grey. Added to the rumpled suit and sweat slicking my face, I felt a mess. Ironic, considering that I'd spent the last few months looking like a tramp and not caring.

Even so, the stocky man waiting on the steps made me look smart. He was sweating more heavily than I was, from the palms of his hands – which he wiped quickly on his creased shorts – to the top of his balding head. He arranged his fleshy mouth into a smile and I couldn't help but relax. If *he'd* got a job, then my chances were better than I thought. I hoped by the time he'd led me to meet Arthur Hodge that I'd cooled down and stopped sweating.

'Elliott?' The man held out his hand. I took it, nodding.

'Arthur Hodge, Head of Tours.' He pumped my hand up and down in his damp, meaty one. 'This way.'

Luckily, he turned away too quickly to register my surprise. I followed him past the entrance building under a stone archway draped with wisteria. Blossoms brushed against my shoulders, releasing a waft of scent that lingered even as we approached a terraced row of old cottages with bright doors. A sign on the wall read *PRIVATE – STAFF ONLY*. He led me across a courtyard, through more archways trailing with greenery, before entering a door. It was so low I had to duck and I barely had time to look around before he ushered me along a narrow hall with doors either side. Each one held a small brass plaque with a name and a title: head of this, or manager of that. Soon we came into a small office and he invited me to sit. As he bent over the desk, a strand of gingery hair flopped from where he'd carefully combed it to conceal his bald spot. He flapped a hand, brushing it back into place. I looked away.

Everything about the room was old. Chunky beams sloped crookedly from one side of the ceiling to the other and there was a cast iron fireplace behind the desk. Arthur Hodge tapped some papers smartly, commanding my attention.

'So, Elliott. Welcome to Past Lives. Like the Black Country Museum and Beamish, we are a *living* museum, an open-air village in which visitors can truly experience historical life. There are now thirty-two buildings on our site, a third of which stand where they were originally built. The remainder consists of historic buildings from around the country which have been moved and carefully rebuilt here. Some of the original buildings – the Elizabethan, for example – were preserved as part of the county council's heritage and arts services for many years before the museum was formed. Others, such as the Victorian school, stand at their original sites but were partial ruins from the wars. Rather than destroy them, they became part of the museum and were reconstructed.'

I nodded. I didn't know much about the place at all, except for one thing: that it was supposedly home to some of the most haunted buildings in Britain.

Arthur Hodge clasped his hands together and smiled his fleshy-lipped smile again. 'Let's begin, then. You've applied for the role of Trainee Tour Guide, the main task of which is providing guided tours, but as the job description explained, this role sometimes involves other duties such as helping out in the shop or tea rooms and such. Is this your first visit to Past Lives?'

'No,' I said. My voice came out thinly. I fought to mask my nerves. 'I've been once before on a school trip. It was years ago though – I was only ten.'

'And what did you think of it?'

'Well, it's a long time ago, but I remember liking the sweet shop . . .'

Arthur's smile faded a little and I mentally kicked myself. I needed to work harder than that – what child *wouldn't* remember the sweet shop? I rushed on.

'And the horse and cart rides . . .' The rubbery mouth began to turn back up, and I clawed at memories, trying to dredge up something that would appease him.

'We watched shoes being repaired by the cobbler . . .' One image slid into another and I smiled, half with relief and half with the memories of that day that until just now, I had entirely forgotten.

Arthur's smile was back, too. He made a note on my application.

'There was a ghost story, too,' I remembered. 'Something about a woman and a window. I wrote about it when we got back to school.'

The smile broadened. 'That story's only the tip of the iceberg as far as the supernatural activity in this place goes. We're careful about how much we reveal, depending on the audience – but we'll get round to that. Now, tell me, Elliott. What do you think you can bring to this particular role?'

I'd found out about the job a week ago. As soon as I got home from The Acorn, I'd started researching ghost hunts and paranormal nights on the internet. Dad was out, and I was grateful not to have him peering over my shoulder, huffing and puffing about 'all that old clap-trap'.

There were a lot of ghost events advertised, most of which looked terrible. Tacky websites dripping blood and hammy videos of people running around in the dark screaming, holding flickering torches. But there were a couple of websites which looked more understated and genuine, with positive reviews from people who'd taken part. There were just two problems with those: the distance (one was a manor house in Cornwall, the other a castle in Scotland), and the logistics of any visit I took. If there *were* any ghosts, I wasn't going to connect with them by running around with a bunch of strangers. I needed to *sleep*. It was then that I had the idea of staying in a haunted hotel.

Another hour spent trawling the net and I had notes on a few possibilities. A couple of phone calls later, it became obvious that even those were a waste of time. One night's stay in any of them would clean out my already pathetic bank account.

I gave up and watched some telly instead. I was seriously

considering taking Adam up on the haunted night at The Acorn, when I idly flicked through the paper to find the TV pages. And the word 'paranormal' caught my eye, on an advert in the corner of the newspaper.

Past Lives – the UK's best living museum!
Step back in time and experience history like never before. Situated at the heart of the Essex countryside, Past Lives is an open-air historical village with something for the whole family. Learn to dance like an Elizabethan, experience life in a Victorian school-room, and witness a real-life joust! For full details of our short breaks and award-winning events, including ghost walks and paranormal nights, visit our website or call us on—

The telly forgotten, I returned to the computer and tapped in the website, intending to look at the admission fee – but the first thing I saw on the homepage was a job vacancy. And the sensible part of my brain asked, why pay to be there when you can be *paid* to be there? It didn't have to be permanent. Just as long as it took for me to find out what I needed, and then I could quit.

Thirty minutes later I'd sent off the online application.

Two days after that an email arrived. I'd got an interview.

The interview quickly went downhill, despite the promising start. I stuttered my way through every question, even the more basic ones. I knew it was going badly when Arthur Hodge stopped taking notes and instead adopted a little nod which he adminis-tered to each of my answers without variation. It was starting to piss me off. Added to that, I'd had another sleepless night and my eyes felt grittier than they'd done in ages, like someone had thrown

34

sand in my face. The gravel dust in the car park hadn't helped and I felt a scratch of irritation with each blink.

'According to your application, you should be halfway through your A-levels,' he said, picking up his pen again. 'Art, History, and Photography. Is that correct?'

By his tone I could tell he thought that I'd lied. It didn't help my mood.

'Yes.' I tried to ungrit my teeth. 'I completed the first year.'

'But not the second?'

'I dropped out. Well, no that's not exactly right . . . I decided to take a year out. It's on hold.'

I'd have exchanged a week's sleep at that moment in return for using Arthur Hodge's smug face as a dartboard.

'Why the change of heart?'

What the hell, I decided. I had nothing to lose by telling the truth. It wasn't like I'd see him again after today.

'I dropped out because I had an accident last year,' I said. 'I got knocked down by a hit-and-run driver and spent weeks in hospital recovering. By the time I went back to college I was way behind. I figured it'd be easier to take this year out. When I go back to do my A-levels everyone will be new. No one will know what happened to me and I'll be able to carry on as normal, without all the questions and staring.' For the first time since coming into the office I realised the tremor had left my voice. It was strangely calming to unburden myself, to be me and not have to think about the right or wrong answers for a minute or two.

It had certainly wiped the smug expression off Arthur Hodge's face. I was half expecting the pitying look I'd come to dread, but instead he looked understanding, and slightly ashamed. Perhaps I was still in with a chance.

35

'Ah.' He cleared his throat. 'Yes, that explains things somewhat.' He rearranged the papers and got up. 'Well, that concludes the interview. If you'd like to follow me, then I'll give you a quick tour and tell you a bit more about the role. It's important that you understand exactly what's required and how tiring the work can be. Much of it is physical and some people have found they can't hack the pace.'

I got up and followed him out to the courtyard once more. He unlocked a wooden gate and, beyond, the museum stretched ahead in a higgledy-piggledy street. It was largely empty, but as I looked about I saw a few signs of life: two gardeners tending flowerbeds along the edge of the cobblestone road; someone washing the windows of a crooked building, and a fair-headed girl mucking out a row of stables further on.

'The museum is tended to by staff who are on-site virtually all year round,' said Arthur. He set off along the cobbles. I hobbled after him, trying not to wince as the stones prodded through the thin soles of my shoes. 'Practically all the food sold in the tea rooms and restaurant is grown and farmed here – we're almost self-sufficient.'

I summoned an enthusiastic expression. I wasn't stupid enough to believe him when he'd told me the interview was over. Everything I said and did was still being noted, and my reaction to the place was especially important.

'There are two staff areas – the main offices we've just left and the Old Barn over there.' He pointed to the crooked building next to the stables. 'There's a common room, and lockers, and a changing room – all our staff are in costume, of course.'

I groaned inwardly. I'd forgotten about that. The costumes were to help maintain the historical feel. If I *did* get the job, Adam would never let me hear the end of it.

36

'What sort of thing do the guides wear?' I asked.

Hodge waved his hand. 'Oh, nothing too elaborate. We keep it simple – we're moving around all day, so it needs to be practical.'

I nodded, relieved.

'Any recollections of your previous visit?' he asked, stopping suddenly.

I paused and looked around me. Straight ahead I saw a well and felt a jolt of recognition.

'I remember that,' I said, pointing. 'The well.' We started towards it. 'This is where all the streets branch off from, and the sweet shop is there . . . and I think the cobbler was . . . there, somewhere.'

'You've got a good memory,' said Arthur, beaming. 'Obviously there have been more additions in the last few years but we've retained each area, or street, of the museum, as a particular era by building from the middle outwards. The central area by the well is known as the Plain. The four streets lead off from there and each represents a different era. Elizabethan, Georgian, Victorian, Edwardian.' He gestured to a huge leaning timber building. 'Calthorpe House and, beyond it, the Swan Hotel are the original Elizabethan structures on Cornmarket Street – the oldest part of the museum. It's also the haunted part, if you're into that sort of thing.' His eyes gleamed. 'Lots of grisly goings on.' He turned and began walking back the way we'd come. 'So that's the very brief tour. If you're successful you'll be fully trained on each of the individual streets to give tours of twenty to twenty-five minutes. Once you're well-versed in the history of the place, you'll work up to full tours lasting just under two hours.' He gestured to the uneven ground. 'As you can probably feel by now, being on your feet all day in a place like this isn't easy. The other thing to mention is the weather. The job involves braving the elements whether it's rain, shine or snow. If you *are* offered the position, please take that into account.'

I nodded.

'Any questions?'

On the way to the interview I'd tried to think of ways that it might be possible to stay on-site overnight, other than paying for a hotel room. 'I was wondering about the ghost walks – whether they're expected of the guides, or if you hire separately for them. Only, I noticed they finish late and it's a long drive—'

'It's not mandatory,' he cut in, 'but it's appreciated. Most staff that are here late are working shifts, but after last year's snow we introduced a few basic rooms for anyone unable to get home in the event of bad weather. That's always an option, provided you're not easily spooked after listening to ghost stories.'

'I don't mind,' I answered quickly. He looked pleased and jotted something down in a small notebook that he produced from his shorts pocket.

'Anything else?'

'No, I think that's it. But I'd appreciate it if you could give me an idea of when I might expect to hear back from you.' As I spoke the words, I was aware of two things: first, that the second, more informal part of the interview had gone much better than the first. And second, that I really, *really* wanted this job.

'I've got a couple of interviews this afternoon,' said Arthur. 'So you should hear from us in the next couple of days – certainly by the end of the week.'

Back in my car I doused my eyes in drops. Peering into the mirror I saw how red they looked. Until then, I'd been feeling more

38

confident about the job, but unless Past Lives liked their employees to look like vampires I didn't hold out much hope.

My mood worsened on the drive home. A wrong turn added an extra thirty minutes on to the journey and, when I finally got back, all I wanted to do was collapse into bed. In my room, the bed was unmade and the sheets still rumpled from this morning. The curtains hadn't even been opened. A stale smell clung to everything.

I went in, drew back the curtains and opened the window, chasing the shadows out. Fresh air billowed into the fusty space. In the living room a light on the answer phone blinked. Dad wasn't home. I decided I'd wait for him to get in, then take a nap to catch up on some sleep.

I pressed 'play' on the answer phone, yanking off my tie. The message was for me, from Adam, asking if I'd go with him to visit Mum's grave. By the time the recording ended, the tie was a tight ball scrunched up in my fist.

I pushed 'erase', wishing that I could do the same for the past six months of my life.

FIVE

Jekyll and Hyde

'Never mind.' Adam leaned over the side of the sofa, lazily reaching for his beer bottle. 'I'll get you a job at The Acorn when you turn eighteen.' His eyes glittered. 'There's plenty to keep you busy in the cellar with old Stacker.'

'Shut up,' said Amy, elbowing my brother. She winked at me, her eyes like melted toffee, and took another sip of wine. I could see why my brother was so smitten.

'He knows I'm joking.' He flopped sideways, nuzzling Amy's neck.

'You were definitely supposed to hear about the job today?' Amy asked.

'He said by the end of the week.' I shrugged and put my unfinished beer on the coffee table. 'It's Friday and I've heard nothing.'

'You leaving that?' Adam asked, eyeing the bottle.

'Yeah.' I stood up and grabbed my jacket. 'It's late. I'd best be off.'

'You've barely touched it. Give it here.'

I pushed the warm beer towards him. I'd had a few swigs on Adam's insistence, but I'd lost interest in drinking since the accident and I rarely finished one if I knew I'd be driving.

My brother hiccupped. 'Oh, did you get my message earlier? About visiting Mum?'

'Yeah,' I said again, zipping my jacket. 'Just give me a call when you want to go.'

Adam got to his feet, swaying.

I made for the door, but he caught me by the arm.

'Elliott,' he said softly. 'I know you don't like going, but ignoring it's not going to change anything.'

'Neither is going.'

He let go of me and sighed. 'I'll phone you, then.'

'All right.' I called goodbye to Amy and left, my mood blackening.

After spending the last few days moping at home, waiting for an email that never came, I'd finally given up at around six and gone to Adam's. Even though I'd enjoyed the evening, it was a bad move. The rest of his housemates were out so it had been just the three of us, larking about, eating takeaway and watching a movie. But I was paying for it now. My entire body begged for rest. I shouldn't even have driven, I was so tired. Thankfully, it was late and the roads were quiet. I drove with the window open the whole way back, cold air blasting in my face to keep me awake. The tension eased for a moment when I reached the green and parked, only to be replaced with a different kind.

I looked up to the third floor. All the lights were out – Dad was in bed. I felt a stab of guilt when I thought of him, coming home reeking of chemicals and other people's dirt. Coming home to an empty flat, a microwave dinner and a note to say I was round Adam's for the evening.

I'll make him dinner tomorrow, I thought, dragging myself up the stairs. *I'll cook him something decent.*

I let myself in. In the kitchen, the cat wound round my ankles. I realised Dad hadn't fed her – the lack of washing up in the sink

41

told me he hadn't even fed himself. He'd walked straight through the door and into bed, probably as tired, if not more so, than I was.

I scraped cat meat into a dish, washed my hands – and paused. The light on the answer phone was flashing. I pushed the button to listen, noting the time of the call. I'd missed it by minutes.

Arthur Hodge's voice bumbled down the phone. I played it twice, but I'd heard it right the first time. He'd offered me the job.

I found myself smiling, weakly, but the excitement I'd anticipated didn't come; I was too tired to be roused even by this stroke of luck. Instead I felt only relief that, finally, I stood a chance of getting some answers.

I didn't bother showering, didn't bother doing anything I should have done – even cleaning my teeth. I just went into my room, stripped and fell into bed without so much as pulling the curtains.

There are two types of tiredness. The first kind – the good kind – is the type of physical and mental exhaustion you get from something like exercise. Your body's heavy and relaxed, and you've cleared your mind. You're in the prime state for some quality sleep.

The other kind of tiredness isn't good. It's the kind you get when you haven't had enough sleep for whatever reason – maybe you got up for an early flight to go on holiday, or you've been stressing out revising all night for exams. You're physically drained, but your mind's buzzing, refusing to wind down.

Like tiredness, my sleep disorder has two sides to it. The first is the out-of-body experience – or astral projection, as it's sometimes called. That's bad enough. Bad because of what I see around me when it happens, the panic of trying to get back into my body, and bad because it's too close to what happened when I nearly died. When I *did* die, for those two minutes.

But the other side . . . that's worse.

In the split-personality of my sleep disorder, I'd grown to think of it as the Mr Hyde to the other side's Dr Jekyll.

And this night, the night I got the job, it was Mr Hyde who paid me a visit.

According to the books I'd read, it occurs as you're either going to sleep or waking up. Your body enters a stage of sleep known as REM. This is when you dream. What normally happens is that your muscles go into paralysis to stop you acting out your dreams and harming yourself or anyone else. But sometimes it's possible to wake a little, not only seeing your surroundings as they are, but while you're still paralysed and experiencing REM. Reality and dream merge. The combination of being powerless and the weight of your paralysed body can result in a feeling of being crushed. This is where the fear starts. Mix fear with dream hallucinations and you're in for an experience you'll never forget.

It's got different names all over the world, depending on the culture. *Devil on your back. Old Hag. Hag-ridden. Witch Riding on Your Back. When the Dark Presses.*

Presses.

Pressing.

Pressure on my chest. Somewhere in the depths of my dream I recognised that I was struggling for breath. The pressure built, grew heavier, and with it I was transported back to the accident, where strangers' hands pumped my body, trying to bring life and air back into it.

But they were pushing too hard, leaving no time for my lungs to fill. Forcing more air out than in. Crushing me. And I couldn't

43

move, not a muscle. The hands that should have helped now felt as though they could harm. Pressing down over my heart with some unknown intent . . . to stifle, to stop?

My eyes opened to the darkened room. As they did, something scuttled away from me into the corner opposite the bed. The pressure on my chest eased. *The cat*, I thought. *Just the stupid cat.* The curtains were open as I'd left them and yellow light from the street lamp outside spilled across the room. For a moment, everything seemed calm.

In the corner, something shifted. *Not* the cat. It was too big for that. And the movement wasn't animal-like. It was considered. Crafty.

I tried to turn over . . . and couldn't.

What the . . .?

My body wasn't doing what my brain told it. I couldn't move. I couldn't do anything. *Not again,* I thought. *Please, not this. Not again.*

I'd read about people who'd woken up during an operation. Their entire bodies were still numb and useless from the anaesthetic, but their minds were alert and clear, the way my mind was now. My mind knew that there was something in the room with me, something not right. And whatever it was, it knew that I couldn't move. It knew I was powerless.

I wanted to curl up, away from the thing in the corner. I wanted to shout for Dad . . . *tried* to shout, but it was like screaming in a nightmare. A pathetic whimper, barely more than a breath, was all I could force out. It didn't matter how hard I tried – it was like someone had shoved cotton wool down my throat, muffling everything. But this wasn't a nightmare. I was awake. My clothes hung off the back of the chair where I'd chucked them; my keys

44

and wallet were in the usual place on the desk. Everything was as it should be, except . . .

The thing moved again. A slow, creeping movement. I strained to see it more clearly but from my position – I was lying on my back – my view was limited. The light from the street pooled in the centre of the room. It didn't reach the furthest parts, the outer corner – and the thing knew it. It kept to the shadowy spaces, melting into them.

I tried to move again, panicking. My stupid, traitorous body lay motionless as a slab of meat on a butcher's bench. I could feel the sheets tangled round my legs, the mattress under my back, but no attempt to move worked.

'*Daaaaad* . . .' My scream came out as a whisper, nothing more.

The thing became bolder. It slunk a little way out of its corner and nearer to the bed. It crept, with pauses that grew shorter. Its shape took on definition. An arm, a shoulder.

Not a thing. A person, on hands and knees. *Crawling*.

It moved into the light. A matted web of waterlogged hair fell across the face.

If I hadn't already been incapable of moving, I would have been paralysed with fear. Was my heart even beating? I wasn't sure any more.

The figure reached the foot of the bed, over on the right. The side I was on. It started to change position, unfurling like a flower. Moving into a standing position. Another attempt to yell resulted in a strangled sound escaping my mouth.

The draggled hair parted with the tilting of the head. I knew that face. I'd seen it before. Like this, now . . . and in the bathroom, submerged in water, lifeless.

Tess Fielding stood at the end of my bed, watching me. She stood, naked and with no shame. Water ran off her waxy skin and on to the carpet and the bed. A droplet glistened on my foot where it had fallen from her body. Revulsion rose within me. She took small steps, closer and closer, until she loomed over me.

Her gaze travelled down my body, then back up to my face again. Water dripped from her hair on to my chest, trickling icily down my sides. She brought her face nearer to mine. Her eyes were red-rimmed, her lips tinged blue. Her outline alternated between flickering and blurred to being solid. I saw her lips moving, but heard nothing.

Move! I shouted to my body. *MOVE! Get out of here, damn you!*

My body ignored me, inanimate as a doll.

Her mouth opened and closed, forming shapes and words that only she heard.

I can't hear you, I tried to say. '*C-can't . . . can't heeeeaaaar . . .*'

I tried to move again. Couldn't. Wanted to close my eyes, to shut her out, and couldn't. I was powerless to do anything except watch.

Her eyes took on a wild look, and her body jerked with the force of her words. She was shouting, now. Angry that I couldn't hear her, or perhaps because she could see that I didn't want to. She reached towards me and I found my attention pulled from her face to her wrists. Slashed, and red, and open without dignity. Her final, darkest hour raw and ugly and exposed.

'*Leave . . . me . . . alone . . .*'

But she wasn't leaving. She came closer still, leaning over me. Putting her hands on me, pressing down on my chest, over my heart, like she was trying to stop it with force or sheer will . . . or perhaps just out of a desire to feel a heartbeat once more. Her face was in mine. She slithered sideways on top of me, squatting like a toad over my body.

46

Slowly, she lowered herself on to me, her knees drawn up to meet her hands on my chest. The air squeezed out of my lungs; the same feeling I'd had as when I'd woken. Only now, it was ten times worse. I felt her weight bearing down and the clammy dampness of her flesh, like a dead fish, touching mine. She had me pinned.

When I was ten, we'd had to have our dog put to sleep. We'd all stood around the vet's table – me, Adam and Mum crying, and Dad trying his hardest not to. We took it in turns to stroke her, from the moment the needle went in to the moment her heart stopped. I remembered the way her body felt different then. How heavy it became when the muscles relaxed and the tension left it. It wasn't called a dead weight for nothing.

That was me, now. A dead weight. The weight of a dead person. My lungs battled to suck in air. I managed tiny gasps that weren't enough. Her lips continued to move, faster, spitting the words.

Blackness crept in from the sides of my vision. She was squashing the air out of me. Crushing the life out of me. The ends of her long hair landed on my thumb, clinging there like a fat slug. Bile rose in my throat. If I couldn't move my whole body, maybe I could just move that tiny part . . . get it away from the dead, waterlogged hair at least.

My vision flickered. Tess Fielding's grey face, grey teeth, would soon be gone. Her wet hair sucked at my thumb. I couldn't see it, but I could feel it. I pictured it in my mind. If I could just move it, move that one, tiny part of me . . .

My thumb twitched and the slug of hair fell away. It was the tiniest motion, yet it had unlocked something bigger. I found I was clenching my teeth, and the realisation sent a jolt through me. Slowly, I was regaining control over my limbs. I stared at Tess with everything I had left in me, willing movement back into my body. My fingers moved . . . then my hands, and my feet. Everything was waking, coming back to life. I shouted, twisting on to my side and threw the thing on my chest clear across the room.

I was on my feet, out of bed, with the sheets around my legs. Awake. I lunged for the light and snapped it on. My own stuff, familiar and messy, greeted me like an old friend. I snatched up a hockey stick that leaned against the wall and held it, ready to attack anything that came near. But I was alone. Wherever Tess had gone, she wasn't here, at least not in any visible form.

Each thump of my heart shook my knees. I trembled, trying to steady my breathing, and rubbed my face, wet with only God knew what. My sweat and tears. The freezing bathwater dripping from *her* . . .

My guts churned. I ran for the bathroom. The last place I wanted to go, but as was often the case after one of these episodes, the adrenaline and fear manifested into nausea. I'd only ever actually *been* sick once, in the kitchen sink, unable to face the bathroom. When Dad came in and saw me, understandably, he'd gone ape-shit. I didn't dare do it again.

I retched until my eyes watered. Nothing came up, but I almost fell into the toilet when something moved behind me.

'What the *hell*? Don't sneak up on me!'

Dad stood blinking in the doorway. My screech sent him back a step or two, but then he came closer, pulling his dressing gown tighter around him.

'Sorry. Just wanted to make sure you're all right.'

'What does it look like?' I straightened up. He watched as I washed my hands and sloshed water on my face, and I was reminded of being five years old again, being supervised to make sure I brushed my teeth before bed.

48

'Do you need a piss, or something? Or are you just here to watch?'

'Just thought you might want . . . thought you might have had another one of those dreams.'

The reference to 'dreams' did it. Forced me to lie, just to wind him up.

'No, I drank too much at Adam's. And in case you've forgotten, I'm nearly eighteen. It's about time you learned to knock.'

Wrong answer.

'*Drinking?* And you drove home?' Dad's finger stabbed the air in front of my eyes, his face contorted. 'You'd better be joking about that. And if you want privacy, you ungrateful little sod, the bathroom door not only shuts, but it's got a lock. *Bloody well use it!*'

He slammed the door. A moment later, his bedroom door slammed as well. My throat ached with the urge to cry, but the need to open the bathroom door overtook it. I couldn't be shut in there, alone. Dad should know that. He should *know*. But it was my own fault, I'd lied and it had backfired.

I yanked it open and it bounced off the side of the bath.

A child's cry rang out from below. I squirmed, dithering in the hallway between the bathroom and the bedroom, growing colder with each passing minute. When I could stand it no longer, I darted into the bedroom, pulled the quilt off the bed and legged it into the living room.

Breathing the stale smell of Dad's cigarettes, I scrunched up on the sofa and tucked myself under the duvet with the remote controls, watching cheesy sitcom repeats on mute, one after another.

Next door, Dad's room was silent but I knew he'd be awake, seething. The child in the flat below grizzled, a low drone mingling with a quiet voice; the parent trying to get it settled. It went on for about half an hour before finally quieting down. I grimaced. No doubt there'd be an irate note stuck through the letterbox in the morning.

When the birds started singing and the first light crept through the yellowed curtains, I allowed my eyes to close, too tired to care if they ever opened again.

I fully expected to grovel for a week to make up for my outburst in the night, but to my surprise, Dad beat me to an apology. He brought a mug of coffee into the living room at ten the next morning and put it down on the carpet next to me. I sat up, moving my legs to make room for him, and he perched on the end of the sofa, sucking heavily on a cigarette.

I picked up the mug and lowered the TV volume. I'd been awake for about an hour, watching the news. It wasn't cheerful viewing but the normality of it helped, somehow. Dad stared at the screen.

'You hadn't been drinking last night, had you?'

I shook my head.

Flakes of cigarette ash floated to the carpet. Dad didn't notice.

'I shouldn't have shut the bathroom door. I'm sorry.'

'It's okay.' I sipped the too-hot coffee, stinging my tongue. 'I was out of order, shouting like that. I know you only came to see if I was all right.'

'Yesterday was just . . . not good,' Dad went on. 'There was a mix-up with the rota – I ended up getting in late. And to top it all off, it's three years this week that your mum . . .' he shook his head slightly. 'Who'd have thought I'd end up doing this poxy job, clearing up after other people?' He chuckled. 'Look at the state of this place. I can't even remember the last time I cleared up after *us*.'

I followed his gaze around the room. A shaft of sunlight cut through the curtains. It should have been cheering and warm. Instead it highlighted everything that was wrong: the dust on the skirting boards, the sticky cup rings on every surface. The cigarette burns in the carpet, and the overflowing ashtrays.

'Mum would have a fit if she saw this place,' Dad whispered.

There was nothing to say. We both knew it was true: the flat was a mess. I looked down at myself, skinny white limbs poking out from under the duvet. *I* was a mess. And poor Dad was trying, and failing, to hold everything together.

'I'm getting better,' I told him, wanting it to be true. 'I've got a job.'

Dad turned to look at me. 'A *job*? Where?'

'At that museum, Past Lives. I've got a job as a tour guide.'

His face fell. 'But it's miles away. All your wages will go on petrol—'

'It's got accommodation,' I cut in. 'If I do extra hours I get to stay overnight.'

'What about college?' Dad asked. 'All your artwork? What about university?'

'I'll go back,' I promised. 'Next year. And this way I can save some money for my fees.'

He nodded slowly. 'What if it continues? You know . . . when you're asleep? What are you going to do if it happens and other people hear you?'

I took a deep breath. 'I'll pass it off as dreams. It'll be embarrassing, but I'll have to live with it. Plus . . . there are stories about that place. They say it's haunted.' I waited for Dad to roll his eyes or walk off in a huff, but he didn't. Perhaps he was too tired to argue.

'I know what you think when I tell you about what I see here when I'm . . . when I *should* be asleep. I know you think it's not real. And I don't know if it is, either. All I know is that it scares the hell out of me, and if I don't do *something*, it'll end up driving me mad.'

'How's this going to put a stop to it? I don't understand. Surely if you think you're being haunted this will just make things worse? Whatever it is that happens to you, this is inviting more.'

'If Tess Fielding is just a dream, then she's a recurring one,' I answered. 'And she'll find me wherever I go. But if she's . . . *real,* then this is the best way for me to figure that out.'

Dad shook his head. 'If you think it's going to help, then do it.' He squashed his cigarette butt into the ashtray. 'But I don't think so. I don't believe in ghosts, Elliott. Never have. What I believe is that the mind plays tricks. And if you're filling it with stories of hauntings, they could trick you just as easily as the story of Tess. Even if you see something, something different, how will you know it's real?'

I didn't answer. The thought was a horrible one and it was entirely possible.

'I won't,' I said. 'But I can't just stay here, in this flat, being afraid. Maybe a change of scenery is what I need. Maybe it won't follow me.'

Dad rubbed his hand over his chin, staring at the telly. 'I hope it doesn't.'

SIX

Ophelia

The first morning at Past Lives crawled by in a monotone of forms, fire exits and health and safety. I trudged over the cobbles after the woman showing me around.

Earlier, when she'd met me at reception, she'd introduced herself as Una. She wore a long, brown dress over an off-white blouse. I thought it looked Victorian, but I couldn't be sure. Even without the historical outfit she was a strange-looking woman: thin, with a scraggy neck and short, spiky brown hair poking out from her cap.

I glanced at my watch. It was nine forty-five. The museum opened its doors to the public at ten. So far the whole place was quiet, with just a few costumed workers bustling about. It was eerie to watch life progressing in the way it would have done all those decades ago. When the hordes of people came flooding in later all that would change, but for now it was a place untouched by time.

Una led me to the Old Barn and entered the door code.

'This is the main staff room,' she said. The entire ground floor had been knocked into one room. A blonde girl in jodhpurs stood in a basic kitchen area in the corner, sipping from a cracked cup with a black horse on it. I caught a whiff of coffee before she turned away, flicking her hair over her shoulder. It fell down her back in a plait that reached her waist.

Three battered settees and a few beanbags surrounded a coffee table. A radio played at a low volume on a ledge by some stairs. Una lowered the sound further.

'It's fine to listen to the radio, but it mustn't be overheard by the visitors,' she explained. 'We do everything we can to reflect the past as accurately as is possible.'

Behind Una's back, the blonde girl glanced over and rolled her eyes. She looked about my age. I chanced a smile, but it died on my lips as she stared at me blankly before looking away.

Stuck up cow, I thought, turning my attention back to Una, who was now halfway up the stairs. I trampled after her.

'Lockers, toilets, showers and changing rooms,' said Una, pointing. 'Costumes are at the front, arranged according to era. Mostly you'll wear the same sort of thing unless you're covering for someone.'

I eyed the rails of clothes. Some were elaborate and vibrant in colour, and others were plain and dull; the colour of mud and moss. The contrast between the rich and the poor couldn't have been clearer.

'You should have received a locker number with your welcome pack,' Una continued.

I hunted through my brown envelope. Locker number twenty-eight. I located it and dumped my stuff inside before pocketing the key.

'Mobile phones are not allowed in the museum at any time,' said Una. 'And that includes on silent. No matter how subtle you might think you're being, our ancestors did *not* sneakily check their phones for text messages.'

When we got back downstairs I looked for the fair-haired girl but she had gone, leaving her empty cup on the draining board.

'That brings us to the end of your induction,' said Una. 'I appreciate it's a lot to take in, but if you have any questions you can find me at the bookbindery on Goose Walk – you might want to mark that on your map.' She looked at a watch hanging from a chain around her neck. 'Anyway, I'm sure you're ready for a tea break. We've got a few minutes before a team member collects you, and then it's over to them. I'll just find out who's meant to be looking after you.' From a cubby-hole in the wall by the door she removed a phone and dialled.

Costumed people wandered in and out of the staff room, making drinks and chatting. I went to make coffee, grabbing the horse cup from the draining board.

'Hello?' I heard Una say. 'Arthur? Who's meant to be training Elliott Drake today?' There was a pause. 'Off sick? *Again?* Who's covering? Oh. Is there no one else? All right, all right, yes. Just send her.' She sighed and hung up.

'Sorry about that. We're a guide down today, and we've several schools coming in. I've arranged for my niece to cover some of the shorter tours, so you'll be with her. She's about the same age as you.'

I nodded. 'What does your niece normally do if she's not a tour guide?'

Una tucked the phone back into the cubby-hole. 'She tends to the horses, giving horse and cart rides and mucking out the stables. Obsessed with horses, she is. Oh – here she is now.'

I stared at the cracked horse cup in my hand, remembering the girl who'd used it earlier. She'd been wearing jodhpurs. The coffee curdled in my stomach.

The door to the Old Barn creaked open and the blonde girl stomped in.

'Arthur said you wanted me?'

Her voice was deeper than I imagined it would be.

'Hello, love,' Una replied. 'I need you to cover Goose Walk –' she matched the girl's sharp intake of breath with an equally sharp warning look of her own, '– and you'll be accompanied by Elliott here. It's his first day.'

'Great,' the girl answered. Her tone suggested the opposite.

Una ignored her. 'Elliott, this is my niece, Ophelia. She knows every inch of this place, so you'll be in capable hands.'

Something passed between them. As Una backed out of the Old Barn, her eyes lingered on her niece's hands, which were gloved, right up to the elbow. Ophelia returned the look with one of defiance. It vanished as soon as the door shut.

'Sorry if I messed your day up,' I said, intending to sound pointed. Somehow it came out like a genuine apology.

She stared at me, expressionless, yet I got the impression I was being assessed.

'You didn't.'

I started to smile before she continued with, '*They* did.'

For the second time that morning I had to pretend I hadn't been smiling because of this girl. I was starting to feel like an idiot.

'I take it you don't like doing the tours?'

Another shrug. 'I'm not a big talker.'

'I can tell.'

'That's my cup you're using,' she said coolly.

'I know.'

She gave me another blank stare. *What is it with this girl?* I thought. Her face was like a mask. I held the cup out to her,

56

expecting her to snatch it, but she didn't. She took it as if she were handling a nervous horse. Her glove brushed my fingers. It was made of some soft material, probably suede. 'There are spare ones in the cupboard,' she said, rinsing it in the sink.

'Fine,' I said, rolling my eyes at her back. 'I'm sorry I used your cup.'

She placed it on the draining board again and turned to me.

'I forgive you.'

It was impossible to tell whether she was being sincere or sarcastic. Either way, she made it sound like her forgiveness didn't come about very often.

'Come on,' she said. 'Time to get changed.'

I followed her upstairs. A horsey smell came off her. It wasn't altogether unpleasant. She led me to the costume area and raked through the women's clothing rail. I stood by the men's, not knowing where to start and determined not to ask for her help. I recalled Una mentioning Goose Walk and pulled out the map I'd been given. Dozens of little buildings spiralled off from each other. A small key at the side indicated the era and, within a few seconds, I worked out that I needed something from the Victorian rail.

I chose the plainest thing I could find: a thick, creamy shirt and dark-brown trousers. As I pulled the hanger out I saw that the outfit came with braces and a flat cap. I grimaced before glancing at the other rails. A hideous Elizabethan doublet paired with stockings caught my eye. It could be a lot worse.

Ophelia made her selection and went into the cubicle to change. I found a second changing room, went in and undressed, then tugged on the unfamiliar clothing. It was scratchy and stiff, the fabric heavy. There was no mirror in the cubicle, but when I came out with my own clothes tucked under one arm, Ophelia's smirk told me all I needed to know.

'You look like something out of *Oliver Twist*.'

I tried to think of a witty comeback, but couldn't.

She gestured to the table by the window. 'We need to log these out.'

I watched as she leaned over the table, filling out the details from a small ticket attached to her hanger. As it happened, Ophelia looked the part. A simple dress drew her in at the waist, giving her willowy figure a curvier shape, and her hair had been twisted into a knot under a straw hat. Her brown gloves had been replaced with a dark-blue pair.

I looked across to a mirror screwed on to the wall. Ophelia was right – I looked like a street urchin. I pulled the cap further down and turned away in disgust. She handed me the pen and stepped away from the desk, tapping her foot impatiently.

Blue day dress, Victorian replica c.1850, she had written in the logbook, followed by a number, the date and her name: Ophelia Knight. Her handwriting was clumsy and childish. I copied the label attached to my own hanger: *Labourer's shirt & trousers. Victorian replica c.1845*.

When I put the pen down, Ophelia was stuffing her other clothes into her locker. I found my locker and bundled my clothes inside.

'What now?' I asked.

'Now we go and meet our group,' she answered.

'What will I have to do?'

'Nothing much. Just keep up, be attentive to anyone who needs help, and listen. Take notes if you want.'

We left the Old Barn. Ophelia glided easily over the cobbles and I hurried to stay level with her. Though I could no longer feel the stones pressing through my sturdy boots, the unevenness of the ground meant that one clumsy footstep could result in a twisted ankle.

A little way back, near the archways, Arthur Hodge stood between two groups of school children. He beckoned, stepping out of earshot of the teachers.

'Come on, Ophelia! For goodness' sake – we've been waiting ten minutes.'

'When you spring a last-minute tour on me, not to mention babysitting –' a jerk of the head in my direction, '– it'll happen,' she said through her teeth. 'Which group's mine?'

I looked over her shoulder at the two groups. The first was a party of teenagers. They looked about thirteen and wore mixed expressions ranging from boredom to downright evil. Worse still was the teacher, a Rottweiler of a woman yelling at them to stand still. The second group consisted of smaller kids aged about eight or nine. They were all shouting and fidgeting, paying no attention to their drip of a teacher who looked like he wasn't long out of school himself. It wasn't much of a choice. Hodge nodded towards the Rottweiler. The teacher had been eyeballing Ophelia since we'd arrived, looking her up and down as if she wasn't convinced someone so young was qualified to do the tour.

I watched Ophelia out of the corner of my eye, but her face didn't give away a thing about how she was feeling. I started to wonder if she'd even blink if a bomb went off. She just nodded and, with that, Hodge took off with the younger party.

Ophelia offered the Rottweiler her hand. 'I'm your guide for this morning.' Her voice was as firm as her handshake. I had to suppress a smirk when the Rottweiler introduced herself as Mrs Barker.

Ophelia addressed the group, her voice clear and confident.

'Welcome to Past Lives. I'm here to make sure you get as much out of your visit as possible, so if you have any questions, please speak up.'

A hand shot into the air.

'Yes?' Ophelia asked.

I craned my neck along with the rest of the class to see three lads falling about and prodding each other. The one who had his hand up wore an irritating smile.

'He asked if you've got a boyfriend.'

'I never! It was him!' his friend protested. Some girls next to them tittered.

'Lucas!' Mrs Barker snapped. 'What did I say to you in the minibus?'

I watched Ophelia for a reaction. She was completely unruffled.

'Why do you ask, Lucas?'

The boy's face reddened, but I could see he wasn't ready to back down just yet.

'Because you're pretty, Miss.'

The class erupted into sniggers.

'LUCAS!' Mrs Barker marched to the back. 'I warned you, didn't I?'

'Well, she is!' Lucas insisted, grinning.

Was she? I looked at Ophelia, intrigued. She definitely wasn't ugly, but there was nothing about her that stood out. Grey eyes, straw-coloured hair and skin. Nothing there that a bit of make-up wouldn't improve. Nice waist, I supposed, but not much up the top to grab hold of.

'I'm glad you asked, Lucas,' Ophelia said. The class immediately shushed, and even Mrs Barker looked surprised.

'One of the buildings you'll see today is the Victorian school, Mayfields. Do you know much about what life was like for Victorian schoolchildren?'

The question was directed at Lucas, but the entire class shook their heads.

'It was grim. They liked their punishments, the Victorian teachers. One thing they might do to cheeky pupils was give them a soap-and-water mixture to wash their mouths out. Would you like to volunteer later?'

His classmates jeered and there were catcalls of '*Cheeky boy!*'

Lucas scoffed. 'You can't do stuff like that nowadays.'

'More's the pity,' said Mrs Barker.

'Right then,' said Ophelia. 'Any *sensible* questions? No? Let's begin.' She set off, slower than before to allow the group to keep up. I stayed level at her side.

'That was harsh,' I said. 'I don't think he meant any harm.'

Ophelia stared straight ahead. 'Maybe not. But if I'd let him get away with it they'd have crucified me.'

We wove toward the Plain, passing the other group, and finally stopped outside a ramshackle building on the corner of a street.

'This,' Ophelia announced, 'is Goose Walk. All the buildings were built from around 1840 onwards. With the exception of the school, which was originally here, they've been taken down, brick by brick, from their original sites all over England and rebuilt.' She gestured to the building.

'We start with the Toll Cottage. Built in 1847, it stood in the village of Old Tiverton, on the road through to London. Anyone passing would have to pay a toll for their wagon and animals. It operated as a tollhouse for just under twenty years. Once the railway line was built, the toll road was no longer needed and the cottage was sold.'

Ophelia pushed the little door open. Everyone squeezed inside. A rocking chair stood by a crackling fire. It smelled of wood smoke and coal.

'The people who lived here were poor. There was no gas, electricity, or running water. Rainwater would be drawn from a pump outside and heated over the fire for cooking and washing. The windows are positioned so that anyone inside can see the road clearly.'

Some of the kids wandered through into the next room. I peered in after them. Inside was a single bed with an iron frame. A patchwork quilt covered it and, next to it, was a table with a candle, another fireplace and a rug. A framed prayer hung on the wall. I went back into the front room.

'Where's the toilet?' a boy asked.

'There's no inside lavatory,' Ophelia explained. She pushed open another door and led us outside to the rear of the cottage. A path led through a vegetable patch and at the end there was a small brick outhouse. She nodded towards it. 'See for yourselves.'

The class rushed toward it, cramming into the doorway. Giggles and exclamations of disgust erupted from them, and I stood on tiptoe to see over their heads. A tin bucket was positioned beneath a wooden bench with a crude hole in the middle.

'This is where you'd have to come to use the toilet, whatever the weather,' said Ophelia.

'Gross. Spiders everywhere,' a girl said, wrinkling her nose. 'But what did they use to . . . you know? Wipe?'

Another explosion of laughter. This time Ophelia joined in. It was the first time I'd seen her lose her blank expression. Her smile lightened her face, but still didn't make her pretty. She pointed to a nail jutting from the wall with torn scraps of paper hanging from it.

'Old newspaper,' she said.

'Was it like recycling, Miss?'

'Yes,' said Ophelia. 'Exactly. Every penny had to count.'

The next stop was the school, Mayfields. It was a grey, gloomy building with a smell of disinfectant about it. Benches and desks stood in rows before a freestanding blackboard chalked with numbers.

'The school was designed to accommodate around three hundred children,' said Ophelia. 'They were aged between three and seven years old. Older children usually had to help with chores at home or work to earn money for their families.

'Now, you might all think that Mrs Barker here is a force to be reckoned with, but compared to Victorian teachers, I guarantee you'd think she was a fluffy little kitten.'

Someone at the back meowed. Mrs Barker smiled thinly.

'You may have noticed how dark the classroom seems. Why do you think that is?'

A hand went into the air. 'The windows are high up, Miss.'

'Correct,' said Ophelia. 'The Victorians were very strict, even down to the way their schools were built. They made the windows high so that pupils couldn't look out and get distracted. Their lessons were not at all fun. Children were made to learn by reciting things endlessly and simply copying things from the board. As a result, they didn't learn properly and got bored. Is there anyone with dyslexia in this class?'

Two hands went up. One of them belonged to the boy who had called Ophelia pretty.

'Ah, Lucas,' said Ophelia. 'Would you like to be a volunteer?'

There were wolf whistles from Lucas's friends. The boy pressed his lips together. Ophelia smirked.

'Don't worry, it doesn't involve soap and water. It's just for a minute.'

Lucas slid out from the back, grinning at his audience.

From a cupboard behind the desk Ophelia withdrew several things: something small made of wood, a paper cone, and a stack of rulers. She set the wooden contraption and rulers on the table and held out the cone.

'You've probably heard of these before,' she said. 'Come here, Lucas.'

Lucas sauntered over. Ophelia handed him the cone. 'The Victorians didn't recognise dyslexia or any kind of learning difficulty. They believed that all children learned in the same ways and at the same pace. The "D" on the cap stands for "dunce", meaning "idiot". Put the cap on and stand in the corner.'

Lucas put it on and slouched off, still grinning.

'Face the wall,' said Ophelia. 'And stand up straight.'

She looked back to the rest of the class. 'You.' She pointed to the other person with their hand still up. The girl edged her way out of the group.

'Put your hand on the table.'

The girl did as she was told. Without warning Ophelia seized a handful of rulers and brought them down, hard. A resounding crack followed a shriek from the girl and everyone in the room, including me, jumped. The girl snatched her hand back.

'Just think how much that would have hurt if I'd hit your knuckles and not the desk,' said Ophelia. 'Not just once, but five, maybe ten times. Now – one more volunteer?' Mrs Barker selected a boy from the front. Ophelia lifted the little wooden object up from the desk. When I looked closer I saw that there were two pieces of wood, each with four small holes in. They were joined by a length of rough string.

'These are finger stocks,' Ophelia explained. 'Pupils caught fidgeting or biting their nails would have to wear these. Turn around,' she told the boy. 'Now hold your hands together behind your back.'

She turned the boy's hands palm out and pushed his fingers into the small holes. Once in position she tied the string tightly around his wrists.

'Ouch,' he complained.

'Uncomfortable, isn't it?' said Ophelia. 'It gets a whole lot worse after a couple of hours.' She tugged at the string to release its captive.

'Can I come out of the corner now?'

I turned. Lucas peered over his shoulder. He'd lost his cocky expression and his face looked grey.

'Hold on, Lucas,' said Mrs Barker. 'You're still in disgrace, remember?'

'But there's a weird smell over here. It's making me feel sick.'

Ophelia put the finger stocks down and went still. 'What sort of smell?'

'Sort of a . . . like . . . like wee,' the boy said finally.

Straight away the jibes began. Some of Lucas's friends drifted over to him, sniffing the air.

'Have you wet yourself again, Lucas?'

'I can't smell anything . . . oh, wait. Yes, I can! It reeks!'

'Come out of the corner,' Ophelia told Lucas. He came towards her, glaring. Behind him, the exclamations continued and I lifted my nose and sniffed. There *was* something, faint at first then fast becoming the acrid, distinctive stench of ammonia. It built steadily, choking and cloying. And yet . . . it wasn't just the smell. Accompanying it was a wave of emotions: suffering, humiliation. Misery. The back of my neck tingled as the small hairs there stood up. The atmosphere in the schoolroom felt thick. Claustrophobic.

I coughed, eyes watering. 'Jesus, what *is* that?'

'Did a wild animal get in, do you think?' Mrs Barker's voice was muffled from behind her hands. Her eyes were wide. I wondered if she, or anyone else in the room was feeling the same things as I was. The jokes and jibes had stopped and most of the kids had edged towards the door. A couple of the girls clutched each other.

Ophelia whipped the dunce's cap off Lucas's head and gathered the rest of the punishment items in her arms before returning them to the store cupboard and locking it.

'Shall I open a window?' I asked.

She shook her head. 'That's not necessary. The smell will vanish any second now.'

'Doubt it!' said one of the kids, pinching his nostrils.

Ophelia moved into the corner, nose twitching. 'It's gone.'

I sniffed again, but already I could tell that the air had changed. It was musty and dank, the way it had been before, but the close, claustrophobic feeling had evaporated along with the smell of urine. One by one the class began sniffing the air again, tentative at first, before escalating into huge, exaggerated gulps.

'That's enough,' said Mrs Barker. 'Settle down!'

'What was that?' Lucas asked, his eyes narrowed. 'Some kind of trick to make me look stupid?'

'Not at all,' said Ophelia. 'There was no trick, I promise you.'

I couldn't be sure, but I thought her tanned face had lost some of its colour. Something about the way she spoke sent a chill over my skin. The entire group was silent, waiting for her to continue.

'What just happened has been witnessed only a handful of times by other tour groups,' she said. 'But this is the first time it's ever happened on one of mine.'

'What *did* just happen?' Mrs Barker asked.

Ophelia nodded to the cupboard. 'Over the past century, the punishments I just demonstrated were carried out in this room countless times, using that very equipment. We know this for fact because there's also a book containing names and details of those that were punished. We don't display the punishment book on the general tour because it's the museum's view that some of the content is a little . . . disturbing. But it appears that one boy in particular was victimised by a certain teacher. We're fairly sure that from the descriptions, the boy had dyslexia. On one occasion he was made to stand in the corner for an entire day, denied lunch and toilet breaks. I'm sure you can all guess what happened.' She paused. 'He was made to stand in his own urine, shivering with cold for the rest of the day.'

'So you're saying we just smelled . . . I mean, it was that boy's *ghost*?' Lucas asked, his gaze fixed in the corner. Whispers rippled around the room.

'I'm not sure "ghost" is the right word,' Ophelia said. 'There's nothing to suggest that the boy died here, but we believe that sometimes events – especially traumatic ones – can leave an imprint on things and places. Sometimes, that imprint manifests through a smell, or a sound, or a feeling . . .'

'I felt something,' said Lucas, in a tight, strained voice. 'It wasn't just the smell. I felt stupid, and small, and . . . angry.'

Even if I hadn't experienced those same feelings, I was in no doubt that I'd have been convinced by what Lucas said. It was obvious that the whole thing had shaken him and, judging by his classmates' faces, a few of them had felt the same emotions, too. I could tell that, like me, at least half of them couldn't wait to get out of the building.

Ophelia nodded. 'Let's move on. There'll be lessons back here at two o'clock if you'd like to return.'

We herded them towards the door, not that they needed much encouragement. I wondered if any of them would have the guts to come back for the lessons later on.

As everyone crowded outside, some of the tension eased and chattering broke out. Ophelia held back, watching them.

'Give them a minute or two,' she murmured.

'You handled that well,' I said. 'How did you know what to do?'

Her expression remained closed. 'Like I said, it's happened before. It's the objects, and talking about them that makes . . . whatever it is manifest. I knew they had to be put away.'

'What would happen if you hadn't?'

Ophelia's grey eyes were solemn. 'One of the guides tried it once.

The man in the corner was in his forties. He could have moved once the smell came up – but it was like he just froze with fear. He pissed himself, right there, in front of twenty strangers. He was hysterical, his wife was hysterical. The tour was stopped – it was awful.'

'You saw it?'

She nodded. 'I was training. After that, I avoided using the punishment devices during my tours. I got away with it until Hodge found out—'

'Hodge? That's what you call him?'

'That's what everyone calls him, apart from Una. Anyway, he was pretty mad – said it was meant to be an authentic tour and the likelihood of it happening again was slim. He'd come up with a theory.'

'Which is?'

'That even though the objects are triggers, it takes something else – a third party – to act as a catalyst. In some of the cases, it came out that a member of the tour group had nearly died. Once it was the guide. He'd had a heart attack a couple of years earlier and died on the operating table before they managed to bring him back.'

Something cold twisted in my gut.

'He swore he'd had a near-death experience,' Ophelia continued. 'Saw a tunnel with light and all that. And there was something similar with another group – a visitor that time. She'd been in a diabetic coma and heard voices of dead family members.'

'So you're saying that it takes someone within the group who's experienced death, combined with those punishment devices being used to act as a catalyst?'

'That's the theory.'

'But you said that the kid hadn't actually died. Why would death be a catalyst?'

'I said there was no evidence he'd died,' Ophelia answered. 'But who knows for sure?' She headed back to the group.

I followed, sick to the stomach in the knowledge that if Hodge's theory was right, then *I* was the catalyst. And any tours I accompanied – or gave – had a high possibility of dredging up things that simmered just below the surface.

69

SEVEN

Dangerous Liaisons

I lingered in the doorway of the Victorian sweet shop, trying to focus on taking notes as Ophelia spoke.

'This building and the bakery next door were built as houses in 1840 . . .'

My head thumped with a need for caffeine and the weight of what had just happened. I stayed near the exit, willing myself to concentrate on what Ophelia was saying in case there were any more ghostly triggers I was likely to set off, but my mind kept wandering to the schoolroom. I stared at the words on the page, hoping they'd make sense when I read them back later on. At the moment they were meaningless. At this rate, I couldn't see the job lasting more than a week.

'. . . with the shop fronts being added in 1870. They originally stood at . . .'

Inside, a plump woman stood at the counter weighing humbugs and explaining how they were made. Jars of boiled sweets lined the shelves behind her and trays of sugar mice sat in the window. The interior smelled warm and sweet, and the schoolchildren crammed around the counter, jingling coins.

Eventually we drifted next door into the bakery. Again, I positioned myself in the doorway. The group crowded into the little shop. I could smell the sweets on their breath, and perhaps it was a sugar rush, or the realisation of what they'd just experienced, but there was a buzz about them. They'd felt something, actually *witnessed* something, and they were hungry for more.

'Are there any more ghost stories?' Lucas asked. A boiled sweet lodged in his cheek and rattled against his teeth.

Ophelia nodded. 'Though most of the stories are associated with the older parts of the museum. You'll hear about those later. Now, let me tell you more about this bakery . . .' Her voice drifted into my head in snatches of dates, names and facts that were only half jotted down in my notes. This place didn't feel like the school. There was a faint, yeasty smell that took me back to my mum's baking days and, like rising bread, a lump formed in my throat at the memory. I shut the notebook and stuck it in my pocket as we left and crossed a small stone bridge over the canal.

Past the bridge, the road widened and led to a cobblestone square which was home to a few more shops. I recognised the cobbler's, but the rest I'd either forgotten or were new additions since my own school visit. There was now a pharmacy, a general store and a bookbinder's shop as well as an imposing grey building. To the left of the square there was a host of fairground attractions, the bright paint and swirling colours alien in the muted Victorian landscape. I read the words curving over the entrance: *Critchley's Travelling Fayre*.

Already some of the kids were begging their teacher to go into it. Surprising really, as it was pretty tame compared with what most of them were probably used to. There was no rollercoaster, no other fast-paced, adrenaline-pumping rides. Instead it was stuff like the coconut shy, hall of mirrors and a helter skelter.

'We'll be coming back this way.' Ophelia waltzed past the fair-ground to a chorus of groans and beckoned us to the huge, ugly unmarked building. 'First, the workhouse.'

Mid-morning, I had a twenty minute break before the next group was due. Already my eyelids were drooping. But when we got back to the Old Barn the last of the instant coffee was gone. Irritated, I made do with tea, only to notice that the box was labelled decaf. No caffeine whatsoever.

I'd barely swallowed the last mouthful before it was time to go and meet the next group. This time, it was a class of college students. Straight away I noticed a girl with glossy red hair and equally glossy lips. It was hard not to – she was staring straight at me. Now *this* was more like it. On impulse, I smiled. She returned it and lowered her eyes, but seconds later they were back on me. I felt a rush of the old excitement. I'd become so used to curious or pitying stares. I couldn't remember the last time someone had looked at me in that way.

By the time we'd reached the school I'd tuned out Ophelia's voice almost entirely. The talk of the punishments jolted me back momentarily but this time, Ophelia merely held the devices up and explained, briefly, how they'd been used. There were no volun-teers and nothing to disturb whatever lay dormant. As we trailed out my gaze found its way to the redhead's mouth. How long had it been since I'd been with a girl? Too long. I hadn't even *kissed* a girl since Juliet – hadn't wanted to . . . but I did now. For the first time in months I felt something like the old me.

When the tour finished we took the group back to the meeting point. It was coming up for twelve.

'It's an hour for lunch,' said Ophelia. 'I'll show you where to go . . .' She broke off to answer a question from someone nearby.

I scanned the group for the redhead but couldn't see her. Then a flash of scarlet from a nearby gated area caught my attention. I headed towards it and saw that it was a smoking yard. I went in. The redhead was one of three people with a cigarette. Her lips curved as I stopped in front of her.

'I'm Kim,' she said.

'Elliott.'

She offered the cigarette packet. 'Do you live around here?'

'No, thanks. And no, I'm not local. I live in Thurrock.'

She slid the box into her pocket and exhaled a cloud of smoke. 'I live near.' She looked at me through thick black lashes, then glanced meaningfully at her friends. They took the hint and left the yard, leaving us alone.

'Yeah?' I knew a come on when I saw one. 'Maybe we could meet when I finish work?'

'Maybe.'

Definitely.

'So how long have you worked here?'

'First day.'

'That explains why you didn't say much during the tour.'

I shrugged. 'Got to learn the ropes.' I found myself staring at her collarbone. Her skin was tanned, but there was a telltale streak on the neckline of her shirt. 'Well, I'd better get back. It's lunchtime and I haven't got a clue where to go, so maybe we should—'

Kim looked over my shoulder. I felt her hand on mine. 'You'll figure it out,' she whispered. 'Come on.'

'Wha . . .? Where?' I glanced back. Through the slats of the gate I saw Ophelia searching the group, no doubt wondering where I'd got to, but Kim was tugging me to the back of the yard where a door led into a corridor off the side of the entrance building. Above it were two logos: a man and a woman.

My knees buckled. Surely she wasn't going to . . .

. . . but she was. I stumbled through the door into the cubicle of the women's toilet. Kim locked it behind us. I stood with my back to the door, heart thudding. I didn't normally get nervous, but then, I didn't normally get girls throwing themselves at me. Not any more. Not like this.

'Won't they wonder where you are?' I croaked.

'It's a big place. I'll tell them I got lost.'

Her hand was still on the lock and her arm rested against my waist. Slowly, she moved it and ran both hands over my chest. I tried not to think about whether my body felt skinny under the shirt. She looked at me with eyes that were too blue. Contact lenses. Then she pressed herself against me, raising her mouth to mine.

I swallowed in surprise but kissed her back. She tasted . . . wrong. The bubblegum sweetness of her lipstick mixed with the sour smoke on her breath. Her tongue slid over mine then moved to my neck . . . the hollow of my throat. Her fingers grappled with my shirt buttons.

'No,' I whispered. Not here, like this, with the stark toilet light glaring down on us.

'Okay.' She moved her hands to my lower back. Her mouth was on mine again. She hooked her thumbs into my waistband, then slid them round to the front. There was a pinch of hair at my navel. My belt buckle rattled loose.

I closed my eyes, then pushed back gently on her shoulders, embarrassed. 'I'm sorry . . . but I can't.'

She looked at me and crossed her arms.

74

I breathed out heavily, rearranging my clothes. 'Listen – I've really got to go, but . . . give me your number. I'll call you.'

She shook her head. 'Phone's broken. I won't get it back for a couple of days. Do you know The Rusty Bicycle?'

'What's that, a pub?'

'Yeah. Five minutes from here. Meet me there tomorrow evening, say around seven?'

'All right.'

She lifted her hand to my face, running a finger under my eye. 'Don't forget to wash your make-up off first.' She rubbed her fingers together, as though she expected to find something on them, and edged out of the door.

I laughed. 'I'm not wearing make-up.'

'Oh, I just . . . You know what? Never mind. I'll see you tomorrow.'

Before I could question her she blew a kiss and vanished into the corridor.

My smile fell away as I emerged from the cubicle, blinking in the harsh strip lighting. My finger traced the path hers had taken, in the dark hollow under my eye. She had thought the shadows under my eyes were fake. Painted on as part of my costume.

She hadn't realised they were the real me.

'I didn't know you smoked,' said Ophelia, when I returned to the group.

'I don't. I just needed the bathroom.' I watched Kim's party moving off into the museum. I spotted her red hair at the back as she giggled with her friends. She didn't look back. My chest tightened.

'Right.'

Was it my imagination, or was there a hint of sarcasm?

'Did you bring lunch?'

'No.'

'I'll show you to the tea rooms,' she said, motioning for me to follow.

'Aren't you coming in with me?'

'No. I go home for lunch.'

'Oh. Is that far away?'

'About ten minutes' walk.'

I waited for her to say more, but she didn't. We walked in silence to the Plain. Ophelia pointed past the well to a chalky-white building with black beams on the outside. 'There it is. Hodge will meet you for this afternoon's tours at one.'

'Won't I be with you this afternoon?'

'Hopefully not.'

'Thanks.'

Her voice softened. 'I just meant that I'll be back at the stables. Another guide should be in to cover.'

'Oh. Well, thanks.'

'I was just doing my job.'

'You should do tours more often. You're good at it.'

'Compared to who?'

I laughed. 'Fair point.'

She rolled her eyes. 'I'll see you.'

'Yeah. See you.'

'Oh, and Elliott? Red really isn't your colour.'

'Huh?'

She smirked. 'The lipstick on your face? You might want to rethink it.'

Shit. Well and truly busted. 'I owe you one.'

76

She raised an eyebrow. 'I don't *want* one.'

'You know what I mean.' I wiped at my face. 'If Hodge had seen me . . .'

'He wouldn't have been best pleased,' she finished. 'No. Especially not on your first day. I doubt you'd have made it back tomorrow.'

I swallowed. 'I . . . thanks.'

She shook her head. 'Don't thank me. Seriously. If that's how you behave you'll be gone before the week's out.'

'Then why bother telling me?'

'I won't, next time.'

'There won't *be* a next time.'

'I've known girls like that,' she sneered. 'There's always a next time.'

'Girls like that?' I mimicked. 'Proper twenty-first century woman, aren't you?'

Her calm smile infuriated me. 'I wasn't being sexist. It applies to boys like that, too – and you're one of them.'

I resisted the urge to shout. 'One of *what*?'

'Do I need to spell it out? You hooked up with someone *in the toilet*. That's classy.'

'We didn't "hook up". We've got a date tomorrow night.'

'Oh, well. That makes it all right, then . . .'

'You don't know anything about me.'

'I've seen enough not to want to.'

I stared at the back of her head as she walked away. Each beat of my blood pulsed in my temple and I found my hands had clenched into fists in my pockets. Uncurling them, I wiped my slick palms against my trousers and stomped into the tea room.

I got a sandwich and some coffee and sat alone on the outside veranda, too pissed off to eat at first. The sun beat down directly above and a trickle of sweat ran out from under my cap. I took it off, staring over the wall at people moving around the museum while I picked at the sandwich. Turned out I was hungrier than I thought. After a couple of bites my appetite kicked in and I finished the lot. When I eventually remembered the coffee it was too cool to drink. As I queued for another, I saw my reflection in a mirror behind the counter and remembered the way Kim had touched the shadows under my eyes. It was enough to change my mind. I took an orange juice instead.

In the distance over by the stables a girl was on horseback.

Ophelia.

Her hair had come loose from the knot and flew over her shoulder. She left the shadow of the buildings and moved into the sun. The light hit her, turning her hair gold just for a second before she vanished from view.

I took a long drink of juice and leaned back, closing my eyes. Ophelia might be a stuck-up cow, but she'd still warned me and probably saved me the humiliation of being sacked on my first day. Much as I hated to admit it, that counted for something.

EIGHT

Seeing Red

I parked behind The Rusty Bicycle ten minutes early. Unheard of for me, but this was the most important date I'd been on in a while. I corrected myself. The *only* date. Adam's advice was to arrive late. Always. Not by much, just a few minutes. Just long enough to make them nervous. But I wasn't in the mood, or position to play games any more, and I hadn't even told Adam I was meeting someone. I hadn't told Dad it was a date either, only that I was going out with a few new friends after work. He'd seemed pleased.

I watched the clock on the dashboard working its way up to seven and thought back over the last two days. The guide I'd been paired with yesterday afternoon was a retired teacher named Len. He was nice enough, but he lacked the control over certain groups that Ophelia had asserted early on. Similarly, today's guide, a local historian, had none of the wit Ophelia had displayed. He'd just reeled off facts without caring whether anyone but himself was actually interested. Between the two I'd got a little more information to add to my notes, but not much.

I hadn't spoken to Ophelia since the dressing down she'd given me. I'd only seen her from a distance, mucking out the stables. She'd given no indication that she'd seen me, but when Hodge

79

called me into his office five minutes before the close of the day my mouth dried up. I went in, convinced Ophelia had changed her mind, and waited for him to fire me. Instead he asked if I thought I'd be ready to start leading tours, under supervision, of the Victorian sector in the next few days. When my heart stopped pounding enough for me to speak, I'd agreed.

Five to seven. I got out of the car. The sun was low in the sky; and having been out in it for the past two days I had some colour, which had gone a little way to camouflage the bags under my eyes. Coupled with the best night's sleep I'd had in ages, thanks to being on my feet all day and staying off coffee, I felt pretty good. I hoped Kim would see a difference.

I went inside and took a stool at the bar, wondering why Kim had suggested here and not somewhere livelier. Perhaps there wasn't anywhere. It was a quiet village, after all. Or perhaps she just planned on some privacy . . .

'What can I get you?'

I looked up. A girl behind the bar waited expectantly.

'Oh. Nothing at the moment, thanks. I'm just waiting for someone.'

She crossed the bar to serve someone else. At five past seven, I called her back and paid for half a lager. At ten past, I remembered to drink some, and took my phone out. I knew there wouldn't be any messages – we hadn't swapped numbers – but I needed to do something with my hands.

Finally, at seven thirty I got up and walked out, the drink virtually untouched. I'd been stood up.

Laughter rang in my ears as I left the building, cutting off as the door swung shut. Common sense told me it wasn't directed at me, but it didn't help the sick feeling rising in my throat on the way to the car. Sweat prickled across my sunburnt forehead. I put the key in the ignition and made myself drive.

Halfway down the road my fist hit the steering wheel. *Stood up?* I'd treated some girls pretty badly, but I'd never, ever stood anyone up. *Payback,* a little voice in my head said. *Now you know how it feels to be discarded. What goes around comes around.*

I'd hoped that wouldn't be true if I wasn't that person any more, but who was to say I'd really changed?

Girls like that . . .

Boys like you . . .

The words looped through my head. I slowed on a corner, recognising the road. The museum was near. I couldn't go home yet, Dad would be there. He was on earlys this week, and if I went back now he'd question me. I couldn't face it.

I looked along the side of the road, searching for somewhere to park. I needed to walk for a bit, to think and clear my head. There was a canal path surrounded by greenery up ahead on the opposite side of the road. The perfect place to be alone. I pulled over, my hand on the door release, when in the rear-view mirror, I caught sight of a group of people emerging from the path. I dropped my hand, waiting for them to pass.

With a jolt I recognised the girl in front as Ophelia. She strode ahead of another girl with short, spiky, black hair and two boys. The three of them were laughing and the shorter of the two boys had his arm slung across the dark-haired girl's shoulders. The other boy was necking beer from a can. I leaned closer to the mirror. Ophelia's face, as ever, had as much expression as a magnolia wall.

'Don't you ever smile?' I murmured. Christ, it was a wonder she even *had* friends.

I sat back as they drew level with the car. Remembering that I'd cracked the window earlier I started to wind it up, planning on getting out once they'd passed. Before the window closed I heard the crunch of the empty beer can and looked up in time to see the guy launch it – straight at Ophelia.

It bounced off the back of her head and clattered along the pavement, mingling with their laughter. I frowned, waiting for Ophelia to turn around and tell them to cut it out, but she put her head down, walking faster.

My hand tightened on the door release. They weren't messing around. And they weren't her friends. The girl kicked the can, aiming it at Ophelia. It missed, but only narrowly, and seconds later she'd lined it up for another go.

Before I knew what I was doing I'd started the car and followed them along the road, swerving across to the kerb just ahead of Ophelia. I wound the window down.

'Get in.'

Her mouth dropped open as she saw me, then abruptly closed. She looked back over her shoulder. In the wing mirror, I saw that the group were only a couple of metres away.

'Just get in,' I repeated. 'I'll drop you off somewhere, away from them.'

She nodded and stumbled around the bonnet to the passenger seat. I leaned to unlock the door, but caught a flash of black in the rear-view mirror. Ophelia made it to the left wing mirror and stopped. I looked at the door. The black-haired girl had got there first and barred it. I tried to catch Ophelia's eye but her gaze was fixed on the girl. I stamped on the accelerator, lurching the car forward. Ophelia caught up, grabbing the handle, but the girl beat her to it once more and blocked it with her body. The two guys watched from the kerb, smirking. I tried again. This time Ophelia reached the door first and yanked it open, only for the other girl to ram into her, shoving her clear.

I slammed on the brakes and leaped out of the car. 'What's your problem?'

The black-haired girl folded her arms on the roof of the car and rested her chin on them. 'Problem's with her, not you.'

'Unless you want it to be.'

I spun round. The smaller of the two guys stood right behind me, looking me up and down. He was a head shorter than I was and thin, but wiry. A few months ago I'd have flattened him without breaking a sweat. His mate, too. Now ... I wasn't convinced. Neither of them looked the type to fight fair.

I turned back to the girl. 'Get off my car.'

She tilted her head. 'You didn't say *please*.'

'Get off my car or I'll throw you off.'

The girl smiled, but shifted off the car.

'Now, that's no way to speak to a lady, is it?' The shorter guy came to stand in front of me. The taller one stayed where he was, behind. I stood my ground, but already adrenaline had started to surge through me. I smelled beer reeking off the one in front. He'd definitely had a few.

'I don't think you should be giving advice on how to treat girls,' I said, staring down at him. 'I just saw your mate throw a beer can at her.' I jerked my head towards Ophelia but kept my eyes on his.

He shrugged. 'Bitch deserved it.'

'I doubt that. Ophelia, get in the car.'

Shorty clicked his fingers at the black-haired girl. 'Don't move.' To me, he said, 'What are you, her new boyfriend?'

'It's none of your business—'

'If you are, you want to watch yourself.'

'Or what?'

'Just leave it.' Ophelia's voice was strained. I stared across the bonnet at her. 'Just go. You're making things worse.'

I shook my head. 'I'm not leaving you here with them. No way.'

'He wants to feel ya, *O-feel-ya*.' The guy behind had spoken at last. I glanced back. He had a flat nose and looked like whatever brains he'd been born with had been punched out several fights ago. He leered at Ophelia in a way that made my skin crawl.

'Shut up,' I threatened.

Shorty didn't react. 'Her last boyfriend disappeared,' he said. 'Isn't that right, bitch?'

'Stop calling her that.'

What the hell was going on? I thought I'd stumbled across some random idiots, but it was obvious something else was happening here.

'Problem is, no one knows why he left,' Shorty continued. 'Or where he is now. Except her.'

'Vince, I've told you already. I don't know—' Ophelia began.

'Yeah, well. You're lying.'

'So what's it to you?' I asked him. 'Why do you care who she goes out with?'

'Mate, I really don't give a shiny shit who she sees.' Vince pointed a calloused finger at Ophelia. 'But her last boyfriend was my brother. And I know she knows something.'

'For God's sake!' Ophelia shouted, her passive expression finally cracking. 'It's not like it's the first time he took off – everyone knows that! You just can't accept that Sean's a coward who runs at the first sign of trouble—'

84

'So there *was* trouble, then?' the spiky-haired girl butted in. 'There! You just admitted it.'

'Piss off, Nina. That's not what I meant. I wasn't the only person in his life – who knows what he was mixed up in.'

'Right. I forgot,' Vince continued. 'The mystery phone calls . . .'

'Something was going on with him,' said Ophelia. 'Something he didn't want me knowing about. I tried to get him to tell me, but he wouldn't.'

'Convenient. No one else noticed him getting these phone calls.'

Ophelia threw up her hands. 'Because no one else gave a damn about anything he did until he went missing.'

'Funny how you vanished off the face of the earth for weeks afterwards though, eh?' Vince sneered.

'Would you want to face everyone?' Ophelia's teeth were gritted. 'With the whole village pointing their fingers? Accusing me of knowing something?'

'But you *do* know something,' said Nina, stepping towards her. 'And the thing is – my cousin who works at the hospital, I spoke to her again the other night and she's sticking to her story. She says she remembers hearing about how you and your aunt arrived at the hospital covered in blood on the night Sean disappeared—'

Ophelia went white. 'And I've told you before that that didn't happen.'

'Whose blood was it?' Nina demanded.

'There *was* no blood!'

'Don't lie.' Something glinted on Nina's face in the fading light – an eyebrow piercing. 'What happened, Ophelia? Come on. You can't hide it forever!'

'I'm not hiding anything.'

'Want to know what I think?' said Nina. Her face wore a cruel smile.

'What?' asked Vince. His eyes narrowed, darting between Nina and Ophelia.

'I reckon her and Sean had a fight . . .'

Ophelia's eyes were wide. 'That's not true.'

'And Sean wanted to leave. Take off again. Or maybe that's what the fight was about—'

'You don't know what you're talking about.'

'He wanted to leave and you didn't. So he told you it was over. And you thought, "Boo-hoo, no one's going to love me now," and decided to get creative on your wrists with a carving knife.'

Ophelia curled her lip. 'Where are you getting this crap from?'

'Prove it, then. Take your gloves off,' said Nina.

'*What?*'

Nina faced Vince. 'I told you, didn't I? She's been wearing gloves for months, even when she's not at work. She's hiding something.'

'Take them off,' Vince repeated.

'No.' Her voice was quiet but defiant.

I frowned, realising Nina had a point. It was a mild evening – why *was* Ophelia wearing gloves when she didn't even have a jacket on?

'Come on,' said Vince. 'Show us what's under there.'

'Told you,' Nina said. 'She's been cutting herself up like a little freak, haven't you? What happened – did you accidentally press too hard, or did you mean to?' Her mouth twisted. 'Just like your—'

Ophelia's arm blurred as it cut through the air. Nina howled, sprawling over the bonnet of the car with one hand on her face.

Ophelia stood over her, fist still raised. 'Don't you *dare* mention her.'

Nina pulled herself off the car. Her hand came away from her face red and wet. 'You bitch! You split my face open!'

I could already guess what had happened: Ophelia's fist had caught Nina's piercing.

'Psycho,' Nina hissed, the sight of her own blood enraging her further.

She launched herself at Ophelia, twisting her hands into Ophelia's hair and trying to force her head down to her knee. Ophelia resisted, aiming wild blows at Nina with no thought for where they landed. Both of them screamed obscenities at each other.

I moved towards the girls, but Vince moved with me.

'Look, let's just split them up before someone gets hurt,' I said. 'If a car comes round that corner they'll get hit.' As I said it, I realised that not one car had passed us since this whole thing kicked off. I looked back along the road. It was quiet, almost deserted. The Rusty Bicycle was out of sight, too far to run to, and there were no houses especially near, only a couple of cottages a few hundred metres away. Both faced away from the road. It would be sheer luck if someone looked out and saw us.

Vince smiled.

'Aren't you bothered?' I asked. 'Who is that girl – your sister? Your girlfriend? Don't you care if she gets hurt?'

'She won't get hurt.'

I glanced at the girls again. It was true. Every move of Nina's was that of a seasoned fighter – Ophelia was just about holding her off. Despite the initial punch she'd got in, her attempts to fight were as pointless as a drowning cat trying to escape a sack.

Worse, I could see she was starting to tire. Nina knew it, and finally managed to knee Ophelia in the forehead.

'That's enough!' I pushed Vince out of the way. Big mistake.

'Damian!'

Thick arms grabbed me from behind and my right hand was twisted and forced up my back. A swift kick put me on my knees.

'Meathead,' I spat, twisting against Damian's hold. 'Do you always do what he tells you?'

'Pretty much,' said Vince.

I couldn't help it. I laughed.

'What's so funny?'

What the hell. He'd obviously decided he wanted to deck me, so it didn't make much difference what I said.

'You,' I answered. 'You're what's funny. A little short arse who picks on girls and can't fight fair.'

'I hope you get to do her after this,' Vince said. 'That's if you haven't already.' He laughed. 'I hear she's good.'

'Screw you.'

Seeing his fist coming didn't make it any less painful. It caught me on the cheekbone, knocking my head to the side. My face throbbed, but I'd had worse.

'Who taught you to hit like that? Your mum?'

Damian released my arm and grabbed my hair. Vince landed another one on me, harder and from the opposite side this time. My vision blurred then cleared. I sensed he was just getting warmed up.

'What's she told you?'

I coughed. 'Nothing.'

'You sure about that?'

'I met her yesterday, if you must know.'

'You expect me to believe that?'

'It's the truth. It was a fluke that I even drove past.'

Vince kneeled down in front of me. 'You know what? I do believe you. But you're a mouthy bastard and I'm gonna waste you anyway.'

I kept my head down, thinking, planning, but it was hard to focus with the girls screaming and swearing nearby. I couldn't see what was going on now – they'd almost disappeared from view on the other side of the car. I had one option: fight dirty.

I threw myself back, butting Damian between the legs. He made a weird, animal howl and released me. I rolled to the side, away from Vince and started to get up, but not fast enough. His boot connected with my jaw, putting me on the ground again.

'Where do you think you're going?' He was breathing heavily now. 'You're not getting up yet.'

He kicked me on to my back and lifted his foot. I waited for it to come down, tasting blood. He stamped on my hand, crushing it into the grass. I yelled and thrashed out with my other arm, grabbing at his leg. For a moment his balance was awkward. I yanked at his jeans, willing him to fall. It looked promising . . . until stupid, dumb Damian came to his rescue.

I groaned as he kneeled on my chest, pinning me to the ground. He leaned over me and I felt his breath in my face. The pressure on my lungs forced the air out of me, triggering all the emotions I felt during sleep paralysis.

He swung a fist at my head. It caught me on the temple. The sky spun above me, streaked with the last dregs of sun. Somewhere nearby, a roaring sound grew louder. A car engine.

Please stop, I thought.

It didn't. Instead it zoomed past, horn blaring. It felt like my head would split open at the sound. Vince's face appeared above me, upside down. My hand throbbed where he'd jumped on it. Even if I'd been able to use it, Damian had both my arms flattened to the grass.

'Bet you wish you'd never stopped now, don't you?' Vince said, grinning.

Damian's crushing weight made it almost impossible for me to breathe, but the anger inside me erupted.

'Yeah. I wish I hadn't stopped. I should have just run you over.'

A punch to the side of the head left me facing the canal. My vision clouded red. Everything hurt. Nina's voice rang out, high and shrill.

'Get back here, bitch! I haven't finished with you yet!'

A figure rushed past, feet pounding the ground. I twisted my head further, gasping for breath. Damian leaned back suddenly and I was able to draw in a lungful of air. Through the red haze I saw Ophelia sprint in the direction of the canal path. Somehow she'd escaped. Her hair had come loose and it trailed behind her like a flame, the last thing I saw before she vanished.

Nina limped towards the path but Vince called after her.

'Leave it. You won't find her. Too many damn places to hide and she knows them all.' He gave my cheek a pat which was closer to a slap. 'Looks like she's deserted you, lover-boy. And don't get any ideas about her coming back with help – the nearest place is that poxy museum and it's over a mile. So let's get comfy, shall we?'

Nina appeared beside him, chewing her lip. Her eye make-up was smeared down her face and her spiky black hair stood out at all angles. It was fair at the roots. I hoped a good portion of it had come out in Ophelia's hands.

'Vince, come on,' she said quietly. 'Let's go.'

'Shut up,' said Vince, examining my face like he was a doctor. 'Can't do much more on the head. Don't want you passing out on us just yet.'

This assessment, in that calm monotone, chilled me more than the threats.

'Get back, Damian,' Vince said, waving a hand at him.

Damian shifted off my chest, releasing my arms. They were as heavy and lifeless as sacks of flour. I watched, helpless, as he repositioned himself on my thighs. Before he'd even settled, Vince punched me in the gut.

Pain blossomed from the middle of my body. I coughed, gasped, spluttered, instinctively wanting to curl up – but Vince's hands on my shoulders held me in place.

'Want me to stop?' he asked. 'Beg.'

I couldn't have said a word, even if I'd wanted to. His fist came down again, too soon. Same spot, but the pain wasn't the same. It was worse, more intense. An image of a bruise swam into my head. Tender, swollen, ruptured blood vessels under my skin. It was all I could focus on.

'I'm serious, Vince,' Nina persisted, fear in her voice. 'That car – the driver was on her phone. We should get out of here—'

'She was probably already on the phone,' Vince growled.

I heard a high-pitched sound, a desperate dragging for air like someone suffering an asthma attack. The sound became synonymous with the purple-red bruising in my mind. I knew I couldn't take much more and stay conscious. My body wouldn't allow it. The red haze flickered at the sides, darkness threatening to swamp it entirely. Another punch and I'd be out. And then what? Would they carry on? Leave me? Throw me into the canal?

Vince knew it too. His upper lip twitched in anticipation.

'Get away from him.'

The voice came from over by the canal path. It was low, empty. I recognised it immediately. Vince arranged his face into a smirk, then turned around.

'How touching,' he crooned, then stopped. He started to laugh. 'You've got to be joking.'

There was a low click.

'Do I look like I'm joking?' Her voice was nearer now.

I heard Damian's intake of breath over my own wheezing and saw Nina's hand fly to her throat, but Vince blocked my view.

'I said get away from him. *Now!*'

Damian scrambled off my legs, his mouth open gormlessly. Slowly Vince got up, still smiling, and moved over next to Nina.

Ophelia stood with her back to the canal, her chest heaving. The breeze lifted her hair and arranged it around her head like a lion's mane. Her eyes were calm, but it only added to the wildness of her, like a creature calculating the best moment to pounce. Her outstretched hands were steady.

The gun she held pointed straight at Vince.

NINE

Stand and Deliver

I didn't know much about guns, but the one Ophelia held looked old. *Really* old. It didn't take a genius to figure out where it was from, but she couldn't have made it to the museum and back in that time. She must have had it hidden somewhere, ready.

'Looks like working at that fleabag museum's paid off,' said Vince. 'Shame you'll be fired when they hear you've been stealing from them.'

'They won't.' Ophelia's voice was steady. 'One, I haven't stolen it. Just borrowed it because I knew it wouldn't be long before you pulled a stunt like this. And two, it'll be back before anyone even knows it's missing, and it'll be your word against mine. Elliott – can you get up?'

'Give me a minute,' I managed, trying not to give Vince the satisfaction of hearing me groan.

'Does that thing even work?' Nina scoffed.

'You can bet your dodgy roots it does,' said Ophelia. 'And before you ask – yes, I do know how to use it. I know more about guns than any of you.'

Nina stared at Ophelia, furious.

'So what next?' Vince drawled. 'Stand and deliver? Our money or our lives?'

93

Damian laughed idiotically. I was pleased to see that it didn't reach his eyes. None of them wanted to lose face, but all three of them were unsure of how far Ophelia was willing to go.

So was I.

'No,' said Ophelia, 'I don't want you to stand and deliver. I want you all to sod *off* and leave me and him alone.' She waved the gun in Nina's direction.

Nina shrieked and jumped behind Vince. 'Don't point that at me, you stupid cow!'

Ophelia kept the gun on her. I got the feeling she was enjoying herself, and I didn't blame her.

'But just so you know, Vince? This particular gun is a duelling pistol. It's . . . oh, let's see. Around 1830 – that's Georgian – and it's killed at least twelve people. No, what you're thinking of is a musket: a century earlier, and much bulkier than this. Next time you swing by the museum I'll show you, if you like.'

Nina's top lip lifted in a sneer. 'You're *so* weird.'

Ophelia smiled. 'I prefer "eccentric", but coming from you, "weird" is fine.'

Vince shook his head. 'Even if you do know how to use that thing, you don't have the guts. If you killed any of us you'd get put away.' He stepped towards her, his hand out. 'Put it down.'

Ophelia stayed exactly as she was. She didn't even blink.

'Don't be ridiculous, Vince. Who said anything about killing anyone?' Her smile widened. 'A shattered kneecap should be more than adequate to keep you out of mischief.'

Vince stopped walking.

'Self-defence,' said Ophelia. 'Pure and simple. Look what you've done to him – doesn't look good for you, does it?' She lowered her arms, pointing the pistol at Vince's leg. 'I've never been shot, but I hear there can be all sorts of complications if you take a bullet in the knee. Worst-case scenario, you could lose the bottom of your leg.'

'You'd still get done for it,' Vince said, but he looked worried now.

'You're right.' Ophelia took the gun off his leg, lifted it, and scratched her head with the barrel before taking aim again. The action was the maddest yet. Vince stiffened. 'But don't worry. I'm sure I could come up with something else. Let's see . . . imagine my surprise when I found this stashed down by the canal one evening. Imagine my horror, when you came along and tried to take it off me . . . and it accidentally went off.' She nodded. 'Yeah. Let's go with that, shall we?'

'You're bloody nuts,' said Vince. 'And you're a lying bitch. You know that?'

She shrugged. 'It's called storytelling and it's part of my job. That's why I'm pretty good at it. But thanks for the update.'

'So why should we believe you when you say the gun works?' asked Nina.

'You don't have to believe anything I say. But then, I don't need to tell you that I've had about as much of you lot over the last few months as I can take. You know that already.' She shifted her aim to Damian. 'Everyone has their limits, don't they?'

Damian's lower lip wobbled. 'Can we go now, Vince?'

'Yeah.' Vince backed off, staring at Ophelia. 'I won't forget this. Next time I see you, it won't be for a friendly chat.'

'That's a shame,' said Ophelia, clicking her tongue. 'I'm such a sucker for a good conversation.'

Vince scowled. He grabbed Nina's hand and they turned and skulked towards the canal path, Damian lumbering obediently behind.

Ophelia moved after them, staring down the canal.

'That's right,' she called. 'Run along, now.' She kept the gun steady, watching until they vanished from sight.

I gritted my teeth and sat up to a wave of dizziness.

'Careful.' Ophelia rushed to my side and crouched down. She put her arm round my shoulders. The gun was still in her other hand, resting on her knee. I wanted to lean into her, but she was so thin and willowy I felt she might break.

'It's okay,' she whispered. 'They've gone. Let's try to get you up.'

'I'll be all right in a minute,' I lied. 'Just getting my breath back. That bastard really winded me.' I couldn't take my eyes off the gun. 'Can you put that thing down? You're making me nervous.'

'Sorry.' She placed it on the grass. 'But you don't need to worry. I was bluffing.'

'You mean . . . it's not loaded?'

'No. It doesn't even work. Used to, but it was made into a replica for the museum.'

I started to laugh, then winced. 'So, was any of that true? About it killing twelve people and everything else?'

'All of it. Apart from the fact that the gun couldn't actually go off. Oh, and what happens when you get shot in the kneecap. I just made that part up. I mean, for all I know it could cause you to lose a leg, but I'm not actually sure, or anything . . .'

A strand of her hair caught the breeze and fell across my face. I felt it catch in the damp space between my lips. Gently, she reached out and pulled it away.

'Is my lip split?' I asked.

She nodded. 'You're lucky your brain isn't.'

I tried to get up again and groaned. 'I'm not so sure about that.'

'Just take a minute,' she said. 'He's messed you up pretty badly. Let me look at you.'

I tensed at her hand on my stomach, pushing my shirt up. The skin there burned from Vince's punches. I remembered Kim's hand in the same place only yesterday, greedy and grabbing.

'It's already bruising,' she said.

Her touch was light and careful. She was the third stranger to have touched me there in the last twenty-four hours. I pushed my shirt down and her hand away with it, swallowing.

'I think I'm okay.' I was aware of her other arm, still on my back, and the warmth of her gloved fingertips through the thin fabric of the shirt. Her hand was shaking. 'You were pretty convincing with the gun,' I said. 'Quite scary, actually.'

Her hand slipped from my back. She smiled faintly, without warmth. 'Yeah. Well, now you can see why I had to be.' She looked at me, her grey eyes serious. 'You've made an enemy of Vince now. If he sees you again . . .'

'I know.'

'You shouldn't have stopped. I would have been all right.'

'I don't think so. And I don't think you do, either. How long have you had that gun stashed?'

She dropped her eyes. 'A few weeks. It was stupid, I know. But I thought if things got really bad I could scare them, then maybe they'd back off. I don't have that card to play any more.'

I frowned. 'Do you think things would have come to that, if I hadn't got involved?'

'Maybe.' She wasn't meeting my eyes. 'With Nina I think it was going that way for a while.'

There was something I was missing here, something she wasn't telling me.

'But you weren't scared to fight her,' I said. 'You hit her first.'

Ophelia's lips suddenly pressed together. I bit back the next question, which I knew she was anticipating, and changed tack.

'Do you think Vince would hit you?'

She hesitated. 'No. He's thrown things before, but I don't think even he'd go that low.'

'Then . . .' I thought back to the moments just after I'd got out of the car. The leering comments and thuggish mentality I'd immediately disliked. It suddenly fitted.

'Damian.'

'He's always given me the creeps.'

'I can see why. But he only does what he's told. He's Vince's puppet.'

'He is when they're together,' she said, pulling up a handful of grass and throwing it. 'But he's not as stupid as he acts.'

'Something happened with him, didn't it? Just you and him.'

Her voice hardened. 'Yes.'

My bruised stomach churned. 'Tell me.'

'Not here.'

I swallowed. 'Right. We should go – I'll take you home.'

Ophelia got up, brushing grass from her sweater. She held the gun loosely by her side. I dragged myself to my feet. Standing was a little easier. Nothing seemed broken.

'Are you sure you can drive?' she asked.

'I'm fine,' I lied. Each step towards the car jabbed at my insides like broken glass. I reached the door. It was still open and the keys were in the ignition. I looked across the roof as Ophelia went round to the passenger side.

In the near darkness, one side of her hair was lit with flashing lights.

'Shit.'

We both glanced up the road and saw it at the same time. A police car sped towards us, the sirens off. 'Get in the car,' I said. 'Stay calm – they might not even be for us. They might go past.'

'And if they don't?' she hissed. 'I've still got the gun!'

I felt like my stomach had taken another punch.

'Get rid of it,' I told her. 'Hurry.'

'Where? They'll see me do it!'

The car passed the cottages and began to slow.

'It's us they're here for. Ditch it – anywhere . . . in the long grass. We'll come back for it – just do *something*!'

But she was on the wrong side of the car – all the grass, nearest the canal path, was on my side. I clenched my eyes shut. If she got caught with the gun . . . Even having a replica was serious, that much I knew.

'I'm sorry about this, Elliott.'

I opened my eyes to see Ophelia striding towards me. My gut twisted. Why was she apologising? Was she about to pass the pistol to me? Ask me to take the blame?

She didn't do either. She did the last thing I would ever have expected.

She stopped in front of me, so close we were touching. I froze as the hand holding the gun slid round my waist and rested on my lower back. I felt the gun's weight, cold and heavy. Her other hand reached up and cupped the back of my neck. She tilted her face up to mine.

'Kiss me,' she whispered. 'And make it look convincing.'

Stunned, I bent my head and touched my mouth to hers, closing my eyes.

Her lips were cool and soft and they tasted sweet, like she'd eaten fruit. My swollen lip throbbed but I was barely aware of it. Instinctively I wrapped my arms around her, one hand on her back, the other in her hair. Behind me, her arm jerked and a dull thud followed as the gun landed in the grass.

The flashing lights were nearer now, painting colours on the insides of my eyelids. My heart pumped faster, but not just because of the approaching police.

It's not real, I told myself. *It's only make-believe . . .*

Whatever it was, it ended with the slamming of a car door. Ophelia pulled away and we stood apart. A second door slammed, then two uniformed figures headed towards us. I watched them as they came into view, feeling woozy, almost drunk with everything that had happened.

Two officers, a man and a woman, walked up to us, adjusting their hats. The man stopped in front of me. I saw him check my number plate. 'We're responding to reports of a disturbance,' he said. 'A witness saw two females fighting and a confrontation between three males. Can you tell us anything about that?'

It wasn't like we had much choice. Nothing says guilty like a split lip. 'I was driving along and I saw her being harassed. I stopped to confront them and it all kicked off.'

The officer looked to Ophelia. 'Is that what happened?'

I glanced at her sharply. Her hand was over her mouth, like she was terrified of what might come out of it, and she was staring past the man questioning us to the female officer, who had wandered over to the bushes.

'Am I right in assuming you two are a couple? You seem to know each other reasonably well.'

Sarcastic bastard.

I dragged my eyes back to the officer in front of me.

'Sort of.' Lie number one.

The officer looked up. 'Sort of?'

'Second date,' said Ophelia, trying to smile. She watched as he made a note and looked over his shoulder again. The policewoman had snapped a stick from a fallen branch and started to poke around in the shrubbery. *Oh, God. What did she see?*

'If you were on a date, do you mind telling me why you were driving and she was walking?'

Shit. THINK. Think of something . . .

'We were supposed to meet at the pub,' I said slowly. 'I was running late. By the time I got there, she'd already gone.'

'I thought he'd stood me up,' Ophelia added. 'So I left.'

'Neither of you have phones?'

'Of course. I tried calling her, but I couldn't get through. So I drove around for a bit to look for her.' *Smart-arse*, I added silently.

'Bad reception,' Ophelia muttered.

Officer Smart-arse's eyebrows lifted. 'Of course. And the pub was?'

'The Rusty Bicycle.' Unanimous answers. Score.

'This is your car?'

'Yes.'

'Talk me through what happened when you saw her.'

I cleared my throat. 'Like I said, I was looking for her anyway—'

The policewoman's shout cut me off. 'Got something over here!'

The male officer glanced back. Ophelia bit her lip as the woman pulled a plastic glove from her pocket and reached into the grass.

No, no, no . . .

'I told you I'd seen her throw something.' She stood up, the gun dangling from her fingers.

'Gum,' said Ophelia. 'I took out my gum before I kissed him and threw it. I've never seen that gun before.'

'Right before you conveniently kissed him.' The woman shook her head. 'Those gloves of yours . . . they look like angora to me. Not the sort of thing you can spit gum into without it making a mess.'

Ophelia's chin trembled.

The officer sighed. 'You can explain the rest at the station. I'm arresting you both on suspicion of possessing an offensive weapon.'

TEN

Invisible Man

I stared at the walls of the cell.

Arrested? I couldn't believe it. What a disaster of an evening. Everything, from the moment I'd left the pub onwards felt surreal, like I was in a dream. I couldn't help but notice the irony there: that I should feel dreamlike being awake, when what I experienced when I was supposed to be asleep felt uncomfortably real.

Through a tiny barred window high in the wall, stars littered a black sky. I had no idea what the time was, but it must be late. It felt like I'd been here for hours, yet still I hadn't been questioned. Since arriving, I'd given my name and address, handed over all my possessions – keys, wallet, phone – and had my fingerprints and a blood sample – for DNA, presumably – taken. After having my wounds looked over and declared non-serious, my clothes had been confiscated. The thing I'd been given to wear instead could only be described as a boilersuit.

I got up and moved to the front of the cell. It took all of two paces. Through the bars a corridor stretched along to the front desk. I counted four other cells. From one I heard slurred, drunken words. From another, muffled sobbing. It sounded like a woman, but I already knew it wasn't Ophelia. Earlier, she'd been briefly placed in the cell next to me, but whisked away for questioning before we'd had a chance to speak – or to get our stories straight.

I gripped the bars. 'Hello?' I called. Seconds later a male officer appeared at the end of the corridor.

'What do you want?'

'What's the time?'

'Nearly half-past eleven . . . Is that it?' He turned to go.

'No.' The knot of nerves in my stomach tightened. 'I want my phone call.'

He grunted. 'Hold on.' He vanished back to wherever he'd come from. I held on for so long that I thought he'd forgotten. Finally he reappeared and unlocked the cell. 'This way.'

I followed him down the corridor, glancing into the other cells. The drunken mutters came from an old, whiskery man who swayed on his feet and glowered out of his cell. Further down, the crying person lay on the brick bed, facing the wall. I couldn't hear any sobs now, but I saw the shoulders shaking under a huddle of scruffy clothing. Both wore their own clothes, not the boilersuits Ophelia and I had been given. Not a good sign.

We exited the corridor and passed the desk where I'd been booked in. A short walk and two sets of double doors brought us to a telephone.

'You've got five minutes.'

I picked up the phone and dialled. It was answered on the fifth ring.

'Adam, it's me.' I closed my eyes, strangely breathless at the sound of my brother's voice.

'Elliott? I didn't recognise the number. Where are you calling from? Have you lost your phone?'

'No, I . . . Listen, I'm at a police station, I've got to be quick.'

'Police station? What's happened? Have you been in an accident?'

'No, not exactly.' I considered telling him about the fight, then decided not to. He'd find out soon enough. 'I'm fine. I . . . I've been arrested.'

'*What?* What for?'

'Suspicion of carrying an offensive weapon.' I winced. God, that sounded bad.

'Bloody hell, Elliott. What have you got yourself into?'

'Nothing, I swear.'

'How long have you been there?'

'About three hours.'

'Three *hours*? Why didn't you call before?'

I swallowed. 'I was hoping I wouldn't have to – that it'd all get sorted out and that I wouldn't need to tell you and Dad about it.' Fat chance. 'I don't have much time, but you don't have to worry—'

'Of course I'm worried, you dick!'

'All right, all right! What I'm saying is that it's a misunderstanding. It'll all get sorted out.' I was babbling now. 'Call Dad and tell him I'm staying at yours.'

'He'll ask why you didn't ring yourself,' said Adam. 'What do I tell him?'

'Tell him the night out was a flop. Say I turned up at The Acorn, got drunk, and now I've got my head down your toilet.'

Adam sighed. 'I'll ring him. Then I'll come down to the station.'

'You can't.' I leaned my forehead against the wall, resisting the urge to head butt it. 'I mean, it's not the local station. It's the one near my work. I think I'll be here for the night – there's no one to question me till the morning.'

'Great. Nice one.'

'I know. Sorry.'

'I'll ask Amy to drive me over in the morning.'

'Sorry,' I repeated, cringing. The officer held one finger in the air. 'My time's nearly up.'

'One last thing.' Adam sounded tired.

'Yeah?'

'Tell me this doesn't involve a girl?'

I answered him with a long, uncomfortable silence.

'Idiot. I hope she's worth it.'

'So do I.' I hung up, feeling worse than I had before.

The officer ushered me onwards to the holding cells. A bitter smell hung in the air. I assumed the drunk had thrown up. He was now sprawled on the blue mattress, rumbling out snores. The other figure in the tattered clothing hadn't moved. When I passed Ophelia's cell she was sitting up with her arms drawn around her knees. She didn't look at me.

The door clicked behind me and I listened as the retreating footsteps faded. I crept past the stinking toilet and sat on the bed. I could still smell vomit and, oddly, it was stronger now. I pulled the neckline of the boilersuit up over my nose and grabbed a thin blanket from the end of the bed. I leaned against the wall, seeing Ophelia in my mind, mirrored on the other side.

Her voice came sooner than I expected, slightly obscured by the wall between us. 'What did they ask you?'

'They haven't questioned me yet.' I pulled the boilersuit down, trying not to breathe the sick smell. 'What did you tell them?'

'Nothing. That's why I was in there so long. They just kept asking the same things over and over.' There was a beat of silence.

'Thank you. I mean it. Thank you for stopping. You didn't have to. Especially after I was such a bitch to you yesterday.'

'I did have to. Anyone would have done. And anyway, you weren't a bitch. Everything you said was true.'

'At least you're honest.' It sounded like she was smiling. Then, more seriously, she added, 'I'm sorry I ruined your evening.'

'You didn't.' I chose my next words with care, aware that there were cameras in the cells. 'Being stood up was just the start of it.'

Her silence confirmed she'd understood that I was now talking about Kim.

'Not the best way to start a date,' she said finally.

'No.' Somehow, I managed a grin. 'I definitely wasn't betting on being kissed at any point this evening.'

'Yeah.' Her voice was flat. 'I meant what I said, just before.'

Just before? Just before the kiss. I thought back to her walking towards me, her hair lit by flashing lights.

I'm sorry about this . . .

'Yeah,' I whispered. I waited for her to say something else, but she didn't. I pulled the blanket over me and slid down on the mattress. My breath clouded the air in front of my face. When had the cell got so cold? I shut my eyes, the only way to shut out my grim surroundings. Well, not completely shut out. The feel of the blanket and unfamiliar clothes kept me rooted in the reality of where I was. And the vomit smell . . . sickly sweet, bitter, washing over me in waves. I stuck my nose under the blanket, trying to imagine I was somewhere, *anywhere*, but here. And I was tired, so tired that it wasn't difficult. Soon my head was drifting, drifting . . .

My eyes opened to a sound. For a few moments I was lost. The cell bars brought everything flooding back. My mouth was dry, my lips sticky. How long had I been asleep?

The noise came again, nearby. A moan. The corridor outside the cell was dim. Through the gloom I saw movement in the cell opposite. I got up and went to the bars.

A figure lay on its side on the floor of the cell. It was a man, probably about the same age as Adam. I raised an eyebrow at his clothes: green corduroy flares and a heavily-patterned shirt – he must have come from some kind of costume party. Wherever he'd been, he didn't look well.

'Hey,' I said. 'You okay?'

At the sound of my voice the eyes opened, startlingly white in his dark face. But they didn't see me. They rolled in his head. Only then did I notice the stains on his shirt. Something glistened stickily on the floor. His afro hair trailed in it.

'Do you want me to call someone?'

No answer. The guy was off his face. Steaming drunk.

'Hey!' I shouted down the corridor in the direction of the desk. Everything was dark. I waited, expecting abuse from the other cells. *Let them shout*, I thought. The more racket they made the sooner someone would come. But the corridor remained quiet. 'Is anyone there? We need help!'

Why was no one coming? Why was no one even *answering*?

I looked back into the cell. His body contracted as he gave dry retches. A thin string of saliva dangled from his lower lip to the floor. He retched again. The movement sent him rolling on to his back. This was not good. This was really, *really* not good.

'Hey!' I snapped my fingers. 'You need to get on your side – you can't stay on your back. Can you hear me?' His eyelids flickered. How much had this guy had to drink? Maybe it wasn't just drink – who knew what he'd taken?

I clenched the bars as he gagged again. 'Is anyone coming?' I bellowed into the corridor. '*Bastards!* Don't you care what's happening in here?'

A gurgling sound forced my attention back on the cell. Liquid bubbled and frothed around his lips, spurting over his chin and cheeks.

'Get up!' I yelled. 'Turn over, for God's sake!'

He didn't turn over. He stopped moving completely.

The smell rose up all around me, bitter and acidic. Choking me with its stench just as it was choking him. It was stronger now, not just vomit, but of shit and urine. Desperate, I turned back to my own cell, searching for something, anything – some water, perhaps that I could throw at him in an attempt to liven him up.

It was then I noticed myself, motionless on the brick bed. Asleep, my mouth slightly open, my forehead creased. And it was then I realised why no one was responding to my shouts, and why there would be nothing, not a thing, that could liven up the poor bastard in the cell opposite.

He was already dead.

It had been right in front of me all along, only I hadn't understood what I was seeing. His hair, his clothes. Even the cell was different – uglier, more basic. He had died a long time ago.

My body's chest rose and fell. I wanted to get back in. So badly wanted to make this stop, to make this apparition go away.

No. That wasn't right. Getting back into myself wouldn't make it go away. It – *he* – would still be there. I just wouldn't see him. I moved away from myself and back to the bars. Remembered how I'd gripped them – or *thought* I'd gripped them. Logic dictated something different. If my body was behind me, then . . .

I held my hand in front of me. It passed through the bars. Not between them, but actually *through* them. Like they were nothing . . . like *I* was nothing. Or at least, nothing physical. I closed my eyes and stepped forward. Opened them.

I stood outside the cell, in the corridor. Still outside myself, sleeping on the brick bed. I turned back to the pathetic, motionless figure on the floor.

'I'm sorry,' I told it. 'I'm so sorry that I couldn't help you.'

The light in the corridor flickered. In the cell, the shadows stretched. The air crackled with static.

No one came.

Somehow I knew the words hadn't been spoken aloud, yet I heard them as clearly as if they'd been whispered into my ear. I stayed still. The air next to me darkened, pooling with inexplicable shadows.

No one cared. They just . . . left me.

The air crackled again and the image before me flickered like a faulty aerial.

'I care,' I told it. 'I was too late, but I tried. I cared.'

The shadow rippled, became thinner. Then the voice came again, this time a wordless harmony of whispers that gave way to soft, sighing breath. It surrounded me like a cloak, then rushed through the corridor lifting dust and cobwebs, whipping them into cloudy swirls before allowing them to settle into some new and unexplored corner.

I found myself staring at an empty cell. Whatever, *whoever* he was, he had gone. I was alone, and for the first time it dawned on me that I hadn't freaked out. I'd been scared, but it hadn't been the same terror that conquered me every time at home with Tess Fielding. Somehow, by listening, I'd helped it. And more than that, I'd escaped from a locked room.

I stared back at myself, the me on the bed. Technically I hadn't escaped. I was still there, and would be until they decided to let me out. But *this* me, the outside me, could do things. Walk through walls, go anywhere. It was power. *I* was powerful.

I moved to Ophelia's cell. She was sitting in the same position I'd seen her in earlier. A few scratches on her cheeks and a red mark on her forehead were the only indications of her run-in with Nina. She didn't look like she had moved, or slept at all. Her knees were drawn up and her hands rested on them, her fingers spread. She stared at them as if lost in thought. With a jolt I realised it was the first time I had seen her without gloves on. I gazed through the bars, trying to see what it was about her hands that she was so keen to keep concealed.

There was something on them, reddish-brown. Not burns, or scars. No reason for her to want to hide them. But there was something. Something drawn . . . tattoos. I stepped forward, gliding through the bars to stand beside her.

Her hands were covered in swirls and dots, woven over her skin in a pattern like intricate lace. It trailed over her fingers and up around her wrists like something organic. Not tattoos in the traditional sense, but henna. I'd seen it before on a girl Adam had dated who'd backpacked around India, but on her it hadn't had the same effect – it had been just another ingredient in a cocktail of make-up and perfume. On Ophelia it was different. There were no distractions. On her, it worked, leaping from her skin like an illustration off a page, telling some secret aspect of a story that couldn't be found in the text. It brought her to life.

I stared and stared, drinking in the images on her hands, committing them to memory. On her right hand was a woman's face, surrounded by flowing hair that cascaded down to Ophelia's fingertips. She wore a crown of stars and was surrounded by smaller swirling symbols and shapes. On the other hand was a pattern of leaves, tracing delicately over her skin. I stayed, mesmerised, trying to work out whatever story was being told. All the while Ophelia sat motionless, as though sitting for a portrait with no clue she wasn't alone.

I could have studied those hands of hers all night, but something had begun to happen. My vision blurred and a wave of dizziness crashed over me. I'd almost forgotten that I wasn't really in the cell with her, not all of me. And I'd never been out of my body for this long before, never felt this odd. With mounting panic I turned and lurched through the bars. My movements grew harder to control, like I was a wisp of nothing, but I clawed my way back through the corridor and to my body. Each step closer to myself lessened the dizziness. I guessed I'd been away for around fifteen minutes, twenty at the most. What would happen if I stayed longer?

I wouldn't wait to find out, not this time. I leaned over my sleeping face. My breathing was slower than seemed natural. I lifted my hand and reached out. A sucking, dragging, weightless sensation took over me as the two halves of myself touched . . .

I was back inside. Real, physical, and with a crushing headache. But it couldn't crush my elation. I'd overcome my fear and for a few minutes, had been like a fly on the wall. The invisible man.

Perhaps something of a ghost myself.

ELEVEN

Muse

The next time I opened my eyes it was to the sound of the cell being unlocked. An officer I didn't recognise stood in the doorway, offering a plastic container.

'Morning, sunshine.'

I sat up, groaning. Everything ached. My head, my face – even my back from the rock-hard bed. I got up and took the box. 'What's this?'

'Your clothes. You're free to leave.'

'I am?'

'You seem surprised.'

'I was surprised to be arrested in the first place.'

He shrugged. 'Your girlfriend admitted to taking the gun. You've been cleared of any involvement. Get dressed – I'll be back in a couple of minutes to get you.'

'Wait – what about Ophelia? What will happen to her?'

He didn't answer.

I struggled out of the boilersuit and stepped into my own clothes and shoes. When the officer returned I followed him out of the cell. Ophelia was nowhere to be seen. The other cells, too, were empty.

At the desk the rest of my things, wallet, phone, and car keys were returned. I shoved them into my pockets with the little dignity I had left, then made my way through to the waiting area.

I saw Adam immediately, though he didn't see me. He was slumped on a plastic chair with his head against the wall, asleep. I went towards him, opening my mouth to speak. Before I got the chance a hand clamped the top of my arm from behind, spinning me round.

'*You.*'

'Wha . . . Hodge?'

He was barely recognisable as the mild-mannered man who had interviewed me. His normally pink face looked like a boiled ham and he was spluttering to get his words out.

'So *you're* the one she was with last night?' His eyes swept my bruised face, but there was no sign of sympathy, only contempt. 'Look at the state of you.'

'I don't . . .' I stared at him, bewildered. What was *he* doing here?

'Don't act like you don't know what I'm talking about. You were with my niece last night. You were with Ophelia!'

'You're her *uncle*?'

'Damn right I'm her uncle – and her legal guardian. And I'm not going to stand by and let the likes of you get her into trouble—'

'Just hold on a minute—'

'She's a good girl, do you hear me? And this is a warning – I don't want to hear you've been sniffing around her after this.'

'*Sniffing around her?*' My hackles were well and truly up. 'Look, if you ask Ophelia what happened she'll explain.'

'Elliott? What's going on?'

I turned. Adam stood nearby, rubbing his eyes. 'Who's this?'

I breathed out heavily. 'My boss.'

'I don't get it,' said Adam. 'What's your boss doing here?'

'Correction,' said Hodge. 'Your former boss. Don't bother coming in again.'

My mouth dropped open. 'You're *firing* me? For what?'

'For getting my niece arrested two days after meeting her,' Hodge spat. 'And God knows what else you had planned, though I think I can guess!'

'What's that supposed to mean?'

'You know what. You lads –' he made a noise of disgust, '– you're all the same.'

'Hey.' Adam's eyes were stormy. 'That's my brother you're talking to and I don't like your tone.'

A burly officer burst through a set of double doors. 'Is there a problem?'

A split second later, Amy appeared at the entrance clutching two steaming paper cups.

'No, no problem.' Adam eyeballed Hodge. 'We were just leaving.'

'But Ophelia—' I began.

'But nothing.' Hodge's voice had reverted to something calmer. 'Don't contact her again.'

'Come on,' Adam told me. He took one of the paper cups from Amy without a word, pushing through the double doors to stalk across the car park. Wide-eyed, Amy followed.

I paused. Hodge stood in the centre of the waiting room, sweating and hunched over, continually wiping his palms on his trousers. A vein had come up in his forehead, like a stalk on the red tomato of his face. Despite the way he'd spoken to me I couldn't help wanting to say I was sorry for what was happening to Ophelia, but I knew that any apology would be seen as an admission of guilt. I left without another word.

I climbed in to the back of Amy's car, shivering. It was a bleak morning and still early, just gone eight-thirty. Twelve hours since I'd been arrested. My stomach lurched as the car pulled off and I realised I hadn't eaten since yesterday lunchtime. No wonder I had a headache.

'I'm starving,' I said.

'There's a café just up the road where I got the coffee from,' said Amy. 'They do breakfast. I didn't see anywhere else.'

Adam slurped his coffee and passed the cup to back to me. 'Well, their coffee's crap but it looks like we're out of options. It'll be nearly another hour before we're home.' He turned to face me. 'Breakfast is on you. And while we're eating you can tell me what the hell happened last night.'

The food was better than the coffee. Over three full English breakfasts I explained the events that had led up to the arrest, with the exception of the kiss. I left that part out, though I couldn't explain why. When I was done, Adam leaned back, wiping his chin with a paper napkin.

'She must have a screw loose,' he said, suppressing a burp. 'And so must you to have covered for her. Every idiot knows you can't carry a firearm and get away with it, replica or not. Still, this Vince sounds a prick. I'd loved to have seen his face when she pulled the gun.' He grinned. 'I'd like to meet her, this Ophelia. She sounds a bit of a feisty one.'

I buttered my last slice of toast and glanced at Amy. She was staring into her cup and didn't react. 'I doubt I'll even see her again.' I bit into the toast then pushed it away, my appetite suddenly gone.

'You like her.' Amy was staring at the discarded food, a small smile on her lips.

I picked the piece of toast back up and forced myself to take another bite. 'I don't. I mean, she's all right – a bit stuck up. And like Adam says, she's got to be a head-case to do what she did. I only stopped because it was, you know . . . the right thing to do.'

Amy's smile broadened. 'If you say so.'

'I do. She's not even pretty.' I put the toast down, for good this time. My face burned as an image of Ophelia's hands came into my mind. Why did I feel like a traitor all of a sudden? 'Not that she's ugly, either. She's . . . interesting.'

'Interesting is good.' Amy sipped her coffee, her eyes fixed on the table. 'Looks aren't everything. Sometimes it only takes a spark of something and a person can grow on you without you even noticing. And then one day, you can look at them and wonder how you didn't see they were beautiful to begin with.'

Adam snorted. 'Clearly that's not what happened with me. Amy wanted my body from day one— Ouch!' He ducked as she hit him. 'Seriously – you must like her. You wouldn't have lied for her otherwise.'

'It's not like that.' My head felt fuzzy. 'She just needed help and I didn't want her to get into trouble. She didn't deserve it.'

'Neither did you.' Adam's voice was sharp. He dropped his cutlery on his plate and stood up, the chair scraping the floor. 'You're better off out of it – especially with that weirdo of an uncle. "*She's a good girl*",' he mimicked. 'What was all that about?' He strode to the door. I waited for Amy to finish her drink and counted money on to the table.

'He said he was her legal guardian,' I said as we got back in the car.

117

'Lucky her.' Adam checked his teeth in the mirror as Amy pulled away. 'Pompous old fart – he speaks about her like she's twelve years old.'

'It's probably worry – she's just admitted to an offence,' Amy reminded.

'What do you think will happen to her?'

Adam yawned and stretched in the front seat. 'Can't see her doing time if it's a first offence, but it'll go on her record.'

I held that thought. Having a criminal record was a sentence in itself: Hodge would have a hard time convincing anyone that Ophelia was a 'good girl' after this.

Amy drove the short distance to where my car had been left. I half expected it to be gone, or vandalised in the event that Vince had returned, but it was there in one piece, plastered with *POLICE AWARE* stickers. I got out and Adam wound his window down.

'Thanks for coming,' I told him.

He grunted. 'I'd invite you back, but I'm in serious need of sleep.'

'It's all right. Dad will be at work. I can get scrubbed up before he's home.'

'You'd better think of something to explain your face, too. You look like you were in a car accident.' He winced as he realised what he'd said. 'Sorry – you know what I meant.'

I watched them drive away then unlocked the car, swearing. My stuff was everywhere, the contents of the glove compartment strewn in the foot wells. Road atlases, anti-freeze, and all sorts of accumulated car junk slid under my feet. The police had ransacked everything. On the backseat even my jacket had been reversed, each pocket turned out to reveal nothing but chewing gum, fluff, and a scrawled note that could have been a phone number. I swept it all aside. It could be dealt with later.

The flat was empty and quiet when I reached it, and the sun had finally burned through the cloud and now filled the rooms with gold. I threw my clothes off and got straight in the shower, leaving the bathroom door open. The steaming spray hit my skin, washing away the cold, hard night in the cell. I relaxed into it, enjoying the warmth for a couple of minutes until the water suddenly ran cold. When I opened my eyes brownish swirls were vanishing into the drain, like dried blood. Chilled, I checked my head for cuts but found nothing. Hurriedly, I twisted the tap off and got out. At some point during my shower the door had silently swung closed.

I frowned and opened it, then dried off, tucking the towel around my waist.

'If that's you, Tess, you can just stop it,' I said into the damp air. 'We live here now, not you.'

I didn't get an answer, not that I was really expecting one. With the sun streaming in it was hard to stay spooked for long and, for now, I had other concerns.

My bruises stood out against the white cotton towel like violet ink on snow. I shaved, assessing the damage to my face. My lower lip was scabbed and there were more bruises to the sides of my face. Just what I didn't need.

I pulled on clean clothes and went into the living room. Despite the aches and bruising I somehow had more energy than I remembered having for a while. And not only that, but something else had surfaced. A desire, one that I'd missed for a long time. Too long.

I ran into my bedroom, rummaging in the bottom of the wardrobe. I found it at the back under a heap of fallen clothes: a black leather folder. I pulled it out, then took a handful of pencils from a tin on the chest of drawers. I carried everything to the living room, where the light was strongest and removed a sheet of creamy paper from the folder. Leaning it on top, I closed my eyes to recall the image I wanted, then opened them and put my pencil to the paper.

Minutes ticked into hours. I shifted around the room with the sun, stopping only once to stretch and fetch a glass of water. Once the phone rang, long and shrill. I didn't stop for it but carried on, lost in the strange, peaceful but intense concentration that only drawing brought me.

Slowly the image took shape like a piece of ripening fruit.

Three hours later it was done, and I set it down on the sofa before stepping back to view it. It was the first time I'd drawn – the first time I'd wanted to draw – since the accident. It was far from perfect, but there was a spark of life about it that shone through the rusty lack of practise. And it was still good.

The phone rang again. I slid the pencil behind my ear and went into the kitchen, only then noticing that the red light was flashing. One new message. I picked up the phone.

'Hello?'

'Elliott? It's me.'

I clutched the phone harder. 'Ophelia? What happened – are you all right?'

'They let me go with a caution. I was lucky.'

My grip on the phone relaxed a little. 'I bumped into your uncle on my way out.'

'He told me. That's why I'm calling.'

I paused, noticing the stiffness in her voice. 'He's there, isn't he?'

No answer. I took that as a yes.

120

'Well, you can tell him I already got the message, loud and clear. He didn't need to go to the trouble of getting you to repeat it—'

'The answer phone message?'

Why did she sound so deflated?

'I haven't heard any answer phone message – I meant what he said at the station.'

'Oh, Elliott – no. That's why I'm calling. He's been trying to reach you, to apologise—'

'*Apologise?*'

'He tried to call, but thought you were avoiding him. So he left you a message. When you hang up, just listen to it. Please?'

I closed my eyes. 'Sure.'

She waited for a moment before speaking. I thought I could hear her breathing into the phone. 'I'll see you, Elliott.'

'Goodbye, Ophelia.'

I set the phone back on the hook, then pressed 'play'. A familiar, blustering voice filled the room.

'This is Arthur Hodge calling for Elliott Drake.' Pause. Clearing of the throat. *Good,* I thought. *He's uncomfortable.* 'Elliott, I'm sorry that I missed you as I'd like to discuss our, ah . . . little misunderstanding.'

I almost laughed. *Misunderstanding?* What a joke. He hadn't even attempted to listen, let alone understand.

'After hearing from Ophelia I now realise that I was completely in the wrong, about everything. She told me what you did for her, and I'm very grateful. We both are, Una and I . . .'

Una? Of course. Una had introduced Ophelia as her niece, but I would never have put her and Hodge down as a couple. They went together about as well as ice cream and gravy.

'. . . and we'd like to invite you to dinner this evening, eight o'clock, at number fifteen Friar's Row – that's in the village. Of course, we understand if you'd rather not, but . . .'

This time I did laugh out loud. In a matter of hours I'd gone from being sacked to a worthy dinner guest. 'Pompous old fart,' I muttered, remembering Adam's summation. 'You need some anger management.'

Hodge rambled on, leaving a telephone number and a post-code. He was still speaking when the machine ran out and cut him off mid-sentence. I listened a second time, scribbling the address down and hitting 'delete' afterwards. Then I slowly walked back to the sofa and sank into it, staring at the drawing.

Ophelia's hands beckoned me into the page like a witch. Every swirling symbol, every curved mark taking on new meaning. Like a spell, perhaps, that had brought her back to me.

TWELVE

Gifts

Fifteen, Friar's Row was a mid-terrace cottage barely a stone's throw from the museum. I parked and got out with a bunch of flowers bought in a hurry from a petrol station. They were already wilting in the heat.

I let myself through a wooden gate into a sweet-smelling garden. The cottage walls were white-washed, and the tiny dark windows hid under the thatched roof like eyes under a fringe. A trellis arched over the door, thick with climbing roses. They weren't flowering yet, but it wouldn't be long.

The door opened before I had time to knock. Ophelia stood barefoot in the entrance. Her hair was in its trademark knot and she wore a plain cotton dress. She gestured with a gloved hand.

'Come in.'

'Thanks.' I handed her the flowers and ducked through the doorway.

'Are these for me?'

'Yeah.' I glanced round, taking in the low, dark beams. We'd stepped straight into the front room. 'Well, for all of you – as a thanks for dinner.'

She lowered her nose and sniffed. I waited for her to come out with the obligatory 'beautiful' or 'lovely'.

'Don't you know it's bad manners to leave the price on a gift?' she asked, peeling off a sticker I'd failed to notice.

Crap.

'Don't you know it's bad manners to look?' I answered, wishing I'd broken into the note in my wallet and not gone for the cheapest bunch purely to use up my change.

She rolled the sticker in her fingers. 'Come through. They're dying to get started.'

'On the food? But Hodge told me to come at eight. I'm not late, am I?'

'No.' She padded over the carpet, her bare feet soundless. 'Dinner will be a few minutes yet. I meant that they're dying to get started on you.'

I followed her through a set of double doors into a second room. Crammed bookshelves lined all the walls except one, where a piano stood. In the middle of the room was a dining table and chairs. Another door stood ajar beyond that, and through it drifted sounds of crockery and smells of roasting food. 'Get started on *me*?' I asked. My newly-ironed shirt started to cling to my neck. 'You make it sound like I'm first course.'

'You kind of are,' she said apologetically. 'You're about to be gushed over.'

A voice trilled on the other side of the door.

'Ophelia? Who are you speaking to?'

Ophelia pushed the door open and motioned me into the room beyond.

Una was bent over the hob, tasting sauce. She glanced up as I entered the kitchen, promptly hitting my head on a saucepan dangling from the ceiling.

'Elliott, how lovely to see you!' she said, reaching up to steady the swinging pan. 'Oh, dear – are you all right? We don't want you getting any more scrapes, do we?' She clucked like a mother hen.

'I'm fine,' I said, rubbing what was sure to be another bruise. 'Just need to watch out for these low ceilings.'

'Thank you so much for coming.' Una gave the pot a vigorous stir. 'We're just so grateful to you for looking out for Ophelia the way you did.'

'Elliott brought some flowers,' said Ophelia, holding the wilted bouquet towards her aunt.

'Oh, how *beautiful*,' said Una, burying her nose in the petals. 'Leave them on the side, Ophelia, and I'll find a vase. Show Elliott to the garden.'

Outside, Hodge was seated at a table beneath a parasol. He stood up when he saw me, setting down a glass of jangling ice.

'Elliott!' He reached towards me. Unsure, I took his hand, and for the second time found myself subjected to a clammy pumping of fists. 'So good of you to come, especially considering . . . the ah, situation.'

'He means especially considering how rude he was to you,' said Ophelia, not looking at her uncle. 'Would you like something to drink?'

'Whatever you've got that's cold,' I answered, awkwardly taking the seat next to Hodge.

'I'll have another one, too,' said Hodge, thrusting his empty glass at her. She ignored it and disappeared into the kitchen.

Hodge turned to me, his pink face damp. 'I'd like to clear the air immediately, Elliott, so that we can enjoy the rest of our evening. From your reaction yesterday I understand that Ophelia neglected to explain that not only am I her uncle, but she's also under my care – mine and Una's.' He lowered his voice. 'Una and

125

I were unable to have our own children, and so Ophelia was always dear to us. Very dear. But she's a private sort of girl, as you've probably guessed. She doesn't much like talking about herself.'

I shifted in the seat, half wishing Ophelia would hurry back to put an end to the conversation, and half afraid she'd turn up to find Hodge discussing her. Part of me was curious about why she lived with her aunt and uncle, but not enough that I wanted to hear it from him. I wanted to hear it from Ophelia herself. Plus the thought of Hodge's reproductive shortcomings was kind of repulsive. An image of him sweating fatly over Una invaded my mind and I forced it away.

'Anyhow, I hope that goes some way to explain why I'm so protective of her. When I got the phone call to say what had happened, I was distraught. Ophelia's never been in trouble in her life, I've made sure of that—' He broke off, wiping his brow. 'And when I saw you, I was tired and worried and I should have listened instead of jumping the gun. No pun intended. I hope you'll understand.'

'I do. Really, it's fine,' I said. 'Don't worry about it.'

'Good,' he said, brightly. 'I don't normally advocate violence but it's the only language some people understand. I don't suppose she told you who they were?'

My mouth had trouble shaping the words. 'She said she didn't know them. They were drunk. Things got out of hand.'

Hodge shrugged. 'That's what she told me, too. Although I can't help but wonder if there was more to it. Why would she hide a gun if something hadn't already happened before?'

I avoided his gaze. 'She never mentioned anything to me.'

Hodge traced the rim of his glass. 'I'd appreciate it if you didn't mention Ophelia's caution to anyone at the museum. Calthorpe's a small place. People talk.'

I nodded. 'I'll keep it to myself.'

'Good.' He winked, like I'd been given a pass into an exclusive club.

Irritation nipped at me like a gnat. This – tonight – none of it was really intended to thank me. It was to question me and buy my silence. Thinking back over Hodge's little speech and the answer phone message, I realised that he had never actually said he was sorry. Not once.

Ophelia returned with two glasses containing ice, and a pitcher of amber liquid. I was glad to see her. It gave me a break from looking at Hodge. She refilled his glass then poured the liquid into the other two glasses, handing one to me and taking one for herself.

I lifted the glass, tasting bittersweet apples. 'Is this cider?'

'Our very own scrumpy from the Past Lives orchard,' said Hodge, draining half the liquid in one swallow. 'Good stuff, eh?'

It was a bit strong for me, but it didn't look like Hodge was about to be argued with.

'Have you seen the orchard yet?' said Hodge. 'Ophelia will show you, next time you're in. Tomorrow, if you're ready?'

I glanced at Ophelia. 'So . . . does that mean I've got my job back?'

'Of course it does.' She gave Hodge a sharp look as he spluttered into his drink.

'Yes, yes.' He wiped juice from his chin. 'I thought I'd made that clear. Everything I said yesterday was in temper. Obviously we didn't expect you in today after what happened – I thought you'd like some rest. But your job is secure, Elliott.'

Only now that I've got dirt on your niece.

'He has a terrible temper,' Ophelia said. 'Most of what he says he either takes back or forgets he's said at all once he's calmed down.'

'And your tongue stings like a nettle, dear,' Hodge said. 'But none of us are perfect, are we?'

Una appeared with placemats and cutlery. She laid the table and began bringing out the food.

'So,' said Hodge, heaping his plate with a mound of potatoes. 'Elliott – do you believe in ghosts?'

My hand froze midway to the bread basket. He couldn't possibly know. 'Why do you ask?'

Ophelia stabbed at something in the salad bowl. 'He asks everyone.'

'At your interview, you mentioned you were keen to work extra shifts if required.'

I relaxed, dropping a crust of bread on to my plate. 'That's right.'

'In that case, I may have a little something for you. We need extra staff for the paranormal events we're running from the end of June through to the autumn. Friday and Saturday nights, from ten o'clock to six in the morning. Ghost walks, séances and a paranormal investigator. It's looking promising that *Haunted Britain* might come to film, too. How does that sound?'

'Pretty good,' I answered, watching as Una ladled meat on to my plate and drowned it in sauce. 'But I haven't actually done any tours at all yet, by myself.'

'Oh, I know that. The events are still a few weeks away, but I thought you could accompany me on the weekly ghost walk leading up to them. That way you'll learn all the stories, and it'll familiarise you with the rest of the museum.'

It was a tempting offer, better than anything I'd ever hoped for. But now I had it, I was hesitant. Firstly, I wasn't sure I needed proof any more. Secondly, because of the firstly, I was afraid. 'Is believing in ghosts a requirement for staff, then?'

'It would be if Uncle had his way,' said Ophelia.

Hodge gave a wave of his hand. 'Let's just say . . . it helps. What these events are all about is the experience. *Atmosphere*. And within every group there's bound to be a cynic – someone who's come along just to sneer and close the minds of others. That's beyond our control. But with the staff, it helps to be open to the possibilities of the paranormal – or at least, not openly dismissive of it.'

'I take it you do, then,' I said. 'Believe, I mean?'

'It's more an obsession than a belief,' said Ophelia.

'It's hardly an obsession,' Hodge said. 'Don't exaggerate. An *interest* is what it is. A healthy interest.'

Ophelia chased a potato around her plate, clearly having difficulty gripping her cutlery with the gloves on. I wondered why she still wore them while she was eating. 'Ghosts are dead people. How can "healthy" and "dead" even go in the same sentence?'

'It's perfectly healthy to wonder what happens when you die,' said Hodge. 'Doesn't everyone?'

'You go up in smoke or become worm food,' said Ophelia. 'End of story.'

I got the feeling that this conversation was a recurring one and guessed that Ophelia's comment was intended to provoke her uncle. She hadn't seemed nearly so dismissive of the subject after what had happened in the museum's schoolroom.

'We all have our little quirks,' said Una. 'Arthur has his ghosts, I have my books, and Ophelia has her horses—'

'Yes,' Hodge interrupted. 'Bloody useless, stinking horses. When her real talent is sitting in that room, gathering dust.' He shoved a lump of bread in his mouth and chewed furiously.

'He means the piano,' Una informed me.

'They're not useless, actually,' said Ophelia, putting her fork down. I watched, transfixed, as she began to remove one of her gloves.

'You play the piano?' I asked. The thought of her hands, with those pictures on, moving over piano keys and making music was mesmerising.

'Leave the gloves on,' Hodge snapped. 'We're in company, remember?'

The glove paused at her wrist and Ophelia yanked it back up. 'Fine.'

I couldn't help myself. 'What's with the gloves? I've never seen you without them.' *Not when I'm awake, anyway . . .*

'Self-mutilation,' said Hodge, spearing a chunk of meat.

'Self-*expression*,' said Ophelia.

'Tattoos,' said Una.

'Not something I want to see while she's under my roof,' said Hodge.

'It's henna,' Ophelia said, the blank look creeping over her face once more. 'It'll be gone in a few weeks.'

'Good for you,' said Hodge. 'I'd hate to see you wearing gloves all through the summer. You'd look even sillier than you do now.'

She stared at her plate. 'I don't care what you think. I didn't do it for other people to look at. I did it for me, and it's still there even if it's hidden.'

'Well, hiding it saves my eyes being offended. And to answer your question, Elliott, she plays piano like some kind of prodigy

– or at least, she used to, until she started letting it all slide in favour of horses.'

'My piano playing is average at best.'

'You could be brilliant again,' said Hodge. 'You could get it back.'

Ophelia didn't say anything. She didn't need to. I remembered hearing the same words from Adam only a couple of weeks ago. *You could get it back.* But like me, Ophelia didn't want it. Something had happened to change her – or perhaps, she had never really wanted it at all. Either way, I understood.

Hodge didn't though. He took her silence as agreement.

'You can play something for Elliott after dinner,' he said, calmer now.

She lifted her hands and waggled her fingers. 'I can't play without taking my gloves off. You can't have it both ways.'

'Stop it, you two,' said Una. 'Honestly.'

I wanted to laugh, not at the situation but at Hodge's expression. It was like that of a child who'd just had its ice cream stolen by a dog. I decided to try and change the subject.

'So, have you ever seen a ghost?' I asked him. 'Or did something happen to make you believe in them?'

Hodge swigged his cider before answering.

'My mother was a medium,' he said.

Ophelia disguised something with a cough. It sounded like 'a large'.

'I heard that.'

Ophelia's blank look gave way to a smirk. Hodge continued.

'Her name was Marjorie Hodge. You may have heard of her – she was well-known around these parts.'

I took care to look as though I was considering this rather than shaking my head outright, but Hodge barely paused before moving on.

'She was very gifted – saw spirits constantly. They were everywhere, she said. I grew up listening to my mother talking to people who weren't there. It was normal for us – my brother and I. She shielded us from most of it, but it must have been difficult for her. Looking back I realise that they must have hounded her all the time – her behaviour was very peculiar.'

My heart quickened. 'Why did they hound her?'

'To tell her things, or ask her to do things for them. Deliver messages to the living, that kind of thing. And she did, for as long as she was able to, right up until her death. Some people didn't like what she did, but many were grateful to her. And she never profited from it. Never charged a penny. Perhaps it was growing up surrounded by it that made me sensitive to it, or perhaps it was something in the blood – who knows. But later, much later, when I reached my teens, I saw my first ghost. Shook me up, it did. Seen a few since – never on the scale of what my mother experienced, but I've seen enough to believe.' He frowned. 'And you? You never answered my question. Do *you* believe in ghosts?'

I'd been trying to figure out what to say to this since Hodge initially brought the subject up, but I still wasn't sure. After so long of trying to convince Dad that ghosts were real, now that I had someone willing to listen and believe, it was perverse that somehow I couldn't bring myself to tell him everything. Well – maybe not perverse, but definitely frustrating. I'd wanted sympathetic ears, but not those of a stranger. I glanced at Ophelia. As usual, her face told me as much as unused newsprint.

'I'm not sure what I believe,' I said eventually. 'I've experienced . . . *something*. A few times.' *Understatement of the year.*

132

Hodge leaned closer. I noticed that Ophelia was picking at a thread in the hem of her dress, but her eyes weren't actually on her hands. She was listening.

'The accident I mentioned in my interview.' God, my mouth was dry.

Ophelia stopped picking her dress and looked up.

'I sort of played down how serious it was,' I said. 'When the car knocked me down I didn't even understand what had happened at first.'

'Were you unconscious?' asked Una. 'In shock?'

'No. I was conscious, but I didn't realise I'd been hit. I . . .' Why was this so difficult? 'At first I didn't know anyone had been hurt. I even watched the car getting away. It wasn't until I turned back that I saw a crowd standing around someone on the ground. When I got closer . . . it was me. I saw myself. It was like my consciousness, or my *soul*, or something, had come out of my body. And I knew I needed to get back in.'

'A near-death experience,' Hodge said. His eyes fixed on mine hungrily, like a dog waiting for a steak. 'What happened next?'

'An ambulance came.' I forced my eyes away and looked at Ophelia. She was still, watching me now. 'Paramedics worked on me. And I just got sort of . . . sucked back in.'

'The mind does strange things,' said Ophelia. 'Just because you thought you were outside of your body, it doesn't mean you really were. It could have been a distancing thing, like a dream or a hallucination to separate yourself from the situation and the pain.'

'Either way it's extraordinary,' said Una.

Somehow I was caught between two things: the need to be believed and the need to retain some of the truth. I wasn't ready to let them have it, not completely. And while I knew Ophelia wasn't being unkind, the urge to convince her outweighed the urge to keep quiet.

'It's happened since,' I blurted. 'When I'm asleep. Sometimes I wake up in the night. Sometimes it's a noise that's disturbed me, or just a feeling. I get up and wander round the flat. Everything's as it was. Then I come back to bed and see myself asleep. It makes me panic, and I have to get back into my body, or . . .'

'Or you're afraid you won't wake up,' Hodge finished.

'Yes.' I stopped there. I wasn't ready to talk about the rest of it, not that I needed to. Hodge seemed convinced, and Ophelia and Una weren't too far behind him. But there was something else. Hodge looked admiring, though slightly put out. Like I'd stolen his limelight.

The conversation ended there and I picked at the rest of my food until everyone else's cutlery had been laid down. Against Hodge's insistence, I helped Una stack the plates and carry them into the kitchen, trying to think of something to say to lighten the mood, and failing. I looked up to see Ophelia in the doorway. Her lips were quirked into a small smile.

'What?' I asked.

'Ghosts.' She rolled her eyes. 'He'll never leave you alone now.'

'Ophelia, don't be silly,' said Una. 'Why don't you show Elliott the rest of the garden, and send Arthur in to help me with the pudding?'

Hodge wasn't pleased at being summoned away from his cider, but he went, grumbling, while I followed Ophelia beyond an ivy-tangled trellis into a wilder part of the garden. Bees hummed in the late-evening sun, and as we wandered among rows of planted vegetables and flowers the air cooled and I got the feeling that she was waiting to say something.

134

'That day, in the schoolroom. It was you, wasn't it? I told you that things sometimes happen depending on who's in the building.'

'People who have been close to death.' I stared across the garden. 'Yeah.'

'Why didn't you say anything?'

'Lots of reasons.'

'Such as?'

She had such a direct stare.

'I don't like to talk about it. And I wasn't sure you'd believe me.'

'I don't know if I believe that you actually *died*. But I believe what you say you experienced.'

'Technically, I did die. The paramedics restarted my heart.'

She didn't say anything. I wondered what her reaction would be if I told her about the other things I'd experienced since, but I couldn't think of how to begin.

'They wanted to make sure that I thanked you for what you did,' she said eventually. 'I mean, I told them I already had, but . . . anyway.' She stopped walking and leaned against a little wooden shed. 'So, thanks.'

'You're welcome.' My eyes lingered on her mouth. The last time we'd been alone together was when she had kissed me. It was weird to think of it now. The kiss itself had been strange, unexpected. Yet not unpleasant. If anything, it had made me realise how toxic Kim's kiss had been the day before, with her smoky breath and her sickly-tasting lipstick.

'So . . . horses?' I said, averting my eyes. 'That's your thing?'

'They're simpler than people.' She was quiet for a moment. 'There's just something about them . . . about putting your faith in a thing so much bigger than you, with a mind of its own, and earning its trust. They don't judge, or hold grudges.'

'Neither does music,' I pointed out.

She made an exasperated noise. 'You can love music. I thought I did, once. But it never loved me.' She glanced back at the cottage. 'They keep pushing me to go to college.'

'You don't want to?'

'School was bad enough.'

I wanted to ask why, but a frosty note had crept into her voice.

'How long do you plan on staying at the museum?'

'Only as long as I need to.'

I frowned as a thought occurred to me. 'If Hodge has such a problem with you choosing horses over music, why does he let you work with them?'

'He knows I could easily get another job at a riding school.' She gave a thin smile. 'But he wants me where he can see me. Plus I've asked around, and the money and hours for stable hands in those places just don't compare to what I'm already doing. Until I'm old enough to train to be an instructor I'm pretty much stuck.'

He wants me where he can see me.

I recalled Hodge's outburst at the police station and his questions before dinner.

'Hodge asked me about the fight – whether you knew them. I told him no, but he thinks you're lying.' I paused. 'I can't imagine anyone being able to tell if you're lying. It's impossible to guess what you're even thinking, most of the time.'

'I'd rather not tell him what the argument was about.'

'You mean your ex-boyfriend?' I tried to recall his name. 'Shane?'

'Sean.' She looked away. 'Hodge never took to him.'

'So, he just disappeared?' I asked.

'Yeah. Just over a year ago.' She gave a wry smile. 'He always said he'd escape this place someday.'

'You never told me what happened with Damian.'

She chewed her bottom lip and looked at me, as though assessing something.

'I saw him alone on the canal path a few weeks back. They'd been harassing me for a while by then – Vince and Nina. They never liked me even when Sean was still here. Said I was stuck up, that I didn't fit in with them. Anyway, Damian came up to me . . . cornered me under the bridge. He said he could make them stop if I . . .' Her lip curled. 'He tried to kiss me. I shoved him away and he got angry. Then someone shouted from the other side of the canal – a couple with a dog. If it wasn't for them I don't know what would have happened. That's why I hid the gun. I knew if he'd done it once he could do it again and I wanted to be ready.'

'That bastard. If I see him again—'

'You'll do nothing,' she warned. 'Don't get involved any more than you already are. Maybe they'll leave me alone now, especially if I tell them the police are involved.'

'You didn't tell the police who they were either?'

She averted her eyes. 'It'd only make things worse – they'd probably get a caution and then harass me even more. At least this way I have something over them. Maybe the threat will be enough.'

'What was Nina about to say before you hit her?' I asked. 'She was talking about someone, your mum?'

But Ophelia's face closed off abruptly. 'We'd better get back before Una calls us.' Before I could protest she turned and wove through the garden. I didn't get a chance to speak to her alone again.

137

THIRTEEN

Neighbours

I thought of Ophelia all the way home.

There were so many questions I wanted to ask her. Like where her parents were and why she lived with the Hodges. What the symbols on her hands stood for. Who Nina had been referring to before Ophelia punched her. Finally, I thought about Damian. My teeth clenched at the memory of him.

I hadn't stayed especially late at the Hodges' but the drive back meant I got home close to midnight. Dad was in bed, and the remnants of the bolognaise sauce I'd made him were congealing on a plate in the kitchen.

In the bathroom I started scrubbing my teeth, then noticed that Dad had left his bath water in. Dirty git. I rinsed, spat, and reached for the plug, then paused.

The water was clear. There was no soap residue and the bath mat, which Dad always managed to soak, was dry. I pushed up my sleeve and reached into the water. The chill of it took my breath away. I left it draining and turned off the bathroom light, listening outside Dad's door. I heard him breathing, slow and deep. He must have run the bath and decided he was too tired to get in it.

In my room I put on the lamp and stared at the drawing of Ophelia's hands, propped on the chest of drawers where I'd left it.

Then I threw off my clothes and got into bed. I'd resisted Una's offer of coffee and my eyelids were heavy now. Finally, I switched off the lamp.

It seemed to start the moment I drifted into sleep, like those times when the alarm clock rings the instant your head hits the pillow. I dreamed that I was little again, sharing a bunk bed with Adam, and in my mind's eye I saw the room as it had been back then. We'd fought over who got the top bunk and I'd won, as usual, by sulking. In the night, I'd woken to the sensation of something splashing my face and the smell of wet plaster. Turned out that the old lady in the flat above, Violet Mardle, had left her bath running and forgotten about it. After that we called her Mrs Muddle, on account of the fact that she was usually in one. Adam of course, found the whole thing hilarious and told me it served me right for whinging to get top bunk.

I felt water droplets hit my face now and stirred. *Not again.*

'Adam,' I mumbled. 'Go and get Mum. Tell her Mrs Muddle's left the water running again. Adam?'

No reply, only more dripping. My eyes opened stickily. Someone was by the door. 'Adam?' I said again, trying to sit up. My limbs were heavy, too tired to move.

'No, it's me, dear.'

Fear shot through me. That wasn't Adam's voice. It was an old lady voice.

'Just popped in to check on things.' The figure shuffled closer and suddenly I was fully alert. Adam wasn't here. Adam was in his own house, with Amy, and I was here with Dad.

Mrs Mardle's wrinkled face loomed over me. A scream stuck in my throat. She tutted, one gnarled hand clutching her cardigan around herself, and the other tucking the sheets around me. Her fingernails dug through the thin fabric, spiking my ribs.

'Now, don't you be silly,' she chided. 'You're a big boy, now. No need to be scared.'

'Wha . . . what are you doing in here?' I managed. My voice came out as a slur, almost drunk sounding. 'You live upstairs, Mrs Mardle . . .'

'Oh, I'm off now,' she said cheerfully. 'Back upstairs to Herb. Just wanted to tell you I'm sorry about the bath, that time. Didn't mean to give you a fright . . .'

I knew I was in paralysis, but like a recurring dream I couldn't remember how to get out of it. I could smell her, an old lady perfumed smell of lavender. She shuffled away from the bed, calling behind her as she went into the hallway. 'And don't you be scared of *her*, either.'

'*Who?*' My voice hissed out in a whisper to the darkened room.

'Poor lass,' Mrs Mardle muttered. 'Such a shame.'

I was so intent on focusing on the door that I almost missed the creeping movement in the room with me. The shock of it jolted me out of the paralysis and my head moved.

Tess stood beside the bed, naked and shivering, watching me through a tangle of waterlogged hair. Her arms stretched towards my face, her slashed wrists upturned like an offering. Icy droplets hit my skin.

'Get out!' I screamed, thrashing to free myself from the sheets. 'GET OUT!' Untangling myself, I scrambled backwards across the bed, pressing into the corner. 'Just leave me alone!'

Slowly, the apparition lowered its arms and turned away. Already she was fading; I could see the drawing of Ophelia's hands through her middle. By the time she reached the door, there was nothing left to see.

I yelled again when Dad skidded into the room, his face grey.

'Elliott, I'm here.' He hurried round the side of the bed. 'Come on, get up. There's no one here.'

'There were two of them!' I shouted, refusing to move. The cold wall pressed in on my back. I didn't trust moving. I needed to see everywhere at once. 'TWO. I can't take this any more!'

'There's no one here,' Dad repeated. He backed off, snapping the light on. 'See? Just a dream.'

'*Don't tell me it's a bloody dream!* It wasn't just Tess this time – it was Mrs Mardle from upstairs . . . Her bath was leaking . . .'

Dad rubbed his eyes. 'Elliott, get up. Listen to me. Mrs Mardle's bath only leaked once, years ago. You were dreaming.' He approached me again and held out his hand. 'Come on. Come into the living room.' I ignored his hand but got up, unsure of my knees' ability to support myself.

Once I was out of the bedroom I felt instantly better. Dad brought me some water and sat beside me. I held the glass to my burning forehead for a few seconds, then sipped. I jumped as something slithered around my ankles, sloshing water over the rim of the glass. I looked down to see the cat hastily retreating in a shower of drips.

Dad prised the glass out of my hand and put it down.

'I was dreaming about how she'd flooded the bath that time. I could smell the plaster on the ceiling and feel the water coming through. I told Adam to go and get Mum. That's when I opened my eyes and saw her. Mrs Mardle. She told me that she was sorry if she scared me and sorry for flooding us that time . . .'

The clock in the hallway tinged the quarter hour. I leaned back to look at it. Three-fifteen.

'Then she left and Tess was there, in the room with me . . .'

Dad sighed, his elbows on his knees and his hands in his hair. 'You know how this works. The REM sleep is interrupted, you wake while you're still hallucinating—'

'I know. I *know* all this. But it just feels so . . . vivid.'

'If anything, seeing Mrs Mardle proves it was a dream,' Dad continued. 'She's safe, upstairs. A little batty these days, but she's fine.'

A horrible thought struck me. 'What if she's not?'

Dad shook his head. 'Don't start. I saw her this evening when I got home. She was taking her rubbish out. She's *fine*,' he repeated.

I sat back on the sofa, calmer. Dad got up and left the room. I could hear him rattling about in the kitchen and a few minutes later he returned, setting two steaming mugs on the coffee table before vanishing again. The second time, he came back with blankets.

'Dad,' I began. 'I'm too old for this . . .'

He hushed me, throwing a blanket around my shoulders. Then he picked up his drink and put it by the armchair, wrapping his own blanket over his legs. 'You're never too old.' He winked. 'And anyway, I won't tell anyone.'

'Just don't tell Adam.' I reached for the mug. It was warm milk with honey and nutmeg, just like Mum used to make Adam and me when we were little. I swallowed a mouthful, swallowing back tears. I didn't even know we still had any nutmeg. It must have been buried somewhere at the back of a cupboard, forgotten since Mum last used it. The taste and smell were warm and comforting, like Mum herself when she'd been here.

I settled back on the sofa, watching Dad. His eyes were closed but every now and then he peeked at me. 'Go to sleep,' he mumbled. 'I'm here. I'm not going anywhere.'

I closed my eyes and allowed myself to drift, the taste of honey still on my lips. It made me think of Ophelia.

I woke with a stiff neck shortly after eight. Stretching, I glanced over at the armchair. Dad's blanket lay in a rumple but there was no sign of him. I yawned, rolling off the sofa and headed into the hallway. Light filled the flat, and already I felt stupid and childish to be seventeen and still needing my dad when I had a nightmare.

The front door was ajar. Beyond it, there were low voices and quiet footsteps. I went towards it and pulled it open all the way. Dad was standing on the doormat, staring up the stairs. Our neighbour Mrs Wilkes, who lived opposite, mirrored his position. She was still in her dressing gown.

I leaned out of the door. Uniformed men were carrying an empty stretcher up the stairwell. Paramedics. Their manner was sombre, unhurried. I turned to Dad and he refused to meet my eyes.

'It's her, isn't it?' I whispered. 'Mrs Mardle.'

Dad lifted his hand to his mouth, pulling deeply on a cigarette. The ash trembled for a second before breaking away. 'She died in her sleep in the early hours.'

I didn't stay to watch them bring her out. The numbness lasted for exactly the number of footsteps it took me to get from the stairwell to my room.

'Elliott?' Dad called after me.

I slammed the door behind me.

FOURTEEN

Discoveries

Wednesday. The day of the ghost walk. It was also the day that Hodge had decided I should give my first tours of the Victorian sector, with another guide to support me if necessary. Part of me looked forward to something new; by now I was sick of trailing the other guides and hearing the same stories repeated. Another part of me baulked at the thought of speaking to groups of strangers.

The evening ghost walk meant a later start. I wasn't getting paid extra because it was classed as training, but Hodge had arranged bed and breakfast on-site to save me the late-night trip back. Up until this morning I'd been considering excuses to come home instead. The idea of spending the night somewhere after learning about its ghosts no longer appealed. Two things happened to change my mind.

I slept in late and woke to an empty flat. Dad was still on the early rota, which suited me. Mrs Mardle's death had done little to convince him. After initially going quiet, he'd stuck to insisting that my vision of her had been a mixture of dream and coincidence. I'd given up trying to figure out if it was me he was trying to persuade, or himself. Either way, we hadn't stopped snapping at each other since she had died.

When I finally got up and went to shower, a full bathtub awaited me. I swiped my hand through the water. It was clear and cold as a river. I emptied it, quickly wiping my hand dry. Five days had passed since Tess had last appeared by my bedside. Five days since I'd come home to a full bathtub. I hadn't asked Dad about it. It hadn't seemed relevant. But now it had happened again I knew it couldn't be Dad. We just didn't have money to waste like that. Now I wondered if it was a warning, a sign that Tess was planning another appearance. My sleep had begun to settle over the past two nights. If she *was* due another visit, a night away from home would only be a good thing.

I showered quickly, gritting my teeth against the changing temperature of the water. It wouldn't stay warm for longer than five seconds. Eventually I jumped out, teeth chattering. My skin was so pimpled from the cold that it felt and looked like raw chicken. I rubbed myself dry. A raw chicken with jaundice: the bruises from last week's beating had ripened to yellow. The only improvement was that I'd put on a couple of pounds. Una's meal, combined with the fresh air and being at work had kick-started my appetite again. I'd woken ravenous every day – except the morning Mrs Mardle died.

I dressed, bolted down cereal and toast and, rather than spend a minute longer in the flat than was necessary, left just after midday. I had an hour to kill before I needed to set off for Calthorpe and I decided to do what I should have done at the weekend instead of spending it brooding at Adam's. I went to the library and booked a slot on one of the computers.

In the fifteen minutes I had to wait, I browsed the health shelves and found a book on sleep disorders. Among the usual subjects such as sleepwalking and insomnia, there was a slim chapter on sleep paralysis. It told me nothing new from the books I already had, only briefly detailing its link to REM sleep and theories of how the paralysis stage triggers a 'threat' alarm in the brain, effectively conjuring the dreamer's fears into the room with them. There was a scant mention of cultural references. My eyes stuck on the phrase 'hag-ridden', printed beneath a picture of a demonic woman crouched on the chest of a sleeping man. *Hag-ridden.* I thought of Tess and shuddered. There was no advice for sufferers. Nor was there anything on out-of-body experiences. I wedged it back on the shelf. The computer was free.

I took a seat, opened up the browser and typed in *Calthorpe police station death*.

It came up near the bottom of the second page.

From the archives: CALTHORPE POST, Friday May 21st, 1971.
POLICE CUSTODY DEATH.
A man has died while being held in custody at Calthorpe Police Station. The twenty-one-year-old, who has not been named, was found unconscious in a holding cell in the early hours of Sunday morning. Attempts to revive him failed and he was pronounced dead at the scene. It is not known how long the man had been in custody or what he was being held for.

'Bullshit,' I said angrily. 'He was dead before anyone even reached the cell.'

The girl on the neighbouring computer shifted her chair further away. I didn't bother to apologise.

I clicked through to a linked article from the same paper, dated several months later.

The grieving mother of a man who died in a holding cell has spoken of her anger at the verdict of accidental death. Oneta Williams, 45, slammed the enquiry into her son's death, branding it a 'cover up'. Her son Eric, 21, choked to death on his own vomit while in police custody last month. He had been detained for being drunk and disorderly after attending a friend's twenty-first birthday party earlier that evening.

Mrs Williams, a widow said, 'It was neglect. He was being held because he was not in a good way. Why then, was he left to die alone? Those on duty failed him. The blame rests with them.'

Calthorpe Police Station declined to comment.

Eric Williams' mother had been right. Her son had died because of neglect. I'd seen it, or at least seen an echo of it. And I'd heard it, too.

No one came. No one cared.

And for Eric it had been that way for more than forty years, until someone had tried to help. Until *I* had cared about what happened to him. No one else but his mother gave a damn.

I tried another search for Eric Williams but came up blank. A final search for his mother brought up an obituary. She had died in a nursing home eight years ago. Like her son, she had been alone. I closed the page and left.

During the drive to Calthorpe, I remembered back to the night in the cell. I'd been afraid, but it was a different fear to what I was used to during an out-of-body experience. When I compared it to a normal episode there were several reasons. First, unlike the times I witnessed Tess sprawled in the bath, the police station hadn't been my personal territory. My fear hadn't been about a dead stranger who shouldn't have been in my home but, in those moments before I realised it was already too late, about *saving* a stranger who needed help. The difference was that I hadn't felt threatened. And after communicating with Eric Williams and freeing him – or whatever it was that had happened – the very fact that I hadn't felt threatened was what had given me the confidence to explore the cells beyond my own.

The feeling of power I had experienced had been dulled by my last bout of paralysis, but now I was starting to see what the real problem was. All the time I was at home, the experiences instantly left me vulnerable. My subconscious knew that no one apart from me, Dad and Adam had any business being in the flat. And so the appearance of a naked, bleeding stranger – and the half-senile old lady from upstairs – triggered only one response: fear. Tess, or whatever remained of her, didn't understand that her home was now someone else's. Until I learned to conquer my fear I couldn't help her – or myself.

I made it to the Old Barn thirty minutes before my tour was due to start. The place was full of staff breaking for lunch and chatting. I nodded to one or two familiar faces and then went upstairs to put my stuff in my locker and get changed. After returning the labourer's costume for cleaning at the start of the week, I'd chosen a gentleman's suit from 1905. It had a waistcoat with an annoying number of buttons. It was smarter than I would have liked but the simplest thing I could find and one of the few that didn't come with a stupid hat of some kind.

My phone buzzed just as I was about to close the locker. It was a text from Adam.

BATTLE OF THE BANDS THIS FRIDAY, ACORN. COMING?

I tapped out *maybe* and sent it. His reply came back almost instantly.

BRING OPHELIA. NO GUNS THOUGH ;)

I threw the phone back in the locker without replying. There was no way I was asking Ophelia out. She might think I meant it as a date, and I got the impression that she didn't see me that way. I shut the locker, reminding myself that she wasn't my type either. I had barely seen her since dinner at the Hodges'. On Monday and Tuesday I'd glimpsed her clearing tables in the tea rooms. Judging from the amount of noise she had been making she wasn't happy to be there and I guessed she must have been filling in for someone.

When I went back downstairs Hodge was in the kitchen drinking tea from the horse mug that belonged to Ophelia. I had a horrible feeling he was about to announce that he'd be the one to accompany me on my first tour. The squirming in my stomach intensified.

'Elliott,' he boomed, 'you're looking very dapper in that suit, I must say.'

'Thanks.' I forced a smile.

'Nervous?' he asked, still looking me up and down.

'A bit.' I recalled the kid who had given Ophelia some lip on my first day. *Please, please don't let it be a school*, I thought.

'No need.' He put the mug down and clapped me on the back. 'I've arranged a couple of good groups for you. Nice easy ones to start with.'

'Are they comatose?' I asked. They would be after listening to me droning on at them.

Hodge laughed and beckoned me outside. 'We've a coach come in from a retirement home. We'll split them into smaller groups as usual and alternate. They'll be interested in what you have to say and they won't ask stupid questions.'

I smiled again, feeling sicker by the second. The last time I'd done public speaking of any kind was an acceptance speech during the school leavers' assembly. I'd collected a sports award for my contributions to the football team. Back then I hadn't worried about what to say because it hadn't mattered. I could have got up on stage and sung *Twinkle, Twinkle, Little Star* and the whole school would have cheered – would have joined in, probably. Now I'd be booed off stage.

I followed Hodge out on to the cobblestones. It was cooler today and overcast. Stuck in the stiff, stuffy suit I was glad. 'Will you be doing the tour with me?' I asked.

Hodge's expression clouded. For a moment I worried I'd sounded hopeful that he wasn't the one I'd be doing the tour with, but then I saw that he hadn't even heard me. I followed his gaze to the nearby stables and saw Ophelia, in a lavender dress, leaning through the door to stroke a horse's nose.

'Give me strength.' Hodge's teeth were gritted. He marched over to the stable like a fat little troll and must have announced his presence before he reached her, for she turned sharply and pulled back her hand like she'd been bitten. The action was almost . . . *guilty*. I tried not to watch as they exchanged words and then Hodge stalked off. Ophelia came towards me, her lips pinched and her skirts rustling like angry whispers.

I wondered whether he'd had a go at her for being near the horses while she wore the costume gown, but her expression suggested it was more serious than that. By the time she reached me her lips were no longer scrunched up and her face was a mask again.

'So I'm with you this afternoon,' she informed me, straightening her gloves. 'Lucky me.'

'Thanks,' I retorted, annoyed. 'And likewise.' I cast a look over my shoulder. Hodge had vanished from sight. 'Look – your uncle's gone. If you're going to bite my head off through the whole thing then I'd rather do it alone. I'm nervous enough.'

She closed her eyes and let out a slow breath. 'Sorry.' The sullen note dropped from her tone. 'I forgot. It's your first tour, isn't it?'

I nodded. 'What if my mind goes blank and I forget everything?'

She shrugged. 'It happens. Sometimes I forget things, but the audience doesn't know that. Anyway, if your mind goes blank I'll be there to fill the gap. If it helps, describe the buildings or rooms by looking around them clockwise. You'll see things which should trigger the information you need to give.'

I calmed a little. 'Okay.'

'Ready?'

'Not really . . .'

She ignored me. 'Come on.'

The afternoon wasn't perfect, but it went better than I could have hoped. After fumbling my way through the first tour I found my stride and even started to enjoy it. The audience didn't seem to notice the accidental pause or two, in fact they used the gaps as breathers to discuss with each other. Ophelia only had to step in for me once near the end. Her suggestion of going clockwise had kept me on track.

151

'You were good,' she said afterwards, once we'd escorted the final group to the tea rooms.

My cheeks grew warm. It was a long time since anyone had complimented me about anything. 'I screwed up the beginning,' I muttered.

'It was good,' she repeated. 'Believe me, I've seen a lot of tour guides. Hodge will think you're even more wonderful than he does already.' Her face twisted at the mention of him.

'Not as good as you. You're only seventeen, yet you're the best there is.'

She shook her head. 'I'm not the best. Hodge is. And there have been many far better than me over the years. I've just watched and learned what to do and what not to do.'

'How long has he had you doing this?'

'I started going with him on the tours when I was twelve. I only began doing them myself last year – you have to be sixteen to lead a group.'

I hesitated. 'How long have you lived with your aunt and uncle?'

Ophelia stared past me, in the direction of the stables. 'Since I was nine.'

I resisted pressing her further. It was obvious she wanted to get back to her horses, and everyone who finished work at six was now trickling in or out of the Old Barn. I remembered Adam's invitation for Friday, thought about asking her, then chickened out.

'What?' she said. 'You looked like you were about to say something.'

'I forgot what it was,' I lied. 'It'll come back to me.'

She smiled, but I could tell she didn't care much. 'I have to go.'

'To the horses, right?'

She gave a low, bitter laugh. 'I wish.'

And from that laugh I got it. 'He's stopped you from tending them, hasn't he? Because of the gun. That's why you've been working the tea rooms and the tours.'

Her grey eyes searched mine and, just for a moment, her misery shone through. 'It's what he always does when he wants to get at me. Keeps me away from what I care about the most.'

'For how long?'

She cast her eyes downward. I noticed her eyelashes were fair and thin; hardly there at all. I'd seen a lot of girls with pretty eyes, and Ophelia's were not pretty, not exactly. But they were striking and the lightness of her lashes emphasised the grey.

'I don't know.' She turned her eyes back up to my face. I wondered whether they had been closed when we'd kissed. My own had been. 'That's part of the punishment, keeping me in suspense. Sometimes it's a week. Sometimes longer. Once it was a whole month, plus piano every night. I felt like cutting my fingers off.'

We both turned at the sound of a horse's hooves clip-clopping over the cobbles. A thin-faced girl pulled up in the cart in front of the stables and proceeded to extract a white horse from its harness before leading it to one of the stalls. It was the same horse Hodge had caught Ophelia stroking earlier. Once the stable door was bolted, the girl vanished into the Old Barn. Ophelia watched, plainly jealous, until the girl emerged, whistling as she headed for the exit. When she was out of sight, Ophelia punched in the code to the Old Barn door. I followed her inside.

'Is that your favourite horse?'

'I love them all,' she answered softly. 'But, yeah. Pippi's my favourite. I was there when she was born. I even named her.'

'Pippi?'

'Like the book,' she explained. '*Pippi Longstocking*. She has one grey leg – I thought it looked like a stocking.'

'Right.' I had no idea what she was talking about, and it must have shown.

'Never mind,' she said, starting to smile. 'It was my favourite story.'

Her teeth were straight and very white, and her bottom lip dipped slightly lower on one side than it did the other, which offset the neatness of her teeth.

'You should smile more,' I told her, realising at the last moment that it sounded slightly corny. 'It suits you.'

Too soon it faded. She shook her head, moving to the staircase. 'I smile when I've got something to smile about. Enjoy the ghost walk, Elliott. I'll see you.'

'See you,' I repeated.

She vanished up the stairs. I went into the kitchen and made a mug of tea. I was still drinking it when I heard the slam of her locker, and a minute later she was gone, leaving me alone in the building. I went to the window and stared out, watching Ophelia heading for the museum exit.

I had an hour before I had to help Hodge set up what he needed for the ghost walk. Yesterday he had given me a token for a free evening meal, but I wasn't hungry yet. I went up to my locker and checked my phone, then rummaged through my things. Earlier in the week I'd had the idea to bring a sketchbook into work with me, with the intention of using it during my breaks. So far, I'd managed a couple of pages' worth of quick drawings; the tea-room customers, plus the well and a couple of the crooked buildings, but now I was ready for something more detailed. And I knew exactly what I was going to draw.

I changed into my own clothes and carefully hung the costume in my locker, ready for later. Then I tucked the sketchbook under my arm, stuck a handful of pencils in my back pocket and went outside.

There were four stables. Pippi's was at the end, nearest to the paddock. I had no experience with horses and not the faintest idea about how to gain the thing's attention, because when I reached the stable door there was no sign of its head. Instead its huge butt greeted me and its swishing tail stirred the damp, earthy scent of wet straw. I pursed my lips to whistle, then changed my mind, grinning. Instead, I whipped out a pencil, opened the book and started to draw.

For a full twenty minutes I sketched. The sun dropped steadily, highlighting motes of dust on the air. Behind me people passed, some pausing to look over my shoulder. I took no notice, hearing only the snuffles and snorts of the neighbouring horses as Pippi gradually shifted around the stable. I drew her in every position she stood for as long as she held it. When she changed, I did. Soon the page was a medley of vignettes; some full body sketches, others just a hoof, a stockinged leg, or a tangled snag in the mane. When the page was full I turned to a clean one, intending to continue, but then the horse lifted her head. She looked right at me and slowly came to the stable door, her head dipped as though she was questioning why I was there.

I clicked softly to her and she nickered in response, stretching her neck through the stable door. Wary, I reached out and touched my hand to her nose, the way I'd seen Ophelia do it earlier. The skin there was soft and covered with a velvety layer of fine hair. Warm air huffed from her nostrils, but she stayed perfectly still, her brown eyes inquisitive.

'Stay there,' I whispered to her. 'Don't move.'

And she didn't, not for fifteen whole minutes. Apart from the occasional blink she remained in position, just gazing toward the paddock as I hurried to capture her on the page. By the time she finally retreated into the stable I'd got her, save a few small details that I filled in from memory without any trouble. When it was done I stood back. Then I returned to the Old Barn and climbed the stairs, thinking.

From my locker I took out a sharper pencil, chewed the end of it, then finally wrote at the bottom of the page of vignettes: *Not as good as the real thing, but the best I can do. Elliott.*

I left the more detailed drawing blank, then carefully tore both pages out of the sketch book and slid them through the gap at the top of Ophelia's locker.

I wondered if they would make her smile.

FIFTEEN

Ghosts

I lay in the narrow, rickety bed, uncomfortably full. I'd eaten too much too late, waiting until the ghost walk had finished to go to the hotel restaurant and use the token Hodge had given me.

Light slipped into the room through an outside lantern. The criss-cross leading of the windows fell across the room, dividing it into a shadowy grid, and a large crack ran above the door. The whole corridor was on a slope. I hoped it was stable. It had stood for more than five centuries yet the thought was little comfort. It might have lasted this long, but it wouldn't last forever. Nothing did.

I was on the third floor, well away from the plusher suites of the paying guests. The room was basic, with only an iron bedstead, a chest of drawers with a mirror, and a table and chair. There was no shower, just a shared washroom at the end of the hall.

My stomach was like a boulder weighing me down. I got out of bed, groaning, then pulled the chair over to the window and knelt on it, resting my elbows on the ledge. The square looked weird at night, like a tiny model or a doll's house lit up by the old-fashioned street lamps. At the centre of it all stood the well. The clock above it read ten forty-five. I'd come to bed too early, not that I could help it. After Hodge had left to go home there had been no one else to speak to.

I'd wanted to laugh when he'd turned up at the meeting point for the tour that evening. His costume wouldn't have looked out of place on Henry the Eighth. It was deep-red velvet, embroidered with gold thread and lacy ruffles. A wig of ringlets perched on top of his head, making his face appear even rounder. He was already sweating.

An hour earlier we'd met to set everything up for the walk, which basically meant sitting in the ticket office printing receipts for customers who had booked over the phone, and trimming and folding ghost-walk maps. Hodge handed me a stash of programmes to sell throughout and told me to take one for myself afterwards.

More than twenty people turned up for the tour. They were quickly divided into two groups. The first had eleven, plus myself and Hodge. The second had the rest and was to be led by a guide called Lyn whom I hadn't met before. She was retired, doing only one tour a week to bump up her pension.

Lyn's group left first. Hodge explained that they would have a headstart of ten minutes before our group followed on. He spoke easily to the visitors, asking if they had come far and whether they had ever had any ghostly experiences. I listened between selling a few programmes, guessing at which visitors would take the evening seriously, and which of them were just there for a bit of fun. There was a young couple, probably the same age as Adam and Amy. She looked nervous, tugging at a Gothic crucifix around her neck. I watched her boyfriend's expression and recognised it. He was being patient, but he wasn't here for fun. He was here to better his chances of getting laid.

Four of the group, two women and two men, were holidaying from Ireland and staying in the hotel. They looked familiar, and I thought I remembered seeing them in the tea rooms during the week. They seemed jovial enough but I could tell that the two men had been dragged out of the pub to come and were likely to be the evening's sceptics, as Hodge had predicted.

The rest of the group consisted of two sisters – the elder, according to the younger one, was psychic; a middle-aged German couple touring England's haunted sites; and a writer researching her latest novel.

Finally, at eight-fifteen, Hodge cleared his throat for attention. 'Welcome to the Past Lives ghost walk, one of the best paranormal tours in the country. Tonight, I'll be sharing with you some of the most fascinating stories of the museum – the ghost stories.'

The anticipation among the group deepened. I saw the young girl clutch her boyfriend's arm. The writer opened her notebook, pen poised.

'Every town, every city in the country has its ghosts, or at least its tales of them,' Hodge continued. 'The museum here in Calthorpe is home to some of the oldest buildings in the country. And with that kind of history, there are stories to be told. This evening's tour begins in the Elizabethan part of the museum – Cornmarket Street. Follow me.'

I tailed the group to ensure no one fell behind. Hodge's smooth introduction had gone down well. They followed him like a litter of eager puppies. Even I was curious to learn more about the older parts of the museum. I'd had a quick walk round during the week after becoming sick of the sight of Goose Walk, but I hadn't learned much about it at all. Hodge led us past the well to a wide, uneven street. There were only two buildings, but both were vast and as wide as they were tall. We passed the first, a heavy timber house, and went further down to the second. Yellow light and voices flooded through the windows.

'This,' said Hodge, 'is the Swan Hotel. Originally two houses – one of which was named the Swan – they were built in or around the year 1562 and were later combined into one in the mid-seventeen-hundreds to become a coaching inn.' He stepped towards two huge arched wooden doors and pushed one open, leading through into a courtyard. 'This is where the coaches would stop and horses were fed and watered for the night.' Here Hodge paused, lowering his voice. 'But some guests – and residents – refuse to leave.'

Someone – I thought it was one of men dragged from the pub – sniggered.

Hodge swept through a side door, beckoning everyone into a low tavern room. The group squeezed past rows of tables, some occupied by drinkers, and came to stand by the bar. 'There are three entities said to haunt this building,' Hodge continued. 'The first of whom is known as our grey lady.'

The group quieted.

'She arrived here one night during a storm. The inn was crowded, but not so much that no one noticed the pretty young woman in the grey cloak sitting by the fire. Seeing that she was alone, several men propositioned her, mistakenly assuming she was a lady of loose morals, shall we say. A diary belonging to the landlord's wife at the time remarked that the young lady seemed deeply troubled and keen to conceal the fact that she was obviously pregnant.

'Once the lady had warmed herself and dried off enough she retired to a rented room upstairs.' Hodge went through a narrow doorway to the side of the bar. 'Take care on the staircase,' he called over his shoulder. 'There are a lot of steps!'

At the top, Hodge lifted his lantern. The dimly-lit corridor was lined with dark wooden doors. There was a musty, airless smell about it. I began to feel hemmed in by too many people in a small space.

'There's no official record of the room she stayed in,' Hodge said grimly. 'But what happened next, and what has occurred since leaves no doubt that it was this one. Some time after the lady shut herself away, a traveller in the next room went downstairs to complain to the landlord about a disturbance. His own knocks and requests for quiet were ignored. He described sounds of somebody tirelessly pacing the room, weeping and talking to themselves in an agitated way. At the same time, another customer reported seeing a distressed young woman at the upstairs window. Concerned, the landlord came upstairs and knocked on the door . . .' Hodge tapped softly. 'But at that moment, screams began on the street outside. Alarmed, the landlord let himself in only to discover that the room was empty.'

Hodge threw open the door. The group filtered into the gloomy room, fanning around a four-poster bed. Beside it a candle burned on a low table and the window opposite was open. I guessed one of the staff downstairs had lit the candle and opened the window before we arrived but the effect of it, flickering in an unoccupied room was eerie.

'The window was open,' said Hodge, moving to the curtains. 'He rushed to it and looked out. A terrible sight awaited him. The young woman lay in the street. She had flung herself from the window to her death.'

The German tourists moved to the window, pointing and whispering. When they moved away the younger couple took their place. The girl rubbed her bare arms and huddled closer to her boyfriend.

'No one ever found out who the lady in grey was,' said Hodge. He began to pace, slowly, up and down the room. 'But she's been seen many times by both staff and guests. Sometimes she's glimpsed in wet clothes, staring into the fire downstairs. Occasionally, a troubled face is seen at this window from the street. And sometimes, she is not seen at all – but guests in nearby rooms have claimed to be woken by the sounds of creaking floorboards and weeping . . .' He paused, and only the rhythmic padding of his footsteps was audible. 'Like someone in distress, pacing long into the night.'

Hodge stopped pacing and bent to blow the candle out. The smoke wreathed into the air. The room was quiet enough to hear a mouse fart.

Bravo, Hodge, I thought. *They're eating out of your hand.*

Without warning, the window slammed shut. Everyone in the room apart from Hodge jumped, and there was more than one frightened gasp. I watched with everyone else as the window flapped like a broken wing.

'Was that . . . *her?*' the writer asked, clutching her notebook to herself.

'Probably just the wind,' Hodge answered, securing the latch. 'But we'd best be on our way. We don't want to upset our oldest guest.' He herded everyone back into the hallway and towards a room further on. 'Now, on this very same floor, and more than a century after our grey lady, another story takes place. Unfortunately we can't go into the room because it's one that's let out, however it was here that the wife of a past owner died after a long illness—'

'I'm feeling faint.' The psychic grabbed her sister's arm. 'Oh, the poor woman. She died in such pain—'

'But the room isn't actually haunted by her,' Hodge cut in.

The woman shut up immediately. *Busted*.

'The story goes that her husband, Mr Joseph Leonard, cared for his wife right up until her death. Every morning, shortly after six, he'd gently shake her awake to make sure she hadn't slipped away in her sleep.' Hodge fixed the 'psychic' with a stare. 'It is in fact the spirit of Joseph Leonard who haunts this room. People who sleep here sometimes experience being woken by a shaking, or rocking of the bed just after six o'clock.'

'But that's the room *we've* booked,' said the girl, wrapping her arms around herself. She looked at her boyfriend. 'Shall we ask to move?'

'You bet I'll ask.'

I could tell he was annoyed; he knew that if he stayed in that room, the ghost was the best chance he had of the bed rocking.

'You needn't worry.' Hodge smiled, leading the way down the stairs. 'He's not scary. In fact it's the opposite – he's our friendly resident spirit.'

'Energy friendly, even,' one of the Irish men commented. 'You won't need an alarm clock.' A few chuckles broke the tension.

Downstairs, Hodge gathered us in the tavern area.

'Our final story before we move on is that of a little girl who haunts this area. She claims her name is Annie, but we can't completely trust what she says because she's known to be a liar and a thief. We think Annie was eight years old when she died, though it's not known how. She used the tavern to provide for her family by pick-pocketing customers. She sometimes makes her presence felt by tugging on people's clothing or even helping herself to their valuables.'

Several hands immediately went into their pockets.

Hodge continued. 'Before we leave here, I'd like to remind you all that your tickets entitle you to a free drink in the Swan after the tour concludes. I hope you'll join us.'

I sold another programme to the writer during the time it took to cross the street to the timber building. It was almost dark now and the house loomed like a cliff, each floor above zigzagging out further than the one below. In the distance I saw Lyn's group moving away, back in the direction of the Plain.

Hodge stood by the door and put his lantern on the step.

'Calthorpe House is one of the oldest timber buildings in the country. Built in 1610, it was the home of the wealthy pastor, William Calthorpe. The house retains much of its original structure and, for safety reasons, I'm unable to show you the upstairs. Before we enter I should warn you that this part of the museum experiences the highest level of paranormal activity.' Hodge picked up his lantern, the movement of the flame highlighting the sheen on his forehead.

'And why is that?' the German woman asked, taking out a camera.

Hodge flicked his tongue over his lips. 'Because terrible things happened here.' He climbed the steps and opened the front door.

I was the last to enter into a dingy hall. The place smelled stale and cold. Hodge's lantern glowed like a beacon, leading us into a wide room. He lit several candles and motioned for us to sit. A long table was at the centre, with wooden benches either side. One by one we sat, but Hodge stayed standing by an inglenook fireplace.

'William Calthorpe and his wife were liked and respected,' he began. 'They had two daughters who were married off quickly with good dowries, and a son who eventually inherited the house.

After he inherited, Simon Calthorpe married a girl named Alice from nearby Bury. She was described as black-haired and very beautiful, but she was cruel and quickly became unpopular with the servants of the house. And with Simon often away on business she was free to do as she pleased.

'Now, the room that we are in was once the old kitchen. And as well as cooks and maids going about their daily chores, these servants often had young children who were also put to work. Children as young as six had to fetch and carry water, light fires and that sort of thing, in return for food and somewhere to sleep. But food was scarce and the lodgings were poor.' He stepped into the blackened fireplace and pointed into an alcove in the side. 'Little boys had to light the bread ovens early in the morning. At night, they slept –' he pointed to two high shelves either side of the fire, '– above those ovens, and for some it was better than the streets. They were warm, at least. But for others, sleeping above the dying fire was a disaster waiting to happen. One misplaced foot, or a turn in their sleep could result in them falling straight into the embers. At certain times of the year, one little boy, terribly burnt, can be seen in this room. And sometimes, the spit for roasting meat above the fire turns, apparently by itself.'

I imagined the smell of burnt flesh and was glad I hadn't eaten yet. Hodge stepped out from the fireplace. The flickering of the lantern played over his wig and, for a moment, I saw the glossy ringlets as a mass of entrails. I forced my gaze away. It was easy to get spooked in a place like this.

'Through the back of the house and into the gardens, we have the orchard,' said Hodge, crossing the room to a door. The benches scraped the floor as everyone stood up. I was glad to get back outside. A light drizzle had begun, lifting the smell of wet earth to

165

my nose. We followed through a flower garden to a gate further back. From there, ancient trees stretched as far as I could see.

'At harvest time the servants were put to work in the orchard. As I mentioned, they were often hungry. The spirits of two such servants, thought to be orphaned brothers, have made their presence known here. Their story is a particularly horrible one.

'One day the younger brother Samuel, aged about seven, stole some bread from the kitchen. The cook noticed immediately and handed the boy to Alice, still holding the uneaten bread. Flying into one of her tempers, Alice ordered that the boy should be hanged from the tallest tree.'

Hodge removed a torch from his pockets and shone it deep into the orchard. The light picked out a sturdy branch. 'Now of course, executions like this were unlawful. But Alice had power and she knew how to use it. Under her instruction the little boy was dragged, kicking and screaming to the tree by the stable hand, who held him while the gardener secured the noose. By now the entire household had gathered. Some were egging it on, eager to gain Alice's favour. Others, including the cook, watched in tears but were helpless to do anything if they valued their own position within the household.'

The tree branch creaked softly. Bile rose unexpectedly in my throat.

'As the noose was knotted around Samuel's neck, his older brother Sebastian raced into the orchard after returning from an errand. He arrived to see Samuel lifted off his feet in one swift tug. In an instant he flung himself at the stable hand, knocking him to the ground and the little boy came crashing back down to earth. The mood became uglier still. The stable hand was angry at being challenged. He insisted that Sebastian was to blame for his little brother's crime because he had failed to teach the boy not to steal. Suddenly the roles were reversed. The noose was removed from Samuel's neck and instead thrown around Sebastian's. And because it was less objectionable for the older boy to die, no one did a thing except watch as Sebastian was hanged until dead. Legend has it that Alice Calthorpe then calmly told the little boy to eat the bread, on account that it had been paid for with his brother's life.'

Hodge paused and shifted position. In that moment's silence I thought I heard a sniff come from one of the Irish women. When I looked up I saw she was crying.

'Is that *true*?' someone asked. 'That really happened here?'

Hodge clicked the torch off and put it away. From his pocket he removed a piece of paper and cleared his throat. 'I'll now read to you from a confession made by the cook, Martha Willis, on her deathbed. "*I cannot go to the Lord with the burden of what we did to that poor boy. He has rested some nine years since in an unmarked grave. His brother, poor child, spoke not a word after watching the murder. Forgive me, O Lord, for my part in this, for it was I who handed him to the wolves. But I did not mean for him to die! Only to be punished. Lord have mercy on my soul.*"'

Hodge refolded the piece of paper to shocked whispers from the group.

'The ghosts of all three are frequently seen throughout the house and grounds. The child struck dumb by his brother's death sits under the tree with the bread that he cannot eat. The cook, Martha Willis, is seen wringing her hands and crying in the kitchen. And the boy, Sebastian, hanged for a crime he did not commit, is seen wandering the gardens or hanging from the tree.'

'When were they last seen?' asked the fake psychic, craning her neck to look into the dark orchard. 'Have *you* ever seen them?'

'I've seen them all,' Hodge replied. 'More often when I'm alone, but last year Sebastian was witnessed by myself and an entire tour group.'

'And we're supposed to verify that how, exactly?' one of the men asked, his arms folded.

Hodge held his hands open in a gesture of submission. 'Those who weren't too shaken up left comments in the visitors' book testifying to it. I'm happy to show you.'

The man's arms remained folded, but he looked less sure of himself now.

'If Alice Calthorpe ever regretted what she did, there was no sign of it,' said Hodge. 'The fear of her spread to the rest of the village. The last part of the story takes us back inside the house.'

I replayed Hodge's words as the group shuffled away from the orchard. There was no question that he was a gifted storyteller: his audience was rapt whenever he spoke. No wonder Ophelia excelled at the tours. She'd learned from the best.

We gathered in a large hall, similar to the kitchen in that there was a huge fireplace, and a long table, but both were grander. Again, Hodge took his place by the fire.

'In 1645, Simon Calthorpe died following a short illness. Nothing sinister about that, you might think, but England was rife with tales of witchcraft at the time. When one of her maids then fell ill, and after a poor apple harvest, Alice Calthorpe became convinced that her household was being targeted by a witch.' He pointed to a glass cabinet on the wall. 'We have evidence that somebody in this house took measures to protect it from witchcraft. Several objects have been found in cavities below doorsteps, in chimneybreasts and other concealed areas. Here we have an onion stuck with pins, a single shoe belonging to Alice Calthorpe, and an iron knife. Historians have verified that all of these items were commonly used to ward off evil. But Alice wasn't content. She began accusing women in the village of cursing her, and even went so far as to try and rebound the witchcraft against those she suspected. She stalked women in the street and stabbed footprints they left with knives. Apparently, this was meant to force a witch into betraying what she was.

'This behaviour escalated into what we now refer to as "witch-pricking", where a pin or needle is used to prick a devil's mark on a woman. Often, these marks were something like a wart or a scar. If they did not bleed, it was a sign of guilt. Alice took it upon herself to jab an embroidery needle into women unexpectedly. To this day, guests complain of a cold presence in this house, followed by a sharp sensation, much like being pricked with a pin.'

A timely draft blew into the room, curling around our ankles. Some of the visitors looked genuinely disturbed. I couldn't blame them. Since the story of the two boys in the orchard I'd wanted to leave Calthorpe House. Perhaps the vibes came from knowing what had happened there, but there was definitely an atmosphere. I could sense it waiting, willing us to believe in it.

Hodge's boots clicked across the floor on his way to the door. I allowed everyone else out first, and couldn't help but let my eyes trail the room before I closed the door. For reasons I couldn't explain, I couldn't get away from this house – from this entire part of the museum – quickly enough.

As I closed the door I realised I couldn't wait for the ghost walk to be over with altogether.

SIXTEEN

Walkabout

I drew back from the window above the Swan, blinking away Hodge's story of Alice Calthorpe. The evening had continued much in the same vein throughout the rest of the museum and, although the remainder of the tales were not as detailed or as grisly as those of Cornmarket Street, they still clung to me like dirt under a fingernail. Most of the Georgian sector, Hodge explained, actually dated back to Elizabethan times but had been rebuilt after a terrible fire. There were a couple more gruesome stories of hangings, and the murder of a man by his servant, and the story of a benign ghost who drifted through the tiny chapel while reading, apparently hovering ten centimetres from the ground. According to Hodge, the museum had puzzled over the haunting for years until they had one day discovered that the floor was reconstructed at a lower level than it had originally been.

In Goose Walk I'd allowed myself to relax a bit. Knowing the surroundings and stories helped, but as it turned out, letting my guard down was a stupid thing to do. Despite taking care to hang back in the schoolroom when Hodge brought out the punishment equipment, the stench of piss and resentment arose so suddenly it sent fits of coughing through the group. The lad who'd volunteered to go into the corner slammed down the dunce's cap and ran past me to the door, gulping huge breaths out on the street. His girlfriend soon joined him and, from the looks on their faces, I doubted they'd stay the night now. After giving him a minute to get himself together I went out to see if he was all right. Secretly, I was glad of an excuse to leave the miserable place. I should never have gone in.

The rest of the group emerged with mixed reactions: some shaken, and others triumphant at having experienced something. As the tour drew to a close, Hodge reminded them all that they were welcome to a free drink in the Swan. With the exception of the young couple, who left as I thought they would, everyone else accepted.

On the way into the tavern I caught Hodge's eye. He grinned and slapped me on the back.

'So, what did you make of it?' he asked, leaning closer. 'Couldn't have gone any better, eh?'

I smiled weakly. Was I the only one who didn't find it entertaining to stir up things that should be left alone? Was anyone else bothered that they had paid to hear about death and murder and suffering? I searched each face, finding little compassion. No. Most of them had relished every word.

I realised I hadn't answered Hodge's question. It didn't matter. He was basking in his success, even accepting a drink from the burly Irish men who had already had their free drink and were now putting money behind the bar, just as intended.

'I'll bet you now that at least half of this group comes back for the paranormal events next month,' Hodge murmured. 'What do you reckon?'

I gave a vague nod. It was another empty question. Hodge was only stating what had been obvious from the reactions when we'd pushed the leaflets at them on the way into The Swan. They'd snatched them out of our hands and snapped up every copy of the programme. I stayed with Hodge for a while, but soon the customers drifted back to him with more questions – and more drinks – and eventually I slunk away to the restaurant, already trying to think of a way to tell him that I didn't want to do another ghost walk.

I rubbed my stomach again, wondering whether I should go for a stroll to help ease it, but I couldn't face walking around the museum in the dark after the stories I'd heard. Eventually, reluctantly, I took my sketchbook out. I drew the view from the window and, using the mirror, a quick self-portrait. My heart wasn't really in either of them. Still, they helped and an hour later, more comfortable, I switched off the light and clambered into the unfamiliar bed.

I lay on my side, listening to muffled footsteps along the corridor beneath me as guests found their rooms, and below that, rowdy voices from those still drinking. The building creaked and sighed along with them. It was better than silence. My eyelids drooped. At some point I must have got too comfortable and rolled on to my back.

I thought it was the clock on the Plain that woke me, its distant chimes piercing the silence. But as I peered through the window I realised I didn't quite remember getting out of bed and, before I even turned around, I knew.

There I was, flat on my back, asleep with my mouth slightly open. I'd kicked the covers back, and lay bare-chested, wearing only thin pyjama bottoms. Looking down at the outside me, I saw that I looked the same. I moved closer to myself, watching as my chest slowly rose and fell. It's the weirdest feeling to watch yourself, not in a mirror, not on a home video, but to actually *see* yourself as someone else might. I fought the urge to panic, fought against the unnaturalness of it. I was here, outside, and I had a choice.

In the dim room, the last of the bruises on my face were swallowed by the shadows. I lifted my hand – my ghost hand, for want of a better description – to my sleeping body's face. I had a choice, I reminded myself. Get back in now, or do as I'd done at the police station. Pulling my hand away, I stared around the room. No shadows in corners, no bleeding girls or choking men. Nothing to threaten me. But what would I find downstairs, if I dared to wander that far?

I went to the door, trying not to think about how I was moving. In the times when I'd only realised I was outside of myself at the last minute, I'd always *assumed* I was walking. But how could I be, when *this*, whatever the outside me was, didn't even have a body? I mean, it felt like I was walking, felt like I was breathing, sweating, all the things I normally felt. But when I reached the door I was faced with a decision. Should I try to open it, or just go *through* it?

I decided I needed to stop thinking like a person who was restricted by the physical. What had happened in the cells had shown me that there were no restrictions. I pressed myself against the door. At first it was solid and resisting. I closed my eyes, reminding myself that my physical body was behind me, and pushed again. There was a thickening of the air, but I forced myself past it. When I opened my eyes, I was on the other side.

Elated, I had another idea: if I could pass through doors, what about floors? I looked down at the dusty carpet. It wasn't like I was really standing on it . . .

As I thought it, I began to sink. Slowly at first, then more quickly. Knee-deep, waist-deep, shoulder-deep, into the floor. The sensation wasn't unlike being in an elevator. I forced my eyes to stay open, then wished I hadn't. Carpet, stiff with grime; the grain of wooden floorboards, the cavity beneath thick with cobwebs, and finally cracking plaster . . .

I emerged in the corridor below, where the paying guests stayed. Alarmingly, I couldn't find a foothold and started to sink once more. *Not again.* I forced myself to focus. *I'm standing, I'm real, I'm standing . . .*

And because it was easier to remember what it was like to be physical than not, it worked. I managed to pull myself back up to floor level and become steady. I took a moment to calm down. The stairs were on my right. I could go back up any time I chose. Or I could explore some of the alleged hauntings here, or even downstairs in the tavern.

While I considered my options, the silence became *not* silence. Beds creaked. Bodies sighed and snored beyond the closed doors. A low hum from downstairs – probably a refrigerator or something – filtered up.

I felt lucid. Powerful. Afraid, but excited. Summoning my courage, I turned and headed for the un-numbered door at the end of the sloping hall. The room where guests were not permitted to stay.

The grey lady's room.

Pausing outside, I listened for the strain of floorboards, the tread of someone in distress, the flap of the window. I heard nothing. Bracing myself, I went *through* the door.

The curtains were tied back and the room glowed from lamp-light outside. The candle was unlit beside the smooth, unrumpled bed. The window was fastened. Everything was quiet, undisturbed. Just an empty room.

The tension building inside me ebbed. If anything, the room felt *un*haunted. But then, even Tess didn't come every night. Correction: I didn't *see* Tess every night. It didn't mean that she wasn't there.

After another turn of the room, it was clear there was nothing to see. I left.

In the corridor I tried to remember which room was haunted by Joseph Leonard. By trial and error I eventually located it, entered it, and found it to be just as empty as that of the grey lady. Upon hearing the clock on the Plain strike one, I realised I was too early anyway: Hodge had claimed that guests were woken by the ghost at around six. I doubted I'd be able to stay out of my body that long but if I could, then this was where I planned to be.

I made my way downstairs. The shutters were pulled at the bar in the tavern area. I ventured a little way in. Dirty glasses were stacked at one end and stools balanced upside down on tables. Behind the bar, the fridges grumbled as though protesting at having to work through the night.

Something glinted on the floor. I stooped to pick up a coin. I didn't recognise it. It must be either something old used by one of the guides, or perhaps dropped by a foreign visitor. I went to leave it on the bar but it slipped from my fingers and fell to the floor.

At the exact moment it hit, the fridges silenced. Instead, the only sound now was the eerie roll of the coin, travelling in a counter-clockwise arc, circles rapidly decreasing. I bent down again, reaching for it as it was about to drop . . .

Then snatched my fingers back with a strangled cry as a tiny, leather lace-up boot came out of the shadows, snapping the coin to the floor.

Falling back, I flattened myself against the bar, my hand pressed against the sticky tiles. My terrified gaze slid up the boot to a stockinged ankle, a tattered skirt hem. One filthy hand clutched a ragged shawl in place over the figure's head and shoulders, leaving the face in shadow. The other hand grabbed for the floor and, with a delighted, girlish giggle that rang in my ears, the coin was secreted away.

In the next blink she moved unnaturally fast, skipping through the tavern. It was like watching an old, jittery film reel. As fast as she vanished from one spot she reappeared in another, dancing over the tiles.

The little pickpocket girl.

And wherever her feet landed the tavern became something else; something forgotten. The upturned chairs vanished and in their places were other tables, other chairs that were much, much older. And God, the *smell*! Putrid and rotten. Old meat, stale sweat. Ale, and sickness and unwashed bodies. The soup of poverty.

I fought to stand, wanting to get out of this place. Back to my body, where I wouldn't have to see or smell this any more. And tomorrow, screw the job, and screw the ghosts. I couldn't do it. Why *should* I do it? Why was it *my* responsibility?

Because who else can? a nagging little voice said. *Who else do you know with this . . . ability?* And then, more selfishly: *If you can't control it, how do you expect to make it go away?*

And it was that selfish little voice I chose to listen to. Crouching, wavering, I watched as she flickered about the room, whispering to herself or perhaps someone that only she could see.

176

'Hello,' I croaked, waiting for her to hear me. Telling myself it would be all right. Not to be a coward. She was only a child. Another thought struck me – what did you say to something that might not even know it was dead?

I tried again. 'Do you need help?' My voice was all wrong. Echoing. Like it knew it didn't belong.

The broken waltz continued. She didn't see me, didn't hear me. And then:

'Annie,' I called, in one last attempt.

The dancing stopped. The head tilted, playful. She turned, crackled, vanished. Then reappeared, her face inches from mine.

I cried out, slipping to my knees.

Two bright eyes burned in a dirt-streaked face. They were alert, watching me like a starling might watch a beetle.

'Money,' she said, holding out her hand. The playfulness had left her now. Her eyes were shrewd, older than her years.

I gestured helplessly. 'I don't have any . . .'

'Pah!' She flounced off to another corner of the tavern. Flames shot up in an empty grate behind her, gone the next instant when she flitted away.

The sawdust stirred on the floor and curtains ruffled as her voice burbled all the while. I shrank back as she swept about the place, whirling and twirling, faster and wilder until, just as I thought I couldn't keep up with her, there was a clatter of tiny heels on the tiles in front of me, and a last hiss of breath in my face with her parting 'PAH!'

The silence that followed was broken by my yelp as the fridges came back on. Shaken, I got up and backed away from the now-empty tavern room, counting the doors to my room, forcing myself through the wooden barrier. I wanted nothing more than

177

to be back in my body and gone from Past Lives as soon as the morning came.

I emerged inside the room and froze. Somehow, I'd miscalculated. Had I entered the wrong one? No. It was mine, all right. There was my wallet, my sketchbook and pencils . . . only the bed was empty.

My body was gone.

SEVENTEEN

Myself and I

Don't panic. Don't lose it. It's a dream. It's got to be a dream . . .

Then why wouldn't I wake up?

The sheets were rolled back like a lip. I stared at them as though they might speak, like they were capable of giving me an answer. I must have got out of bed. It was the only explanation – but then where was I? Had I imagined or dreamed the entire out-of-body experience? It had never happened this way before. With a yell, I threw myself at the door. Not caring if I got hurt, not caring if I woke anyone, just wanting to feel something solid.

I passed straight through it, like it was no more substantial than wet newspaper. In terror, I hurtled back again, willing myself awake. Nothing had changed. The bed was still empty and I was still the outside me. Desperate, I dropped to the floor, peering beneath the bed. Had I fallen out, rolled under?

Nothing.

If it had been possible to throw up, then I would have. If I could have cried I'd be sobbing. A hollow nausea grew inside me, spilling into dizziness. What was happening to me? Had I gone mad? Or was I paying the price for wandering away from my body and defying the laws of nature? The thought hit me like a shovel striking a coffin. What happened when a body was deserted for the length of time I'd been away? I wondered if my heart was still beating, whether my lungs still breathed.

I'd never believed in God but I was willing to give anything a go now.

Please, God. PLEASE, don't let me be dead. Don't let it be too late. I swear I'll never, ever mess around like this again.

If God was there, He or She wasn't listening. I was on my own. Totally alone in the void between sleep and waking – unless the spirit of the child in the tavern downstairs could be counted. The thought filled me with horror.

A door closed somewhere below me. Who could be moving around the hotel at this hour? Unless . . .

I'd never sleepwalked as far as I knew. But then, I'd never wandered so far, or for so long away from my body before either. Could it have got up in search of the rest of me? I went for the door, noticing for the first time since I'd returned to the room that the key wasn't in the lock. Seconds later I saw it on the floor, resting against the skirting board. Someone else, besides me, had been through the door.

I moved into the corridor. A swift check of the hall held no answers: all the other rooms were empty or occupied by other staff members. I edged down the stairs. The entire building seemed poised, holding its breath with me. I searched the guests' corridor then the ground floor, my fear of a repeat appearance by Annie overridden by other, deeper fears.

I was starting to feel odd, like an hourglass running out of sand.

You're panicking. That's all it is.

I wished I could believe that. But every moment the sensation intensified. I felt . . . misaligned. Like a jigsaw piece forced into the wrong slot.

The movement came out of the corner of my eye, catching me off-guard. I shrank back. From what, I didn't immediately know – it had been something small, but familiar.

Something . . . *human*.

Through the tavern window a half-naked figure lurched, bare-foot along the cobblestones, away from the Swan.

Me.

I bolted. Out of the tavern, past the reception area. Through the entrance hall to the double doors barring me from the street. I leaped through them, the shadowy world I was in blurring around me.

Outside in the open air, low clouds crowded the sky. The cobble-stones gleamed wetly, coated with a drizzle that was steadily building into something heavier. Ahead, my body slowed. Had it sensed the nearness of its other part? Or was it in danger of waking in the rain?

I had never considered what might happen if I woke up while part of me was separated from myself. Until now, I hadn't believed it possible. But this, seeing myself moving around, made me realise exactly how little a grip I had on it. I thought I'd been so clever, so invincible. I'd thought wrong. And now, somehow, I had to unpick the stitches of my mistake and get back in. But how do you get back into something that has a motion of its own? How do you jump on to a moving train?

I approached, stealthily. Unsure of any other way to do it. From what little I knew, sleepwalkers were supposed to be handled care-fully, not woken or frightened. I was happy to go along with that. If the logical, thinking part of me was outside, then surely all that remained was the most primal of instincts.

Then my body raised its arms into the rain and its face to the sky, slowly spinning. Rejoicing in the downpour in a way that was anything *but* primal.

181

It was considered, awed . . . and, as its gaze levelled with mine, *aware*.

Those eyes were focused, awake.

And not completely mine.

I felt I was slipping, grasping at that sand in the hourglass as reality slid further through my fingers and away. This was worse than Tess, worse than seeing myself on the road after the accident.

Because it wasn't me in there.

Whatever it was, it could see me.

'Who . . .?' my voice cracked. '*What* are you?'

The other me – *it* – didn't answer immediately. Instead it leaned its head back, closed its eyes, and opened its mouth to catch the droplets of rain. When its mouth closed again, it was smiling.

'Alive,' it answered.

Alive. One little word. It was the most terrifying word I'd ever heard spoken. The voice, *my* voice, was different. Rasping and slow. Like it was being used by something that had forgotten how to speak.

'How long have you been dead?' I whispered, so quietly I thought it had surely been lost in the rain. 'Who are . . . who *were* you?'

'A long time. Feels like forever.' Confusion replaced the smile. 'But I was . . . like you, once. A boy.'

Not an *it*, then. A *he*.

'Why have you stolen my body?' I asked.

'I didn't steal it.' The eyes flashed darkly, darker than mine really were – closer to grey or green than blue. 'I saw you, moving around. And I saw your body, just . . . lying there. Still breathing, but not sleeping. Just *empty*. Vacant.' The eyes met mine, curious. 'How?'

'I had an accident. I almost died . . . I *did* die, just for a few minutes. Ever since then, I – part of me – can come out of my body when I sleep.'

The other me looked around the deserted museum slowly.

'And so you explored.'

I swallowed. 'Yes.'

'One day it will be your turn, your time.' He shook his head. 'More time than you know what to do with.'

'So . . . you're not . . . I mean, you'll give me my body back?' I croaked.

He laughed, low and bitter. 'I only . . . *borrowed* you. I just wanted to feel and remember. I don't want your body, or your life. I want my own. It wasn't my time.' He broke off. 'But I'm not meant to be *here*, either.' He looked pale now. Sweat shimmered on his upper lip. 'I have to go.'

I watched, helpless, as he sank first to his knees, then on to his side. His eyelids flickered, pupils dilated like someone slipping under anaesthetic. Then his eyes closed. He took a shuddering breath. The face – my face – constricted with some kind of spasm. A shadowy wisp streamed like vapour from my body, twisting into the air. I waited for it to take some kind of form, but no sooner had the last of it filtered out there was a feeling of weight from all around, like gravity itself pressing in. Then a crushing and dragging. If I'd ever struggled to get back into my body before then the thought now seemed alien to me. This time, there was no resisting. I could no more have stayed out than a wasp could have stayed away from marmalade.

I was back inside, choking in strangled, grateful gasps that racked my body. I rolled on to my front and stood up, shivering.

183

My thin pyjama bottoms were sodden, clinging to my skin. I felt odd and sick, like I'd taken medicine that I shouldn't have. I ran to the Swan, the rain numbing my feet against the spiteful ground, but I knew tomorrow would bring bruises.

I arrived at the door, shoving it harder than I meant to. It didn't budge.

Great.

For the first time since I'd rushed outside I stopped to consider the way I'd left. I'd gone *through* the door. And although whatever had occupied my body had left the building this way, too, the door had closed behind it. I was locked out, half naked, with no way of getting back inside. Added to that, I had absolutely no possessions that could help me: my phone was in the room upstairs and so were my keys. I couldn't even sleep in the car.

I prowled the perimeter, looking for any possible way in; an open window or unlocked side door. Nothing, and the rain showed no signs of letting up. I squinted through the downpour towards the clock above the well. Two-thirty. I'd been out of my body for almost an hour. Every other time it had been a matter of minutes.

At the very least I needed somewhere to shelter. Even without the rain it would still be cold. If only there was somewhere I could wait it out with a blanket, or some clothes . . .

Clothes. The Old Barn . . .

I raced towards it, my hand outstretched even before it reached the door. I punched in the code, already imagining how I'd happily wear the most ridiculous frilly costume I could find so long as it was warm, and that there would be tea or maybe even hot chocolate . . .

The door didn't move. Halfway through keying the code in a second time I saw why. There was another lock below the keypad, one that required a key I didn't have. I smacked the door, calling it every name I had. My hair plastered my face, rain coming off it in icy rivulets. I pushed it back, thinking. There was bound to be someone operating the gates at the entrance lodge: with guests and staff on-site there had to be access in case of emergencies. But how could I explain being outside, half dressed at this hour? The only feasible explanation I could give was that I'd been sleep-walking, but I had no idea if anyone I went to for help could be trusted. I'd had enough of being pointed and stared at over the past few months. I didn't need it again, not here, yet at the same time I knew I couldn't stay outside in the elements because of my pride. I turned towards the exit, resigned.

One of the horses neighed in the nearby stables. A new idea came to me. The stables would be warm and dry. If I could hide in one until early morning, there was a chance I could make it into the Old Barn when the cleaners opened up. Then I could sneak inside, grab some clothes and wait until the hotel opened. No one would know any different and I'd be saved from humiliating myself.

I crept towards the stables, praying that they wouldn't be locked. I couldn't think why they would be – it wasn't like these were racehorses or anything. For once my luck held: all that fastened each stall door were two outside bolts on the upper and lower section of the door. I fumbled with the lower bolt of the first door I came to. It opened smoothly, releasing a warm waft of hay and horse.

Squeezing in, I pulled the lower half of the door closed and felt for an inside bolt. Locking it, I stood up, instantly warmer, and

185

began skirting the edge of the stable. I could hear the horse breathing and snorting, but it was too dark to see anything. My hand stretched out blindly, trying to find some corner that wasn't too draughty. It found something warm and muscular.

A bellowing snort froze me in place. Then pain shot through my knee, once, then once more. I was too stunned even to cry out. The bloody horse had kicked me. Twice, in the same spot. Somehow I managed to stagger back to the door, feeling my way and moaning softly. No way was I staying in here with that thing. I grappled with the latch and scrambled out.

I wasn't ready to give up yet. That stable had been *warm*. I gritted my teeth and limped along to the one at the end: Pippi's. She'd been calm earlier when I'd drawn her – maybe she had a better temperament. Maybe I could convince her to share.

I heard the rustle of straw as I slipped in, bracing myself for another kick. She nickered softly, as though in greeting.

I clicked to her, trying to put her at ease. 'Hey,' I whispered, 'it's only me. I was here earlier.' I reached out and found her flank. She was warm, solid. I gave her a firm pat. 'I drew you, for Ophelia. Remember?'

Please don't kick me. Or bite.

I continued to stroke her, talking all the while. She seemed restless and was pawing at the ground. Slowly, I moved along until my hand was in her mane, scratching it. The straw beneath my feet crackled – and was dry, thankfully – but I could feel the cold seeping through from the stone floor. As my eyes adjusted I picked out shapes and shadows. There were a couple of things hanging up on the far wall.

I moved over to them, still murmuring to Pippi. One of the items was a scrap of sacking. The other was a thick horse coat. I

186

unhooked both and slung them over my arm, my toes nudging through the straw. After my luck tonight I fully expected to step in something horrible, but somehow I made it to the corner unscathed. I took off my bottoms and wrung them out, then hung them on a nearby hook. There was no chance they'd be dry by morning but it was better than wearing them. I dried myself with the sack as best I could but the fabric was rough and scratchy. With my good leg I kicked a pile of straw into the corner, before wrapping the horse coat tightly around myself and curling up.

Pippi shifted position, chewing on something. My knee throbbed in time with her munching. I couldn't stop shivering, not just with the cold but with everything that had happened. At first I couldn't bring myself to close my eyes, fearful of whatever else might be lurking, unseen.

Something, *someone*, had entered my body. Actually occupied it, and used it. Been alive again, through me, for those few minutes . . .

With a jolt, I realised that I had no idea exactly how long it had been. I'd assumed it had been just for those moments I'd witnessed, and shortly before, but how could I know for sure? I'd been away from my body for far longer than that.

I was like you, once. A boy . . .

I hadn't asked his name. Or even how he'd died.

It wasn't my time.

I'd been too afraid to do anything except wonder how I was going to get my body returned. Now I looked back I saw that I hadn't found out much about the ghost at all. I hadn't asked enough questions.

And the ones I had asked hadn't been the right ones.

187

I lay there, warmer, a little drier, allowing myself to doze but not to drop off fully. *Just a few hours. Just need to hang on until they start opening up, then make a run for it . . .*

But there's nothing more difficult than trying to stay awake when your body craves rest. Now that I was finally generating some heat, and with the comforting snuffles and earthy smell of the horse, I'd had it. I was gone.

It wasn't a restful sleep. I dreamed of lost children, hanged servants, and a dark-headed woman reaching for me with a pin—

Something pricked the sole of my foot.

'Go away!' I shouted. 'I don't have any devil's marks!'

Another jab swiftly followed. I woke properly this time, blinded by light streaming through the open stable door. In the centre of the light a figure stood silhouetted over me.

'What the hell do you think you're doing?'

EIGHTEEN

Exposed

The voice was low. The figure lunged forward and once more I felt the stabbing sensation in my foot.

'Hey!' I sat up, one hand clasping the horse coat tightly to preserve what little remained of my dignity. The other I used to shield my eyes from the light. I wished I hadn't. Ophelia stood over me, brandishing a pitchfork.

'*Elliott?*'

'Did you just stick that in my *foot?*' I asked furiously.

'I'll stick it somewhere else in a minute – and it won't be your foot. Get up.'

I hurried to my feet. Every part of me ached. *This cannot get any worse.*

'Did he hurt you, darling?' she murmured, glancing at the horse.

'*Hurt her?* Of course not. Why would you think that?'

Ophelia's head snapped up. 'Let's see. It's seven-thirty a.m. and you're holed up in a stable. It's obvious you've been here all night – and oh yes! You're not just semi-naked, you're wearing a horse coat!'

For the first time, I looked down at myself. Then I looked from my saggy pyjama bottoms hanging up nearby, to the horse. Finally, I looked at Ophelia.

'I can explain.'

Her eyes narrowed. 'Yeah? You've got exactly thirty seconds. Depending on what I hear I'll then call Hodge and get you kicked out. Or I'll beat the crap out of you, then I'll call Hodge and the police and get you kicked out.'

'Oh, come on. I've seen you fight—'

She raised her arms. 'Twenty-six seconds.'

'All right, all right! Look – remember what I said the other night? About the out-of-body experiences I have?'

She frowned. 'Yes. So?'

'I had one last night. And . . .' I trawled my mind for something, anything that I could give her that was remotely plausible – which I guessed discounted the truth. In the end all I could think of was my own first assumption when I'd discovered my body was gone. 'At some point I sleepwalked. I don't know how – it's never happened before.'

Her glare softened. 'And you just happened to wake up *here*?'

'I . . . no.' I wished she'd turn away. Her gaze was dissolving me like salt would a slug. Plus it was difficult to keep the horse coat wrapped around everything. God, this was humiliating.

'I woke up on the Plain, drenched with rain and all I had on was what I went to bed in. I couldn't get back into the Swan – I'd locked myself out.' I gestured to my pyjama bottoms. 'I just thought if I could wait it out until the Old Barn opened I could sneak in and get some clothes and no one would know.'

'Why didn't you just call for help? There are phones all over the place.'

'I was hoping to save myself the embarrassment of anyone finding out.' I scowled, rubbing my temple. I could feel a headache coming on. 'Least of all *you*.'

Ophelia's lips twitched. I thought she was about to swear at me, but then a gasp of laughter bubbled out of her. She dropped the pitchfork and clapped her hands over her mouth, shaking silently.

'What?' I said, unimpressed.

'Sorry . . . I'm sorry . . .' she managed, through another peal of laughter. 'You just look . . . so . . . so *ridiculous*!'

'Well, I'm glad you're amused,' I said huffily. 'I feel like hell, but next time I'm locked out, half naked, freezing and kicked by a horse, I'll be sure to let you know so I can brighten your day.'

She stopped laughing and wiped her eyes. 'Wait – Pippi kicked you?'

'No, not Pippi. That bloody thing at the other end. I went in there first and it got me twice in the knee.'

'You must have scared him,' said Ophelia. 'He's young, still nervous. Poor Jasper.'

'Poor *Jasper*!' I exclaimed. 'What about poor me?'

She unhooked my pyjama bottoms and tossed them at me. 'Put those on and let's get into the barn.'

'Can you face the other way?' I snapped.

'I was going to!' She turned around, but not before I caught her smirking. 'Keep your pants on.'

I scowled harder. The soggy fabric clung to my skin as I shivered into it. Worse, it didn't leave anything to the imagination. I decided to keep the horse coat wrapped around me for now.

'I'm ready. Is the Old Barn even open yet?'

'I've already been in – the caretaker gets here at seven.' She patted the horse on the rump. 'Come on.'

I limped around Pippi and outside. Ophelia secured the stable door and strode past me.

'Why are you even here so early, anyway?' I asked as we reached the door. As soon as it was out of my mouth I had a pretty good idea – she was in jodhpurs and riding boots. 'Oh, I get it. You were planning on a sneaky ride before Hodge gets here. What if he turns up and catches you?'

She shrugged, pushing the door open. 'I'll be finished before he turns up. Got to get my kicks somehow.' She cast a sly look back at me. 'I take it you won't be telling anyone you were here to see me?'

'Very funny.'

Once we were inside, Ophelia walked over to the kettle and filled it at the sink. 'Do you want a shower? There's a clean towel in my locker. Come on, I'll get it for you.'

I nodded. 'Thanks.'

The shower didn't make up for the hellish night, but it helped. Afterwards I dressed in another Victorian labourer's costume that had appeared on the rail and limped downstairs. Ophelia handed me a mug. 'I made you some tea. Let's have a look at your knee.'

I eased myself back into the beaten-up sofa, trying not to bend my leg too much. Ophelia knelt in front of me. I pointed.

'It's this one.'

Gently, she pushed my trouser leg up. I wished I wasn't so thin. Her gloved fingers pressed down.

'That hurts.'

'Sorry.' She pushed again. 'You were kicked by a horse. What do you expect?'

I gritted my teeth. 'Have you ever been kicked by a horse?'

She didn't look up. 'Lots of times. Trodden on, too. The trick is to let them know you're there – keep your hand on them and talk to them as you move around. Don't surprise them.'

'I figured that out.'

Her hand was warm on my knee. I felt better just for it being there, imagining the henna under the gloves working some kind of ancient healing spell.

'I don't think any real damage has been done. You'll have a whopper of a bruise though – it's coming up already.'

I peered down. The skin was bluish-purple. 'I've had more bruises in the last week than I've had in my entire life so far,' I complained.

Ophelia tugged my trouser leg back into place. 'Keep an eye on it. And ask Hodge if you can do something else today. You should rest it.'

'I can't tell him I got kicked by a horse.'

'Say you twisted your ankle on the cobbles.'

I pondered. It was a good idea. I waited for Ophelia to get up but she stayed where she was, crouched below me.

'Those pictures in my locker,' she said. 'You really drew those?'

My heart did a funny little trot. I'd forgotten all about the drawings I'd left for her. 'When did you find them?'

'This morning, just before I found you.' She went quiet, pulling a thread from the couch. I got the feeling she didn't want to look at me, like there was something she wasn't saying.

'Don't you like them?' I suddenly felt the ache in my knee more fiercely. Until that moment I hadn't known how much I wanted, *needed*, her to like them.

'I love them.' The thread came loose. I released the breath I'd been holding. 'They're her. They're just . . . *Pippi*. You got her exactly right. They're perfect.'

'I'm glad.' My voice emerged too croaky.

'And it's not just because they're good. When I found them this morning . . .' She stopped, shaking her head. 'I mean, they *are* good. Better than good.' She met my eyes finally. I was shocked to see they were glistening. 'But I love them because you did them for *me*.' She blinked quickly and stood up. 'Thank you.'

'You're welcome.'

She took our mugs to the sink. 'I seem to be thanking you a lot lately.'

'And threatening to beat the crap out of me.'

'Shut up.' She had her back to me but I could tell she was smiling. 'Anyway, I only threatened you once.'

'Once was enough.' I stood up, feeling bold. 'What are you doing for lunch?'

'Eating.'

'Ha ha. Where?'

'I don't know. The tea rooms. Or I might go to the orchard. Why? Do you want to join me?'

'I've been here since yesterday afternoon. I'm kind of sick of the place. I was thinking about maybe driving out somewhere, just to get away for an hour. Coming?'

She turned and looked at me for a long time before answering. 'I'll meet you here at one.'

It didn't happen like that.

I found Hodge shortly before nine-thirty, sniffing around the stables like a suspicious bloodhound. He took one look at me limping towards him and hurried over, his round face creasing with what I thought at first was concern.

'Elliott, what's wrong?'

Not concern, I realised. Irritation.

'My ankle. I must have jarred it last night, somehow.'

He tutted, then sighed. 'Well, it happens. When do you think you'll be well enough to return to work – after the weekend?'

'I wasn't asking to go home.' A note of annoyance had crept into my own voice. 'I just wondered if you could give me something else to do today.'

'Ah.' He looked sheepish. 'Yes, of course. We'll find you something – come with me.'

I hobbled after him, feeling bad for snapping. In his line of work, Hodge must be used to hearing excuses. Even so, I decided to hold my tongue about my thoughts on the paranormal events when he raised the subject.

'So, what about last night, eh?' He clapped and rubbed his hands together. 'I'll bet you can't wait until next week's walk!'

I avoided the question. 'I wonder if we'll get any more pretend psychics?'

He snorted. 'She was terrible, wasn't she? I don't know where these charlatans get off. Gives those of us with the genuine gift a bad name.'

We bumped into Ophelia, literally, passing through the stone archways near the museum entrance. She came hurtling past, bouncing off Hodge and brushing against my arm. Her hair was loose and damp, and a strand flicked under my nose and left a scent of oranges there.

'Sorry I'm late.'

'Hold on a minute,' Hodge commanded.

Ophelia stopped. 'What?'

'You weren't in your room when I called you for breakfast.'

She looked him straight in the eye. 'I woke up early, so I went for a walk.'

'Nowhere near the stables, I hope?'

'Of course not.' Her voice was emotionless. 'I'm banned, remember?'

'I remember. Just make sure you do.'

She rolled her eyes skyward then turned and went on her way. Hodge took me to an office adjacent to his own and pointed me to the desk.

'Not very exciting work, I'm afraid, but with my assistant on holiday this is all piling up. These invoices need filing.' He slapped a stash of papers in front of me. 'After that, this post needs opening, stamping and sorting into the relevant pigeonholes. If you get through the lot, then I'd be grateful if you could check the visitors' comments,' he nodded to a black leather book, 'for any obscenities that schoolchildren are so fond of leaving.' He tapped a bottle of correction fluid on the shelf. 'Just shout if you need anything.'

A dull hour was spent filing before I moved on to the post. Sounds of people going in and out of other offices nearby filtered through. I was glad of them. Being alone made it too easy to dwell on what had occurred in the night.

Had I been possessed? It seemed too strong a word. Everything I knew about possession, the majority of which came from bad movies, suggested that whatever force was occupying the body did so at the same time as the owner. Thinking about it that way actually changed the perspective, for if there were two forces in one body, then neither of them could completely possess it.

I hadn't even been *in* my body at all. I'd been a bystander with no control, until the thing, the ghost, had given my body back. Until then, the ghost had owned me completely. I sat back in the chair, staring at the wall. 'Possession' no longer seemed too strong a word. It was the *perfect* word.

I jumped forward at a bang from Hodge's office and groaned. I'd bashed my knee against the desk.

'Ophelia, for God's sake!' Hodge snapped. 'Must you charge in like that?'

I couldn't see her, but Ophelia's voice drifted through the door. 'It's Pippi,' she said, offering no apology. 'I'm worried about her.'

'Why?'

'She's not herself. I think there's something wrong.'

Hodge made an exasperated sound. 'How can you know what she's acting like when you're not even supposed to have been near her?'

'I can still *see* her,' Ophelia said defensively. 'She's restless and I saw her pawing at the ground. I need to spend a few minutes with her – it could be colic.'

'You really will say anything to get near that damn horse, won't you?'

'You think I'm lying? I'm not! Let me go to her.'

'Ophelia, I don't have time for this. Lydia's on stable duty today. Let her know – she can deal with it. Now get back to work.'

'I've told her already. She says she'll check on her after lunch, unless I can go first . . .'

'After lunch is fine.' Hodge's voice was curt.

'You don't understand. Lydia doesn't know them like I do. And the other day I saw her putting their feed out all in one go, rather than spacing it out in smaller, regular feeds like you're supposed to—'

'Oh, for heaven's sake, girl! Stop telling petty tales.'

'It's not petty.' She spoke through gritted teeth. 'That sort of change to a horse's diet can make it ill.'

There was a loud crack and Ophelia gasped. I guessed that Hodge had brought his fist down on his desk. Neither of them said another word. A moment later his door slammed. Ophelia had gone.

I listened for sounds of movement from Hodge's office. There were none but I could hear his breathing: short angry little bursts.

I lifted the next letter from the pile. It was a plain white envelope addressed to Hodge. In the almost-silence, the tear of the paper knife through the envelope was unbearably loud. I removed the contents and tossed the envelope aside. My other hand hovered above the sheet of paper, searching for a space to stamp with the date.

Without meaning to, my eyes rested on a sentence within the typed text:

I *will* expose you.

What was this? I glanced towards Hodge's office, my heart quickening. Unable to stop myself, I started to read.

Arthur,
Since you do not return my phone calls and emails, and have refused me entry to Past Lives, it seems a more old-fashioned approach is needed to get your attention.
 This is your last chance. Remember that I have nothing to lose but you have every-thing: your family, your job, your good name. One word from me and they will all be gone. If you value them then you know what to do.
 Under a false name I will book a place on the ghost walk on the evening of 5th June. You will allow me entry and will not make a fuss. Afterwards, you and I

shall have a long overdue chat about what
the future holds.

Do not ignore me this time, or I will
expose you.

S.D.

A heavy tread crossing the room next door had me stuffing the letter under the desk. Hodge peered around the door.

'Break time,' he said gruffly.

My hand shook underneath the table. I coughed to disguise any crackle of paper. I was afraid to hold it too tightly in case I creased it, and afraid that I wasn't holding it tightly enough. An image of it slipping from my fingers and floating to Hodge's feet wavered in my head.

'I think I'll stay here,' I said, forcing a smile. 'By the time I get over there it'll be time to come back again.'

'Fair enough. Can I bring you anything?'

I swallowed. 'Coffee would be good.'

I kept my hands where they were until I heard the click of his office door. Then I took the letter out and read it again. What could Hodge possibly be mixed up in? What could he have done that, if exposed, would ruin him?

The obvious answer was an affair. I put the piece of paper on the desk. Who'd be desperate enough to have an affair with Hodge? I knew it was a cruel thought even as it came into my head, but I couldn't see why anyone – apart from Una, who had been with him for years – would look at him in that way. He was ugly as a run-over toad and had a temper to match. His only real quality was his charisma when he was telling a story – when the attention was fully on him.

Whatever it was, it was none of my business, and my time at Past Lives was likely to end prematurely if Hodge had the slightest idea that I'd seen the letter. My only option was to make it seem as though I hadn't.

I grabbed the envelope it had arrived in and examined it. There was no repairing or disguising the slit in the top. I flipped it over. The name and address had been typed directly on to the envelope. There was no postmark. It had been delivered by hand.

I searched around the office, eventually finding a white envelope similar in size to the one I'd opened. So far so good. Now I had the problem of getting the address typed on to it. The computer on the desk was off. Hodge hadn't given me permission to use it but I could probably get away with saying I'd looked something up if he came back and caught me. I switched it on and waited for it to load.

I hadn't counted on being asked for a password. I swore and shut it down. Stupid Hodge and his stupid letter. I should just bin it. I probably would have, had I not spied a reel of labels on the shelf. Suddenly, I had one last idea. I grabbed the envelope, a pencil, a ruler, and a glue stick. I drew lightly around the name and address in a square, taking care to round off the corners. Then I cut out the square and stuck it on to the new envelope. It worked like a charm. To anyone else it would just look like a printed label.

I sealed the envelope and put it to the bottom of the pile. The rest of the old envelope I stuffed into my pocket. I breathed out slowly, finally relaxing. All I had to do now was remember to leave a couple more envelopes unopened to make it appear that I hadn't got through all the letters. The visitors' book would have to be left, too.

I glanced at it, remembering that Hodge had mentioned it on the ghost walk last night. Apparently, Sebastian's spirit had manifested a year ago and been seen by the entire group.

I picked it up and flicked back through the pages to last May. There were not many entries, but there, among the usual niceties and blanked-out swearwords, was a spate of dramatic comments all taking place on Wednesday, 17th:

Chilling. A night I'll never forget.

Should come with a health warning! NOT for the faint hearted.

Privileged to have witnessed this supernatural phenomena – but won't sleep for weeks!

Think I need counselling now.

On they went, and on. Most had left a name but others had included their town or city. Sandwiched between them on the same date, a short comment that could only be a single word had been blanked out. Strangely, in the space adjacent, a name and address was intact: *Lesley Travis, The Sanctuary, Weeping Cross.*

I wondered why someone would put their name to an offensive comment. Most of the concealed remarks were anonymous, apart from those names that were filthy and obviously invented. Perhaps Lesley Travis's thoughts had been censored because they were offensive in another way. Could she have dared to find fault?

I heard Hodge returning and closed the book as he came in with a steaming mug of coffee. After he'd gone, I drank it slowly and dawdled over the rest of the unopened post. At five to one I began transferring the ones I'd opened to the correct slots out in the hallway. I'd just taken out the last stash when the thin-faced girl I'd seen at the stables yesterday came hurrying up the hall and rapped on Hodge's door. He called her in, by which time I'd re-entered the adjacent office and taken my place at the desk again.

'Lydia,' he said, 'what can I do for you? And please don't tell me Ophelia's making a pest of herself again.'

I leaned forward to see through the gap in the door. Lydia had her back to me but I could see her hands. They fidgeted by her sides.

'I think Ophelia's right. I've just checked on Pippi and signs of colic are there. She's tossing her head back and curling her lip. Ophelia's walking her in the paddock—'

'She's *what*?'

'I told her to, Mr Hodge. The horse should be kept moving until the vet arrives, but because we delayed he's two hours away.'

Hodge's expression was thunderous. 'That horse is spoilt. Are you sure it isn't just playing up because it hasn't had Ophelia mollycoddling it for the past few days?'

Lydia shook her head. 'The horse is ill. I should have listened to Ophelia earlier, but after what you said, about being prepared for her to make excuses I . . . I just hope it's not too late.'

'Very well.' He stood up, scratching his head. 'Go and wait for the vet to arrive. I'll be along shortly.'

I heard her leave. Seconds later Hodge entered the office where I sat, gnawing his lower lip. 'Take your lunch now. I've got something that needs attending to. You'll be with Una this afternoon – she needs help with preparing some materials for her book-binding demonstration.'

I got up, pointing to a pile of three unopened envelopes, at the centre of which was Hodge's letter. 'I didn't manage to open them all . . .'

'It doesn't matter.' He was distracted, impatient. He followed me out and locked the door behind him, then rushed past me without another word. He was probably preparing himself to face Ophelia. I didn't envy him.

NINETEEN

Confessions

The bookbindery smelled of musty paper and leather. I sat at the workbench, stapling handout sheets while, opposite, Una unpicked the binding of a crumbling book. Her hands trembled, making her clumsy. I knew why: I couldn't keep Ophelia from my thoughts, either.

I'd known lunch was off the moment I'd seen her in the paddock, leading Pippi slowly up and down, her mouth murmuring words only she and the horse could hear. Every now and then, the animal forced her to halt by digging its hooves in and turning to bite at its flank. Every time, she coaxed it to move again.

I edged slowly alongside the paddock, eventually falling into step with her.

'I can't come for lunch,' she said, barely looking up.

'I know.' I was surprised she even remembered. 'Can I bring something to you here?'

'I'm not hungry.'

I limped along in silence. 'So . . . it's colic, right?' I said eventually. 'Is that treatable?'

'Depends. Colic's a symptom, not an illness. We won't know more until the vet arrives.' She glared into the distance. I looked ahead and saw Hodge and Lydia by the stables. 'They should've listened.'

'Is there anything I can do?'

She shook her head. 'I just need to keep her moving.'

'Oh.' Suddenly I wished I knew more about horses. 'Why?'

'At best, walking her could help get her digestive system going. If it's something small like trapped air, problem solved.' She paused. 'At worst, keeping her moving helps stop her from rolling. If she rolls her gut could twist and that can be fatal.'

'But she was fine this morning, wasn't she?' I asked, lowering my voice. 'I mean, she seemed a bit restless, but I thought it was just because I was in the stable with her.'

Ophelia shook her head. 'She wasn't right even then. I didn't notice straight away, not until I tried to saddle her. She was unco-operative, not herself. I left her in the stable and decided to keep my eye on her but she's got worse throughout the morning.'

I wracked my brains for something to say. The only thing I could think of was: 'Want me to keep you company?'

She gave a watery smile. 'A lot of good you'll be, Sir Hop-along.'

'I'm good at hopping.' I turned a grimace into a grin. My knee was really hurting now. 'A champion hopper, actually. I can keep up.'

'I'd only bite your head off every five minutes.'

'I wouldn't expect anything less.'

'Hey!' she reached over the fence to punch me lightly in the arm. Her smile faded. 'If you really want to help, draw me another picture.'

I forgot to walk for a second, then frantically hopped to catch up. 'What of?'

'Anything. Whatever you want.'

I swallowed. 'How about you? I could do your portrait.'

She shrugged. 'That could be interesting.' She looked at me again, trying to smile, but her forehead was creased at the same time. 'Now go on,' she said softly. 'Hop it.'

I hopped it.

For the next hour I sat in the Old Barn, picking at a sandwich and staring at a page in my sketchbook. It was still blank when I closed it. I was no good at drawing faces from memory; to get a true likeness of Ophelia then I'd have to draw her from life. My face tingled at the thought of looking at her for any length of time.

A muffled ringing brought me back to the present. Una shot up from the bench and grabbed the phone. 'Yes?' Her voice was high. 'Another twenty minutes? Where's Ophelia?' Her eyes were fixed on the door. 'I'm coming now.' She slammed down the receiver and left.

Above the door a clock ticked towards half past three. Outside, a group of visitors peered in but didn't enter. Alone with only my thoughts, I was in bad company. Even being around Una with the knowledge of Hodge's secret was better than being by myself. Alone, it was too easy to remember watching the thing that hadn't been me wandering barefoot in the rain and uttering that first, terrifying word: *alive*.

After ten minutes I couldn't stand it. I left the bookbindery, closing the door behind me. I already knew where I was headed, but when I got there I wished I'd stayed where I was.

Lydia and Hodge were either side of Pippi, leading her around the paddock. Hodge was in his own clothes instead of costume, but he wasn't dressed for it. Mud caked his shoes and the bottoms of his corduroy trousers. At the side of the paddock near the stables, Una stood with her arm around Ophelia.

I'd never seen her looking so pasty. Her normally tanned skin was grey. As I got closer I saw her teeth were chattering. Neither of us said anything as I arrived at her side. Her hands were locked around her horse mug. Every now and then Una tried to encourage her to drink from it but she wouldn't. I doubted she even knew it was there.

'Where is he?' she kept asking, looking towards the entrance. 'He should be here by now!'

'He's on his way.' Una rubbed her arm helplessly. 'It'll be any minute.'

Even I could see that Pippi was in a bad way now. It was taking everything to keep her moving. She dipped, going to the ground. Somehow Hodge and Lydia managed to get her up. Her coat gleamed with sweat and her eyes rolled as she blundered clumsily toward the fence.

'She's getting tired.' Ophelia's own eyes were wide. 'They should rest her again. Tell them to rest her!'

Una glanced at me, then hurried around the side of the paddock. As she reached them the horse's legs buckled and she sank to the mud. This time, Hodge and Lydia's efforts to raise her were in vain. Bellowing, she rolled on to her side, kicking at her gut.

'No!' Ophelia dropped her mug and ran. It landed at my feet in two pieces, dark liquid trickling away. All I could do was watch as Pippi rolled herself from side to side, legs kicking the air. Beside me I noticed a tour group had lagged behind to watch. The guide herded them away. In the paddock, Pippi stopped rolling and lay on her side.

Her legs and head twitched, convulsing. Foam frothed at her mouth. I forced my eyes away, unable to watch, and instead found my focus on Ophelia. Hodge held her back, struggling against her flailing arms.

I turned to a shout behind me. A bearded man with a black case ran towards the paddock. One look at his face made me back away. I couldn't watch any more of the horse's suffering or Ophelia's grief. I took myself back to the bookbindery and sat there, alone. Hoping for a miracle.

An hour later Una returned, her face blotchy. I knew what she was about to say before she even opened her mouth. Her voice was quiet, fighting for control and losing.

'She didn't make it.'

I nodded mutely, concentrating too hard on the bench and following the wood grain with my fingers.

The paddock was still and quiet on my way back to the Old Barn. At the far side a large canvas sheet covered a motionless shape.

Ophelia was nowhere to be seen.

She didn't show up for work the next day. I toured Goose Walk as usual, tolerating my bruised knee to look out for her. Pippi's body remained in the paddock, hidden beneath the canvas. At lunchtime I went to Hodge's office to ask after Ophelia. He was more dishevelled than usual and a stale odour lingered about him. Paperwork spread across his desk like a layer of fallen dominoes.

'She's been in her room all night. Won't see me, talk to me. Nothing less than I deserve, I suppose. Maybe if I'd just *listened*...' He wiped his hand across his face. 'Una's with her, trying to get her to eat something.'

I felt a stab of pity for him but it was overridden by annoyance. I'd known him little more than a week yet already I disliked the way he acted first, thought later.

He sniffed and rubbed his nose. 'Una says she won't let go of those drawings you did.'

My body tensed. 'She won't?'

'She's just lying on her bed, holding them.' He looked up at me, his eyes pleading. 'Would you . . . would you look in on her later? I don't want to impose on your time – leave as early as you like – but . . . but perhaps you could, on your way home?'

'If you think it'll help. I don't know if she'll speak to me, though.'

'But you'll try? She might open up to you. She's . . . I don't know. You've obviously connected with her through your drawings, somehow.'

'I'll go.' The words stuck in my throat. Being civil was like choking on them.

'You will?' He seized his wallet, fumbling through it. 'Here. If you could get her out of the house into the fresh air . . .' He pushed a twenty-pound note at me. 'Maybe take her somewhere, just for a little while. I'd consider it a favour.'

'I don't want money.' I put the note on the desk. As I did, my fingers accidentally brushed against a familiar white envelope. I snatched my hand back. 'I asked how she was because I care, not as a favour.'

'Oh.' His face fell. He stuffed the money back. 'I see. I'm just not used to . . . that is, Ophelia doesn't have many friends.'

No, I thought grimly. *They'd have to get past you.* Aloud I said, 'So I can take her out somewhere, if she'll come?'

He jerked his head up and down. 'Yes.'

I stole a second glance at the envelope between us. It hadn't been opened.

'I'll leave at four-thirty.'

I opened my locker to a text from Adam.

BAND NIGHT! 7.30. DON'T BE LATE.

I stuck the phone into my pocket without replying, mildly irritated. Every message from Adam was like a foghorn. He always used capitals and refused to get into text speak on account that it was 'lazy'. What annoyed me more was that he just assumed I'd be there, like I had nothing better to do. Usually, he was right.

I got my wallet, keys and sketchbook and closed my locker.

In the car I rode with the windows down and the radio up, wholly glad the weekend had arrived. It had been a weird, horrible few days and I couldn't wait to forget them.

By the time I'd pulled up outside the Hodges' I'd started to have doubts. I cut the engine but stayed where I was. Ophelia was unlikely to thank me for showing up if she wanted to be alone. She'd probably slam the door in my face. Worse, if I *did* manage to speak to her I could imagine Hodge grilling me on Monday for a detailed 'he said, she said' account.

I got out of the car before I could change my mind. I wasn't here for Hodge, and I hadn't promised him anything. I was here for Ophelia. And if slamming the door in my face made her feel better, then at least that was something.

The door opened before I was even on the path and a floury-aproned Una beckoned me in. The cottage was warm with the scent of baking.

'Oh, Elliott,' she said, guiding me into the living room. 'Thanks for coming. Arthur said you'd agreed to visit.' Her voice was almost a whisper. I felt like I'd walked in on a wake. I supposed it kind of was, in a way. 'Help yourself to anything.' She gestured to the table. It was laid with dozens of jam tarts, scones and things I'd only seen on cookery programmes but didn't know the name of. I took a warm scone and bit into it. 'I thought I might get her to come down and help with all this,' Una explained, tucking a wisp of poker-straight hair behind her ear. 'She used to love baking with me.' She shook her head. 'At the very least I thought she might eat something, but the last thing I took up ended up on the wall.'

The scone stuck in my cheeks like sawdust. 'Really?'

'You try, love.' She took my arm and led me to the stairs. 'Straight up and second on the right.'

I coughed, managing not to swallow as I climbed the stairs. I went right and stopped outside the second door, listening. There was nothing. No angry music, no sounds of crying or things smashing. Only silence. I lifted my hand and knocked. The snarl came instantly.

'I don't *want* a bloody jam tart, Una! I am not *bloody six*!'

'Ophelia?' Was that squeak really my voice? 'It's me, Elliott.'

There was a creak. Silence. Another creak, then footsteps and a scuffle at the base of the door. It opened a crack. Swollen red eyes glared through a tangle of hair.

'What do you want?'

'To see you.' I chanced a smile. 'I haven't brought any jam tarts. Promise.'

She moved back, holding the door open. I stepped into the room. 'Are you sure it's safe for me to come in? You haven't got any Freddy Krueger-style gloves in your collection, have you?'

'I wish.' She closed the door behind me and, with her toe, nudged a wooden wedge between the bottom of it and the carpet.

'Inventive. Doesn't it lock?'

She walked past me, flopping on to the bed in the corner. 'It did, until the key went missing. I know Hodge hid it, even though he swears he didn't.'

'That's pretty extreme. Why'd he do that?'

'I can't remember,' she said tiredly. 'I'm sure you can tell by now that it doesn't take much to upset him.'

'No.' I gave up waiting for her to offer me a seat and glanced towards a chair piled with clothes under the window. A white bra draped over the back of it made me reconsider. I sank down on the end of the bed instead, trying not to look at the chair. Ophelia sat hunched with her back to the headboard, knees drawn up in front of her. She wore jodhpurs and a baggy T-shirt with a hole in the neckline. Her hair was lank and loose.

My sketches were on a table with a lamp at the side of the bed. Next to them was a framed picture of Ophelia on Pippi, but it was the drawings Ophelia hadn't stopped staring at since sitting down. I leaned forward and held out my hand. 'Can I see them again?'

She blinked then lifted my pictures from the table like they were fragile as a baby bird. I took them from her. It was hard to believe that they'd been done only two days ago. Pippi had been so calm then, so full of life. Now she was cold in a field, shrouded in canvas. One of the corners of the vignettes was buckled. I ran my thumb over it.

'I cried on it a bit,' she said. Her voice was flat, empty. 'Sorry.'

'It's all right.' I handed them back to her, looking around the room in the silence that followed. It wasn't especially like any of the girls' bedrooms I'd seen before. There were no heartthrob posters, no scattered jewellery and make-up, or photographs of girls' nights out. A framed print was the only thing on the walls.

211

It hung above a large CD collection and an even larger bookshelf. Under the dressing table a pair of muddy Wellington boots were askew where they'd been kicked off. On top of it a strand of blonde hair caught in a hairbrush gleamed in the sunlight.

'I thought you'd be sitting in the dark with the curtains closed,' I admitted.

'Maybe if I wanted to depress myself even more I would be,' she remarked. 'But the outside is about the only thing that keeps me sane. I'd suffocate without it.'

A breeze flew in through the window. It lifted her limp hair and stirred up a horse-like smell that I guessed was coming off Ophelia herself. She looked wild, like some kind of fey woodland creature.

I shifted on the bed. 'How did she die?'

'Twisted gut.' She stared at the drawings. 'Well – the shock from the twisted gut is what actually killed her. The vet sedated her and tried to operate but it was too late. He says her intestine was already distended through trapped air.' She looked at me suddenly. 'You're not afraid to talk about it, are you?'

'Afraid to talk about what?'

'Death. Why is that?'

I met her gaze, concerned that I'd upset her with my directness. But there was no anger or hurt in her eyes, only curiosity. Why wasn't I afraid to talk about death? It was a good question. *Because it's inevitable,* I thought. *Because I've experienced it. Because it's all around me wherever I go and I don't know how to stop it.*

'Because my mum died three years ago,' I blurted out. 'And there's nothing more lonely. People – friends, relatives – avoiding you. Not because they don't care but because they don't know what to say. And when they do talk about it they use words like "sleeping" or "passed over" or "in heaven". It never made things easier. It was like pretending it wasn't real, that she wasn't gone. That she would wake up. Or that heaven was just a place she'd nipped into for a chat, like a neighbour's house, but she'd be back soon.'

The words rushed out of me in a torrent, like a carefully constructed dam had been broken. I hadn't even known they were coming. And now they were out I couldn't seem to stop talking. 'Adam – that's my brother – he still goes to visit her grave. On her birthday and on the anniversary of the day she died. Every time I tell myself I'm not going to go, but somehow he always talks me into it. And I hate it. I come back feeling worse because I sit there listening to him talking to the ground and I know it's not really her under there. It's not her or who she was.'

'How . . . what happened to her?'

'Cancer. She'd already beaten it once, but then it came back and she just couldn't . . .'

I stopped. Ophelia had leaned closer. Her gloved hand rested on top of mine. My hand burned under her touch. I realised I wanted to lace my fingers with hers. The only thing stopping me was the thought that she might pull away. 'Sorry,' I whispered. 'I didn't come over to go on about my dead mother.'

'Don't say sorry. I'm grateful.'

'Grateful that I've depressed you even more?'

Her hand hadn't moved. 'Grateful that you use real words like "died". That you asked about Pippi but didn't ask me if I was okay – I'm *not* okay. But you knew that. And I'm grateful that you offered to keep me company yesterday, even though you could barely walk.'

'I would have.' I slowly spread my fingers, allowing Ophelia's to drop into the spaces between. Our fingers intertwined. I closed my hand around hers, drawing her fingertips into my palm. My breathing quickened. 'If you'd wanted me to, I would have.'

'I know.' She was so close I could see the faint tear tracks on her cheeks. In places, tiny fibres from the tissues she'd used to wipe them clung to her like frost. I lifted my other hand and ran my thumb over her skin. It was soft and damp. Pulse racing, I tilted her chin. We looked at each other for a long moment. I brushed my lips against her cheeks, tasting the saltiness there. She trembled as my mouth met hers, closing her eyes just before I did.

We broke apart at the sound of a light creak outside the door. I kissed the finger she pressed to my lips. Her pupils were wide, dilated. '*Una,*' she mouthed.

I slid off the bed, still holding her hand.

'Want to go somewhere?'

'Depends,' she whispered, staring at the door.

'On?'

'On whether I'll be able to kiss you some more. Or otherwise swear and scream about how unfair life is.'

I nodded. 'I know somewhere you can do both.'

PART TWO

I grant I never saw a goddess go;
My mistress, when she walks, treads on the ground
— William Shakespeare

Sleep — those little slices of death, how I loathe them.
— Edgar Allan Poe

TWENTY

The Empress

Ophelia slept most of the way. I had the radio on low, stealing glances at her as I drove. She'd kept her hair loose. The ends of it still dripped from the shower she'd taken before we left. Her lips were parted slightly, like she was waiting for me to kiss her again. I still couldn't believe I had, or that I'd fought it for so long. It felt *right*. More than right. It was like waking up and seeing her properly . . . or seeing her for the first time.

She stirred as I pulled on to the green, but didn't wake. I stopped the car and touched her shoulder.

'Hmm?' She burrowed her face into my hand. Her eyes opened, bleary but less red and swollen than they had been earlier. For a moment she looked peaceful. Then sadness flooded her eyes. She'd remembered. 'Sorry.' She stifled a yawn. 'I didn't mean to fall asleep. Guess I was exhausted.'

'I know the feeling.'

She turned her head to look through the window. 'Are we here?'

'Not yet. Thought I'd stop off for a change of clothes. We've got plenty of time until the first band starts.'

Our footsteps echoed through the block. The cat yowled a greeting when I put my key in the door and wove around our legs.

Ophelia knelt and made a fuss of her. I dumped my keys and wallet in the kitchen.

'So you live here with your dad and your brother?' she asked.

'Just my dad. Adam moved out last year. He lives with his girl-friend in a house-share.'

'Where's your dad now?'

'If he's not here he's at work.' I opened the fridge and took out a carton of apple juice, pouring two glasses. I downed mine in one then leaned against the counter, watching as she drank hers more slowly. 'Do I ever get to see what's under there?' I asked.

She spluttered into her glass. 'Pardon?'

'Your gloves.' I took her hand, pulling her closer. 'You're still wearing them.'

'Oh.' She put her glass down. 'It's just . . . habit. Hodge was furious when I had the henna done. He said it made me look like a cheap tart, and he didn't have tarts under his roof. So this is the compromise.' She looked up at me, defiant. 'Until I'm eighteen. I'll be gone from there before my birthday candles are even lit. And in a way the gloves are kind of helpful – they keep me hidden when the henna's fading and I can get it re-done without him knowing.'

'How often do you have it re-done?'

'Every three weeks.' She laughed. 'I told him it lasted six months – he's got no idea I've had it re-done four times already. And by the time he thinks it'll fade I'll be gone.'

I took her other hand. 'He's kind of overprotective, isn't he?'

She nodded. 'He always has been, ever since I was little. Back then, it suited me, I suppose. They spoiled me because they had no children of their own and, with a mother like mine, I was happy to let them.'

'Where is she?' I asked. 'Your mother?'

'Some kind of writers' retreat in Paris, last I heard. That was four months ago. I haven't heard from her since. Before that, it was Vienna, and before that, Berlin, I think.'

I gave a low whistle. 'She gets around.'

'In more ways than one. With whatever waif or stray she's picked up along the way. A novelist this time.' She snorted. 'She thinks she's some kind of muse again.'

'Again?'

'How do you think I ended up with the name Ophelia?'

'Let me guess . . . she hooked up with another writer, or – an artist?'

'A painter in Florence, eighteen years ago. He was part of some group – there were three of them, apparently. They thought they were going to be the next Pre-Raphaelite movement or something. She spent the summer modelling for them, prancing around half naked and telling anyone who'd listen that she was going to be the next Lizzie Siddall.'

'The artists' model?'

'Right. And she messed that up like she does everything else. Arrived on Una's doorstep five months pregnant with nowhere else to go.' She gave a tight little smile. 'The group fell apart after they found out she was sleeping with all three of them. I don't think even she knew which one of them was my father.' Her hands tightened on mine. 'She stuck around until I was nine, on and off. She still had her fads. Sometimes she'd take me halfway across the country, or even to Europe, on whatever mad scheme she'd dreamed up. Other times, she dumped me on Una and Arthur if she was in one of her depressions. I was in and out of schools, homeschooled, not schooled. That's why my handwriting's a mess.

Why at school, everyone thought I was slow and stupid. Always the outsider and never around long enough to make friends.

'Then she had one of her depressions that seemed to go on and on. One day I was with Una. We went to visit her. When we let ourselves in, she'd locked herself in the bathroom. Una told me to wait in the kitchen, but I could hear Mum crying and moaning about how trapped she felt. How she wasn't meant to be a mother. When Una finally got her to open the door she screamed, so of course I came running. Una tried to hide her from me, but not before I saw the spots of blood on her . . . and the kitchen knife.'

'Shit. She tried to kill herself?' I shivered involuntarily. At that exact moment the kitchen tap whooshed on. Freezing water bounced off a stack of dishes in the sink, spraying us both.

'Jesus!' Ophelia jumped back, releasing my hands.

No. Tess, actually.

I grappled to turn the tap off. With my back to the counter I'd caught the worst of it and now water dripped down my neck and trickled along my spine like an icy finger.

Ophelia laughed. At least that was something. I felt about as far from laughing as I could get.

'Does that happen often?' she asked, shaking water off her arm.

'It's starting to,' I said under my breath.

'What?'

'Plumbing problems,' I said more clearly. 'These flats are old.' I handed her a tea-towel, then peeled off my drenched T-shirt and threw it in the washing machine. I knew Ophelia's eyes were on my bare chest. Somehow it didn't matter. I wasn't self-conscious or uncomfortable with her any more. She'd seen me half naked, in just a horse coat, only yesterday. And she'd still wanted to kiss me. That thought chased the shivers away.

220

'So anyway,' she said, blotting herself, 'it looked worse than it was. Just surface cuts, really. She hadn't pressed hard enough. With the knife, I mean. After that, they all decided – Una, Hodge and Mum – that it would be better for everyone if I stayed with Una and Hodge permanently.' She folded the tea-towel and put it aside. 'She comes back sometimes. When she's feeling guilty. Or when she's out of money.'

'She sounds like a wild child.'

'I used to think that. That she's a wild child, a dreamer. She was always so bohemian, doing what she wanted whenever she wanted. I still try to think of her that way but it gets harder. Mostly I just think she's a selfish bitch.' She moved close again. 'Sometimes I'm scared I'll end up like her.'

'What do you mean?'

She stared at her gloved hands, before looking up at me. 'The henna. It's typical of the sort of thing she'd do. Maybe that's the real reason Hodge hates seeing it – it probably reminds him of her.'

Her eyes were so grey, like a storm cloud. I pulled her to me, tucking her head under my chin. Her arms folded around me. I could smell her hair, the fresh scent of oranges lingering on it. It wasn't shiny but it was soft. Touchable. I ran my fingers down the length it, following the curve of her back. Halfway down, my hand froze.

Wet footprints glimmered on the tiles. Just two at first, over by the sink. I watched in horror as more appeared, each one faster than the last, in a watery trail that rushed past us and out into the hall. I realised I was gripping Ophelia too tightly and forced myself to release her.

'Come on,' I whispered, trying to stop my teeth from chattering together. I led her out of the kitchen, blurring the wet marks into unrecognisable shapes with my own feet and praying Ophelia didn't notice. In the living room I flicked the TV on. 'I'm going to get a quick shower and then we'll get out of here.'

Before she had even sat down I was in the bathroom, closing the door with my back to it. The air in there was freezing, forcing goosepimples to rear up on my skin. My breath froze in white clouds in front of my face. The bathtub was filled again, right up to the overflow.

'Tess,' I whispered, 'I know you're here.'

A draught wound around me.

'I'm begging you. Please, don't do this now.'

The coldness intensified as a word came into my head, unbidden. Not spoken or heard, just there.

When.

I wrapped my arms around myself. 'Later . . . tonight. When I'm asleep. Whatever it is you need to tell me, tell me then. Just *please* . . . not now.'

Frost particles formed on the mirror above the basin, spreading like hairline cracks over the glass. I shuddered then lunged at the bath, pulling the plug. It was like breaking a curse. Instantly the air warmed and the frost on the mirror began to thaw. I still couldn't stop shivering even though I knew Tess was gone. In my head I could see the footprints trailing through the flat, leading to her watery grave.

I couldn't decide what bothered me more: the things she was doing, or the fact that she was no longer confined to haunting me when I slept. She'd managed to break through into my waking life, and it seemed the more I feared and believed in her, the stronger she got. Or perhaps, I wondered, some barrier had been breached when the dead thing at Past Lives had entered my body.

222

If that barrier was broken, how could I repair it, if it even *could* be repaired?

A knock on the door had me sucking in a sharp breath.

'Elliott? Can I put some music on instead?'

I released the breath in a hiss. 'Sure.' I opened the door, too fast. Ophelia looked at me strangely.

'Are you okay? You seem pale.'

'I'm fine. Probably just reacting to the city fumes again after getting used to Calthorpe.' I managed a smile. 'All that fresh air.'

She pursed her lips, following me down the hall. 'I'd trade the fresh air to live somewhere you can walk down the street without everyone knowing your name.'

I went ahead of her into the bedroom, hastily shaking the bedcovers into place where I'd left without making it in the morning. I pointed to a rack of CDs next to the chest of drawers. 'Help yourself. I'll be back in a minute.'

'The moment of truth.' Ophelia brushed past me and kneeled down.

'Huh?'

She grinned. 'Where I get to dissect your taste in music.'

'Now I'm nervous.'

'You should be,' she teased. 'I might not be here when you get back.'

'I'd better kiss you goodbye just in case, then.' I leaned down, closing my mouth over hers before she pushed me away, laughing.

Grabbing some clean clothes, I went back into the bathroom. Miraculously I managed a decent shower, with the water staying hot the whole time. Tess was obviously saving her talents for later. I pushed her out of my head and vigorously soaped myself,

223

rubbing colour and warmth back into my skin. My teeth clenched when I touched my bruised knee, but it was slightly better. I twisted the water off, humming over the silence as I dried and dressed. I frowned and stopped mid-hum. Why was there silence?

'Ophelia?' I called, stepping into the hall.

'In here.' Her voice was quiet.

I went into the bedroom, still towelling my hair. 'It's so quiet I thought you were serious about leaving . . .' I trailed off. She was sitting on the bed, away from the CDs. In her hands she held a large, thick sheet of paper.

Oh, no . . .

'I . . . I don't understand.' She sounded small, lost. 'These . . . these are *my* hands. But I've never taken my gloves off in front of you. I *know* I haven't.'

I stared at the drawing. I'd been so caught up with Ophelia herself that I'd forgotten all about the sketch of her hands, propped up on the top of the chest. The patterns on them swirled and looped, like a fingerprint convicting me of stealing something I shouldn't have seen.

'No,' I said hoarsely.

'Then . . . how?' The paper shook, betraying her. 'How is this possible?'

I sat next to her before my knees buckled. 'Please don't freak out.'

'I'm *already* freaking out.'

Slowly, I reached over and took the drawing from her, resting it on the floor. I took her hands, swallowing as I slid off first one glove, then the other. She said nothing but I could feel her shaking. 'That night in the prison cells,' I began, 'I had one of my . . . When I went to sleep, I came out of my body. I saw myself on the

224

bed. For the first time I faced my fear. I stopped myself getting straight back into my body. I came out of my cell and—'

'Into mine,' she whispered, looking down at her hands. My fingertips traced the woman's hair, the sycamore seeds and fallen leaves.

'You had your back to the wall. It was late – everyone else was asleep. You just stared straight ahead. I saw your hands in your lap and I couldn't stop looking at them.'

Her eyes went to the drawing. 'You must have looked for a long time.'

'I did.' I met her eyes with difficulty, afraid of how she would react to learning she hadn't been alone in what she'd thought was a private moment.

'Why?' was all she asked.

My heart crashed against my ribs like it was trying to escape. 'Because I'd never seen anything like them before. And because in that moment you stopped being a blank canvas and became something else. Mysterious. Beautiful.'

'So . . . it's real?' Her hands gripped mine harder. 'When you come out of your body . . . it's not just a dream. What you see is real?'

I swallowed. 'Yes.' The urge to tell her *everything*, to unburden myself of the full horror of it goaded me. I searched for the words, wondering how much more she could take and still be here. She hadn't left yet. And then . . .

'No one's ever looked at me for that long before.'

Her voice was only a whisper but it may as well have been a gale, sweeping away any notions I had of speaking out and risking losing her. Instead I lifted the hand with the image of the woman to my face and held it there, against my cheek.

In unison we leaned back, sinking into the rumpled sheets face to face.

225

'Who is she?' I murmured. 'The woman on your hand?'

Ophelia looked up at me through her lashes. They were so fair they were almost translucent. 'Do you know anything about the tarot?' she asked softly.

'Only that there's a death card.'

'It doesn't mean death, not literally. It's more about one door closing and another one opening. New beginnings.'

'I didn't think you'd be into the tarot.'

'I'm not. It was one of my mum's "things" for a while. I only know what I remember from her readings. She was so secretive about the cards to begin with. Hiding them away in a wooden box. She wouldn't let anyone touch them but herself and whoever she was reading for. The energies would be tainted, she said. But as usual she grew bored with them and moved on to the next thing.' She gave a wry smile. 'Eventually she gave them to me to play with. I was so careful with them – I thought they were magic. But it was the pictures I loved. There was this one card . . . the Empress. A woman wearing a crown of stars. She told me it was a powerful symbol of motherhood. I slept with it under my pillow sometimes when she'd gone away. Wishing on it for her to come back.'

I lifted her other hand. 'And these pictures? What are the falling leaves for?'

'Loss and time passing. Reminding me that I have to let go.' She lowered her eyes. 'Sounds so gloomy, doesn't it? I bet you wish you hadn't asked.'

'No.' I kissed one hand, then the other. 'I wish I'd asked sooner.'

'You're late,' Adam said over his shoulder, weaving through the crowded hall at the back of The Acorn.

'Not by much.' Clutching Ophelia's hand I followed him, doing my best to avoid elbows and drinks.

'You haven't missed anything, anyway. One of the bands was stuck in traffic but they're going on last now. It'll be starting any minute. We're on second.'

He stopped at a table next to the stage, slopping beer as he put down the three pints he'd been carrying. I'd managed to spot him at the bar from the door. It was never that hard to find Adam, even in a busy place. You only had to look where most of the girls in the room were facing.

'So, the famous Ophelia.' He gave a curious smile, his eyes lingering on her hands. She'd left her gloves in my car. 'We meet at last. I'm Adam.'

I cringed, hoping he wouldn't mention the gun incident. Thankfully he didn't.

'We saved you seats – over there, next to Amy. What do you want to drink?'

I left Ophelia with Amy and went with Adam to the bar.

'Not bad for a country bumpkin,' he said, once we were out of earshot. 'Not your usual type, though.'

'Maybe that's why I like her.'

'You've finally admitted it, then. Her hands are cool.' He waved a note over the counter. 'Come on, Pete! It's my night off, don't keep me waiting – staff perks and all that!' He turned to me. 'Sure you only want a Coke?'

'I'm driving.'

He handed me a bottle of cider for Ophelia. 'Well, don't get her pissed. If she throws up it's my neck on the block. And I'll probably get stuck with clearing it up.'

The first band started as we took our seats. The music crashed around the room, swelling inside it. All around us people were drinking, dancing, talking. The singer yelled into the microphone, the words unintelligible.

I leaned over to Ophelia. 'See? You can shout and scream all you like here – no one will hear!'

'What?' she shouted back, laughing. It took three attempts before she heard me.

We finished our drinks as the band stopped playing. Adam bought us more. On the way back from the bar he jerked his head towards the dance floor.

'Over there – isn't that the girl you were seeing a while back?'

I glanced to the left. 'Juliet,' I muttered. She stood with two of her friends, giving me what could only be described as the stink eye.

Adam sniggered. 'She's stopped feeling sorry for you, then.'

'And gone back to being pissed off.'

'You're here with another girl. What do you expect?' He swigged his beer with a slow smile. 'Was she always this tasty, or just when she's mad?'

I elbowed him to keep going. 'Shut up. And concentrate on Amy. I haven't seen you speak to her all night.'

He rolled his eyes. 'I see her every day.'

I took my seat as Adam and the rest of the band got up to change over. Apart from the drummer, Chris, I only knew the others from sight. Within minutes they were ready. Adam took his place at the mike and they kicked off with a Kings of Leon cover. The mood in the place was electric. On stage, Adam was practically a god. I knew the routine: his eyes swept the dance floor, singling out pretty girls to sing well-chosen lines to. By the third song, something twisted in my gut. He hadn't looked Amy's way once.

Halfway through their set I leaned over to Ophelia.

'Want to dance to the next one?' I asked her.

'You want to empty the building?'

I laughed. 'Why not? It's way too crowded in here.'

'I'll make a deal with you. If I like the song, I'll dance.'

'Deal.' I got up.

'Wait – where are you going?'

'Putting in a request with Adam.' I grinned slyly. 'I seem to remember a lot of Kate Bush in your CD collection.'

Her mouth dropped open. 'What? When did you—?'

'When you were in the shower. You weren't the only one dissecting musical tastes today.'

'Cheat. Anyway, I never got to see yours. The drawing distracted me.'

'Too bad.' I slid away from her. 'Looks like I've got you for a bit longer, then.'

Even through the swarm of people, Juliet's eyes burned into me as I crossed the dance floor. I made it halfway without looking at her, but every step further away felt like my feet were stuck in tar. I halted, then took a breath and turned around, approaching her. Her eyes widened.

'Hello, Juliet.'

'What do you want?'

Not the friendliest of greetings, but at least she hadn't told me to get lost. Yet.

'Can I speak to you alone?'

She glanced at her friends. 'Could you get some more drinks? I'll meet you by the bar.'

Her friends glared at me then sidled off, whispering.

'So what's up?' Her voice was pointed. I'd forgotten how pretty she was.

'Look, this is awkward . . .'

'You made it awkward.'

'I know. And I know how I treated you.' I wished I hadn't left my drink at the table. My mouth was dry. 'You didn't deserve it.'

'So why, then?'

I forced myself to meet her eyes. 'Because that's who I was and what I did. I wanted fun, no strings.'

'But you're not like that now. Is that what you're saying?'

'Yes. I don't want to be that person any more.'

'Is this the part where you try to get back with me?'

'No,' I said, gently as I could. 'It's the part where I tell you I'm sorry.'

She nodded, lowering her eyes. 'Accepted.' When she looked up again she was trying to smile. 'So . . . that girl you're here with. Are you two together?'

I glanced back at Ophelia but someone blocked my view.

'I'm not sure. I think so. I hope so.'

'Then be nice to her, Elliott,' she said, glancing at the bar. 'Listen, I'd better go. But . . . thanks. For coming over. I appreciate it.'

'No problem.'

She smiled, a proper smile this time. 'I'll see you.'

'Yeah. Take care of yourself, Juliet.'

And just like that, the tar under my shoes disappeared. I strode to the stage feeling lighter. Better. Adam was mopping his face with a towel when I got there.

'Hey.' He bent down at the edge of the platform. 'What did you say to her?'

I stuck my hands in my pockets. 'That I'm sorry.'

Adam's top lip curled. '*What?* Have I taught you nothing? Don't ever apologise! Now she'll stop thinking it was her fault and tell everyone it was yours.'

'It was.'

He flicked the towel at me. 'You're not supposed to admit it.'

'So? I acted like a dick and she didn't deserve it. I apologised and now I feel better and so does she. The end.'

He made a disgusted sound and grabbed a bottle of water next to him.

'Speaking of acting like a dick, how much more of your flirting do you think Amy's going to stand?'

'Bloody hell, Elliott! Shut up, will you?' He took a belligerent swig. 'It helps with votes. Amy knows the score – look but don't touch.'

'Well, just make sure *you* do. Amy's not the one giving half the room the come on.'

'Since when do *you* lecture *me*?'

'It's not a lecture, just an observation.'

'Look, just because you've pulled Ophelia doesn't make you bloody Romeo.'

'That would be Hamlet. Romeo was with Juliet.'

'Whatever. I can't keep up with all these Shakespearean girls of yours.' He raised an eyebrow. 'Was that it?'

'No. I need a favour.'

'So you lecture me and now you've got the cheek to ask for favours?'

'I'm your brother, I'm allowed to be cheeky.' I grinned. 'Plus I nearly died so that means you can't say no to me. Ever.'

'Glad to see you're not above emotional blackmail. I was starting to worry that you'd had a complete personality transplant. What do you want?'

'Know any Kate Bush songs?'

'Yeah, unfortunately. Why?'

'Can you play one next?'

'What – *now*? Here?'

I enjoyed the way his voice rose. It was distinctly un-Adam. 'Yeah.'

'Are you winding me up? We're trying to win this thing, or had you missed that?'

'So do something unexpected. Stand out.'

'We've got a set, you know. I can't just change it.'

'You can do whatever you want. The band listens to you. Come on – please?'

Adam shook his head disbelievingly. 'Kate Bush?'

'You can pull it off. Or are you scared of a challenge?'

His eyes narrowed to pinpoints. 'Is this for Ophelia? Because that really would be tragic.'

I winked. 'I owe you one.' I legged it back to the table before he could protest.

When I glanced back Adam had taken the mike. He eyed me, shaking his head again but he was smiling.

'So this next one,' he drawled, 'is for Ophelia.'

I bowed and offered her my hand as the band launched into *Running Up That Hill.* 'I'd like to request this dance with the Lady Ophelia,' I said, struggling to keep my face straight.

She stood up, cheeks flushed. 'The lady accepts.'

We squeezed our way on to the dance floor. Contrary to Adam's fears, the song was going down well. Everyone seemed to be crowding into the small area, pushing us closer together.

'I haven't got a clue how to dance to Kate Bush,' I confessed. Ophelia's thighs pressed against mine, making my skin tingle. It did nothing for my coordination.

Her hair tickled my ear. 'Just dance how she dances. Like whatever you feel, whatever the music's telling you. Like it's the last dance you'll ever have and you don't give a toss what anyone else thinks.'

And so I did. We moved together, laughing, spinning, and in my case limping and stumbling a few times. But it didn't matter. The song blurred into the next and we blurred with it; lost in the night, lost in the moment. Too soon it was over to a thudding applause. I looked up at Adam. His chest heaved and he pulled an arm across his forehead. 'We're going to slow it down now,' he said breathlessly. 'And this last one's for my girl.' He looked straight at her. 'This is for Amy.'

He caught my eye and nodded. I returned it, and smiled. I took Ophelia's hand. 'Want some fresh air?'

'Okay.'

We headed towards the exit. Outside, the sweat on my skin cooled in the breeze. A handful of people lingered at the door, their faces lit by the glow of cigarettes. More were dotted around a small beer garden beside the car park, wreaths of smoke twisting into the night. We kicked through the too-long grass to an empty table then straddled the bench, our knees touching.

Gnats buzzed above us in the halo of an overhead lamp. In the pale light, Ophelia glowed. Her hair was damp at the temples and her face had a slight sheen. Her skin, now that the redness and tear-streaks had subsided, was incredibly clear. Flawless. My hands twitched with wanting to touch her. I shuffled closer and rested them on her waist. Beneath her thin top her skin burned damply.

'Are you having a good night?' I asked.

'The best,' she said, lifting her head to search the sky. 'In a long time.'

'Me too.'

She looked at me, then down at her hands. They rested just above my knees.

'Who was that girl you spoke to earlier?'

I slid my hands away from her waist, tracing the henna on hers with my fingers. 'Her name's Juliet. We went out a few times.'

'She's pretty.'

'Yes, she is.'

'Do you still like her?'

'No. Not like that. She's a nice girl, but . . .' I trailed off, lifting my hand. I cupped her face, running my thumb lightly over her bottom lip.

'But what?'

'We got paired once in art class. I had to do her portrait. Afterwards, the only thing she said to me was, "You drew my nose too big".'

Ophelia huffed out a laugh. 'That's hardly a crime.'

'No,' I admitted. 'And I'd forgotten all about it until yesterday, when I said I'd do your portrait. I expected you to come out with some request. Don't make me too this or too that. But you didn't. All you said was that it could be interesting.'

'So?' her voice was soft.

'I want the girl who wants an interesting portrait, not a beautiful one. I want the girl who's crazy enough to pull a fake gun on her enemies, who starts fights she knows she can't win. Who doesn't fall at someone's feet the minute she meets them. The girl who dances like she doesn't give a toss what anyone else thinks.'

'Not a toss,' she whispered.

I kissed her hard, hungrily, until my lips throbbed and the need for air was the only thing that stopped me. And she kissed me back, matching my need, my urgency.

234

When I pulled away her lips were red, swollen like ripe berries. Her breath was warm on my face.

'So where is my portrait?'

'I haven't drawn it yet,' I said. My voice tangled in her hair. 'But I will.'

It was almost perfect.

Almost.

Until I got home later, alone and grit-eyed from driving. And though I fell into sleep with every intention of dreaming of Ophelia, in the back of my mind I knew Tess would come. How could she not, when I'd invited her?

She stood over me for most of the night, screaming silently above my pillow. Cold water gushed from her mouth and dripped off her hair into my face. Any words were lost in the torrent.

What? I screamed back at her in my head. My stupid, unmoving, unspeaking head. *What is it you're trying to say? What is it you want from me?*

But she could hear me no more than I heard her. Every time I brought myself out of it, coaxing slow movement back into my limbs, she faded, only to reappear in another corner of the room, or there was a dreaded, sinking feeling of weight at the end of the bed, like someone sitting on it.

I eventually woke – properly – at five, dragging myself out from the sheets more exhausted than I had been when I clambered into them.

TWENTY-ONE

Strangers

Monday morning, as I arrived at the gates to the museum entrance, I saw a man leaning over a billboard fixed to one of the pillars. Ordinarily I'd have taken no notice, but the fact that he was taping something over the Past Lives poster caught my attention. Once I'd looked at him, his appearance held it. He was slight and scruffy and stood with the aid of a stick. Spiky blond hair, so bleached it was almost white, spread across his head like a dandelion. He wore a brown leather jacket with tassels, ripped jeans, and a silver cross dangling from one earlobe. None of it looked good, especially on someone who had to be pushing sixty.

Averting my eyes, I fumbled in my wallet for my swipe card to operate the gates. When I finally found it and looked up again it was to see a stocky figure coming towards the gates from the inside, eyes bulging. Hodge.

I wound down the window and swiped my card, ready to acknowledge him, but he didn't look my way. The moment the gates were opened wide enough he squeezed through with an expression that would have seen off a Doberman. The man turned in surprise, his eyes wide. They were pale, bleached-looking like the rest of him, but defiant.

I heard Hodge speak, something low and growled. His fist shot out, snatched the tape from the man and tossed it into the bushes. I caught sight of the word *SANCTUARY* in bold letters on the piece of paper just before Hodge ripped it away and crushed it in his fist.

His other hand jabbed the man in the chest, forcing him to take a step back. A noise of disgust left my lips. Had Hodge really just *prodded* someone with a walking stick?

I lowered the passengerside window. Barbed words drifted in.

'. . . and if I see you here again with your pathetic little propaganda attempts it won't be me you're dealing with. It'll be the police. Got it?'

'It's not a crime to distribute flyers.' The man's voice was as thin as the rest of him and as much of a match for Hodge as a flea against a comb.

'It is when it's on paid advertising space!' Hodge yelled. 'Now, I suggest you get back to that hovel you call a business and forget whatever it is you seem to think you know.' He leaned closer, hissing into the man's face. 'No one's interested.'

The gates were fully open now, with nothing to stop me passing through them. I wondered if Hodge was even aware I was there. I guessed he must be, but I was reluctant to leave. If he was prepared to jab a man with a walking stick in the presence of a witness, what could it escalate to if there was none? And if I was honest there was another, less noble reason I hadn't left: I was curious.

I got out of the car. Hodge jumped at the slam of the door.

'Everything okay?' I asked, more for the benefit of the stranger.

'Fine.' Hodge shoved the balled-up paper in his pocket. 'Just sending a troublemaker on his way.'

The man chuckled mirthlessly and backed off, his stick clicking on the road.

When I turned back to the car a uniformed man had appeared from the lodge next to the gates. He strolled up to Hodge, fiddling with the radio on his belt. I got back in the car, wondering why Hodge had come all the way down here when security was more than capable of handling things. I wasn't wondering for long. With a trademark handshake Hodge stuffed something into his top pocket. I remembered the way he'd shoved money at me on Friday. Clearly, here was a man who didn't mind paying for things to go his way.

I took my time fastening my seatbelt, ears straining for any exchange between the two men. I caught a terse 'Call me if he comes back' from Hodge before they went their own ways: Hodge back on to the drive to the museum and the security fellow to the lodge. Only as I started the engine and edged forward did I glance at the billboard Hodge had torn the flyer from. It was an advert for the forthcoming paranormal weekends. I regretted not getting a better look at the flyer Hodge had referred to as propaganda.

Forget whatever it is you seem to think you know . . .

In the rear-view mirror I watched the back of the spiky head moving down the lane in the direction of a bus stop. Could this be the writer of the mystery letter? Hodge had seemed rattled enough and his threat to summon the police had been an empty one. This was something he wanted to deal with alone. If I was right, then the man intended to return for Wednesday's ghost walk. I doubted he'd make it past the front gates. I considered going after him, asking what he knew – or thought he knew – then dismissed the idea. The security lodge had too clear a view of the road. I'd be seen and Hodge would probably hear about it before I'd even parked.

I set off, thinking of the word I'd caught before Hodge had torn down the flyer. *Sanctuary*. Where had I heard of that before? *The Sanctuary, Weeping Cross* . . .

It came to me: the visitors' book, and the single-word comment that had been removed. I even partially recalled the name: Lesley something. Did Lesley and the spiky-haired man have some sort of vendetta against the museum?

Once I'd parked, I pulled out the road atlas. Weeping Cross wasn't hard to find. It was three miles north of Calthorpe. I could drive out and back in my lunch break. I closed the book, thinking. Whatever was going on with Hodge was no concern of mine, but a small part of me couldn't stop asking why he seemed to have so many enemies. If I planned on spending any amount of time around Ophelia it might be in my best interests to find out why.

I got out of the car and locked it. A visit to The Sanctuary, whatever it was, could be useful. But for now, I had more important things to worry about, such as Tess and how to make her go away.

I found Ophelia in Jasper's stable, raking fresh straw into place. Leaning on the door, I watched her for a moment. Her hair was scraped back and she wore peat-coloured jodhpurs and a white shirt. The colour of the skin at her neck reminded me of honey.

'Hey.'

She carried on with what she was doing, barely looking up. 'Hey.'

I felt the smile on my lips crumble. All weekend long I'd thought of practically nothing but her and now she was acting like

I was no one. 'I see your ban from the horses has been lifted, then.' My voice sounded odd even to myself, like it was sticking to my throat.

'Yeah.' The pitchfork scraped the stone under the straw, setting my teeth on edge. 'Hodge has been grovelling all weekend. He even promised he'd never stop me from working with the horses again, can you believe that?' She continued without waiting for an answer. 'Too little, too late.' She stopped and leaned on the handle, staring at the ground. I suddenly realised the reason for her distance. She was trying not to cry.

'I called you yesterday,' I said, edging into the stable. 'Una told me you were here. With Pippi . . . and Hodge.'

She sniffed, facing me. Her eyes glistened. 'I know. I was going to call you back, but . . .'

'It's okay. I thought you'd probably want to be alone.'

'I . . . thanks.' She dipped her head. 'I just wanted to be here. To say goodbye before they took her, you know?'

'Yeah.'

'Only . . . I wish I hadn't. When I think of her now, that's how I see her. A slab of meat being lifted into a truck. There's nothing else, only that.' She dropped the pitchfork as I went to her, folding her in my arms.

'It'll fade,' I told her. 'I promise. The good memories will come back.' We stood like that, time slipping away too fast until I reluctantly released her. 'I'd better go. I still have to get into costume.'

She nodded, her face still buried in my chest.

'Are you doing anything for lunch?' she asked.

I instantly erased my Weeping Cross plans. I'd go after work instead. 'No. You?'

'Apart from making a Hodge-shaped voodoo doll and being a miserable cow, no. I'm free.'

'Sounds like fun,' I said. 'Can I join you?'

By lunchtime I was struggling to function properly. A weekend of broken, fearful sleep had taken its toll and I'd resorted to the very thing that aggravated my problems more: caffeine.

Beyond Calthorpe House and out of sight, Ophelia and I moved hand in hand through the orchard. I hadn't relished the thought of returning to the place – not after what I'd learned on the ghost walk – but I had to admit it seemed different in the daytime. Rather than eerie, the silence felt peaceful.

Until I saw the rope hanging from a tree.

'What's that – a prop?' I asked.

She stared into the branches. 'No. It's what's left of an old swing.'

I relaxed, allowing her to pull me onward. 'You could get lost in here.'

She shook her head. 'At night, maybe. It's not as big as it seems.'

It wasn't a bright day, but it was mild. We settled on thick, springy grass beneath a tree out of view of the house. After eating, we leaned back and I gazed up through the craggy branches to the sky, my eyelids drooping. Ophelia's head was a comforting weight in the crook of my arm, her breath warm on my neck.

'You smell of coffee,' she whispered.

'And you smell of horse.'

She laughed.

'It's so quiet.'

She nodded. 'No one else really comes here, apart from at harvest time.'

241

'Why's that?'

'I don't know. It's not open to the public anyway, they can only view it from the house. You might get one or two staff up here with a book on a nice day, but generally they prefer the Old Barn for convenience. Maybe it's superstition that keeps some of them away. The tale of the hanged servant, and all that.'

'But not you?' I asked.

'I'm not scared of ghost stories.'

I wished I could say the same. Instead I said, 'So, we're really alone?'

'Totally.'

'Take off your gloves.'

Silently, she did. I traced the maze of henna with my fingertips, then pulled her palm to my cheek and held it there. In response she drew herself up on her elbow, shifting her weight on to me so we were face to face. Her knee pressed between mine. Suddenly I wasn't just awake. Every part of me burned. My hands went to her waist. Her shirt had come untucked. Beneath it her skin was warm but she shivered as I moved my fingers over her, exploring the small of her back, the smooth space between her shoulder blades. Her tongue slid over mine and a strand of loose hair fluttered against my cheek. Her hand moved from my face to my chest. Lower.

As lunch breaks went, it was the best I'd ever had.

Featherlight touches on my face. Ophelia's fingertips? Her eyelashes? No. Something lighter, even. Snowflakes drifting down from a grey sky.

But it doesn't snow in June . . .

Apple blossom, I realised. I was in the orchard, beneath the trees.

Where I had let myself fall asleep.

And now I couldn't move.

My body was heavy. Lifeless. I tried calling out but my lips wouldn't respond. Was Ophelia still here? I could feel the grass under my hand, a pebble digging into my back. But I couldn't feel *her*, or see her. All I could see was the gnarled tree stretching across the air above me. Why had she left?

Something moved in the corner of my vision. A figure. *Ophelia . . .?*

He edged into view. A boy, about my age or slightly younger. His lips were thin, his eyes dark and watchful. There was a familiarity about him, but I was certain I hadn't seen him before. He wore a ragged tunic. Something long and serpentine slithered in the grass behind him as he moved towards me. I recognised the movements: fluid one moment, quick and jerky the next, like a faulty film. Even through the paralysis I knew the hairs on the backs of my arms were standing on end. He moved the way Tess moved. He wasn't in costume.

He was one of *them*.

There was no breeze, but the air grew cooler with every step he took. He crouched at my side, leaning over me. I saw now that his face was streaked with dirt and tears. Apple blossom fluttered past his filthy fingers on their way to his neck. He pulled the tunic lower.

The scream resounding in my head amounted, physically, to no more than a hiss of breath. Every inch of me recoiled. Every inch of me had no choice but to stay exactly where it was.

The rope looped around his neck was thin, but knotted tightly. Above his dirt-caked fingernails, bruises the colour of plums spread across his throat. He lowered his chin, eyes levelling with mine. As I watched, the whites slowly vanished. Blood vessels bloomed and burst in miniature vines that crept across the surfaces. Pain and fury and sadness rolled off him in waves.

He opened his mouth, trying to speak. Soil spilled out instead of words. Rich and dark as ground coffee, falling into my face, my eyes, my mouth. Choking me, blinding me. I tried to lift my hand to brush it away but like the rest of me it was dead, numb like it had been slept on for too long and the life had left it.

Something small, I remembered through my panic. *Just . . . a little finger to start.* I focused, holding the thought in my mind. My finger twitched. Curled. Dirt continued to tumble into my face. *It's not real it's not real it's not real . . .*

'Elliott?'

Footsteps pounding the ground. Another face in mine. A flesh-and-blood face oblivious to the dead one that was so close in the veil between sleep and waking.

'*Elliott!*' Ophelia gripped my arm, shaking me. 'Wake up! What's wrong with you?' She brought her gloved hand to my face. Smacked it hard. 'Elliott, *please!*' Her voice was almost a sob.

A choked sound gurgled from the apparition's mouth. His features were contorted with anger. Saliva and blood and dirt spewed out on to his chin as his arm reached over my body towards Ophelia. His lips formed a single, soundless word. *Mine.*

My finger curled again, bringing my hand with it. Above me the boy's fingers passed straight through Ophelia's arm. '*Noooo!*' I yelled, thrashing out of it. I rolled away on to my front, coughing up dirt that was no longer there. In that eye blink, he too was gone.

'What the hell happened to you?' Ophelia grabbed me, spinning me over to face her. She was whiter than I'd ever seen her. I clung to her, shaking, and buried my face in her lap. Words I couldn't control spilled out.

'He's here . . . I *saw* him.'

'Who's here?' She shook me. 'Elliott, you're scaring me . . .'

'The boy. The hanged servant – Sebastian. I saw him . . .'

'There's no one here, only us. You were dreaming.' Her fingers smoothed through my hair like I was a frightened horse she was trying to tame. I squeezed my eyes shut. *Get a grip.*

'Why did you leave me?' I twisted my head to look up at her. 'Where were you?'

'You fell asleep after we . . .' She gestured helplessly. 'You looked so peaceful I thought I'd let you rest. I went to get coffee.'

I pulled myself up, still tasting soil somehow. I wanted it gone. 'Where is it?'

Ophelia jerked her head to the ground a few metres away. Two empty paper cups lay on their sides on the grass. 'I dropped them when I saw you. I panicked – I thought you were having some kind of fit. Your eyes were open . . . and you were twitching.'

'I could see you,' I said, 'and hear you. I just couldn't wake up.' I climbed to my feet, unsteady as I brushed grass from my clothes and tucked my shirt in. The panicked feeling was diminishing now, but embarrassment was all too ready to take its place. I couldn't believe I'd lost it in front of her like this. 'What time is it?' I asked gruffly.

'Nearly two. Time to get back.'

I let her take my hand despite how clammy it was.

'Are you sure you're all right?' she asked.

'Yeah.' *No.* I forced a smile, tugging her away from the orchard. 'I'm fine. It was just a dream.'

TWENTY-TWO

Weeping Cross

I mumbled my way through the afternoon's tours in a monotone, for once glad of the repetition that I normally resented. It was now the only thing that kept me on track. Even so, my delivery was awful. I expected complaints. It wasn't long before I got them.

During my last break of the day I made coffee in the Old Barn and took it outside to the stables, the clip-clopping of hooves ringing my ears. In the distance I saw Ophelia with the cart and horse, taking visitors across the Plain. Briefly, I closed my eyes and replayed those earlier moments in the orchard; the softness of her skin, the taste of her. Before Sebastian had appeared and ruined it all.

I opened my eyes but still I saw his contorted features. His hand lunging to push Ophelia away, like a wolf growling over the last scraps of a kill.

Mine.

Fingers closed around my arm. I jerked my cup, almost spilling the dark liquid.

'Steady.' Hodge's voice was low. He whistled, releasing my arm. 'What's rattled you?'

'Nothing.' I reached towards the stable door for support.

Hodge peered at me. 'Doesn't look like nothing to me.'

I stayed silent. He sighed.

'Listen, Elliott. I hate to nag, but that last group you took – the school? Well, they weren't happy. They said you weren't engaging, the children weren't listening. I had to refund them. You're supposed to be *earning* us money, not losing it.'

'I'm sorry.' My voice was flat. 'I'm not . . . feeling myself today.'

Hodge shook his head. 'On the contrary, I had excellent feedback about you this morning. Now, either you tell me what's happened since then, or I'll have to seriously consider your employment beyond the probation term.' His tone softened. 'I don't want to do that. I can see you're good, but that's not enough. It must be *consistent*. Do you understand?'

'Yes.' I gripped the cup, hesitant. My mistrust of him took a step back to hide behind the need to redeem myself, as well as speak about what I'd seen in the orchard to someone. *Anyone*, so long as they believed me. And I knew Hodge would. Besides, it wouldn't be like I was telling him anything he didn't already know.

'I thought I saw something today. A . . . a ghost.' There. The words were out. Too late to take them back now. 'A boy, about my age. There was a rope around his neck. He was wearing old-fashioned clothes . . .'

Hodge seemed to have stopped breathing. He said nothing, only nodded for me to continue.

'He was in the orchard, under the trees. His throat was all bruised and crushed . . . and his eyes were bloodshot—' I broke off, shuddering. 'I think it was Sebastian.'

Hodge's eyes were round and wide. 'Did he . . . say anything?' he asked at last.

'No. I think . . . I think he was trying to, but his mouth was full of dirt.' I gulped. That was enough. I couldn't bring myself to say more.

Hodge patted my arm roughly. 'No wonder you're shaken!' He glanced about us then lowered his voice. 'Come with me. I've got just the thing.'

Numbly, I followed him over the cobbles and through to his office. He locked the door behind us then crossed to a safe beside the fireplace. As he fiddled with the dial I stood awkwardly behind him, noticing charred remnants in the grate. Something had been burned there recently. The acrid smell of smoke still lingered along with an untouched shred of white paper. It didn't take a genius to figure out what had been burned.

'Here we go.' Hodge turned back from the safe, a decanter filled with golden liquid in one hand and two glasses in the other. He set them on the table and rubbed his hands together. 'Doctor's orders, eh? Can't beat it for frazzled nerves.'

I didn't have time to protest as he slugged a generous measure into each glass. He handed me one and took the other. I lifted the glass and sniffed. The smell alone made my eyes water.

Hodge knocked his back in one swallow. 'Cheers.'

'The thing is, I'm driving later,' I began.

'One won't hurt.' He was already pouring himself another. It vanished just as quickly. 'Not a word to Una, mind.'

'Sure.' I tilted the glass, sipping a tiny amount.

'Come on,' Hodge goaded. 'You've just seen your first ghost! Get it down you, lad.'

I hesitated then drained half of it. It burned all the way, settling in my belly like fire. Hodge looked approving.

'Better?'

'Yeah,' I lied. There was no way I was drinking the rest.

He walked to his window, one hand in his pocket and the other holding his empty glass. I took the opportunity to dump what was left in mine into a plant pot on the mantelpiece. I hoped he wouldn't insist on a refill.

'So – are you up to doing the last tour of the day?' he asked.

'I think so.'

'Good.' He turned around. 'Relax, lad. There's nothing to be scared of in the spirit world. You could even consider it an honour – a *privilege* – that one of them appeared to you.' He set the glass down on top of the safe. The door remained open and I couldn't help glance inside. At the front sat a small, fat notebook, stuffed with cuttings. 'Some people spend their lives in search of answers and never experience anything.'

I looked away from the notebook, distracted. 'What kind of answers?'

'To whether or not there's an afterlife.' He returned the decanter to the safe. 'Now you've seen for yourself that life *does* go on after death. It's a rare gift.'

I couldn't answer. To me, there was nothing gift-like about watching someone trapped in their last moments, in pain, in suffering, alone. Nothing gift-like for either party: them or me. An afterlife? What a joke. It was afterdeath. Again and again and again.

'Were you with Ophelia in the orchard?'

The question caught me off-guard. I wondered if it was a trick and decided not to lie. 'Y-yes. She showed me the orchard, like you suggested.' Heat rose in my neck. If he knew what we'd *really* been doing . . .

'And did she see . . . anything?'

'No. It was just me.' I made a mental note to warn Ophelia that I'd discussed it with her uncle. I was starting to wish I hadn't.

'Right.' He locked the safe. 'You know, I haven't seen you properly since Friday. It was good of you to visit her . . .' He trailed off, his expression thoughtful. 'I wasn't expecting her home quite so late, though.'

'Sorry.' The alcohol took effect, making me bold. 'I didn't think midnight was late for a weekend.' *Or for a seventeen-year-old.*

'Ah, well. No harm done. She did return much happier, I noticed.'

'Good.' *No thanks to you . . .*

Hodge smiled. 'Una and I are very grateful to you. Your friendship will be good for Ophelia.'

And there it was, that word: friendship. Only it was served as a warning, one I'd heard many times and in many guises: *Stay away from my daughter, my girl, my princess. You're not good enough. Hands off.*

Too late for that, Hodge, old chum.

'I'm glad,' I said, smiling back. The whiskey galloped through my veins like the Trojan horse it was. 'I think she needs a friend.'

My first impression of Weeping Cross was that it had good reason to feel sorry for itself. It was a grey, grassless little town only three miles from Calthorpe in distance, but about a thousand in every other way. I bit my tongue bumping over potholes in the road and tried not to make eye contact with the bored group lurking around a graffiti-covered monument that I suspected was the 'Cross'. It took ten minutes before I saw someone whose appearance I deemed trustworthy enough to ask for help and another ten before someone was willing to extend the same trust in answering my question.

'The Sanctuary?' The woman wrinkled her nose. 'What do you want with that place?'

I waited politely, hoping it was an empty question but she

continued to stare. I pointed to my jacket on the passenger seat. 'Just . . . returning some lost property.'

'Well, mind they don't ask you in.' She wrapped her own coat around herself more tightly. 'They don't call it the nut church for nothing.'

'"They" who?'

She frowned. 'Anyone with any sense. It shouldn't be dabbled with, all that.'

'All what?'

'Ghosts. Psychics, or mediums, or whatever they call them-selves. It's stirring up trouble.'

I smiled a smile I didn't feel. The Sanctuary was some sort of centre for mediums? I wondered what Hodge's problem with the place was. He'd told me that his own mother had been a medium.

The woman gave me muddled directions which I muddled further, eventually arriving at a shabby town hall that looked neither nutty, nor like a church. Frustratingly, it was closed. I scanned the notice board and found a timetable of events. Under today's date were the words: *Developing Psychic Awareness – Workshop with Resident Psychic Lesley Travis. Doors open 7.30 p.m.*

I checked my watch. There was no way I was prepared to kill an hour in this dump. Checking up on Hodge could wait. I went back to the car and was fishing in my pockets for the keys when I saw him. Or rather, heard him.

His stick tap-tapped the pavement with every other step. A plastic shopping bag swung either side of him. He wore the same clothes he'd had on this morning: the ripped jeans, the brown jacket. He saw me seconds after I saw him, the bleached eyes piercing even over the distance between the car and the town hall. I removed my hand from my pocket and jogged towards him.

'Excuse me,' I began.

He regarded me warily. 'Yes?'

'I wondered if I could ask you a quick question.'

He grunted, brandishing his walking stick with surprising ease and pointed it to the notice board. 'Doors open at half past seven. I'm only here early to set up. Come back later and you can ask all the questions you want. Entrance fee's seven-fifty.'

'Seven-fifty? Wait – no. I mean, it's not that kind of question.'

He cackled. 'No, never is when money's involved.' He lowered the stick. 'Go on, then. I haven't got all day.'

'I work at Past Lives—'

'Oh, Lordy, here we go. Has old Podge sent you?'

I liked him already, despite the dodgy dress sense.

'I saw you there this morning, at the gate. You stuck something over the poster but Hodge tore it down. I wondered what it was.'

He frowned, unlocking the door. 'I thought I recognised you. You got out of the car.' He tilted his head, indicating that I should follow him. 'Here. Hold these.' He handed me his shopping bags and pushed the door open to a large hall. It was empty apart from tables and chairs stacked neatly around the edges. He hit the lights and headed towards another door inside.

'Bring those bags in here.'

I followed him into a kitchen with the bags. He took his jacket off and hung it on a peg, then went through the pockets.

'Here.' He handed me a sheet of folded paper. 'This is a copy of what I had this morning.'

I unfolded it. 'Paranormal Claims,' I read, 'a Lecture in Critical Thinking with Lesley Travis and guest speaker, acclaimed medium David Morse. Topics covered in this ninety-minute session are: A Brief History of Fraudulent Mediums; Prayed For or Preyed

252

Upon . . .' I glanced down the rest of it. 'I don't get it. I thought The Sanctuary was *for* this stuff, not against it.'

The man began unloading milk, tea, coffee and biscuits on to the counter. He chuckled. 'Oh, we are, provided it's genuine. The trouble is that nowadays there's so much information available through books and the interweb, it's easier than ever for the bereaved to be taken advantage of. And other times it's used for entertainment, for people looking for a cheap thrill. I don't see what's entertaining about some poor soul's death being exploited for a quick buck to be made, know what I'm saying?'

I did. And more to the point, I agreed.

He tore open a packet and offered it my way. 'Want a biscuit?'

'Um, no. Thanks.'

'Suit yourself.' He crammed three into his mouth, crunched and swallowed. 'And *that's* where my problems with that museum start. First it was the ghost walks. Now it's entire paranormal weekends with so-called psychics and séances. Treating it like it's bloody Halloween all year round.'

I frowned. 'But aren't you charging people for the same sort of thing here?'

He gave me a stony look. 'You think I make a profit from seven-fifty a head? That barely covers the hall hire and refreshments. Don't even get me started on guest speakers' travel fees.' He made a scoffing noise. 'The Sanctuary isn't about money. It's about guiding people, helping them move on. Not a circus to raise the dead.' He attacked another biscuit. 'He tells people I'm jealous, you know. Jealous of his events and the revenue they bring in. And most people, they don't look too close. Some of that money could have been mine – if I'd wanted it.'

'What do you mean?' I interrupted.

'He asked me to come onboard. Offered me a tidy little sum to get involved directly, or a commission for any contacts I could send his way. He wasn't amused when I told him to jog on.'

'Right. So . . . that's where the hostility began?'

'Pretty much. Now, was there something else I could help you with?'

'Actually, there is.' I looked at the leaflet again. 'I came across a comment left in the visitors' book last year by a colleague of yours – Lesley Travis. It was in relation to one of the ghost walks, but I couldn't read it – it had been wiped over. I'd like to speak to her about it. Do you have a contact number for her? Or perhaps she mentioned something to you—'

The silver eyes regarded me curiously. 'You work there, you say?'

'That's right.'

'I take it Podge doesn't know you're here, asking questions?'

I hesitated. 'No.'

'Hmm.' He shuffled out of the kitchen, beckoning me into the hall. 'Well, if you value your job it's probably best to keep it that way.' He lifted a chair from a stack and pushed it towards me, then took another for himself, leaning his stick against the wall. 'So why *are* you asking questions?'

I wasn't entirely sure myself. Apart from my earlier thoughts about getting involved with Ophelia, all I knew was that Hodge was being blackmailed and the only suspect I had was right in front of me. I wasn't prepared to admit to either of those things just yet. Luckily I'd had the sense to pre-empt the question on the drive over and I had an answer ready.

'On the night the comment was left, a spirit was said to have been seen by the entire tour group. A servant boy, hanged for stealing bread. Today, I thought . . . I thought I saw him. I wanted to know how my experience compared with what Lesley saw. And what she thought about it was so bad that someone hid her comment.' I paused. 'Do you know where I can find her?'

'Yes,' he said. 'Only, Lesley's not actually a "her" but a "he". Me, to be precise.'

'*You're* Lesley Travis?'

'According to my bus pass.' He gave a weary sigh. 'And my birth certificate, thanks to my father's lousy spelling, in case you were wondering.'

'Do you remember that night? What you wrote?'

Lesley pursed his lips. 'I remember the gist of it.'

'It was short. One word.'

'It would have been something along the lines of "act", or "show",' he mused, tugging absently at the silver cross in his ear. 'Got it. I *do* remember. It was "staged".'

'*Staged*? You mean . . .'

'That's right. I thought the whole thing was a set-up. That there was no ghost . . . it was a hoax.'

TWENTY-THREE

The Silver Cord

'But I saw him,' I whispered. 'I know he was there. It *can't* have been a hoax.'

'I'm not saying what *you* saw wasn't real,' said Lesley. 'I'm saying that I have doubts about what *I* saw – and heard – that night.'

'So what exactly happened?'

'I'd already told Hodge I wasn't interested in getting involved in his events,' he said. 'But he kept trying to persuade me to reconsider and even sent me free tickets for the ghost walk. In the end I used them, partly to shut him up and partly, I admit, because I was curious. He seemed surprised when I turned up – I think he'd given up on me coming. And as the night went on, he seemed increasingly . . .' He paused, thoughtful. 'I'm not sure that "nervous" is the right word. Agitated, perhaps.'

'Why do you think that was?'

'At the time I thought it was down to me being there.'

'You said he'd invited you . . .'

'He did. But he wasn't expecting me to misbehave.'

'Misbehave?'

'A few eye rolls here and there, a couple of whispered comments. I could see he was getting narked – I was starting to enjoy myself. Then we got to that house on the Elizabethan street.'

'Calthorpe House?'

'Right. He took us to the orchard and told the story of the hanged servant and the crying cook. It was dark, and the mood at the end of it . . . well, the entire group was on edge. I don't mind saying that a shiver even went up my spine. And then Hodge took a torch out and shone it into the orchard, pointing out the tree the boy had been hanged from. It was just for a split second, but we all saw it – every one of us.'

I leaned forward in earnest. 'What? What did you see?'

'A body, hanging from a rope. It was swinging, very lightly. I remember hearing the creak of the branch. It was horrible.'

A prickle of dread rippled over my skin. 'What did it look like?'

'It was so quick, hardly a glimpse. And it was far away, within the trees. All I remember is a tattered tunic. And bare feet, covered in dirt.'

'Dark hair? Kind of long – shoulder-length?'

'I don't know. It was too dark to make out the head, thank God.'

'So then what happened? Did it vanish?'

'Someone laughed, at first. They obviously thought it was set up to make us jump. But it was Hodge's reaction that changed things – he wasn't laughing. He dropped the torch. Then people screamed – I don't know how many. More than one. It was pitch-black – people were grabbing at each other. I heard Hodge telling us to keep calm as he searched for the torch. Someone started crying behind me – a woman. Hodge shouted that he'd found the torch and put it back on. I turned to ask the woman behind me if she was all right, but I saw that she wasn't crying after all. She looked scared, but her eyes were dry. At that moment it came again – we all heard that, too.' He paused. 'A woman crying. It seemed to be behind us, near the house or from it, but I couldn't pinpoint where, exactly. Hodge shone the torch around. His hand was jerking about everywhere – I started to feel dizzy.'

'Did you see her?' I asked. 'The crying woman?'

'No. No one did. And just as quickly as it started, it stopped.' He clicked his fingers. 'Hodge shone the torch around some more, at windows, through the gardens. There was nothing. Then he shone it back at the tree where we'd seen the boy – but he was gone.'

'Just – gone?'

'Yep. Vanished.'

'Then what happened?'

'We got out of there. Everyone was pretty shaken. Hodge led us back to the hotel, where he ordered drinks for everyone. By the time we got there the group was a couple short – the experience was too much for some people and they left. But the others – once we were inside the tavern, people began to calm down. Everyone was discussing what they'd seen – the mood was electric. They became excited, greedy for more. When the drinks were finished Hodge took us out again to continue the tour. Nothing else happened, but it didn't need to. There was this . . . *energy* about the group, a sort of . . .'

'Buzz,' I whispered, remembering my own experience after the awful smell had come up in the school.

'Yes, a buzz. And there was this moment when I caught Hodge's eye afterwards. He looked so pleased with himself. I suppose he was thinking of how far the news would spread – and how much more custom it would bring in. But that wasn't all. He looked . . . *relieved*, too. It was that, more than anything, which made me begin to question what I had seen.'

'You hadn't until then, though?'

'No,' he admitted. 'But once I'd started, I couldn't stop going over it in my mind. The fact that *everyone* present saw it also made me suspicious – it's believed that some people never have the ability to see the dead. *I* have never seen the dead—'

'But you say you're psychic . . .'

'It's two different things,' he snapped. '*Mediums* communicate with the dead. Psychics work off living energy. Some say it's just finely attuned instinct and I agree. Most people could tune in if they tried, if they were open enough.'

'Is that why you were the only one who had doubts?'

'Perhaps, perhaps not,' he said darkly. 'I was probably the only one present who knew just how desperate Hodge was to make the thing work. The more I thought about it, the more convinced I became that it had just been a very clever, well thought-out trick. There were no fancy effects. Just what we saw and heard, and an impeccable but convenient time lapse between each.'

'But if someone was pretending to hang from the tree, then surely you'd have heard or seen them climbing down afterwards?' I asked.

'I think that's what we were meant to believe,' said Lesley. 'That it would be impossible. But I've thought about it – a lot. As soon as the torchlight picked the figure out, Hodge dropped the torch. People were screaming – any sounds would've been easily masked. As soon as the torch went back on, the sounds of the crying woman began, drawing our attention *away* from the trees. By the time the light went back to the orchard, over a minute had to have gone by – more than enough time for someone to have carefully climbed down – or even further up the tree – and hidden.'

'What about the woman behind you?' I said. 'You mentioned that you heard someone crying close to you before it began over

259

by the house – do you think she was near the group and then moved further away?'

'No. I think that was another distraction trick. The group were strangers. Any of them could have been a stooge – someone in on it from the start. My guess is that this person never left the group. The other noises were either made by someone else in the upstairs of the house—'

'But Hodge said it's off-limits for safety reasons . . .'

'For large groups. Not for a single person. Hell, it could even have been a recording left to play.'

'Seems a lot of trouble to go to. Why bother?'

'Same reasons anyone bothers to hoax,' said Lesley. 'Fame, or publicity. Money. Think about it – you'd only have to pull something like that once and it'd ripple. Those people told people, who told other people and so on. There were mentions in the local papers and I think it even made it into one of the nationals.'

'Did you tell Hodge what you suspected?'

'I congratulated him on a good performance, or words to that effect. He acted like he didn't know what I was talking about. He wasn't about to admit it, now, was he?'

I decided to try a direct approach. 'Did you ever attempt to make him?'

Lesley looked confused. 'What do you mean?'

'Like, say . . . a letter? Threatening him with what you knew?'

'No, of course not. I don't *know* anything – that's the whole point. I only have my suspicions. I don't have any proof.'

I sat back in the chair. I was no expert but I felt sure he was telling the truth.

'Why are you really here? Eh?'

'I told you,' I muttered. 'I wanted to compare your sighting of the ghost with mine.'

'And has it changed your view on what you saw, or thought you saw?'

'No.'

'Tell me what happened. To start with, were you in a group?'

'I was alone.' As briefly as I could, I described what had happened. 'I know what it sounds like,' I said, once I'd finished. 'But it wasn't a dream.'

'You seem quite certain of that.'

'It's happened before. Not just with this boy, but . . . others.'

'Have you always had these . . . visitations when you sleep?'

'No. They started recently, after I was in an accident.'

Lesley studied my face for a long time. 'The mind is a complex thing,' he said eventually. 'As far back as history goes there are tales of prophets foretelling things in their dreams. Who knows what's real and what isn't?'

'You don't believe me.'

'I didn't say that. But in any case it doesn't matter what *I* believe, boy. If it's real to you then it's real enough. And the only thing that matters is how you deal with it.'

'I've tried. Nothing works. It won't go away.'

He gave a crow of laughter. 'Let me give you some advice. This sort of thing, once it starts, won't just "go away". What have you been doing, trying not to sleep? Pretending it'll go away if you ignore it?'

'Trying not to sleep?' I blurted out. 'That's a laugh. When I'm meant to be sleeping I'm too afraid, or it's disrupted, and when I'm meant to be awake all I can think about is sleep. I know the triggers, I try to avoid them, but sooner or later it comes. *They* come.'

'Ever tried asking them what they want? Trying to help?'

'Yes. It doesn't always work. In fact, it's only worked once.'

'What was different about that time?'

I thought back to the night in the prison cell. 'It wasn't at home. And at first, I didn't realise what I was seeing. I tried to help before I even knew what it really was.'

'How did you feel?'

'Worried. Scared for him, not for myself.'

'And normally? What do you feel then?'

'Afraid. Terrified, more than I've been of anything.'

'There's your answer. Your fear is what's holding you back.'

'It's hard to feel much else towards a stranger who appears in your room at night,' I retorted, 'dripping water and blood on to you when you can't move a muscle.'

'Communication between a spirit and a medium is a two-way thing,' he said. 'You have to show compassion and the same measure of trust the spirit is showing you.'

I frowned. 'I'm not a medium. I didn't ask for this.'

He chuckled. 'I'm afraid I disagree. The term "medium" means "vessel", which is exactly what you've become, whether you want it or not. They've found a way through to you and it seems to me you don't have much choice except to listen to them.'

'What about something else? I don't know . . . exorcism,' I said.

'Exorcism is for demons, or spirits that can't be helped. It's not a resolution – it's more like a door slamming in their face. Is that something you want on your conscience?'

'I can handle my conscience. What I can't handle is being haunted.'

Lesley's silver eyes bored into me. 'I think you'll find that some-times, the two go very closely hand in hand. What exactly is it you're so afraid of?'

I gave a hollow laugh. 'How about possession?'

'I've never heard of anyone becoming possessed through sleep paralysis or dream visitations . . .'

'What about out-of-body experiences?' I demanded. 'I get those too and I can't control it. And the last time it happened, my body wasn't where I left it when I went back. Something was in it – a ghost. I couldn't get back in until it chose to leave.'

'That's impossible.'

'Trust me, it's not.'

'I think you'll find that it is.' Lesley's tone was cool, clipped. 'You had me going there, for a moment. But I'm afraid you just went that little bit too far.'

'What are you on about?'

'What you're telling me isn't possible. There have been numerous studies of people who experience astral projection or out-of-body experiences, and the overwhelming majority of them report a silver cord which tethers them to their body, ensuring that they never get lost and can always find their way back.'

I laughed harshly. 'Right. You think I haven't read about it? You think I haven't done my homework? I've never had this mystical silver cord appear – never seen it once.'

'The cord not only tethers your psychic self to your physical self, it also maintains a connection between you and your body while you're away from it,' Lesley continued, his eyes now like flint. 'That connection means that your body isn't vacant, there-fore it can't be possessed. It's believed that the only time the connection breaks is at the moment of death.'

His words sent cold fear rushing through my veins.

'So you see,' he said quietly, 'I think we both know you're lying. And I'd like you to leave.'

263

'No,' I whispered. 'You don't see. You don't understand . . . The accident I told you about. Where it all began. My . . . my heart stopped beating. Not for long, just a couple of minutes. I died, but they brought me back.'

What little colour remained in Lesley's face drained right then.

'Out,' he said hoarsely. 'Get out. Now.'

'It's the truth, I swear—'

He stood up so quickly his chair toppled and crashed to the floor.

'I believe you.'

'I don't understand . . .'

'I'm sorry.' His eyes were wide, fearful. 'I need you to leave. Right now.'

TWENTY-FOUR

Protection

Forty minutes later my hands still shook as I tried to put my key into the front door. On the third attempt it opened to a waft of warmth and roasting food that washed over me like a balm. Dad peered out of the kitchen, a carrot in one hand and a peeler in the other.

'There you are. I was just going to call you – dinner's ready in twenty minutes.'

'Fine.' I moved past him, head down, and went towards my room.

'Elliott? Has something happened?'

'No.' I paused at the door. 'Yes. But I don't want to talk about it, not yet. I need to think.'

There was a short silence. 'I'll shout when it's ready,' Dad said eventually.

I nodded but didn't look back as I went into my room. It was still light, just. I switched on the computer. While I waited for it to load I dug out everything I had on out-of-body experiences: books, newspaper clippings, internet printouts. There wasn't much and soon I found what I was looking for:

During astral projection, some claim to see a thread connecting the astral form to the physical body. This thread is known as the silver

*cord and it assures projectors that they will not become separated or
lost. It can also aid a swift return to the body.*

My eyes lingered on *swift return.* Apart from the last couple of times
I'd been out of body, every other experience I could remember had
proved a challenge in getting back in. I put the book aside and
typed *SILVER CORD* into the search engine. It returned thousands
of results. Among those of movies, bands and numerous others that
were irrelevant, I found more definitions, Biblical references, blogs
and forums relating to astral projection. As I clicked through, I was
reminded how descriptions of the thread itself varied, ranging from
sparkling like Christmas tinsel to something like an umbilical cord.

Some claimed the cord would appear simply if it was looked for,
while others maintained that it could remain intact for days after
death. *Like anyone could know,* I thought. The more I looked, the less
comforted I was. According to many, possession was impossible if the
silver cord – or fragments of it – were intact. I cleared the search field
and stared at the blank screen. I'd learned nothing, apart from that
every person had an opinion, and that every opinion was different.

If it's real to you, then it's real enough. The words came back to
me, but this time they resonated. In the end, the only opinion
that mattered and the only facts I could count on were my own.
Those facts were: one, I'd been clinically dead for two minutes at
the scene of the accident. Two, I'd never seen any evidence of a
silver cord. Three, I usually had difficulty in getting back into my
body when I left it. And four, *something* or someone had entered
my body when I was out of it.

All of those things combined had frightened Lesley Travis. Now
they frightened me. *This sort of thing, once it starts, won't just go
away . . .*

Lesley was right. I *had* been trying to make it go away. All the time I'd spent trying to understand the paralysis and avoiding its triggers had been wasted. It could be held off for days, weeks even, but eventually it returned. It always came back. And in doing those things I'd actually avoided what mattered the most: the thing I'd known all along.

I was being haunted.

My fingers hovered over the keys then slowly typed in another phrase: *PROTECTION AGAINST GHOSTS AND POSSESSION.*

I hit 'search' and sat back. The page loaded with thousands of results. Most articles on possession referenced demons. I dismissed them.

I was like you, once. A boy . . .

The same lists and items came up time and again. I took a pencil and began noting them down in the back of my sketchbook.

Spirits cannot pass lines of salt, or nails prised from coffin lids and hammered into door frames.

Walking backwards through doorways will prevent being followed by spirits.

The Bible, holy water and prayer are effective in warding off evil.

Graveyard dirt in a pocket repels the dead.

Spells, amulets, plants and herbs I couldn't pronounce, much less imagine looking for. My head swam with information overload. Then I came across something else:

The most important aspect of any defence method is your belief in it.

I looked back over my list. Then I began crossing things out. The first three went on the basis that I could only prevent *new* ghosts from following me. For existing ones they'd be useless – if they even worked. Reluctantly, I crossed out the Bible, holy water and prayer. Three years ago things might have been different, but I wasn't sure I had faith any more. Prayers hadn't saved Mum. I doubted they'd save me.

That left me with precisely one possible defence: graveyard dirt. *Great.* Perhaps a visit to Mum's grave was on the cards after all. I moved on to possession. There was plenty on the subject, most of which was religious and again, related to demons and evil spirits. I tapped the pencil against my teeth. I wasn't sure that I'd encountered anything *evil*, exactly. Scary, yes. Tess was definitely that. But evil? No. Nevertheless I reminded myself that something didn't have to be evil to harm me. A spirit's desire to live again, by using *my* body, was harm enough.

I clicked off one site and on to another.

Illness, trauma, depression, drug or alcohol abuse, or being physically or spiritually drained may lead to vulnerability and increased risk of psychic attack. Fear is a gateway that allows negative entities to bring harm.

Trauma. Depression. Physically drained. Fear. Not to mention that I couldn't control when I was in or out of my body. No wonder Lesley Travis had wanted me away from him. I was wide open.

I shut the computer down. Under the list I'd made I wrote another heading.

Reasons I'm afraid.

Under that I wrote the following:

1. I never know when they'll appear.

2. I don't know what they want.

3. It's usually dark when they're here.

4. I'm physically vulnerable both in paralysis and out of body.

Then I put the pencil down and stared at the list. Number three was the easiest to resolve, I realised. All I had to do was leave the light on. I grimaced, wondering whether seeing Tess in more detail would be a good thing or not. At the very least it would prevent those few moments of fear manifesting at her approach, when she was still only a shadow in the dark.

Number two I was already working on. I'd asked Tess what she wanted the last time she appeared – well, screamed it at her inside my head. Perhaps if I had been calmer, like I was with the ghost in the prison cell, it would stand a chance.

I was still staring at numbers one and four when Dad called me for dinner. We sat in the living room with trays balanced on our knees, watching the TV. I shovelled down mouthful after mouthful of food, barely tasting a thing. I watched Dad picking over his own meal without much enthusiasm. He looked tired again. Guilt pricked at me like a pin. A weekend of disturbed sleep for me had meant the same for him. I wished I had a better way of coping, but he was the one thing that let me feel safe—

Fear is a gateway for negative entities . . .

I stopped chewing. If fear was my biggest threat, then feeling safe was my strongest asset. *Dad* was that asset. Dad was safety. Perhaps that was all the protection I needed. With that knowledge, the answer to the final thing on my list came to me.

I never know when they'll appear.

I didn't know for sure, but I knew what triggered them. And more importantly I knew that I had one element under my control to some extent. Sleep. I controlled when and where I slept, only until now, I'd been doing it all the wrong way. I'd allowed Tess to manifest on her own terms, dreading each time she visited and willing her away. But what if the roles were reversed? What if *I* went looking for *her*?

'Dad?' I said. 'What do you know about Tess?'

Dad lowered his fork. 'Elliott, I don't think—'

'Please, Dad. It's important. I – I know you don't believe she's here, but I do. And if I'm ever going to make it stop I need to know why she won't go away.'

'Is this about the bath?'

'The bath?'

He put his plate down. 'A couple of times this week I've found it full of water. At first I thought it was you, but—'

'It wasn't. It's happened to me, too. It's her, Dad. She's angry. It's like she's trying to tell me something but she can't because I'm always too scared to listen. That's why I need to find out about her. If I know more, then maybe I'll be less afraid.'

Dad stared at the floor. I couldn't tell what he was thinking.

'I'm not mad.' My voice was small. 'I went to see someone today. A psychic—'

'Oh, Elliott!'

'Please, just *listen*! I told him what had been happening. He believed me, but he was scared.'

'Of what?'

'He wouldn't say. But I think I know. He . . . he told me about this thing. A silver cord that's supposed to appear during out-of-body experiences. It keeps you connected to your body.'

Dad's voice was strained. 'A silver cord?'

'Yeah. Only, I've never seen it. I don't have one. And apparently, it only breaks when you die. Which would make sense because of . . . what happened. The accident.'

270

'They brought you back.' Dad's face was colourless and, somehow, a decade older in the space of a few minutes.

'Dad?'

'I wasn't going to tell you,' he whispered. 'I didn't think it mattered.'

A cold sensation travelled from the top of my head to the tips of my toes.

'Tell me what?'

'It happened before. When you were little.'

'What are you talking about?'

'You were only about two years old – you hadn't long been speaking in proper sentences. One morning while we were having breakfast, you told us that Granddad had visited you when you were asleep.'

My breath caught in my throat. 'Go on.'

'Adam started crying and wanted to know why Granddad hadn't been to see him as well. We explained to you both that it was only a dream – Granddad had been dead a month by then. But it happened again a week later and this time you said that Granddad had taken you to the pond to feed the ducks. Adam was at school that time, so we let you carry on, even laughing at one point when you described a line that had come out of your tummy button. You pointed to your mum's silver necklace and said it looked like that and that it had pulled you home when it was time to go back to sleep.'

'A silver line?' I said hoarsely.

Dad nodded. 'It sounded so bizarre, so typical of a dream that we thought nothing of it. But then you said Granddad kept telling you to ask me about the watch. Why I wasn't wearing it.'

'Whose watch?'

'His watch.' Dad looked away. 'He'd left it to me, but I hadn't been able to bring myself to wear it. I was still too cut up. The thing was, neither you nor Adam knew about the watch. So when you came out with that, it shook us up.'

'Why don't I remember any of this?'

'You were so small. There was so much else going on, you were learning new things every day. And we decided not to make a big deal of it. Mum told you that if Granddad came again you were to tell him goodnight and stay in bed. After that . . . I started wearing the watch. You never mentioned anything else and over the years – the few times we spoke about it – we put it down to coincidence.'

My head reeled. The food in my stomach sat like pebbles.

'It happened before, and you never told me? Even after all this – months of it?'

'I'm sorry.' Dad's eyes were pleading. 'I didn't know what else to do. I thought that if it had gone away once, it might go away again.'

'But it hasn't,' I said. 'It's only got worse, little by little.'

'I know that now. But when it started up again, your descriptions of it were different. More threatening. You never seemed scared when you were a baby – and you never mentioned the silver line again.' He shook his head helplessly. 'I thought it was just some sort of stress thing, that it had evolved. And then with Mrs Mardle, I started to wonder. I didn't know the silver line was significant, I—' he stopped abruptly. 'What does it mean, now it's gone?'

I wanted to be angry but couldn't. Dad had lost too much and tried too hard. He didn't deserve my anger.

'It means that I might be in danger. Without it, it's harder to get back into my body and . . . it leaves me vulnerable.'

272

'Vulnerable how?'

'To whatever's trying to get through to me.'

'What are we going to do?' Dad asked. 'We could get someone – a priest, to come here and—'

'No. That wouldn't be helping.' I remembered Lesley's words. 'It'd be like slamming a door in her face. And anyway, it's not the flat – it's me. It doesn't matter where I go. They'll be there. I'm the one who has to find a way to deal with it. Starting now.'

'What do you mean?'

'I'm going to find her. Tess. Now. This evening. I'm going to find out what she wants.'

'How's that safe? You just said you'd be vulnerable.'

'I am. But I'm starting to think Tess isn't a threat, not in that way.' My mind raced back over the last six months, recounting every time I'd seen her. 'I've been out of my body countless times – if she'd wanted to hurt me she could have by now. But she hasn't.'

'What about the shadow thing, watching you when you come back into the room?' Dad asked.

'I think that's her, too. Waiting for me to return to myself – trying to make contact.' I remembered the ghost of Eric Williams, the shift of form from the dying boy in the cell to the shadow whispering to me. And I remembered the spirit of the boy at Past Lives. *It wasn't my time . . .*

He hadn't chosen to die. But Tess was different. I was starting to understand that while she may not have wanted to die, she hadn't wanted to live, either. But then I had to ask whether she regretted that decision. Had she had a last-minute change of heart, after she'd already cut too deep? When it was too late?

273

'I need to know about her, Dad. If I just knew *something* it could help me break through.'

Dad's head was in his hands. 'I don't know much more than you do – mostly gossip about how she did it and that she was here for days before anyone found her. The only person I ever spoke to who was here at the same time as Tess was Mrs Mardle.' He lifted his head suddenly, a spark of something in his expression.

'What is it?' I asked.

'She said something once, soon after we moved in. It was probably nothing, but she seemed so insistent . . .'

'Tell me.'

'She said she'd called Tess several times across the green one day to give her a letter that had come through her door by mistake. At first she thought Tess was ignoring her, but as she got closer she tapped Tess on the arm. It apparently frightened the life out of her.'

'I don't understand.'

'Mrs Mardle thought the reason Tess wasn't answering wasn't because she didn't hear, but because she didn't realise she was being called.' Dad paused. 'She was convinced Tess Fielding wasn't her real name. Do you think it's important?'

'I don't know. Maybe.' I gripped the arm of the chair. 'I need you to do something for me.'

He nodded. 'What?'

'Just . . . stay here. Don't leave this room.'

'Where are you going?'

'Technically, nowhere.' I put my empty plate down on the carpet beside the sofa and lay down, reclining on my back. 'I'm going to sleep. I'm going to try to find her while it's light and while you're here. While I'm not afraid.'

'Are you sure about this?'

'No. But I've got to try. And I need your word that you won't leave this room. Not for a minute. Promise?'

'I won't move, I promise. But . . . there's just one thing I don't understand. Why her – why Tess? Why not your mum?'

I turned my head to look at him. He looked so sad, so broken.

'I don't know, Dad,' I told him. 'But I think . . . I think it's a good thing. They don't stay unless they need to. Mum said her goodbyes. She was ready, even if we weren't.'

He nodded and glanced away, but not before I saw his eyes glistening.

'I should have listened to you before. I'm sorry.'

'You're listening now. That's all that matters.' I turned away again to face the ceiling, allowing my eyelids to fall closed. They were so heavy, despite the increased thudding of my heart.

I was ready.

TWENTY-FIVE

Lucid

I fell into sleep almost immediately. It began with paralysis, which I'd been hoping to avoid. If Tess appeared I didn't want to feel trapped.

She didn't show, but that didn't mean she wasn't here. I fought my heavy limbs, familiar panic rising in my chest. Through half-open eyes I viewed the living room and forced myself to remember my breathing. In, out. In, out.

This is my choice . . . I chose this.

From my position I saw the TV playing a soap, the living-room window reflected in the screen. I heard a lapping noise down by the side of the sofa where I'd left my plate. The cat was licking the gravy up. The sound was stupidly comforting. And Dad, still in his chair, his legs stretched across the carpet. I heard the crackle of newspaper, smelled the struck match as he lit a cigarette.

As the fear left me I started to relax. My thumb twitched. One by one I flexed my fingers. The paralysis was over, but I had to take care not to wake up completely, nor go to sleep completely. I had to stay lucid.

I imagined, then felt, the lucid part of me sit up. Looking around the room . . . walking to the door. Looking back at Dad, at myself . . . and I was out. Moving lightly over the carpet, I stared at my sleeping body, taking a moment to remind myself that I was safe, with Dad. Then I stepped into the hall.

The bathroom door was open. I went to it and found it empty.

'Tess?' I whispered. Nothing answered me. Part of me was relieved, another part disappointed. I'd only half expected to find her – why should I, when she always appeared at three in the morning? I wandered along the hallway, preparing myself for wet footprints. None appeared.

The atmosphere shifted. Became colder, damper. Dead.

She was here.

A muffled sob echoed from back down the hallway. I turned and edged towards it, fear tightening like a band around my chest. Water vapour crept underneath the bathroom door and rose. I moved past the bathroom, my back flat against the wall. The living-room door was open. My body lay sprawled on the sofa, eyes closed. Dad hadn't moved. Warmth and light radiated from the room, beckoning me. It would be so easy to go in. Escape was just a few steps away.

There would be no escape for Tess if I turned my back on her. I knew that. She'd be here for ever, trapped.

I turned my back.

On Dad, on myself, and on my own fear. I stepped away from the living room and went towards the bathroom, my hand stretched out. The door opened soundlessly beneath my fingers. Damp air curled around me, rising from the bathtub. I heard rushing water before I saw anything. The bath was running, but the sound was weaker than the sobs that filled the small space. I wanted to close my eyes, but forced myself to look into the water. It was empty.

A face loomed out of the mist, startlingly close. I let out a cry and staggered backwards, clutching for the door handle. Its

277

features were twisted, the eyes dark with pain. Another sob escaped her mouth.

I forced myself to let go of the door. The mist cleared a little, though the water continued to fall into the bathtub. She stood there trembling, half undressed.

'Your name isn't Tess, is it?' I whispered. 'I . . . I'm ready to listen to you now.'

Slowly, she reached her pale hands towards me. I braced myself, preparing not to flinch at the sight of her wrists – but this time they were intact.

I glanced at the bath, the water still running.

She hasn't done it yet.

'Talk to me,' I said softly.

She shook her head. Tears held her eyelashes together in thick, dark spikes. 'Come with me,' she whispered. 'I'll show you.'

'Come with you where?' I asked.

She raised a finger to her lips. The other hand remained in front of me. I reached through the tendrils of steam before I could change my mind. Her skin felt like chilled meat. Her fingers closed around mine. The bathroom walls peeled back on themselves like fruit to reveal another layer, an older layer, beneath. The cream paint became mildewed wallpaper. The plain blind split down the middle into pale-green curtains. The mirror above the sink grew outwards and upwards, framed by plastic instead of wood. The layout was the same, but I was no longer looking at the bathroom I shared with Dad.

I was looking at Tess's bathroom.

TWENTY-SIX

Shedding Skins

Her grip on my hand intensified. She brushed past me through the door and I stumbled after her into the hall. It too was different, but I barely had time to glance around as she tugged me onwards to the front door. It opened before we reached it and, instead of the grey concrete floors and faded walls of the communal stairwell, we walked out into a warm, wide room with low, dark beams. Instantly I saw that we were in a pub, but it wasn't one that I knew. I glanced behind me, but the flat had vanished and been replaced by tables and chairs dotting the alcoves, some occupied and some not. The place hummed with low chatter and, beside an open fire, a Christmas tree twinkled in a corner.

Tess led me past it to a couple sitting in an otherwise empty partition. They leaned towards each other confidentially, speaking in low voices. As we neared, I saw that the girl seated at the table looked familiar. It took a few seconds to realise that it was Tess – or whoever she had once been. The version in front of me was younger, about twenty, with shorter, reddish-coloured hair. The man seated opposite was blond and rugged. He looked older than her, in his early-thirties if I had to guess. He had the wine list open in front of him, and as his hand ran down the page a gold band on his finger glinted.

The other Tess noticed it, too.

'Do you have to wear that when you're with me?'

He glanced up. 'What do you want me to do – take it off when-ever we're together? Risk losing it and face more questions?' His voice was low. 'That's how mistakes are made, Lorna. I can't afford any more mistakes – she's already suspicious.' He reached across the table for her hand. 'Look, I know it's hard. I hate all this sneaking around as much as you do – I'm living a lie. Deceiving everyone—'

'So end it!' Her fingers turned white around his. 'Do what you promised you'd do two months ago.'

'Don't you think I want to? I'm in agony here! My boys have just lost their grandmother – I can't leave now. I need to wait until everything's settled. Then I'll tell her and we can be together. For good.'

'How long?'

'It depends. Six months, maybe.'

'Six *months*?'

'Maybe sooner – I don't know.'

'Robert, I can't do this any more. It's wrong.' She pulled her hand away and stood up, grabbing her coat from the back of the chair.

'Where are you going? Look, at least stay for one drink—'

'No. One drink will lead to two and then I won't leave. And I have to, for my own good.' Her eyes shone with tears. 'I'm not being the other woman any more. I want more.'

'Lorna, I'm begging you – don't go. I need you.'

She buttoned up her coat. 'I'm going now,' she said softly. 'But I'm giving you one last chance. I'll be here at this time exactly a year from today. If you want to see me again you'll be here, too.'

She looked him in the eye. 'You won't be wearing that ring. Until then you don't contact me at all. Do you understand?'

'I . . .' He rubbed a hand over the lower part of his face. 'A *year*?'

'That should be plenty of time for you to make up your mind. Goodbye, Robert.' She fastened her last button and shook her hair over her collar, then left without looking back.

He remained at the table, staring at the wine list. At the top of the sheet the name of the pub was proclaimed in a fancy script: *The Mask and Mirror.*

He was still staring at it when a waitress came and stood next to the table.

'Would you like any help choosing, sir?' she asked.

'No. Thank you.' He stood up and shrugged into his coat. 'I'm afraid I need to cancel the room I booked. The reservation's in the name of Bradley. Robert Bradley.'

In silence we followed him as he walked to the exit. Icy air blasted in. He stepped out into the night and, with the slam of the door, the scene changed again.

This time Tess and I were in a plain room, which at first I thought was a cheap hotel. As I looked round it became clear that it was a hostel. Opposite a single bed was a washbasin and, next to that, a tiny kitchenette. The room was light: the windows were thrown open in an attempt to draw a breeze into the warm space. Through them I saw busy roads below and trees and flowers in bloom. The old Tess – or Lorna – stood by the window with a glass of water. She looked like she hadn't eaten properly or seen the sun in weeks.

The glass slipped through her fingers at the sound of a knock. She stepped over the puddle of water and glass fragments, and crept to the door. 'Yes?'

281

A deep voice filtered into the room. 'Miss Clements? It's Detective Sergeant Lockwood.'

She fumbled the chain and slid back two bolts. A large man in plain clothes stepped into the room. She pointed him to a chair and he sat while she bolted the door again.

'How are you doing?' he asked.

'How do you think?'

'Sorry. Stupid question.'

'I just want tomorrow over with. Are you sure I need to be hidden away like this? It's making me more nervous.' She collected a dustpan and knelt to sweep the broken glass.

'Miss Clements, I—'

'That makes me nervous, too. Just call me Lorna.'

He hesitated, wiping moisture from his forehead. 'Lorna. I'm afraid it's essential that you're here until the trial's over. As the key witness, your evidence is vital. We told you from the start that what you saw would place your life in danger if you were to testify—'

Her head snapped up. 'I saw my sister killed – no, *executed* – in front of my eyes. What kind of person would I be to let that bastard get away with it?'

Lockwood sighed. 'Some would.'

'I want him behind bars.'

'That's what I'm here to tell you.' Lockwood's voice was gentle. 'We've had intelligence through which suggests that Billy Lynch has put a price on your head whether a conviction is brought against him or not. With his contacts we've reason to take the threat seriously. If you testify tomorrow, your life as you know it will be over.'

She dropped the dustpan. 'What are you saying?'

'I'm saying that if you go ahead you'd be unwise to go back to your old life. Our advice would be for you to accept police protection – permanently. That would mean a new identity, new home, new *everything*, far away from here. It would mean telling only the essential few that you're leaving. They wouldn't be allowed to know where you were going, or any details about your new identity. Contact – letters, phone calls, visits – would be severely restricted and monitored.'

'Why are you saying this?' she whispered.

'I'm stating the facts. Your sister got involved with the wrong man and she knew too much. It cost her her life. It could cost you yours, too. But you have a choice: walk away and he goes free. Or testify and run.'

'*Choice?* What choice? If Billy walks, I lose. If I disappear, I still lose. And I don't think my father's heart can take either outcome. He's already lost one daughter. Now I have to tell him her killer goes free or he loses the other one.' She laughed bitterly. 'Some choice.'

Lockwood stood up and touched her shoulder. 'You have until morning to decide. A car will collect you either way.'

'I've already decided.' Her voice was low and steady. 'I'll go on the stand. Billy Lynch can rot in jail.' She got to her feet and walked Lockwood to the door. As it opened the air cooled and the light in the room changed to late evening. The two figures vanished then reappeared from the opposite side of the door, this time dressed formally.

'We don't have much time,' said Lockwood. 'Get changed and packed. Leave anything you can do without.' He went to the window and tactfully looked out as Lorna stripped off the cream suit she was wearing and stepped into jeans and a shirt. She began throwing stuff into a large hold-all: clothes, hair brush, purse.

'Do you think he'll go down?'

Lockwood shrugged. 'It's in the hands of the jury now. But with your evidence I don't see how they can clear him.' He smiled. 'You did well.'

She zipped the bag and put on a cap. 'Where am I going?'

'We won't know until we're *en route*. All I know at this stage is your new name, which you'll have to adopt as soon as we leave this room.'

Her voice trembled. 'Which is?'

Lockwood turned to face her. 'Sally Painter.'

Her jaw clenched. 'And when do I get to say my goodbyes?'

'You don't. You leave tonight and once we reach our destination your father will be contacted and informed of the decision to move you.'

'I don't get to see him before—'

'I'm sorry. The same goes for your close friend Sarah. Your employer will be contacted also.' He paused. 'Is there anyone else?'

She lowered her gaze. 'Yes.' Her voice was a whisper. 'A . . . a man. We were involved.'

Lockwood frowned. 'You never mentioned anyone.'

'He's married.' She looked ashamed. 'We broke it off. I haven't seen him since just before New Year's Eve. Before all this happened.'

'Does this man . . . have a family?' he asked. 'Children?'

'Yes.'

He sighed. 'Miss Clements – Lorna – my advice to you is to let him go. Start afresh. We wouldn't be taking these measures if we didn't feel that it's not just your safety, but those you're connected with, too. Any leak of information could prove disastrous – not just for yourself.' He looked grave. 'Those children need their father. You don't need me to spell out what Billy Lynch is capable of.'

A tear dropped on to her cheek. 'I know. I'm ready now.'

Lockwood smiled sadly. 'Say goodbye to Lorna Clements.'

She wiped her face. 'I just did.'

The room swayed around us. I was aware of Tess's hand, still clamped around mine as the vision shifted and took us somewhere else, but this time, what I saw and what I heard didn't go together.

I saw Robert Bradley sitting alone at a table, checking his watch. He was thinner in the face and his wedding ring was gone. Behind him was a Christmas tree and another table with a family seated there. I didn't hear their words or laughter. Instead two other voices, high-pitched and angry, played out in my head.

'I don't want to go to Essex. I hate it!'

'It's not negotiable. Your identity has been compromised somehow and you're at risk. Are you sure you haven't called anyone, anyone from . . . before?'

Her voice was tiny. *'I never spoke. I just let him answer, so I could hear his voice—'*

'Jesus, Sally!'

'I was lonely! I've got no one, now Dad's gone. How can I make friends, talk to anyone, when I'm so terrified I'm going to slip up?'

'Do you know how much work has gone into protecting you? How many lives are at stake? Billy Lynch is plotting your murder from his prison cell right now, in case you've forgotten, and you risk it all for what? Another woman's husband who's probably shacked up with someone else by now.'

'He wasn't like that—'

'It doesn't matter how he was. It's over. OVER. You've got twenty minutes to get your things together. Then you shed this skin and become someone new.'

'Another life built on lies.' I felt the defeat in her voice. 'Who am I this time?'

'Your name will be Tess Fielding.'

Tess Fielding.

The name brought us crashing back into the last place in Lorna's memory. The bathroom. The suicide room.

Her grip on my hand loosened. My arm fell to my side, cold and numb. The air was clear of steam and the bathwater was still as a millpond. I didn't recall her turning off the taps. My vision of her shuddered and, for a moment, the bathroom merged with its present day version – mine and Dad's version.

A new panic shook me. I was in danger of waking up. I focused on the mildewed wallpaper, pushing the version I knew away.

The bathroom wavered, then reverted. When I looked back at Tess she was naked, stepping into the bath. Her foot, so pale it was almost blue, broke the water's surface. It didn't ripple as she slid under it.

'Tess – Lorna,' I said, 'I'm running out of time. And I still don't understand. You have to tell me what you want me to do. Is it something to do with Robert, is that it?'

A tear travelled over her cheek and fell, meeting the bathwater.

'Yes,' she whispered. 'Robert . . .'

'You still love him? Is that what's keeping you here?'

She looked at me with hopeless eyes. I watched her hand reach for the razor, doomed to play out until the end.

'No, not yet . . . Tess, please don't . . .'

'I'll always love him.' She lifted the blade, watching the light play along its edges. 'But I let him go a long time ago. When I became Tess.'

'So what is it?' I urged, desperate to avert my eyes from the razor but unable to. 'Why are you here?'

'Because *he* won't let *me* go. He doesn't know what happened to me.' She brought the blade closer to her skin. A dot of red appeared on her fingertip. 'And he's searching for the wrong girl. She doesn't exist any more. He needs to move on . . . before I can.'

'You want me to find him? To tell him what happened to you?'

'Yes.'

'All right . . . I'll do it!'

Swear it.

The voice – *her* voice – came from inside my head.

'I swear – I'll find him!' I yelled, backing away from the bathtub. 'Just *please* – stop hurting yourself!'

'One last time,' she whispered. Her arms moved under the surface. The clear water clouded. She leaned back, her expression content. 'It doesn't hurt any more.'

The bathroom wavered – and Tess with it. Choking on tears I retreated, pressing through the bathroom door and away from the cold. The living room drew me in with its warmth. Dad stood over my sleeping body, hesitating. I sank to my knees, reaching my hand towards my face, willing myself to wake up.

My eyes opened to Dad's face looming in mine. 'You're awake, finally. I was getting worried,' he said.

'I'm awake. I'm back.' Tears leaked down my cheeks.

'Elliott?' Dad said, his voice low. 'Is it over? Did you . . . find her?'

'Yes. I have to do something for her. Deliver a message. But I think that's it . . . I think she's gone. I sprang up, wiping my eyes, and ran to the bathroom, pushing the door open.

The water in the bath was deadly still, as though frozen over. I stood quietly for a moment. Then I plunged my hand into the icy bathwater.

'I hope you're at rest now, Lorna,' I whispered, pulling the plug. 'I'll keep my promise. I don't know how yet, but I will.'

The water gurgled and sucked away down the plug. And over it, I heard the faintest of noises. A peaceful sigh.

TWENTY-SEVEN

Intruder

I slept, deeply and dreamlessly and better than I had in a long time. So well, in fact, that I woke groggy rather than refreshed. I downed my first – and what I vowed would be my last – coffee of the day, took a long, hot shower, and ate breakfast alone before setting off early for work. Though still tired, the knowledge that I was now free of Tess was a burden lifted, but already I was wondering how to tackle my new problem: finding Robert Bradley. All I had to go on was his name and the name of the pub in Tess's memory: The Mask and Mirror. I tried not to think about how far away it might be, or if it was even still there.

I drove a different route than I normally took, taking a small turning off the high street instead of heading straight to the motorway. I hadn't wanted to think about it last night after my small victory, but deep down I knew I couldn't rely on Dad to act as a safety net every time I went to sleep. I had to find other ways – and I'd decided that my first stop would be the cemetery. I'd come prepared with a jar to scoop some graveyard dirt into, hoping I'd arrived early enough to avoid an audience.

Unfortunately, I was *too* early. The gates were still locked.

I swivelled on to the drive anyway, manoeuvring the car around in the opposite direction. For a moment I held the brake, staring through the iron railings. The place was more overgrown than I remembered. The last time I'd come here was under duress and well before the accident. I hadn't planned on returning and, now I was here, I felt guilty that it was with another agenda. I put the car in gear and sped off.

The next set of gates I stopped at were those at Past Lives. With my staff card clamped between my teeth I rolled down the window, ready to swipe it – then froze.

A figure appeared seemingly out of nowhere, blurred through the early-morning mist. I recognised the tasselled suede jacket and spiky hair instantly. But whatever I'd gained in sleep last night, Lesley Travis appeared to have lost. His expression was tormented. He leaned heavily on his stick, the clicking muffled by the grass beneath it. He lowered his face to my window.

'I've been waiting for you,' he croaked. 'I hoped you'd turn up today. I was just about to go.'

I snatched the card from my teeth. 'What do you want?'

'Got something for you—'

A furious roar erupted nearby. Lesley's head snapped to the side, his eyes squinting past the gates.

'Oh, no . . .'

A stocky figure was running full pelt towards us. Though silhouetted by the sun I knew as well as Lesley did that it was Hodge.

'Here!'

His hand came through the window without warning, wrinkled and brown and paw-like. My skin crawled. There was something in his fingers; I caught a glimpse of feathers and a slash of red before he dropped it and fled.

'What the hell—?' I yelled. I leaped out of the car, brushing the thing off me. My swipe card flew out of my hand. Lesley hobbled off down the lane, grunting like a madman with each step.

'HEY!' Hodge bellowed after him, slamming through the gates. 'I told you not to come back, you bloody lunatic!'

Lesley vanished beyond the bushes. Hodge stamped to a halt. A vein had risen in his temple and once again I was reminded of a stalk on a ripe tomato.

'If he wasn't a cripple already I'd make him one,' he said, his chest heaving. 'What did he say to you?'

'Not a lot.' I gestured to the ground. 'He threw something at me. It rolled under the car when I got out. I think . . . it looked like a dead bird.' I knelt and peered below the door. Hodge bent down beside me, craning his neck.

'There.' He pointed to the wheel.

Something small and round huddled beside the tyre. Stomach churning, I reached for it. It gave beneath my touch, not solid as I expected, but light. I gasped as it suddenly unravelled in my fingers, and I dropped it once more, wiping my hand against my jeans to get rid of the feel of it.

We stared at it in silence. I'd been right about the feathers. Small and brown, they were knotted into three pieces of string. One strand was black, another blue and a third – which I'd mistaken for blood – red. My initial relief at realising that it wasn't a dead bird was rapidly disappearing. Instead it was replaced with dread. There was something indescribably menacing about the object.

'What is that thing?' I whispered.

Hodge's eyes were wide. He grabbed a nearby twig, using it to lift the thing up. Unfurled, it was about the same length as one of my feet.

291

'Nine knots,' he said quietly, lowering it. 'Each with a hen's feather tied into it.'

'Do you know what it is?' I asked.

He nodded. 'It's a witch's ladder.'

The words were like a malevolent spell spoken into my ear.

'I've seen one before, a few years ago. It was found during some restorative work on Calthorpe House, hidden below a doorstep. We don't know who made it but it supports the theory that someone in the house – most likely Alice Calthorpe – was unpopular. Hated.'

I stared at the witch's ladder. The feathers danced in the breeze, as though malice had breathed life into them. 'Hated?'

'It's a form of cursing someone. Each knot is made with a hex . . . a wish for some kind of injury or illness, even death.' He let out an angry breath. 'Crazy old fool.' He glanced at me. 'But why would Lesley Travis want to harm *you*? Have you even spoken to him before?'

'No,' I lied.

'No, of course not.' Hodge's face darkened. 'He probably meant for you to give it to me. Did he say anything when he threw it?'

I've been waiting for you . . .

'He didn't have time to. As soon as I saw him you appeared.'

Hodge scooped it up again, still using the twig.

'What are you going to do with it?' I asked.

'I know what I'd *like* to do with it, but unfortunately it's not legal.' He paused. 'In the old days they believed that each knot had to be undone to release the curse, but I think the fire will do.' He scowled and got up. 'If only for the enjoyment of watching hours of his work go up in flames.'

I felt his hand on my shoulder.

292

'Sorry about all this,' he muttered. 'I expect with what you saw in the orchard, and now curses being thrown at you, things are feeling strange here.'

'A bit.'

He took his hand away. 'If you don't want to do this week's ghost walk, I'll understand. It's probably not the best thing if you're feeling jittery.'

The ghost walk. I'd almost forgotten about it – it was tomorrow. I didn't want to do it, but Hodge offering me an easy way out niggled me. If I accepted it was like admitting weakness, admitting defeat. And I still had enough pride left to defend it.

'I'll think about it.'

I got back in my car, not knowing what else to do. I couldn't exactly tell Hodge the truth: that the witch's ladder had been meant for me. If I did he'd know I'd been sniffing around The Sanctuary. I picked my card up off the seat and swiped it. The car lurched through the gates. Hodge remained standing outside, the string and feathers still fluttering from the twig like a dying bird.

Not once had he touched it with his bare hands.

I parked, but stayed in the car, willing my racing pulse to slow. I watched in the rear-view mirror as more staff turned up, yawning and clutching steaming flasks.

Crazy old fool.

He hadn't seemed crazy yesterday. Afraid, maybe. But today he'd seemed manic. Unhinged. I couldn't decide whether to feel angry or sorry for him. Either way I'd picked the wrong person to ask for help. I wasn't sure I believed in curses, but if Lesley did then maybe the witch's ladder had exorcised whatever fear he harboured towards me.

I switched the radio on, glad of something normal to listen to. A song I liked by a now-defunct band was playing and I leaned back against the headrest and shut my eyes, trying to calm myself. I still had a couple of minutes before I needed to go and get changed.

It was warm inside the car. Sunlight filtered through the trees leaning over the car park and dappled the insides of my eyelids. My thoughts drifted, became muzzy . . .

Scratching. A jumbled confusion of words and sounds. My eyes flew open and I tried to reach for the garbled radio. My hand remained in my lap, unresponsive. My body stayed frozen.

Not again.

The radio settled suddenly, blaring out a song I didn't recognise:

> *'Sometimes I sense I'm not alone*
> *Still hear your voice, it's as real as my own.*
> *Echoes of the past stir my dreams,*
> *They told me time heals, they were wrong it would seem . . .'*

I caught a movement in the rear-view mirror. Someone was in the backseat.

'Who's there?' I tried to say. The word emerged shapeless, a weak hiss of air.

Dark eyes fixed on mine.

'*You . . .*' Another useless word left my lips as I struggled against the paralysis.

The boy stared back at me, tears streaking through the dirt crusted on to his cheeks. His eyes reddened and bulged. Blood vessels swelled. He was choking . . . and so was I.

I couldn't see the rope but I could feel it, thin and deadly, crushing my windpipe. If I could just get my fingers to my throat then maybe I stood a chance but fear had me gripped even more firmly than the rope did. My vision flickered and blurred. Still I saw the soil spilling out of his mouth . . . tasted it in my own. Thick, gritty, earthy. Something fleshy and alive writhed its way over my lips. I felt it hit my thighs and coughed, spraying the windscreen with dirt and tiny white grubs. Maggots. My stomach heaved.

I felt his voice by my ear, a cold draught.

'*Leave.*'

The rope tightened another notch. My vision reddened. Blackened. Vomit rose in my already-tight throat, prevented from entering my mouth by the rope holding it down. I wanted nothing more than to be away from this, from myself. For the pain to end.

'*Go.*'

And I didn't care where. I just had to get out, anywhere. With the last of my strength I pushed my consciousness out and away, clawing through the car and falling to my knees on the gravel. The pressure on my throat eased instantly. I brought my hands up and felt only my skin. There was no rope. I got up and looked back into the car. My half-sleeping body reclined on the seat, eyes open a crack. There was no rope, no dirt. The windscreen was clear of earth and squirming maggots.

And the backseat was empty.

I have to get back in . . .

Too late.

The me in the car twitched. Blinked. Then sat forward and stared in the mirror at myself – *itself* – touching its face. In awe, in wonder.

I thumped the side of the car ineffectually and tried grasping the door handles. 'Get out. GET OUT!'

The door creaked open. My body climbed out and stood up, watching me warily.

'Get out,' I repeated, gritting my teeth.

'I am out,' he said, in that rasping voice I remembered. That voice that wasn't used to speaking . . . or perhaps just found it too painful because of an injury inflicted long ago.

'You know what I mean. Get out of *me*.'

He didn't respond but merely looked up, drinking in the sky with his eyes the same way he had drunk in the rain before.

'It was *you*,' I whispered. 'You were the one that got into me before. And you were the one in the orchard . . . Sebastian.'

He flinched at the name, his eyes finding mine.

'You can't stay,' I shouted. 'You can't do this – you've got no right!'

'I was like you, once,' he said softly. 'Then I became *this*. I was only a boy.'

'I can help you,' I said. 'But not like this. Tell me how to help you. Tell me what you want.'

He held his hands – my hands – out either side of him, like he was holding the air itself. '*This*,' he said simply. 'And revenge.'

'But you can't —'

Footsteps approached in the gravel behind me. I saw Sebastian look up and I turned.

Ophelia stood there, shielding her eyes against the sun. 'What are you doing here?' she asked, staring at Sebastian. 'Do you know what time it is?'

For the first time I realised the car park was empty of people apart from us. I glanced through the car window at the dash. It was after ten.

'I'm sorry,' he said. 'I . . . must have fallen asleep.'

'Hodge sent me looking for you,' she said, moving closer to him.

'No,' I whispered, helpless. 'That's not me. That's not *me* . . .'

'You scared me yesterday.' Her voice was soft.

'I did?'

She reached out and brushed a strand of hair away from his eyes. 'Yeah. That dream you had in the orchard. About the hanged boy.'

Sebastian's eyes glanced my way, then back at Ophelia. 'Just a dream,' he whispered, catching her hand.

'I missed you,' she said, leaning into him. Her arms twined around his neck. 'I mean, I know it was only yesterday that I saw you, but . . .'

His hands moved around her waist. He bent his head, inhaling her hair. 'I missed you, too.'

I felt as though a snake had taken nest in my stomach and was slowly eating its way to my heart. 'Get away from her, you bastard,' I whispered. 'I'm warning you. If you *touch* her . . .'

But he was already touching her. And I couldn't stand it.

'Your voice sounds croaky,' she murmured in his ear. I watched her lips trail his neck.

He looked over her shoulder at me. 'I've got a sore throat.'

Her fingers snagged in his hair, pulling his mouth to hers. I watched, every kiss a punch in the gut. He reached up her back and tugged her hair loose from its knot. It tumbled free, golden in the sunshine. Suddenly he was spinning her round, pushing her up against the car.

'What are you doing?' she mumbled through his kisses. 'Someone might see.'

'I want you.' His breath clouded the air.

'Not here. We have to go . . . We're late already . . .'

I couldn't bear it a second longer. Watching her in the arms of this creature, this stranger with my face. I swung out with my fists, aiming for his head. Each blow passed through him like air through a cobweb.

'You think she wants this?' I yelled. 'Your hands all over her? It's me she wants. *Me!* You're nothing, do you hear me? Nothing but a parasite!'

My words were as useless as my fists. Tears of rage burned my eyes. I would have taken a thousand beatings to get her away from him, to protect her. Instead I could only watch as his lips crushed into hers with each kiss hungrier, needier. 'How long have you been watching her?' I spat in his ear. 'How long? You probably watched her growing up, didn't you? You sick, twisted—'

His tongue snaked along her top lip and entered her mouth. Her eyes opened wide, and her hands came down on his shoulders. Pushing, forcing him away.

'Elliott, I'm sorry – I . . .'

She stopped as Sebastian staggered, off balance. I watched, transfixed as he took another step back. For a second he appeared almost drunk. Streams of vapour curled away from him, twisting and writhing into the air. He toppled, and in that second I saw my eyes deaden. Sebastian had vacated my body, leaving it about to crash to the ground.

I rushed at it, fierce with rage. Claiming it with everything I had. Forcing myself in. It wasn't enough to save me completely. I went to my knees, landing heavily on the gravel, biting my tongue on impact.

Ophelia stood over me, her hand on my shoulder. 'Elliott, what's happening – do you need me to get someone?'

'No.' I stood up shakily, eyes darting around for any sign of Sebastian. Even though there was none I doubted he could be far away. Despite the morning chill, my skin was damp with sweat at the thought of him watching us.

'You don't look too good,' she said, uncertain.

'Head rush.' I breathed in a lungful of cold air. I felt feverish and spaced out, like there was some kind of virus in my body.

Or the remnants of a parasite.

'I just got a bit . . . carried away there.'

She nodded and looked away, rubbing her fingers over her lips. There was a look on her face that I didn't recognise or understand, and it bothered me.

I swallowed with difficulty. It hurt to talk all of a sudden and I realised my throat felt tender.

I watched as Ophelia swept her hair back and fastened it once more. She wouldn't meet my eyes. 'Come on. We're late enough.'

'Ophelia, wait.' I reached for her hand. 'I'm sorry. I didn't mean to upset you.'

Her gloves were soft under my fingers.

'You didn't upset me.' Her expression softened but I still couldn't read it.

'Then what?' I hesitated. Had she sensed there was something not right? That those kisses hadn't been mine? 'Why did you push me away?'

She let out a long, slow breath. 'You just . . . nothing. Forget it.' She turned her face up to mine and stared at my mouth. 'You didn't do anything wrong. I thought someone might see us, that's all.'

I wanted to kiss her, badly, but didn't dare to. I couldn't risk her pushing me away again. She tugged my hand and we walked, more slowly than we should have, away from the car park towards the museum entrance. We stopped outside the Old Barn, awkward and wordless for a shade too long.

'Meet me for lunch?' I asked.

She nodded. 'Where?'

'Anywhere but the orchard.' I tried to smile. 'Let's drive out somewhere, like I said before.'

'All right.'

We parted, still awkward but with little else I could do about it. I entered the door code and went upstairs, changing clothes and dumping everything else in my locker. The costume hung heavily on me, itching. Sweat poured off me and I couldn't seem to cool down. I went back past the changing rooms to the washroom, rolling up my sleeves and splashing cold water on my face. It helped a little.

I turned off the tap and stared at myself in the mirror. My eyes were bloodshot and felt gritty, but in a different way than usual. I was used to feeling tired but now it almost felt like I had sand in my eyes.

Or dirt.

I shuddered, undoing my top button to loosen the high collar. And then I leaned closer to the glass, my hands gripping the sides of the basin.

'Oh, my God . . .'

The thin red line on my neck stood out starkly against the pale skin. As I watched, it deepened in colour, a mixture of bruised and chafed flesh. The outline of a thin rope, pulled tightly and cruelly, was unmistakable.

The sweat on my skin chilled from within. I fumbled with my top button, fastening it again, then backed away from the mirror until I hit the door.

'No,' I whispered. 'What are you doing to me?'

A word echoed in my head: *Parasite, parasite, parasite.*

I'd thought it couldn't get worse than watching Ophelia being violated, *molested* without her knowledge . . . but this came a close second. I too, had been violated. Used. And now I wore someone else's marks, someone else's injuries.

I squeezed my eyes shut. Sebastian wanted revenge, but how could something dead for five centuries avenge itself? Unlike Tess, there was no one from his time still living, no one I could help bring to justice for their actions against him. In any case, revenge wasn't the same as justice. And perhaps Sebastian didn't care who paid, only that *someone* did.

I remembered his face as he'd reached out to Ophelia in the orchard.

Mine.

I'd assumed he was pushing her *away,* attempting to prolong the contact he'd made with me. Now I reconsidered. He could just as easily have been reaching out for her.

Staking his claim.

TWENTY-EIGHT

The Witch's Ladder

I stirred milk into the stewed tea and scratched my thumbnail over a chip in the mug.

'What would you do if he came back?' I asked.

Ophelia looked up from her omelette. 'Who?'

'The boy you were seeing. Sean.'

She put her fork down and wiped her mouth. I envied her appetite. I'd hardly touched my own food.

'Why are you asking about him?'

I took a mouthful of tea, wishing it were coffee. 'No reason. I was just thinking of that night.' My voice was hidden beneath chatter and the clattering of plates. 'With the gun, and Vince and everything. I came to this café the next morning with Adam and Amy after the police let me go.'

She stared at her plate. 'Oh.'

'You said to Vince that he'd run away before,' I persisted.

'He did. He was underage the first time. They found him and brought him back. If anything it made him more determined.' She smiled faintly. 'He said he'd make sure he got it right the next time. Disappear for good.'

'Sounds like he gave it a lot of thought.'

She shrugged. 'With a family like his I didn't blame him.'

'Vince seemed pretty rough.'

'They all were. His younger brothers were little toe-rags, and their dad was a bigger one. Knocked them all about, according to Sean. I felt sorry for their mum. She got the worst of it – Vince and Sean used to try and protect her, but they just got thumped as well. I lost count of the times he turned up with a fat lip.'

'Do you know where he is?'

'No.'

'You knew he was going though, didn't you?'

She picked up her fork again and began crushing the remainder of her food into the plate with it.

'God, Ophelia. You bloody *did*, didn't you?'

She let the fork fall. 'Yes, all right? I knew. Can we drop it, please?'

'But why not tell that to Vince and Nina? Why not get them off your back?'

'Because I was meant to go with him!'

'*What?*'

She looked up finally, her eyes clouded with pain. 'We were going to leave together, get out of here for good. Make a fresh start where no one knew us. He wanted to leave his family's reputation behind and I wanted to experience life for once without being wrapped up in cotton wool by Hodge and Una.' She shook her head. 'Don't get me wrong, I'm grateful for everything they've done, but it's like they don't want me to grow up, ever. Not Una, so much. But Hodge – he treats me like a little girl because that's what he wants me to be. His little girl. He can't accept me growing. *Changing*.'

I stared at her, dumbstruck. The truth – or the partial truth – was that I'd asked to distract myself from thinking of what had happened in the car park this morning. The rest of it, which I hadn't consciously known until this moment was that I wondered where I'd stand with Ophelia if Sean came back. Now I wished I'd never opened my mouth.

'Can we go?' she muttered.

I nodded, peeling a note out of my wallet and leaving it beneath my still-full mug. We left the café and walked to the car further up the street in silence, slamming the doors in unison. But the subject was like a scab I couldn't stop picking.

'I think you should tell Vince where Sean is. If only for their mum's sake—'

'I've already said I don't *know*,' she snapped.

'If you were going with him you must know.'

'We hadn't thought that far. I mean – *I* wanted to but he said it was best we didn't. If we made plans like that they could be found out. His only worry was to get as much money as we could before we left. He said if we had money, we had options. So we saved every penny.'

'So why didn't you go?' I asked. 'Cold feet?'

'No.'

'Then what?'

'I'd packed,' she said softly. 'I waited, like he told me. And he didn't show.'

I exhaled sharply. 'He went without you?'

'I guess he decided it'd be easier on his own.' She faced me, her eyes shimmering. 'Especially with my share of the cash.' She laughed bitterly. 'That's right, I was that stupid. *That* gullible. And that's why I haven't told anyone I was supposed to go with him.'

I tried to imagine Ophelia a year ago. Full of hope, waiting to escape. Waiting for her life to really start. A life without me.

'I'm glad you didn't.' My voice was hoarse. 'I know that's selfish. I'm sorry – I didn't mean to drag it all up and upset you.'

'You didn't.'

I hesitated. 'Do you miss him?'

'I used to.'

'What if . . . What if he came back?'

'He won't. Even if he did . . . Things are different now.'

'Like how?'

'You're here.'

'And?'

'And I hope you carry on being here.'

I reached across the back of her seat, threading my fingers into the soft hair at her nape. 'Ophelia.' Did that trembling voice really belong to me? 'You know I'm falling for you, don't you?'

She turned her face into my hand. 'I bet you say that to all the girls.'

'I've never said it to anyone.' I traced her cheekbone with my thumb. She closed her eyes, and I realised I could have sat there all day, counting every one of those fair lashes. 'I've never felt it before.'

With her eyes still closed she leaned into me and in that kiss the last of any awkwardness melted away. Everything was as it should be and, for now, the lie I'd just told her didn't matter.

Because the truth was that I'd fallen for her already.

We were almost back at the museum entrance when I spotted a lone figure lurking by one of the hedges, out of view of the lodge. *Lesley Travis.* Instinctively I slammed my foot on the brake.

'What's the matter?' Ophelia gasped.

'Nothing.' I pulled over a little way ahead of the bus stop. 'Do you mind walking back from here?'

'Where are you going?'

I nodded in Lesley's direction. 'I want a word with him. I won't be long.'

She gazed into the lane. 'He's from The Sanctuary, isn't he? Why do you want to speak to him?'

'I just want to ask him something. Do me a favour – don't tell Hodge you saw him.'

'All right.' She undid her seatbelt. 'But does this have anything to do with that dream you had yesterday? In the orchard?'

'Yeah. It sort of does.'

She slipped out of the car without asking any more questions. I watched her cross the road then clambered out. Lesley shielded his eyes from the sun.

'Hey!' I jogged towards him, by which time Ophelia vanished. 'I wasn't impressed with that stunt you pulled earlier.'

He looked even worse than he had this morning. 'Have you still got it?'

'If you mean your little hocus-pocus witch ladder, then no. Hodge took it.' I enjoyed his reaction. 'It's probably ash by now.'

'I didn't mean to get you in trouble with him.'

'Trouble?' I laughed harshly. 'No, course not. You just threw a string of curses at me, but you wouldn't want to get me into trouble or anything.' I looked him up and down. 'What have you got for me this time? A crucifix? A silver bullet?'

'Curses? No, I . . . no. You've got it all wrong.'

'Like I had it wrong coming to you for help yesterday, I suppose?'

He looked haggard. 'I knew the moment you left that I shouldn't have behaved that way, but I panicked. You came to me for help, and that's why I came back – to help you.'

306

I stared at him for a long time. 'Help? Hodge said the witch's ladder was a way of hexing someone . . .'

'He would. Takes everything to a negative place, he does.' He scoffed. 'Fair enough. Witch's ladders – or witch's garlands, whatever you want to call them – they *are* sometimes used for darker means. But they're also used for good.'

'You expect me to believe that?'

'Listen to me! Yes – the only difference is the intent with which they're made. They can be used for protection as much as to harm.' He swiped a hand over his chin. The stubble there was grey, battling against the peroxide of his hair and winning. 'I felt terrible after you'd gone.'

'After you kicked me out,' I corrected.

He nodded dully. 'I thought about you all evening . . . and what that silver cord, or the absence of it could mean. I needed to let you know that you're in danger.'

'I knew that already,' I retorted. 'Your reaction was a pretty clear indication.'

'Because you're open, that's why,' he snapped. 'I wasn't only thinking of myself – there were dozens of people due into that building yesterday evening, people who were ready to open their hearts and minds. I've got a duty to them to make sure they're not made vulnerable – and if you'd brought something in with you then that could well have happened.'

'So where does the witch's ladder come in?'

'When I got home last night I went through every book I own that deals with psychic protection.' He squinted up at me. 'I suspect you did the same. Anyway, forget the usual stuff – walking through doors backwards and all that malarkey. That only works with haunted places, and the problem with you, son, is that you've

307

already let something in. They'll be . . . closer to you now. More powerful. Does that make sense?'

I thought of the visions I'd seen with Tess. The way she'd been capable of showing me her memories. Ever since Sebastian had been in my body, things had escalated. The realisation made my blood turn to sleet.

'Where did you find out about the witch's ladder?' I asked, trying to keep my voice steady and failing. 'I didn't see anything about that.'

'It's not a protection against the dead, not traditionally,' he answered. 'But it's something I stumbled across a while ago. And the thing that brought me back to it was the very way it's made.'

The most important aspect of any defence is belief . . .

'With intent?' I asked.

'Yes, but also something more literal – the physical form it takes.' He snapped his fingers. 'Cord!'

My heart sank. 'You *made* me a cord for the one I lost?' Hodge was right. Lesley Travis was a crazy old fool.

'I made you a starting point,' he said. 'An example. And yes, I wished for your safety and protection as I made the knots, but really it was a template for you to make your own.'

My silence spoke volumes.

He frowned. 'You've got a better idea?'

Short of sleeping in the same room as Dad for the rest of my life, I hadn't.

'I was going to get some dirt,' I said sourly, 'from my mother's grave.'

Lesley's eyes narrowed. 'Mmm. Placed under the bed, or in your pyjama pocket . . . Yes. It could work.' He shrugged. 'If you want to risk of waking up with bits of cemetery in your mouth.' He leaned forward and poked me in the chest. 'But if you've got faith enough to trust in that, then why not something of your own making?'

'I . . .' It was a good question. Last night, I'd trusted in nothing more than Dad's protection and the feeling of safety it brought me. That alone had been enough.

'Three pieces of cord,' Lesley said firmly. 'One black – this represents earthly matter, to keep you grounded. One red – to symbolise blood—'

I recoiled. '*Blood?*'

'Life,' he said, impatient. '*Energy.*'

'Oh.'

'And the last . . .' He paused, thinking. 'They say a colour of your choice, but many people go for blue. Healing, that is. Sometimes people even weave in a few strands of their hair. But for you . . .'

'Silver,' I guessed.

'Exactly. Now, the more personal you make it, the better. Old clothes, bedding—'

'Where do the feathers come in?' I interrupted.

'They're for counting. If the maker wants to chant their wishes, their knots, they use the feathers. In your case the feathers could symbolise something else – a connection to your sleep.'

'I'm not following.'

'What do you sleep on at night?'

'A pillow. A feather pillow . . .'

'Good. Take your feathers from that, then braid the three cords and knot them into it as you go along.'

'Nine knots, nine feathers?'

Lesley wrinkled his nose. 'Traditionally it's three, nine or thirteen knots. However many or few you do, you need to make your requests specific. Most people adapt their wishes from a certain chant.' He leaned his stick in the crook of his elbow and fumbled in his pockets. 'I wrote it down for you, but Podge came along before I could hand it over.' He pulled out a crumpled piece of paper. 'Here.'

I unfolded it to read the spidery handwriting.

'*By knot of one, my spell's begun,*' I read. '*By knot of two, my will be true. By knot of three, so shall it be* . . . I'm supposed to think of *nine* of these things?'

'Doesn't have to be nine. If you can do it in three, fine. Just be clear about what you're asking for.'

I folded the paper. 'You really think this could work?'

Lesley's eyes narrowed. 'Anything works if you believe in it. The mind can work wonders by itself, but sometimes it just needs a little help to focus it.'

'What am I supposed to do with this thing once it's made?'

'It's up to you. Sleep with it under your pillow, or in your hand if it makes you feel safer. If you're out-of-body and you feel threatened you can use the chant to reassure yourself and ward off any negative spirits.'

'After I saw you this morning he came again. The boy,' I blurted out. I held the written chant tightly, like the words alone could protect me. 'But this time he got to me in a different place – I'd dozed off in my car. I saw him dying, felt it. Then he . . . he forced me out. I had to wait until he weakened and left, but I don't understand how he could have found me there.'

'Haven't you listened to what I said? You let him in! He's no longer tied to a place, he's connected to *you*, now!' Lesley's face was grim. 'And he'll get stronger each time until you're locked out. And then you'll be the ghost.'

'There's this, too,' I croaked. With my other hand I undid my top button.

Lesley's eyes widened as he took in the marks on my throat. '*Christ* . . .' he breathed, stepping back. 'You need to make that witch's ladder, boy. You make it as soon as you can, do you hear? And then you find out what's keeping him here and you get rid of him before he gets rid of *you*.'

'That might be easier said than done.' I hid my shaking hands in my pockets. 'I already asked him. He wants to live again – and he wants revenge.'

Lesley shook his head. 'Well, he can't. And once you're protected – once he realises he can't control you – then he might change his tune.'

'And if he doesn't?'

'We'll deal with that if it happens. You'll come and find me. Sometimes the door has to be slammed, know what I'm saying?'

'Yeah.' I paused. 'Lesley? Thanks.'

He pursed his lips. 'Don't thank me yet,' he said gruffly. 'I've only told you what I know. You're the one who has to make it work, but you need faith, son. Have you got faith?'

I didn't answer immediately. My faith had been shattered by Mum's death, but last night I'd had a newer, different faith in Dad, and it'd worked. And it was that faith, *love*, I realised, that I needed and which drove me. Because it wasn't just myself I needed to protect now. It was Ophelia, too.

'I'm working on it,' I said. 'And I'll get rid of him.'

Starting with the ghost walk tomorrow.

Later that evening I sat on my bed, staring at the objects in front of me. The first was an old football boot of mine. Something I used to wear before, when I was strong. When I'd felt invincible.

The second was a red woollen scarf of Dad's. Mum had knitted it for him the Christmas before she died.

The third item was the box I kept under my bed. I took off the lid and lifted out some of the things inside. The half-empty bottle of perfume that would never be used up. I held it to my nose and sniffed the fresh, grassy scent that reminded me of Mum. I poked past other things: cards we'd made her, milk teeth she'd kept, two tiny hospital wristbands issued to us when we were born. And then I found it; the silver necklace that she'd always worn. The one, Dad had said, that I'd pointed at when I was little, likening it to my silver cord.

I put everything back except the necklace. I laid it out carefully then unthreaded the black shoelace from my football boot. Finally, I cut a length of red wool from the end of Dad's scarf where it hung in tassels.

One black cord, one red, and one silver.

I took my pillow, freed it from its case and made a small incision in the stitching. A downy feather escaped immediately, floating across to the window.

I began.

TWENTY-NINE

Meetings

I knocked a second time, stepping back to check the upstairs window. Adam's curtains were drawn. Weird. It was after twelve and I'd already been to The Acorn looking for him.

Something moved behind the glass. The latch clicked and the door opened. Adam squinted out at me wearing only a pair of shorts.

'What are you doing here?' he grunted.

'I need a favour.' I moved past him into a fug of stale air. 'Bloody hell, Adam. It stinks in here.'

'Does it?' He stumbled to the kitchen and reached past a pile of pizza boxes to the kettle. 'Coffee?'

'I'm not supposed to drink it, remember?'

'Yeah.' He coughed. 'Well, we all do stuff we're not supposed to.'

'What's that mean?' I asked. Already I had a horrible suspicion. 'Where's Amy?'

He moved a stack of dirty dishes to get to the tap. 'Gone.'

'Gone where? Why?'

'Her parents' house.' He turned, not meeting my eyes.

'What have you done?'

'Nothing,' he snapped. 'Technically nothing, anyway.' He sighed, scratching his head. 'She turned up the other night when I was at work. I didn't see her come in.'

'What were do you doing, Ad?'

'I was with a girl,' he mumbled. 'Not actually *doing* anything . . . I just took her number.'

'And Amy saw?'

'Yeah.'

'You *idiot*. What's wrong with you?'

'I don't know.'

'I do. It's called being a stupid, selfish arse.'

He nodded. 'Want to know what the really stupid part is? I wouldn't even have called her – it would've gone in the bin. I was just playing her.'

'What *for*?'

He shrugged. 'Because I could. And now Amy thinks I was playing *her*.' His voice shook. 'I've really messed up this time, haven't I?'

'You're a shit,' I told him. 'Doing this right before her exams.'

We stared at each other. My stupid, handsome, popular brother. Everything I used to be and now wasn't. And that was all right, I realised. I had changed, but not for the worse. Now Adam had to decide if he wanted to.

'You're right.' He hid his face in his hands. His voice was muffled. 'What am I going to do? I don't want anyone else. Now I've cocked everything up.'

'Tell her.'

'I tried. She said she couldn't believe anything that came out of my mouth any more. That actions say more than words.'

'Show her, then. Use the words differently – write her a song.'

He went silent, then finally looked up. 'You think it'll work?'

Anything can work if you believe in it.

I shrugged. 'I think you should try.'

314

Adam put the kettle on to boil and grabbed a screwed-up T-shirt from the back of a chair. 'So why are you here, anyway? Shouldn't you be dressed up as Henry the Eighth right about now?'

'I don't start till two. I'm working late tonight.'

'Right. The ghost walk.' He pulled the shirt over his head. 'Speaking of ghosts, how's everything at home?'

'That what I'm here about. The thing with Tess . . . it's over. She's gone, but I need to do something for her. I promised.'

'Are you serious? You're doing things for ghosts, now? I thought I was the one with problems.'

'Forget it. I knew I shouldn't have said anything.'

'No, wait – what? Come on, I'm sorry.'

'I need to give someone a message.'

'What's the message?'

'None of your business. The point is, my one clue to where this person might be is a pub. I looked it up this morning – there's only one with its name in the country. And it's in Oxfordshire.'

'That's miles away.'

'Yeah. A good three hours each way. I wondered if you'd come with me – keep me company on the drive.' I stopped, gesturing to the mess of a kitchen. 'I can see you've got your own problems, though.'

Adam nodded. 'Sorry, Elliott. I'd be about as good company as a fart in a blanket at the moment.' His eyes lit with a familiar spark. 'But what about Ophelia? Perfect chance for—'

'Don't even say it,' I groaned. 'She doesn't know about any this. And even if she did I doubt her uncle would let her come. He's a pain in the arse.'

'You need to make friends with him.' Adam handed me a black coffee. 'Milk's off.'

We sat down at the table, blowing on our steaming mugs. Adam chanced a sip and swore. 'What a shitty few days,' he said bad-temperedly.

'Why, what else happened?' I couldn't help smirk at his sour expression. 'Apart from getting dumped and burning your tongue?'

'It's Mum's birthday next week.'

That wiped the smile off my face.

'You'd forgotten, hadn't you?'

No point lying. 'Yeah.'

'I'm taking her some flowers. Are you coming?'

I stared into the black depths of my mug.

'Well?' His voice was terse.

I looked up. 'No.'

His eyebrows bunched together. 'Just . . . *no*?'

'It's not "just no", though, is it?' I said. 'I told you from the start that I didn't want to keep visiting the grave. You kept pushing, so I went along with it.'

'So you just want to forget her, then?'

'Don't be stupid. I want to remember her as much as you do – as much as Dad does. But I can remember her by thinking of things that happened. Looking through photos and stuff she kept. And maybe that's no healthier than going to where she's buried but that's how I want to deal with it.' I kept my voice level but firm. 'If you want to go there, if it makes you feel better, then I respect that. But you need to respect my reasons not to.'

I waited for him to protest, to explode, but he didn't. In the silence that followed I thought of Mum's box that I'd looked through last night. 'Remember the silver necklace?' I asked eventually. 'The one we bought her?'

Adam smiled faintly. 'Yeah. She always wore it.'

316

And with that the tension between us snapped. We drank our coffee, reminiscing. Somehow, even without milk it tasted good, like the memories we spoke about took away its bitterness. Soon it was time to leave. Adam walked me to the door, looking marginally less sorry for himself.

'So, the thing with the uncle, then,' he said, folding his arms. 'Does that mean you haven't, yet?'

I knew what he was getting at but chose to ignore it. 'Haven't what?'

'You know. With Ophelia?'

I let myself out, jangling my car keys. 'It's like you always taught me, Adam. A gentleman never tells.'

'Yeah, but that doesn't count, not with me. Come on, we always tell each other . . .'

I got into the car, grinning. 'Not this time.'

I left Adam's miserable face only to exchange it with another. A school coach on its way to Past Lives had broken down, leaving the afternoon virtually without tours and Hodge pouting as though he were one of the children on it. He grumbled all the way to his office and gave me a sheet with a list of catering services on it.

'Extra hours for you next week, if you want them.' He tapped a poster on the wall. 'Last year it was packed – should be even busier this time.'

I glanced at the glossy paper, nodding. It was an advert for a Tudor event week beginning on Friday. A collage of images showed jousting, dancing, and some sort of feast.

'What's this?' I asked, referring to the list.

'Oh . . . one of the food stalls has dropped out. We need a replacement – and fast. Would you ring around and see if you can find someone who can fill the slot?'

'Sure.'

'Great. After that you can take a residential seat on Goose Walk and assist anyone wandering about. It's likely to be a quiet afternoon.'

I caught a waft of something as he whisked past me out of the offices. Had he been on the whiskey again? He seemed distracted and sweatier than usual.

He returned a few minutes later when I was halfway through the list.

'Any luck?'

'Not so far.' I crossed off the last number I'd called and checked the next, ready to dial again. Something made me pause and look up. Hodge was staring at me.

'Your accident,' he said.

I felt on edge all of a sudden. 'What about it?'

'Do you think it's made you sensitive to things?'

I lowered my eyes.

'It's just that Sebastian is one of the less . . . forthcoming spirits, shall we say. I was surprised when you said you'd seen him.'

He leaned past me, picking up a set of keys from his desk. I caught the smell again. Definitely whiskey. I got the distinct feeling that I was being challenged. Had Hodge had time to think about what I'd told him and decided I'd lied? Or didn't he like the fact that I'd seen something, something *real*? If Lesley was right about Sebastian's appearance last year then Hodge had to be involved. Either way, it rankled.

I put the list down. 'I wasn't completely honest with you before,' I said, watching his face carefully. I felt sure he thought I was going to retract it; say it was a dream. 'Sebastian wasn't the first ghost I've seen.'

His eyebrows shot up. 'No?'

'A woman died in my flat. I've been seeing her ever since the accident.' I averted my eyes, reluctant to divulge more than I had to. Weirdly, after fearing, even *hating* Tess for so long, I now felt a strange sense of loyalty to her and her secrets. 'Anyway. I found out what her . . . why she stayed. And I have to do something to help her – I have to *tell* someone something for her.'

'Really?' Hodge sank into his chair. I couldn't tell if he believed me or not.

'Thing is, I have to go to Oxfordshire to do it.' I shrugged. 'And I don't even know if I'll find him.'

Hodge looked up, his eyes suddenly bright. 'Oxfordshire, you say?' He crossed to his safe and spun the combination, taking out the cluttered notebook. He turned to the back and ran his finger along a page. 'How about you and I take a little field trip out there? In work time, with full pay?'

I blinked in surprise. 'To *Oxfordshire*?'

He grinned. 'Every now and then I take research trips around the country. Check out the ghost walks and events, pick up some ideas. Even poached a tour guide or two here and there. I was planning on Glasgow next, but there are plenty of places in Oxfordshire I could visit. Two birds with one stone – I do my research, you get to deliver your message and we both get paid. We could share the driving. What do you think – it'd be like a lads' road trip!'

I forced a smile. A road trip was what I'd envisioned for Adam and me; talking about girls, driving with the radio as loud as it'd go and sinking a few beers before bed. A road trip with a hot-tempered, pot-bellied forty-something wasn't what I had in mind. But I had to admit, a paid day in work time didn't sound bad. And this could be my chance to take Adam's advice and make a friend of Hodge.

'Sounds good,' I replied. 'When do you want to go?'

'How about Friday?'

'*This* Friday?'

'Why not? Weather's meant to be good all weekend. If we leave early enough we'll be back in time for the Tudor banquet in the evening.' He winked. 'Plus avoid the aggravation of helping set up during the day.'

'All right,' I said. 'Let's do it.'

It wasn't until much later, when I sat alone in the tollhouse on Goose Walk, that Hodge's mood prior to our plans for the trip made any sense. Today was the fifth of June.

The day the writer of the threatening letter had promised to show up.

Ophelia and I sat in my car in the hour before the ghost walk was due to start. The car park was mostly empty now the majority of staff had finished for the day, Ophelia included.

Her jodhpurs were mud-spattered and there was hay in her hair. I reached over and gently pulled it out, watching her pulse flutter under the honey-coloured skin at her throat. A shaft of early evening sun hit her hair, turning straw into gold.

'Did Hodge tell you we're going away on Friday?' I asked.

'Road trip, right?' She made a face. 'He'll bore you to death.'

I shrugged, relieved that Hodge hadn't mentioned my part in things. 'It's worth it if it makes things easier for us to be together.'

'After a day around Hodge you might not want to.'

'I will.'

'You're coming back for the banquet, aren't you?'

'I'll be here.'

'Good.' She grinned slyly. 'Afterwards there'll be dancing. You need the practise . . .'

'Hey!' I tugged her hair. 'That's not fair. I was injured. Listen – let's do something this weekend. Just you and me, somewhere away from here. Dinner and a movie?'

'I'd like that.'

She lifted her face to mine, her hand cupping the back of my neck as it had the first time we'd kissed. I shivered as her fingers slipped under my collar, threaded into my hair . . .

A blast of screeching static forced us apart. I jerked backwards, scrabbling for the radio to turn it off.

Ophelia pressed her hand to her heaving chest. 'How did that come on?'

'I-I must have knocked it with my knee,' I stuttered, punching it off. 'Either that or it's broken—'

Ophelia's gasp silenced me.

'What?'

'Your neck – what are all those marks on it?'

I grabbed the rear-view mirror and tilted it down. My shirt had come open at the top when Ophelia had touched me, exposing my throat.

'It's nothing.' I grappled with the buttons, tucking my collar into place. 'Just an allergy.'

'It looked like bruises.'

'No, really.' I kissed the tip of her nose. 'Don't worry. It'll be gone soon.'

I gripped the mirror and searched for the right position, hitting several angles before I found the right one.

Dark eyes glared back at me.

Sebastian.

I whipped round. The backseat was empty. When I turned back to the mirror there was nothing.

Ophelia looked at me strangely. 'Are you sure you're all right? You seem kind of . . . twitchy.'

'I'm fine.' I snatched my keys out of the ignition. 'Just worried about the time. Don't want to be late.'

'Okay.' I heard the confusion in her voice, but didn't dare touch her. If I did she'd feel me shaking. 'Well, I'll see you tomorrow.'

'Yeah.'

She got out, slamming the door. I watched her walk across the car park.

'You can't have her,' I whispered to the empty car. 'She's mine.'

Nothing answered me.

I observed them one by one as the sun set over the museum.

Eighteen had shown up for this week's ghost walk, split evenly between Hodge's group and Lyn's. Hodge's nine consisted of four double-dating teens slightly older than me, a retired couple, and three people who each had come alone: two women and a man. I hadn't got a good look at Lyn's group before they moved off, but I guessed that if Hodge's pen-pal had shown up he'd want to keep them close and be more likely to put them with his own group.

I listened carefully to their questions and, even more carefully, tracked their eyes for any meaningful or snide looks. I kept a closer watch on Hodge. His manner was normal, excitable only when relating a grisly fact. When the story of Sebastian and Samuel was related I drew back from the group, goosepimples rippling over my skin. But nothing happened and, by the time we'd finished with the Elizabethan sector, I was convinced that none of them were the guilty party. Whoever it was hadn't shown.

322

In the Victorian schoolroom I tried to slink back and remain outside, but Hodge called me in. My stomach churned as he demonstrated the punishments. The stench came up as I knew it would – and as Hodge knew it would. He gave me a triumphant smile as we led the shocked group back to the Swan for their free drink.

I refused to return it, too livid even to look at him.

Back at the Swan, Hodge sank several pints of ale before most of the hotel guests and ghost walkers drifted away home or to their rooms. At the final bell for the bar, only a handful of us remained, including the man and two lone women, and a few stragglers from Lyn's group.

'Right then, ghost-hunters.' Hodge clapped his hands together. 'It's been a lovely evening, but it has to end some time. If we're all finished here I'll escort you to the exit.'

Glasses were drained, coats were shrugged into. I tagged behind all the way over the cobblestones, silent as they laughed about what they'd seen. *There it was again*, I thought bitterly. *That buzz.*

We bypassed the main visitors' entrance, now closed for the evening, and headed for the archways leading to the parking lot. They were almost out. Hodge and I were retreating through the archways when it came:

'I've lost my necklace.'

The younger of the two women patted herself down, shaking out her coat. The rest of the group trickled away. Car doors slammed in the distance.

'I know I had it earlier – it must've come off somewhere.' She gazed at Hodge, her eyes wide. I felt my pulse quicken. Was it the truth, or could she be the letter-writer?

'Ah. Perhaps our little pickpocket Annie's been up to her old tricks, eh? Well, no good looking for it in the dark,' Hodge replied.

'If you come with me and fill out a slip I'll have it sent on if it turns up.' He glanced at me. 'I'll take care of this, Elliott. You take yourself off to your room. Oh,' he winked, 'and thanks for your assistance.'

He took the woman in the direction of his office. Her dark hair gleamed in the overhead street lamps, bobbing against her red coat. Neither of them looked back, too sure of Hodge's authority. I waited thirty seconds. Then I followed.

Inside the cottages I crept along the limestone floor. Every door was closed, and every light off – apart from the yellow glow under one. I edged along the wall, pausing outside to listen and at the same time praying that what I heard was only words.

At first there was nothing and I almost backed away, afraid of what was happening on the other side of the door. But then I heard it, a faint shuffling sound. Like cards being dealt . . . or money being counted.

'That was quite the performance,' she purred. 'Seems I'm not the only actor here tonight. If I hadn't known, even I would've sworn that you didn't know me at all.'

The counting sound stopped. 'Just take it and go.'

'*Five hundred?*' The purr was gone. In its place was something ugly, clipped.

'How much did you expect?' Hodge growled. 'It's taken me weeks to skim that off the ghostwalk profits, and there's an audit next week. Now, I'm warning you, this is the last time—'

She cut across him harshly. 'It's the last time when I *say* it's the last time. It didn't have to come to this – you're the one who shirked on the deal, remember? You forced my hand, Arthur. I was happy to carry on doing what you told me. I quite enjoyed your little scripts . . .'

Her voice changed, became dreamy and soft: 'I see a woman, wringing her hands . . . She's wearing a cook's outfit. She's . . . she's trying to tell me something . . . What's that? I can't hear you, my love. A hanged boy, you say? You want to confess?' She giggled, reverting to her normal tone. 'Yes, I quite enjoyed being the psychic. It was a neat little arrangement. I'd go back to it tomorrow, if you want to . . .'

'There was no arrangement!' Hodge hissed. 'I never said it'd be regular. Anything regular would *cheapen* it, not to mention risk mistakes.' He sneered. 'But then, that's all you are, isn't it? Cheap. You don't care where it comes from.'

'There's worse ways to make money.'

'And I'll bet you've tried the lot of them.'

She ignored him. 'Those paranormal events you've got coming up. You could've put something my way there. You know I'd do a good job. I did last time—'

He made a scoffing noise. 'You know something? I probably would have. But you'd already started with the demands, hadn't you? The threats. You think I'm putting more your way, having you sitting there with my colleagues, my family, around? And that *letter*? It's sheer bloody luck my secretary didn't open it!'

'You shouldn't have ignored me. I told you I wouldn't be ignored. I'm in control here, Arthur, for as long as you want your dodgy little dealings kept secret. Remember that. It'd only take a few words and everyone would know what a fraud you are.' She gave an exaggerated sigh. 'Just think of the shame you'd bring on your poor mother if she was still alive—'

I caught her gasp before a thud came, so loud that I expected to see a crack in the wall next to where I stood. I backed away, adrenaline rushing through my body. Had he punched the wall? Thrown her against it? I couldn't tell.

'*Don't you dare mention my mother, you little bitch!*'

'I – I'm sorry! Arthur, please . . .'

Something slid. Her heels clicked as she staggered to the door.

'Take the money and go.' Hodge's voice was low, barely contained. 'If I see you again, if I hear *anything* from you . . .'

I didn't stay to hear any more. Instead I crept away, my breath coming heavily in the silent corridor. I made it outside with barely enough time to press myself into a wisteria-covered archway when the main door to the offices slammed. I watched from the shadows as Hodge frogmarched the woman to the exit and shoved her through it without another word. From his coat pocket he pulled a small bottle. His hand shook as he unscrewed the cap. He took a couple of swallows, coughed, and stalked back to the offices.

I waited, then slunk away, starting to run once I reached the stables. I saw no one as I crossed to the Swan. I took out my room key and let myself in through the guest entrance. Voices and rattling crocks filtered from the restaurant area as staff cleared the night's work away. I left them behind me, climbing the stairs to the staff quarters. It was a different room this time, but it felt no safer. It was now me that Sebastian haunted. Wherever I went, he could go.

I put the light on and shut the curtains. My overnight bag, which I'd brought up earlier, was on the chair. From it I took out a plain T-shirt and faded combats, and changed into them. I wasn't risking getting locked out half naked a second time. From the front compartment of the bag I carefully lifted out the witch's ladder.

I closed my eyes against the harsh light and lay on the bed with the knotted cord and feathers twisted between my fingers. Lesley was right. Hodge *had* been faking things. *Paying* people to re-enact

326

the ghost stories. Lying, cheating, and conning. Exploiting death and misery for profit.

I fell into an uneasy sleep, dreaming jumbled dreams of Hodge, hanging from a three-coloured rope knotted with feathers. His eyes were bloodshot and glassy, his mouth slack. I tried to scream but found my mouth clogged with something gritty and thick. One of Hodge's eyes winked at me, sending a bloody tear down his cheek.

The lightbulb overhead fizzled and went out, waking me.

Half waking me.

I lay paralysed in the darkened room, my breath misting the air in front of my face. A shadowy outline waited in front of the thin curtains, still and watchful. Though it didn't move, the curtains slowly, slowly peeled back. Yellow light fell into the room from outside, highlighting the torn tunic, the tear-stained face. Then he moved.

Sebastian prowled round the bed, circling it like a fox would a rabbit. Soil spilled from his lips as he mouthed angry words I couldn't read. Dirt-caked fingernails reached for me, stopping short of my face.

The witch's ladder trailed over my fingers, feathers animated in the icy draught. And I forced myself to remember, to say it even if the words in my head were clearer than those in the room.

'*By knot of one, the day is done,*
By knot of two, my rest is due,
By knot of three, sleep comes to me,
By knot of four, I'll fear no more,
By knot of five, I am alive,
By knot of six, my cord is fixed,
By knot of seven, with thread and feather,

327

By knot of eight, there is no gate,

By knot of nine, to what is mine . . .'

Sebastian's hand recoiled, his eyes darkening. I knew that he had heard it and the knowledge strengthened me. He couldn't force me out and he couldn't get in, not if I didn't let him.

I repeated it, over and over. On the third recital he backed away, toward the window. My little finger twitched; I was starting to come out of it.

'Talk to me,' I instructed. 'Tell me another way to help you.'

Fresh dirt fell from his mouth, staining the tunic further. He grew angrier, frustrated. He turned to the window, foggy with condensation, and wrote a single word:

SEBASTIAN

'I know,' I shouted at him. 'I *know* who you are!'

He screamed silently, sweeping a hand through the word from top to bottom, partially obliterating it. On an untouched part of the window he wrote again. And I watched, only to see the same word appear. Once more he dragged his hand through it.

SEBASTIAN SEBASTIAN SEBASTIAN

Soon the glass was covered with the name, every one of them destroyed with a swipe of his hand. Beads of liquid linked each word to the next, one running into another.

My hand moved properly, gripping the witch's ladder. The rest of me followed, breaking the paralysis. I sat up to an empty room, still breathing clouds of air. The window dripped, any words now unreadable.

I pressed myself back against the headboard, whispering.
'*By knot of one, the day is done,*
By knot of two, my rest is due,
By knot of three, sleep comes to me,
By knot of four, I'll fear no more . . .'

The witch's ladder, or the faith I'd placed in it, had worked. I'd
protected myself, but I was no closer to laying Sebastian to rest.

I hadn't lost, but I hadn't won yet, either.

THIRTY

The Mask and Mirror

Another snore rumbled out from the passenger seat. With one hand still on the wheel I unzipped my CD case, pushed a disc into the player and nudged the volume a notch higher. Hodge didn't stir.

It was after ten and I'd been driving two hours. Hodge had slept for more than half of that time, after suggesting we switch midway. Ten minutes ago I'd pulled over and taken a leak before finishing the coffee we'd brought and resigning myself to driving the rest of the way. I hadn't seen much of him yesterday but, judging by his bleary eyes and sour breath, he was sleeping off a hangover. At first he'd made small talk, then nodded off before we were even out of Calthorpe. Not that it bothered me – after Wednesday night I didn't have much to say to him. For me, the trip was just a means to an end.

Dazzling sunshine bounced off the wet road. It had rained in the night but already my T-shirt had started to cling to my skin. It was set to be a scorcher. The car at least, was decent – Hodge had arranged for us to take a company vehicle. Though it was no bigger than mine it was smoother, with air con.

Thirty minutes later he groaned and stretched.

'Is that the time?' He sat up straighter, rubbing his eyes. 'Want me to take over?'

'It's fine,' I said evenly. 'We're nearly there.'

'Sorry about that – I was knocked out.' He blinked and peered out of the window. Miles of countryside surrounded us. 'Where are we?'

'Just passed Brackley. We should reach Steeple Aston in about twenty minutes.'

He slumped back. 'And this pub's in Woodstock, you say?'

I nodded.

Our first stop was the Holt Hotel, apparently frequented by the ghost of a highwayman from the eighteenth century. By the time we arrived Hodge had perked up and was armed with more questions than a four-year-old on a sugar high. I half listened, feigning interest as he scribbled notes and bobbed his head enthusiastically, even photographing areas of sightings and standing in supposed cold spots, but sensing nothing.

I trudged from room to room feeling a strange mixture of tiredness from the early start and impatience to get gone. The Mask and Mirror was next on our list of places to visit, and I had my own questions that needed answering. I doubted there was even a one-in-a-million chance that my path would cross Bradley's, but perhaps someone there would know him and give me a new lead.

I sensed from the moment we arrived that I was out of luck. Besides Hodge and me, there were only four people in the place. Two were staff and both were young. I approached them anyway then went on to ask the two old men who were grumbling into their beers. None of them knew, or knew of, a fair-haired man named Bradley. In desperation I mentioned Lorna Clements and got the same answer. I hadn't expected any different – the pair were hardly likely to flaunt their affair close to home. They'd chosen this place for a reason – because nobody knew them.

'We may as well stay for lunch,' said Hodge, nodding at the blackboard behind the bar. 'They start serving it in ten minutes. He could still show up.'

'I don't think so.' I ignored the curious look on Hodge's face. 'But let's stay anyway. I'm starving.'

I found the alcove a minute later. It was set back, away from the bar and prying eyes. I stepped into it with the feeling I was intruding somehow and stared at the table Tess – or Lorna – had sat at. Many, many people must have been seated here, before and since. Eaten and drunk. Laughed or argued. I wondered if any of them had as strong a connection to the place as she did; if any had plotted, loved or lost here.

'You want to sit at this one?' Hodge came up behind me, grabbing a chair. Tess's chair.

'No,' I said quickly. 'Not this one. Let's go here.'

I took a seat at the table behind. In Tess's memory, it had been where the Christmas tree stood. Hodge sat opposite and took a menu.

The food came. So did more people. I got up every time I heard the door go, wandering from room to room, scanning each face. None of them was Bradley.

We ate, paid and left. I took the passenger side and Hodge took the driver's seat. 'Listen,' he said, 'how about we come back this way and pop in on the way home, just in case?'

'Won't that be out of the way?'

He shrugged. 'A bit. But the route I have planned is quite circular – it'd only mean an extra half an hour.'

I nodded, grateful and more than a little guilty over my earlier thoughts. I didn't agree with a lot of stuff Hodge had done or the way he was with Ophelia, but he'd gone out of his way to help me today.

It didn't make the rest of the day pass any quicker. From Woodstock we went to Blenheim, from Blenheim to Eynsham, from Eynsham to Oxford. Each place and its stories blurred into the next; a mist of weeping women, monks and murders. Houses, halls, and churches. Each place brought a brief respite from the searing heat outside, but by mid-afternoon I felt sluggish. Hodge wasn't faring much better judging by the glow of his skin, but he was in his element. His notebook grew fatter, my attention span thinned. Absently, I played with the witch's ladder in my pocket, running the feathers and knots through my fingers like a rosary. I looked into the face of everyone we met, wanting it to be Bradley's. It never was. He could be anywhere, I realised. Anywhere at all. How was I going to keep my promise to Tess? And what would happen if I didn't – would she come back?

At four Hodge loaded his camera into the backseat and we began our journey back towards The Mask and Mirror.

This time it was busier, with people keen to celebrate the weather and the weekend. While Hodge stood at the bar with a small cider, I prowled the gardens, the alcove, and every table in the place. It was as big a waste of time as it had been this morning and, with every face I looked into, a little more of Bradley's was forgotten. I started to wonder if I'd even recognise him if he walked straight past me.

'It's a shame we didn't have longer,' Hodge said, as we finished up our drinks and prepared to leave. 'Next time I'll book somewhere overnight and make it a two-day trip.'

I lingered at the door, scanning the place one last time.

'It wasn't to be, lad.' Hodge patted my arm and moved past me.

I turned to follow, then stopped. Because there he was: Bradley. Gazing back at me from just a few feet away. I glanced around for

Hodge but he was outside now, in the car park. I stepped closer to the notice board on the wall, heart drumming.

He was older, but it was definitely him, one of four men in a moody black-and-white poster pinned to the board. I must have walked past it six or seven times today and not looked at it once.

WILD BOYS, it said at the top. *THE ULTIMATE DURAN DURAN TRIBUTE BAND*. At the bottom there was a website address, and a blank box into which a handwritten date had been added in: *Saturday 20th July*. I scrounged a pen from the bar and wrote the date and website on my hand. Then I ran out to the car.

'I found him – I actually *found* him!'

A bemused look crossed Hodge's face. 'I thought you said he wasn't there.'

'He wasn't.' I held my hand up and explained about the band. 'Now I've got a way to contact him. Even if the website's no good, I know where he'll be next month.' I leaned back in the passenger seat, relief washing over me as Hodge turned out of the car park and got back on the road. 'That's why she sent me there.' The tension I'd carried around with me all day melted like ice cream in the summer heat. 'She knew it'd be enough to find him.'

'Do you think he'll want to hear whatever it is she has to tell him?' Hodge asked.

'Not at first. I don't even know if he'll believe me. But he has to.' I rested my head against the glass. 'He *has* to.'

Fields of wheat rushed past the window.

'Why do you think she chose you?'

'I don't think she had a choice. I was the only one who could see her.'

'Tell me something,' Hodge said. 'When you came to work at the museum – knowing it was haunted – were you worried that other spirits might try to make contact?'

'I was hoping they would,' I admitted. 'Until then, I didn't know if it was real or not. Sometimes with Tess . . . I thought I was going mad.'

'But now you know you're not? That it's real?'

'It's real to me.'

'And apart from Sebastian, have there been others?'

'Just one.' I hesitated, my skin creeping at the memory. 'Annie.'

'*Really?*'

I caught Hodge glance sideways at me.

'I've never seen her myself,' he said. 'But lots of people claim to.'

'And the thing in the schoolroom,' I said. 'I've *felt* that, whatever it is. I know that it happens when there's someone nearby who's been close to death.' I watched Hodge's eyes, back on the road. 'If it's all right with you, I'd rather not be nearby when you're showing the punishments in future. I mean, I know it's an experience for the tour group, but whatever it is, I don't like being the one responsible for making that stuff happen. It just makes me uncomfortable.'

'I see.' Hodge's face was unreadable. 'Yes, that's fair enough, I suppose.'

I couldn't tell if he was sulking or not. But with the sun on my skin and renewed hope of delivering Tess's message I was suddenly too exhausted to care. The day had sapped me of strength. My eyelids drooped. I pushed my hand into my pocket and entwined my fingers with the witch's ladder, allowing my eyes to close.

When they opened again the sun was weak and low in the sky, and my bladder was full.

'How long before we're back?'

The words came out as a series of little grunts with no shape or meaning. I tried to turn my head towards Hodge. Couldn't.

Couldn't move a muscle.

It'll be all right, I told myself. *Just relax and you'll come out of it. There's nothing here to harm you . . .*

So why was the skin on the back of my neck tingling? Why had the temperature in the car plummeted?

On the edges of my vision, something was happening to the window beside me. I strained my eyes, trying to focus, but my head was angled the other way slightly, towards Hodge. The glass was clouding gradually, as though someone were breathing on it. Slowly, letter by letter, a familiar word appeared.

SEBASTIAN

Oh God oh God oh God no . . .

I forced myself to focus on the witch's ladder in my pocket, still wrapped around my fingers. *By knot of one, the day is done . . . By knot of two, my rest is due . . .*

The cold seeped closer, creeping over my shoulders and back. Down my arm. I tasted damp soil and rot in each breath.

By knot of three, sleep comes to me . . . By knot of four, I'll fear no more . . .

Filthy fingers slid around the top of my arm. A scream filled my head but went no further. *By knot of six . . . no, by five . . . NO!* The fingers tightened. And the conscious part of me, the lucid part recoiled.

Recoiled violently enough to separate itself from the helpless, sleeping part of me. I felt myself loosen and emerge, twisting round to face the backseat. The act of moving, even if it wasn't my physical self, gave me courage. Strength enough to face the monster.

But there was no monster. Only a boy, choking on dirt and tears.

'*By knot of five, I am alive,*' I whispered. '*By knot of six, my cord is fixed.*'

He stared back, beaten.

'Hands off, Sebastian,' I warned.

Slowly, he withdrew his hand from my sleeping self.

'*By knot of seven, with thread and feather. By knot of eight, there is no gate.*' I stared him straight in the eye. '*By knot of nine, to what is mine.*'

We regarded each other, like two opponents about to fight to the death. Only, one of us was already dead. Long dead.

'You've got no claim on me, Sebastian.' My voice was hollow, almost drowned by the hum of the engine. Beside me, Hodge continued to drive, oblivious. 'But if there's another way I can help you, I will. This is your last chance. Is there something you need to tell me?' I grimaced as he coughed, spraying soil into his lap. I tried again. 'Something you want to *show* me?'

He nodded, his bloodshot eyes fixed on mine.

I reached towards him, offering my hand. He mirrored the action. Our hands met, one coloured by the sun, the other coloured by the earth. One alive, one dead.

The car flickered and vanished. The night melted around us, a cocktail of trees and fields and headlights and fading sun. I steeled myself for a dead boy's past and whatever awaited us there. But this time, I wasn't a bystander as I had been with Tess.

This time I saw it all through his eyes.

THIRTY-ONE

'Sebastian'

Trees . . .

Trees in blossom, releasing scent and petals with each breath of wind. I kicked through the grass between the gnarled old forms. It was late, almost dark, but the air remained warm. I was in the orchard, but I wasn't alone. Someone else was there, walking just behind me.

'This way.' The voice was familiar, one I'd heard many times before. I turned back to see him heading further left, to a taller tree more solitary than the rest.

Arthur Hodge stopped at the foot of the tree and dumped a tangle of thin rope on the ground. He pulled an arm across his gleaming face, managing to plaster a strand of thinning hair across his forehead like a caterpillar. I forced myself not to laugh.

He pointed into the darkness. 'Grab that, will you?'

In the fading light I saw a set of ladders propped against a nearby tree. I collected them, stumbling under their weight.

'Careful,' he hissed.

'You try carrying them in the dark.' The voice that came out wasn't mine. It was not as deep, and instead of my own accent came something a little softer. 'I can't see one foot in front of the other.'

'All right, just get on with it. And keep quiet. Someone might hear us.'

338

I dragged the ladders into place and opened them up, securing them in a steeple shape. Hodge kneeled down and extracted something from the mass of rope.

He threw it at me. 'Put this on, like I showed you. Do you remember?'

'Yes.' I stepped into the harness and pulled it up over my shoulders, clipping it into place.

'Needs to be tighter.' Hodge came closer, roughly grabbing the harness and pulling on the cords.

'And I need to breathe . . .'

'You will. But it has to be firm or it won't hold you properly.' He stepped back, nodding. 'There. Now this.'

He passed me the noose. I slid the rope between my fingers. It was thin and the knot was basic, looping back on itself to be easily tightened or loosened.

'It looks real.'

'It is real.' Hodge grappled with the rest of the rope. 'We can't make a proper hangman's knot on the noose itself, so I had to do it this way.' He lifted the main length of rope. About a foot from the end of it another smaller section of rope was tightly coiled, giving the impression of a complex knot. The bottom section of rope hung free, fitted with a clip.

I slipped the noose over my head and tightened it as much as I could stand to. It left a tail of rope hanging free down my back.

'Tuck that in and hide it down the back of your shirt,' said Hodge, watching me. 'Good. Now put the end of this rope down your back and clip it on to the harness.' He looked up, surveying the thick branch over head. 'After that, stand there and don't move. I need to get the position right.'

I stood beneath the branch, waiting. Twigs snapped under Hodge's weight as he shuffled round, moving the ladder to various spots, looping the rope over this branch and that. He returned, his shirt untucked from repeatedly reaching up, and repositioned the ladder under the branch.

'Climb up four or five steps and wait.'

'How will I get up tomorrow?' I asked suddenly. 'If I use the ladder, someone might hear if I kick it away.'

'That's exactly why you won't use it. You'll have to climb up there, attach the clip, then drop.'

The ladder creaked and wobbled. I perched uneasily, staring through the branches. Calthorpe House glowered back at me, its windows like dark eyes seeing something I couldn't.

'Hodge? This can't go wrong, can it?' I swallowed against the tightness around my throat. Suddenly the rope attached to the harness became taut.

Hodge reappeared before me on the ground. 'It'll only go wrong if you don't cut the rope in time and you're still dangling there like a fool when I shine the torch back on you. Remember, you'll have about a minute to sever the rope, drop, and hide. I'll attach a weight on the other end that will bring the rope down over there. Cut the lot off and bring it with you – don't leave any behind. Got that?'

'Yes.'

'Right. Let's have a trial run. Ready?'

I stepped off the ladder. It gave a few inches but I was still a good couple of feet off the ground. Hodge moved the ladder out of the way and stood back, his round face breaking into a grin.

'It's bloody brilliant!' he breathed. 'From here you can see the noose isn't attached, but with the distance from the house there's no way they'll be able to tell. No way at all. And tomorrow, with the make-up and everything . . .' He changed angles, circling like a vulture. 'Let your head go limp – that's it. Keep your eyes closed – if they're open the torchlight might make you blink.' He grinned up at me. 'If we pull this off,' he said softly, 'people will talk about this for years.'

'And if we don't?' I fidgeted in the harness.

The smile left Hodge's face. 'Don't even think about it. Failure isn't an option.'

A breeze lifted the hair off the back of my neck, stirring loose apple blossom from the branches and whipping it in front of my eyes like a freakish snowstorm. When it cleared, I was no longer in the orchard. I was somewhere else, with someone else.

It was dark. Musty and damp, but daylight danced either side of my vision. I was under a bridge, with cold stone at my back. Green-brown water lapped at the edge of the path. A barge was moored in the distance.

'So, this is it? We're really going – for good?' Ophelia looked up at me, her bottom lip trembling. She looked younger, softer.

'For good.' I kissed her forehead, stroking damp hair back from it. 'Don't look so worried, I've got it all figured out. This time tomorrow we'll be halfway to . . .' I broke off, shaking my head and grinning.

'To . . .?'

'I don't know. To our future, wherever it'll be.'

'I still think we should've decided.'

'Don't be stubborn,' I murmured against her forehead. 'We can go anywhere, anywhere we want.'

'Paris? Milan?'

'Don't be daft. I was thinking more along the lines of Brighton. Maybe Falmouth.'

'Oh.'

I tilted her chin up. Her grey eyes were wide, darting everywhere but mine.

'You haven't changed your mind, have you?'

'No, it's just . . .'

'Good. Now, I'll be a bit later than I thought I would but we can catch the later train. I'll meet you at the bus stop near your house, yeah?'

She frowned. 'Okay, but . . . why?'

'That thing I told you about?'

The frown deepened. 'You mean the thing you didn't tell me about—'

'Well, yeah. But it doesn't matter. All you need to know is that it's going ahead and the pay-off will be—'

'Why won't you tell me? It's not . . . it's not illegal, is it?'

'No. Course not.'

'Promise?'

'I promise.'

'Then why won't you—?'

'It's just better that you don't know.' I tucked her head under my chin and stroked her hair. 'It's not illegal. But it's not exactly moral, either. I don't want you to think badly of me.'

'I could never think badly of you.'

'You're the only one.' I pulled her closer, feeling her heart against mine. 'You're all I've got. All I care about.'

She looked up, her eyes shining with tears.

'Hey . . . What did I say? Come on, don't cry. What is it?'

She gulped noisily. 'There's something . . . s-something I need to tell you.'

'What?'

'You won't like it. Oh, God, I've messed everything up, I . . .'

342

'You haven't. And whatever it is, it can't be that bad. As long as you still love me then there's nothing we—'

'I'm pregnant.'

The only things that broke the silence were her sniffs and the rasp of a nearby bird roosting under the bridge.

'Shit, Ophelia. Are you sure?'

'I did three tests. I'm sure.'

I let go of her, turning to lean my head against the clammy stone wall. I felt her warmth at my back. Waiting, needing.

'I'll understand if you've changed your mind.'

'No – just . . . give me a minute. I need to think.'

'I'm sorry. I thought I'd better tell you now. Give you a chance to get away if that's what you want.'

'Don't say that. And don't say sorry.' I turned back finally, pulling her into my arms. 'We'll work it out.'

'You mean it?' Her hot tears soaked into my shirt. 'You don't want to go without me?'

'Listen to me – I'm not going anywhere without you. You hear? Never. It's you and me now. Say it.'

She looked up, smiling through her tears. 'You and me,' she whispered.

I closed my eyes, and kissed her.

When I opened them, the scene changed.

I was on my back in total darkness, with something covering my face. An engine purred all around me.

'Can I sit up?'

'No.' Hodge's voice came through gritted teeth. 'Stay there until I tell you to get up. We're not clear of the gates, yet.'

'I'm getting car-sick.'

'Hold on – we're nearly out.'

343

The car rolled to a halt. I heard his window go down, the scratch of the gates opening. My stomach heaved as the car turned out on to the road and began picking up speed.

'We're out.'

I threw back the blanket and sat up, breathing deeply.

'For God's sake don't throw up.'

'I'll be all right. It's just in the back I get queasy.' I clambered between the two front seats and squeezed myself into the passenger side, fastening the seatbelt.

'Are you sure no one saw you get in the car?'

I shrugged. 'As sure as I can be. I went the way you told me.'

'You got straight in and covered yourself with the blanket?'

'Yeah.'

He released a slow breath, his shoulders lowering. 'Good.'

'So . . . how did it go? Were they impressed?'

'Impressed? They couldn't get enough of it. Well, all apart from that damn Sanctuary fellow – Travis. But he can't prove a thing. The others were fooled. And you know why? Because they wanted to be. They wanted to believe it.' He slapped the steering wheel and laughed. 'You looked bloody hideous hanging up there, I have to tell you. You even had me fooled.'

'Shame it's only a one time thing. Could've been a nice little earner.'

'You can't over egg the cake with this sort of stuff. It has to be rare, unexpected. Just a flash, just enough to scare them shitless. And they love it.'

A light drizzle spattered against the windscreen. I shivered, staring out of the window. My breath clouded the glass. 'It's cold. Can you turn the heat up?'

'It'll warm up in a minute.'

I traced a word on the window with my fingertip: S E B A S T I A N.

'Was he real?' I asked.

'Who?'

'Sebastian.'

Hodge's mouth twitched. 'Who knows? There are so many stories with that place. The tale of the servant boy is only one. I just added a few bits on, here and there. The brother, the cook . . .'

'Was his name even Sebastian?'

He snorted. 'He probably never even had a name. It was me who gave him one.'

I stared at the letters on the window. Already they'd started to run.

'Hey, did you notice?'

'Notice what?' Hodge glanced at me. He face twisted. 'Get that off the window, will you?'

'I will, but look . . .' I swiped my hand through the middle section of the word, leaving only the beginning and end letters: S E A N.

'Sean.' I chuckled. 'Like I was part of him all along.'

'Very amusing. Now wipe it off.'

I cleared the window and fidgeted. 'You locked my bag in the boot. I could've got changed while I was waiting – I swear this tunic's given me a rash.'

'No. If someone had seen you moving about in the car the whole thing could've been blown. We did it the best way.'

'What about the costume? Don't you want it back?'

He shook his head. 'I ordered it specially. Didn't want any of the museum's unaccounted for.'

I pulled the mirror down. 'Have you at least got anything I can clean this muck off my face with? I look like I haven't washed for a week.'

'You're a servant. That's the idea.' He nodded at the glove compartment. 'There're some wipes in there.'

I pulled them out and scrubbed at my face. Layers of dirt streaked away.

I wiped around my neck, then began to laugh.

'What's so funny?'

'The noose. I'm still wearing it – I forgot to take it off.' It wasn't tight now, I'd loosened it a little after dropping from the tree. The rope was warm against my throat.

'Chuck it in the back.'

I lifted the tail-end of the rope out of my shirt. It slithered up my spine like something living, then flapped free on the outside. I worked my fingers into the cord at the front, starting to widen it enough to get my head through.

'Did you tell Ophelia you were leaving?'

The question caught me by surprise. I stopped what I was doing, blindly reaching for an answer. 'I haven't told anyone,' I lied. 'What do you care anyway? Your wallet said it all – you want me gone.'

'Nothing personal.' Hodge flicked the wipers on a little faster. The rain had got heavier. 'I just think the two of you are too young to be spending so much time together.'

'Bullshit. You think I'm not good enough for her.'

He sighed. 'Fine. I thought I'd play it nice, part on good terms and all that. But if you want the truth? No. You're not. But like I said, nothing personal, not really. No one's good enough for her.' He smiled faintly. 'She'll think her heart's broken for a while, after you've gone. But soon she'll realise it wasn't love, and you'll both have been saved from what's inevitable.'

'And what's that?'

346

'Being another teenage statistic. Your lives over before they really began. You know what I'm talking about.'

Dread uncurled inside me. *Does he know?* I wondered. *But how can he? I only found out myself this evening . . .*

And for the first time I allowed myself to wonder, to think about how it would be. To be alone. Her news this afternoon . . . I hadn't been able to take it in properly, not yet. It would be tough with two of us, let alone three. But I could do it. I could cut and run if I wanted to. My future lay ahead, but there was a fork in the road. Which one should I take?

A sign rushed past us outside. And with that, I knew. There was no way I could do it, no way I could leave her. I sat bolt upright.

'Where are we going? We just left Calthorpe.'

'You're catching the train, I assume?'

'Yes, but—'

'Then I'll take you to the station. What's the problem?'

'We arranged for you to drop me at the bus stop.'

'I know what we arranged,' he snapped. 'You think I don't know what's going on? That I don't know she's waiting for you back there?'

I stared at him, frozen. 'I don't know what you're talking about—'

'Oh, I think you do. She's been acting odd for weeks, even if she doesn't realise it herself. Emotional, even obedient. Guilty, in other words. So I'm taking you to the station, boy. And you're getting on that train alone.'

I thought of my phone, in the car boot with everything else. I couldn't even call Ophelia to warn her, to tell her to take the bus without me. 'Let me out. Now.'

'In the middle of nowhere? I don't think so.'

'Stop the car. I want my stuff and I want to get out.'

'Forget it.'

I grabbed the handle. 'I'll jump.'

He laughed. 'Jump, then. Say goodbye to the money. It'd make my life easier.'

I gulped back tears of rage as Hodge calmly reached forward and put the radio on. He adjusted the tuner, sifting through static until settling on a station.

'Oh, here's a good one.' He turned the volume up. 'My mother's favourite.'

The radio played a familiar song.

'Sometimes I sense I'm not alone,
Still hear your voice, it's as real as my own.
Echoes of the past stir my dreams,
They told me time heals, they were wrong it would seem . . .'

The rain eased once more to a drizzle. The car wound through lane after lane until I saw the sign for Weeping Cross. Soon we were passing houses, some lit, some not. It was late now.

He turned off and swung into the deserted station car park. I glanced at the clock on the dashboard. There was thirty minutes until the train, but by now Ophelia would have missed the bus by waiting for me. And even if I called her once I was out of the car, told her to take a cab, Hodge knew exactly where she'd be headed.

Hodge reached into his inside pocket and withdrew an envelope. He threw it at me. 'Go on, then. Piss off.'

I flicked through the envelope. 'There's only half of what we agreed here.'

'Count yourself lucky there's anything at all.'

'Where's the rest?' I yelled.

'You said goodbye to that when you tried to screw me over by taking my niece. Now get lost.'

'I'm not going anywhere without that money.'

'We'll see about that.' He snatched the keys and got out, walking round the back of the car in the rain. I heard the boot lift. A moment later my door opened. My bag lay in a gravelly puddle.

'Out.'

'I want my money, you bastard! And I'm not going until I get it!'

I anticipated his lunge and grabbed across to the steering wheel, kicking him away. He grunted as my foot hit his gut, then I felt his grip on my ankle. He swore as I kicked again, but managed to pin my legs down with his weight. At first I thought he was going for my hands, to pull them off the wheel. Then I felt my neck jerk as the rope tightened around it. My eyes bulged. Instinctively my hands left the wheel and went to my throat, clawing to free the noose.

The stupid, bloody noose. I'd so nearly removed it before. Nearly . . .

He grabbed my feet and hauled me out, on to the ground. The car door clipped my head as he slammed it, then without a backwards glance he stalked around to the driver's side. I lay there, fingers prying the noose looser, gulping great breaths of air, when I heard his door thump shut and the engine roar to life.

And I saw the rope, trapped in the door.

'No . . . WAIT!' I yanked the noose, coughing, panicking.

He released the brake. The noose jerked tight. Gravel sprayed in my face. Peppered my eyes.

I tried to lift myself to my feet but the speed took me, dragging me off balance.

Dragging me . . .

My neck snapped backwards.

Pain. Like nothing before. Everything burned: my neck, my lungs, my eyes. The skin surely hanging off my back.

The one light in the car park suddenly changed to red. No, it wasn't just the light, it was everything.

And just as quickly as the pain began, it stopped. I couldn't feel any more. Couldn't hear. Had the car halted? He must have felt it . . .

And then he loomed over me.

'Jesus . . . oh, Jesus . . .'

Beads of sweat dripped off his face into mine. I wanted to wipe them away but I couldn't move my arm. Couldn't feel it.

He fumbled with the rope, great clumsy paws on my neck.

'Sean, can you hear me? Breathe, damn you! Oh, God what have I done!'

Blackness. A void, in which something rumbled. Like a purr of a giant cat. Air . . . there just wasn't enough air. I drifted. In and out. Swaying, like being rocked. On and on. Minutes? Hours? I couldn't tell any more.

Then cold. Damp on my face. How come I could feel that, but not my legs?

Everything red again, why?

Hodge's face in mine. Behind him, stars. When did the rain stop?

Not enough air. Never, never enough.

'I'm sorry,' he whispered. Something glinted in his hands. A shovel.

Darker. Where did the stars go? Something was in my mouth. Gritty, earthy, what? Breathing it . . . So hard to breathe now. All the air, gone, but still my lungs dragged in . . . out.

In . . .

Out.

THIRTY-TWO

The Ringmaster

I snapped back into the present as the figure in the backseat released my hand.

Not Sebastian. There *was* no Sebastian, only a boy playing his part.

But there was a Sean.

Ophelia's missing boyfriend. Ophelia's *murdered* boyfriend. And apart from those in this car, here, now, no one else knew he was dead.

Thoughts flashed through my mind. The name on the window, over and over. The song playing in the car. Sean's final moments, replaying through me. The anger, the rage and longing he'd felt upon seeing Ophelia again in the orchard that day.

Mine.

She'd been his before she was ever mine. Maybe, deep down, she still was.

An image of her hands swam before my eyes. The woman in a crown of stars: the Empress, and falling leaves. Motherhood and loss. Ophelia hadn't lied. But she hadn't told the complete truth, either. It wasn't just the loss of her own mother painted on to her hands, I realised. It was the loss of her chance to be a mother to Sean's baby.

351

So what had happened to the child?

I twisted back, fighting to re-enter my body. Terror made me clumsy and the swaying of the car kept me off balance. Sean sat motionless in the backseat, flickering from one side to the other. One moment behind me, the next, behind Hodge.

I closed my eyes and threw myself at my body. My stomach lurched in a wave of nausea, like riding an elevator double speed. Then I was in, but something – fear perhaps – had me locked in paralysis for a few crucial seconds. I focused on my little finger, trying to force the smell of wet earth out of my nose. He was still there, behind me. So close . . .

My finger bent. The rest of my hand twitched and fell out of my pocket, the witch's ladder still in it. I saw Hodge glance down. His eyebrows knotted together.

'What's this?' He pulled the witch's ladder out of my fingers.

'*No!*' The protest gurgled out of me, too late.

And Sean saw his chance. The fingers gripped the top of my arm again, clamping down. Whatever progress I'd made I lost right then, in that second. All that existed for me was fear, and he knew it.

Leave. The word was unspoken, only in my head.

NO, I told it. *You can't make me.*

'Has that bloody Lesley Travis been giving you his trinkets again?' Hodge fumed, crushing the feathers and cord in his fist. He elbowed me. 'What's wrong with you? Wake up!'

My hand twitched again. So close. So very close . . .

A gust of fetid air filled my lungs. I tasted rot and blood and earth. And then memories, crashing against each other, crashing against my own, all cramming into a space too narrow in a jumble of confusion and grief and loss.

Children crying. A man shouting, pummelling something, someone, in a corner. A boy's face, pinched and tight, his nose bleeding. *Vince.*

'Just leave it, Sean.' He spat blood on the kitchen tiles. 'He'll only start on you as well . . .'

And then Ophelia. Ophelia's face, smiling. Her hands, bare and pale, weaving through a horse's mane with no trace of henna in sight. Ophelia with grass in her hair, eyes closed. Throwing her head back, biting her lip.

Do you want more? Sean's voice asked in my head. *I can give you more.*

No, I screamed. *Just get out, go!*

I'm not going anywhere until he pays.

A door slamming. Neck jerking. Gravel spraying, scraping. Crushing pressure on my throat, the burn of the tightening noose . . .

With a cry I forced myself free, tumbling into the backseat of the car.

Hodge's hand was on my shoulder – my body's shoulder, still in the front. My head turned, animated by something that wasn't me.

'You all right? I thought you'd gone into a coma!'

Sean stared back at his murderer with my eyes. 'I'm fine,' he said, in a dry, slow voice. 'I must have slept deeply. Really deeply. But I'm awake now.'

'What was this doing in your pocket?' Hodge asked, flapping the witch's ladder. 'Was it meant for me? Did that crazy bastard give you another one?'

Sean shook his head. 'I've never seen it before. But I don't want it.'

353

Hodge rolled his window down. Warm summer air blasted in.

'No!' I shouted, but it was too late. The witch's ladder flew past the window into the night. Mum's necklace . . . gone.

I caught the curve of Sean's smile on my lips and knew I'd lost.

'What are you going to do?' I croaked behind him. 'What are you planning?'

'Mind if I put some music on?' Sean asked.

'Be my guest.'

I watched his hand reaching for the buttons. Flicking through songs and news. Already I knew what was coming.

'Echoes of the past stir my dreams,

They told me time heals, they were wrong it would seem . . .'

Hodge's hand shot out, fumbling for the controls. 'Not that.'

'I thought you liked that one. You said it was your mother's favourite.'

In the rear-view mirror I saw a crease appear in Hodge's forehead.

'I don't remember telling you that.'

Sean shrugged. 'Maybe Ophelia told me.' I heard, rather than saw him smile.

Hodge found another station. 'It was one of Mother's favourites,' he muttered. 'But sometimes memories are . . . difficult.'

'I can imagine.'

'Stop it,' I hissed. 'What are you doing? Trying to cause an accident? You'll kill us both!'

My words made no impact.

'How long until we're back?' Sean asked.

'Five, maybe ten minutes. We've made good time – and the Tudor banquet will be worth the wait. Hungry?'

'Starving.' Sean stared straight ahead. 'Hungrier than I've ever been. I feel like I haven't eaten for a year.'

I sat, helpless. Watching, waiting for Sean to do something. To grab the wheel and force Hodge off the road. Attempt to strangle him with his bare hands. But he did nothing except gaze out of the window into the darkening red sky, and with every moment that passed my innards twisted a little bit tighter.

Soon we passed a sign for Calthorpe. Sean sat up straighter as Hodge slowed the car for the turning into the museum. The gates were open and, before us, cars queued to get in and people on foot made their way down the drive.

We pulled through and Hodge manoeuvred the car off to the staff parking area. He cut the engine, stretched and yawned.

'It's been a good day,' he said. 'But a long one.'

'And it's not over yet,' Sean answered. He got out and walked around to the front. Hodge's door slammed. I scrambled past him as he opened the back of the car to collect his camera and notebook.

'Did you bring anything?' he asked.

'No.' Sean smiled. 'Got everything I need right here.'

The words sent a chill through me.

'What are you going to do?' I repeated. '*Answer me!*'

'Where do you think Ophelia will be?' Sean asked, as they started on their way towards the entrance.

'Probably saving us seats,' said Hodge. 'We should hurry before all the food goes.'

I trailed behind them, unseen, as they made their way through the stone arches. Already I could see movement and hear laughter up ahead. Lanterns glowed through the darkness, illuminating bodies jostling for space up by the well on the Plain. They stretched like a row of fireflies from Goose Walk to Cornmarket Street, and above the hum of conversation I heard the strains of a harpsichord.

'You'd better get changed,' Hodge told Sean. 'Even the visitors will be in costume tonight. I'll be over shortly. If you see Una, tell her I'm in my office getting ready. I'll be there in a minute.'

'Sure,' Sean said. He stayed exactly where he was. His eyes were glassy, fixed on Hodge. Once again they were darker than mine and I didn't like the look in them.

Hodge glanced at him. 'Is there something else?'

'You asked about Sebastian, before. When I saw him, in the orchard.'

I heard Hodge's breathing pause. 'Yes. Did you remember something else?'

Sean came a step closer. 'I don't think it was the noose that killed him.'

A trickle of sweat ran down Hodge's cheek. 'Then what did?'

'Suffocation.'

'Suff— *what*?'

Sean nodded. 'Yeah. All that dirt coming out of his mouth? That could only have got in there if he was still breathing when he was buried.' His eyes narrowed. 'You should've checked, Arthur. If you had, would you still have buried him alive?'

A strangled sound emerged from Hodge's lips. He staggered backwards, dropping his camera. The lens cap bounced off and rolled away. He made no attempt to pick either piece up. 'Why are you saying these things?'

'Because they're true.' Sean smiled. 'You weren't sure whether to believe me at first, were you? That's okay. Something tells me you believe it now.' He gestured towards the crowd. 'I wonder how Ophelia will take it when she finds out what really happened that night? When she hears the truth about why Sean didn't come for her?'

The name was the final nail in the coffin. Hodge's face twisted.

'Where did you . . .? Don't you spread lies about me! I want you out, *now*—'

'Wrong. *You're* the liar. *You're* the murderer.'

Hodge lunged for him, but Sean darted out of reach and ran through the arch.

'Get back here!' Hodge yelled.

I froze between them, not knowing which way to turn. Hodge stood visibly shaking as Sean sprinted towards the crowd. I hesitated. Should I go after him and try to reclaim my body, or stay with Hodge? Either was a gamble. Now that Hodge knew what I'd discovered, how far would he go to shut me up? He'd killed once already. Would he do it again to cover his tracks? And what did Sean have planned for him at my hands? Would he sacrifice me, make me a murderer to get his revenge?

Worst-case scenarios jostled for space in my mind. All the while, the intruder in my body was getting further away. Any second now he'd be lost in the crowd and then the real game of cat and mouse would begin.

And then Sean was gone, swallowed in the maze of bodies, making my decision for me. Hodge grabbed the pieces of his camera. I followed as he stumbled into the cottages and hurried towards his office, slamming the door before I reached it.

But doorways were not a problem any more. I stepped through it, joining him at his desk. His breathing was loud and fast. He threw the camera on to the chair and the notebook on to the table top. It fell open, papers scattering from it. Some went on to the floor. I leaned over and scanned the pages. There were photos, diagrams, printouts and handwritten notes in neat black ink.

The Castle – coaching inn, Devon. Guest room reputedly haunted by weeping woman who threw herself to her death from the balcony. Seen regularly by staff and guests. Visited October 21st 2009.

The story was familiar. It sounded strangely similar to the grey lady in the Swan. I glanced at Hodge. He was grappling with the dial on the safe. I knelt over one of the loose pages on the floor and read quickly.

The Bear and Peasant – public house, Stafford. Rooms above rented to students. Repeated stories of being 'woken' early by non-threatening spirit believed to be former owner.

There were hundreds of them going back some five years, from all over the country. And this was just one, I realised with sickening clarity. How many other notebooks had there been before? Most of the stories were snippets or sentences. Some were almost essays. A few had words or paragraphs underlined or circled. I recognised only a fragment, but I knew the majority of them had to be in here: the stories of the ghosts at Past Lives. He'd collected them. Dissected them. Reinvented them. Tried to make them real, just as Lesley Travis had said, in a bizarre circus of the dead. And Hodge was their ringmaster.

Aside from Sean and whatever it was in the schoolroom, Annie was the only exception. The one ghost who *was* real here.

He swore, snatching the papers up and stuffing them back into the notebook before jamming the whole lot into the safe. From the back of it he took the whiskey bottle and drained it dry. His face crumpled into a sob but he growled, forcing it away.

'Calm down, Arthur,' he whispered to himself. 'Just take it easy.' He held the glass decanter to his forehead, closing his eyes. Then he opened them, put the empty bottle back and removed something else.

A gun. It looked like the one Ophelia had used to warn off Vince and his crew, but as Hodge loaded bullets into it, I knew it wasn't.

And I didn't need to know any more. I ran.

THIRTY-THREE

In the Orchard

The streets heaved with costumed figures: men, women and children, a mix of staff and visitors. Tables laden with food and drink circled the Plain and an area around the well was set up for music and dancing. I weaved between the tables. Some faces I knew: Lyn and the staff from the tea rooms. Most were strangers.

I found Una and Ophelia on a table near to Cornmarket Street, an empty chair either side of them. Una had gone all out in an embroidered dress, jewels and feathered hairpiece. Ophelia wore her hair loose over a simple green dress, with no adornments. She didn't need them. Next to her, Una looked like a trifle. To see her and know I was on the verge of losing her made me ache.

She stiffened suddenly, sitting up straight in her chair like a fox sensing danger. I followed her gaze across the Plain.

Three people stared back at her. Even from here I could see their own clothes barely hidden under cheap fancy-dress store cloaks. Vince and Damian wore plastic swords at their sides and perched on Nina's black hair was a gaudy crown.

'What is it, love?' Una asked.

'Nothing.' Ophelia stared at her plate. 'Where're Uncle and Elliott?'

'They should be here by now.' Una stretched her neck, ostrich-like, above the sea of heads. 'Oh, there's Arthur. He's just come from the Old Barn. What was he doing in there? I left his costume in his office for him.' She got up and started towards her husband. 'Over here, love!'

Looking for me, that's what he was doing, I thought grimly.

I was so intent on watching him that the voice at my back shocked me.

'What have I missed?'

My voice. And yet, not.

Sean took his seat beside Ophelia. He'd changed into a peasant shirt and brown trousers. The shirt hung open at the neck. Fresh marks ringed my throat.

'Your neck's all red again.' She took his hand, grimacing. 'Where have you been?'

Good question. Not the Old Barn, that was for sure. He'd appeared from behind us.

'The orchard.' His eyes never left her face. 'God, you're beautiful.'

She snorted. 'What are you, a poet tonight?'

'No. Just a boy. That's more than enough.'

'Sean,' I whispered, 'I know you loved her. But you can't stay in there for ever.'

A flicker of recognition crossed his face but he kept his eyes on Ophelia.

How long could he last before he had to leave? Each time it had been a little longer. Each time he'd gained strength.

I tried again. 'Hodge has a gun. If you don't leave now Ophelia won't have lost once, but twice. He's going to kill me. Do you want to do that to her? *Do you?*'

361

He gave an almost imperceptible shake of his head.

'You have to let her go. Say goodbye. And then show me where your body's buried. If we've got that, we've got evidence.'

Another shake of the head.

'What do you mean, no?' I yelled.

He didn't answer. Instead he gazed across the table at the wealth of food, and began loading his plate. Cheese, grapes, bread, meat. He tasted a little of everything, pleasure flashing across his face. He paused only when Una returned to the table with Hodge. They regarded each other wordlessly. I wondered where Hodge had stashed the gun; there were plenty of ruffles and frills on his costume. For now, Sean – *I* – was safe. Hodge couldn't say or do anything with others present, and they both knew it.

'So how was Oxfordshire?' Una asked, pouring herself wine. 'I want to hear everything.'

'Good.' Hodge twisted off a chicken leg, his eyes on Sean. 'Found out lots, didn't we?'

Sean nodded. 'Things you wouldn't believe. Ghosts everywhere. Right, Arthur?'

Hodge's eyes widened as he took in the bruising on my throat. He reached for the ale jug with trembling fingers, managing only to nod.

Throughout the meal Una coaxed and wheedled, teasing out details. With each one Hodge's answers grew shorter until he snapped, 'Enough, Una! I don't want to talk about it.'

In the silence that followed, no one but me noticed Sean slide a carving knife into his sleeve. Moments later, on the pretence of dropping his fork, he transferred it into his boot.

'Come on,' said Ophelia, glaring at Hodge. She tugged Sean's shirt. 'Let's dance.'

362

Hodge watched them cross the Plain. I went with them, helpless as Sean gathered her into his arms. He held her tight. Inhaled
her hair. Then without warning, he drew back.

'Listen . . . we'll dance later. I need to do something.'

'What? Where are you going?'

'Back to the orchard. There's something there, I can't explain—'

'Is this to do with that dream?'

'Yes. He's trying to tell me something.'

'You're scaring me . . .'

He kissed her gloved hands and released them. 'Come and find
me in five minutes.'

'Let me come now! Vince is here – he's watching us. He's going
to do something, I know it . . .'

'He won't do anything after tonight. Trust me.'

'But—'

'Five minutes!' He broke from her, hurrying away from the
festivities into Cornmarket Street. I followed, glancing back to see
Hodge excuse himself and rise from his seat. He wouldn't follow
directly, I knew. But he'd follow.

I ran, leaping past running, laughing children, dodging dancers,
not always successfully. They felt nothing as they whipped through
me like I was no more than air, or breath. I hurtled down the side
of Calthorpe House, through the gardens and into the orchard. A
single light in an upstairs window of the house reached weakly
through the branches, too far and too faint to penetrate the darkness beneath.

'Where are you?' I demanded. I got no reply.

Something crackled nearby. I strained to see through the murk.
Then a figure one shade darker than everything else became
visible.

Sean stood beside the wooden ladders.

'It's impossible to be quiet again when you're used to not being seen or heard.' He sounded almost apologetic.

I moved between the trees, trying to get my bearings. Nothing snapped or crunched beneath me. I was weightless. 'Why have you come here?'

'Because this is where it ends.'

I arrived beside him. Only then did I see the rope swing, dangling from the branches above. But this time it was shorter, higher off the ground. Instead of a knot it ended in a noose.

'You've been busy.' The voice came from a little way off, blanketed by the trees. A click followed, then a torch beam picked out the rope overhead. It moved to my body's face. Sean squinted back, raising a hand.

The torchlight flickered as Hodge neared, moving with a practised stealth. He flashed the light around quickly. 'Who the hell were you talking to?'

'Ghosts.'

Hodge chuckled. 'It's a shame that your obsession has come to this, Elliott.' He played the light over the noose. In the distance, the music lilted and swelled.

'I'm not Elliott.'

'Oh? Then who are you?'

'Sean.'

'*Don't keep saying that name!*'

'Which name would you prefer? Sebastian?'

'Stop this! What do you want? Money? Is that it?'

It was Sean's turn to laugh. 'You'd love that, wouldn't you? That's how you made all your little problems go away – before you killed me. Sorry, Arthur. Been there, done that. And you couldn't

364

even keep your word about the money, could you? You had to try and stitch me up.'

The torch shook in Hodge's hand. 'How do you know this?'

'The same way I know that, before now, you've never seen a ghost in your life. The way I know which song played just before you grabbed the rope around my neck and forced me out of the car, the way you drove off with the rope in the door—'

'SHUT UP!'

'Truth hurts, doesn't it?'

'You're not him . . . You *can't* be him . . .'

'Didn't anyone ever tell you to be careful what you wished for?' Sean mocked. 'You wanted ghosts, Arthur. Now you've got one.'

Hodge licked sweat from his upper lip, his free hand snaking beneath his coat.

'Watch out!' I shouted.

He whipped the gun from his waistband.

Sean didn't flinch.

I shoved at him, pummelled him uselessly. 'Move, damn you! He'll shoot!'

'Is it easier this time?' Sean asked him. 'It must be. You've lived with being a killer for a year.'

Hodge trained the pistol on Sean. On *me*.

'How are you going to get away with it again?' Sean continued. 'You were lucky with me. No one looked hard enough, or asked the right questions. One boy can disappear – but two?'

Hodge shook his head. 'You don't need to disappear. You just need silencing. All I have to say is that I caught you with this gun. Challenged you. You turned violent and there was a struggle. Neither of us knew it was loaded until it was too late.' He stepped closer. He couldn't miss. 'I'll make it quick.'

'Run!' I yelled. 'For God's sake, *run!*'

'You're forgetting something,' Sean whispered.

A muscle in Hodge's cheek twitched. 'What's that?'

'I'm already dead.' Sean launched himself at Hodge, clawing at the gun. The torch flew out of Hodge's other hand and spun in an arc, hitting a tree then the grass. They wrestled, grunting, feet scuffling for a hold on the ground.

Sean's elbow jerked up, smashing Hodge's temple. He staggered but didn't lose hold of the gun. I saw my head snap back as he forced his arm across my throat. Sean stumbled and Hodge pushed harder, kicking his leg behind mine to sweep Sean off his feet.

They landed nose to nose, Hodge on top. Beneath him Sean was flailing. Perhaps, in his life, his body, he'd been stronger. But now he was in mine and my strength was no match for Hodge's. Not only that, but I sensed he was weakening. He couldn't stay in me for much longer. If he left, it was all over. For both of us.

I did the only thing I could. I leaped through Hodge, forcing my way back into my body.

'*No . . .*' Sean hissed through gritted teeth.

I felt the full force of Hodge's weight. The breath being crushed out of me. Sean's thoughts, Sean's memories tangling with mine. I hit back with my own. I thought of Dad, Mum, Adam, Ophelia. And I thought of the cord. The witch's ladder. I didn't have it any more, but I'd created it. I believed in it. And it was still out there, somewhere. It still existed, just as I did. And this time, I didn't force Sean out. *Don't fight me,* I told him. *We're not strong enough to fight each other and him.*

His memories retreated to some far corner of my mind. Still there, like an itch I couldn't reach, but bearable, leaving me to turn my will to the real fight. Combined with Sean's rage a burst of energy surged through us. Together we brought Hodge's hand down, knocking the gun free. He yelled as I batted it away into the long grass, crawling over me to search for it.

The knife, Sean reminded me.

I pulled it from my boot and pressed it into Hodge's fleshy side. 'Stop there.'

He froze, panting.

'Turn over. Slowly.'

He rolled on to his back, his hands raised in surrender.

'Get up.' My mouth, Sean's words. He was still weak, but our dual strength had him holding on. Hodge stood. 'Now, dig.'

'Dig?' Hodge's eyes darted about. A bead of saliva hung from his lower lip. 'Dig where?'

'You know where!'

His face crumpled. 'How do you know . . .? Please, don't make me. *Please . . .'*

'Do it.'

'There's nothing to dig with.'

'Then use your hands,' Sean snarled. *'Your murdering hands.'* The knife jabbed Hodge's side again. He yelped.

'I'm not sure exactly where—'

'Yes, you are. Go!'

Hodge stumbled through the trees, over the uneven grass towards the house. He paused by the little stone wall and knelt beside it.

'Dig,' Sean repeated. He kicked a stone at him.

Hodge took it and thrust it into the earth, peeling away a layer of dirt.

'Dig down,' Sean growled. 'Not across.'

Hodge obeyed, glassy-eyed, panting in quick rasps. Deeper he dug, and deeper, beneath the dried crust into the moist earth below. A foot down, then two. The stone struck something.

A sob bubbled out of him. And then he lost it, dropping the stone to claw at the dirt with his bare hands. Something pale appeared. A row of teeth, like milky pearls.

'Oh, God, oh God . . .' Hodge babbled. 'Don't make me do any more . . . I can't, I swear *I can't* . . .'

'You can stop there. It's nearly over.'

Hodge scrambled away, crying and heaving like an overgrown fat baby.

'Get up. It's nearly time.'

Time for what? I asked.

Voices broke away from the music, coming nearer.

'Hurry,' said Sean. 'The tree.'

I waited for Hodge to resist, to run. But he complied, stooped and snivelling, willing to do anything but remain by what he had unearthed.

'Climb the ladder,' said Sean. 'Then I want you to put the noose around your neck.'

Hodge stared at me, dull-eyed. Then he started to climb.

'*No,*' I began, then tasted blood as Sean bit the word back.

Obedient as a puppy, Hodge lifted the noose and slipped it over his neck.

'Tighter,' said Sean. 'Good.' He flung the knife away. 'Now we wait.'

'Let him down!' I hissed.

Sean fought back. 'Not yet.'

The voices grew louder, overlapping.

'She came this way, I'm sure she did . . .'

'Where are you, Ophelia? Don't be shy!'

'You can run, but you can't hide!'

Nina's laugh rang out in an echo.

And then Ophelia's voice cut through the darkness by the house, broken and breathless. 'I tried to lose them but they kept following. We need to go – I'll tell Uncle to make them leave . . .' She faltered, peering through the branches. 'Who's there with you?'

'Call her over,' Sean whispered.

'Ophelia? C-come here . . .' Hodge's shoulders shook with fresh sobs.

'Uncle?' Her voice was sharp. 'Is that you?'

Sean's tears ran over my cheeks. 'Now, you tell her what you did,' he whispered. 'Tell her, and I'll let you down. Lie, and I'll kick the ladder. Your decision.'

Ophelia edged closer, her eyes darting from mine to her uncle's. 'What's going on here?' she whispered.

Footfall pounded the grass. Figures tumbled, laughing and gasping. Then Vince leered through the orchard, a short way behind Ophelia.

'Are we interrupting something?' he began. His face fell as he saw the ladder and the noose. 'What is this?' He shoved a giggling Damian. 'Shut it, will you?'

'Ophelia,' Hodge croaked. 'I'm sorry. It . . . it was an accident, I swear.'

'Come down.' Ophelia took another tiny step, her face pinched and white. 'You're frightening me. Please, come down.'

'It's too late.' Hodge wrung his hands. 'I never meant it, though. You have to believe me . . .'

I clung to the ladder, terrified it would slip.

It's done, Sean, over. Leave. NOW.

He weakened further, hanging on by a mere thread.

By knot of one, the day is done. By knot of two, my rest is due . . .

'Come down, Hodge,' I said. 'Take the noose off.'

He seemed not to hear.

'What was an accident?' Ophelia pressed. 'What have you done?'

'Sean . . .' Hodge whispered, his face contorting. 'I just wanted to give a good show, that's all. To bring Sebastian to life. Sean wanted the money. It seemed so simple.'

'Sebastian?'

By knot of three, sleep comes to me. By knot of four, I'll fear no more . . .

Vince pushed past Damian and Nina. 'Did he just mention my brother?' he demanded. 'You know where he is, old man?'

'Over . . . by the wall.' Hodge's voice was a whisper.

Vince stared back at the house. 'What's he talking about? There no one there – he's lost it.'

'Someone do something,' Ophelia cried. 'Call an ambulance – there's something wrong with him!' She turned to Vince. 'Find Una. *Please!* I don't know what to do . . .'

Vince's eyes went to slits. 'I'm going nowhere. Nina, get her aunt.'

By knot of five, I'll stay alive. By knot of six, my cord is fixed . . .

Nina hesitated, then ran towards the house. Back past the wall and the piled-up dirt that they'd failed to see on their way in. She paused. Knelt. Then jerked away, screaming.

'What is it?' Vince yelled, rushing to meet her.

'There's someone . . . Oh, Jesus . . . Someone's buried back there . . .' She fell against him, shaking. Vince passed her to Damian and edged towards the grave.

By knot of seven, with thread and feather. By knot of eight, there is no gate . . .

'I didn't know,' Hodge said. He was calm now, his voice sing-song. 'I didn't know he was still breathing when I buried him. I thought the rope had killed him already . . . But it was an accident. An accident . . .'

Ophelia stared back at her uncle. 'Sean? *You . . .* you *killed* him?'

By knot of nine, to what is MINE.

'I'm sorry,' Hodge whispered. 'Forgive me.'

Sean's memories loosened, unfurling from mine.

Look after her. The words echoed in my head as he released me. A shadow-like wisp hovered in front of my face. In an eye-blink it was gone.

He was gone.

Ophelia sank to her knees, rocking. 'He didn't leave me. *He didn't leave me.*'

I heard Vince retch and moan. So did Ophelia. She twisted around and I ran to her, pulling her into my arms. 'Don't go over there,' I murmured into her hair.

She turned her face up to Hodge. 'How could you? How *could* you? All this time . . . I thought it was my fault. That he'd left because of the baby . . .'

Hodge's head snapped up. '*Baby?*'

'I'd only told him that afternoon. When he didn't come . . . I waited and waited. My insides, everything was churning, *twisting.* Because I *knew.* I don't know how, but I knew he wouldn't come. And I started to bleed.'

'You let him *touch* you? You let him . . .' Hodge wept softly. 'You were my little girl.'

'Una called the ambulance – but it was too late. I'd lost it.' Ophelia trembled, the tiny hairs on her skin standing upright. 'I lost it the same time I lost him. Una swore we'd never tell.'

'Come on.' I lifted her up. She was limp in my arms. 'Let's get away from this place.' I glanced at Hodge. 'Take the noose off and come down, slowly. It's over, Hodge. You can't hide from what you've done any more.'

'No,' he whispered. 'You're right.' He stared straight at Ophelia. 'I love you. I'm sorry.' He kicked the ladder away and dropped.

'NO!' I ran towards him, grabbing his legs, lifting. His eyes bulged, but there was enough life left for him to kick me away.

Ophelia watched, emotionless.

'Let him die!' Vince screamed. '*Let the bastard hang!*'

Part of me, *most* of me, wanted to. It was no less than he deserved. But another part wouldn't let me, if only for Ophelia's sake. There had been too much death already.

I scrabbled in the grass and seized the knife, grappling to set the ladders straight. Scrambled up them as Hodge's legs stopped thrashing and twitched instead. Two, three strokes of the knife and the rope came apart.

Two, three seconds too late.

Arthur Hodge was gone.

Epilogue

I wait until the interval to tell Robert Bradley.

The evening sun is still strong when I leave him in the alcove and make my way out of The Mask and Mirror for the final time. Outside, July heat softens the tarmac and warms the back of my neck.

Ophelia lies on the bonnet in the shade, legs stretched out in front and a damp T-shirt knotted at her waist. She sits up as I cross the car park.

'Did he believe you?'

'Not at first.'

'No one really does until they have to. Until it happens to them.' She hands me a downy white feather. 'Think he'll stay for the rest of the set?'

'I don't know. He's been looking for her for so long . . . I think he'll need some time before he can lay her to rest.'

'At least he's not still wondering what happened to her. Waking up every day and not knowing.'

I nod and twirl the feather between my fingers. 'What's this for?'

'It landed on me while I lay here waiting for you. I thought maybe you could use it. If you ever make another witch's ladder.'

I tuck the feather into my shirt pocket, just in case. 'Let's go.'

We drive out, past fields and farms. Past towns and churches and into more open land either side of the road. And then she shields her eyes and points.

'Here?' I ask, slowing.

'Here.'

I pull over and we get out, walking hand in hand past thorny hedgerows and jumping stiles to the solitary tree in the middle of the field. Ophelia shakes out the blanket over the grass and we sit, staring at the sun dipping on the horizon. The only sounds are bees humming and birds chirruping in the hedges.

'They'll be stories, one day, won't they?' she says eventually, hugging her knees. 'Sean. And Hodge. I mean, I know they're already stories, but one day, in a hundred years when no one that knew them is alive . . . that's all they'll be. Ghosts.'

She turns to me, her eyes are bright and damp. I touch my fingertips to her wet cheeks. Kiss the teardrops off her mouth.

'Maybe it's too soon,' she murmurs under my lips, breaking away.

'No.' I lean back, studying her. 'You're perfect.'

She sniffs and laughs all at once. 'Hardly. My nose is running, my eyes are all puffy . . .'

'Exactly. It'll be . . . *interesting*. Just like you wanted.'

She tries to smile. 'Do I still look sad?'

'Yes.' I open my sketchbook. 'Sad, but hopeful. Real.'

She reclines on the blanket, her hair rippling around her.

'Bring your hands up by your face,' I tell her. She does. The henna is fading now, but I'm still in time to capture it. I take a moment to just look at her. The way her pulse beats under her skin and how her breathing quickens as my gaze travels the length of her body, taking her all in.

Then I lift my pencil and start to draw.

For now, there are no ghosts. There's only this moment; her and me. Alone, alive, with the rest of summer stretching ahead of us.

Author Note

The idea for *Unrest* came from a relative who has lived with sleep paralysis and out-of-body experiences for most of her life. Like Elliott, waking paralysed to see strange and terrifying figures watching over her in bed is a regular occurrence, and the episodes described in this book are inspired by her accounts.

Though her out-of-body experiences are less frequent, it was this that led me to wonder what would happen if a person who had come out of their body found it missing upon their return. Elliott's descriptions – of not immediately realising that he is out of his body and of his difficulty in returning to it – are again based upon those of my relative, though I've taken more liberties with this aspect of the story.

Sleep paralysis spans the world and its cultures. In some areas of the USA and Canada it's known as 'Old Hag' syndrome; in Hong Kong it translates as 'ghost oppression'; in Africa, 'the witch riding your back'. The common element that unites these experiences is the presence of an apparition or shadow-like figure and the sense of fear that accompanies it.

As Elliott discovers, the cause of sleep paralysis is thought to be linked to the REM (rapid eye movement, or dreaming) stage of sleep. A brief period of muscle paralysis occurs naturally during